Thank you for purchasing this book. Sign up for Nicholas's *spam-free* newsletter to learn more about future releases, how to claim a book patch, special offers, and bonus content. Subscribers will also receive access to exclusive giveaways.

eepurl.com/bggNg9

You can also sign up for Anthony's newsletter to receive info on his latest releases and free short stories exclusive to subscribers.

http://bit.ly/ajmlist

EXTINCTION CYCLE: DARK AGE 2

EXTINCTION INFERNO

AN EXTINCTION CYCLE STORY

NEW YORK TIMES BESTSELLING AUTHOR
NICHOLAS SANSBURY SMITH
AND ANTHONY J. MELCHIORRI

Extinction Cycle: Dark Age
Book 2: Extinction Inferno
By Nicholas Sansbury Smith and Anthony J. Melchiorri

Cover Design by Deranged Doctor Design
Edited by AJ Sikes

GREAT WAVE INK
PUBLISHING

For all that serve or have served in the
United States Military, thank you for the
sacrifices you have made to protect our freedoms.

We are forever grateful.

"The cost of freedom is always high, but Americans have always paid it. And one path we shall never choose, and that is the path of surrender, or submission."

John F. Kennedy

— 1 —

The Black Hawk circled low over Scott Air Force Base (AFB) ten miles east of the apocalyptic ruins of St. Louis. A crew chief opened the side door, revealing the sight of Variants darting down the streets toward the walls of the forward operating base (FOB).

"Jesus, they're everywhere!" the crew chief yelled.

Master Sergeant Joe "Fitz" Fitzpatrick leaned out, one hand on a rail, his prosthetic carbon-fiber blades creaking. The rest of Team Ghost sat impatiently behind him.

Sunlight pierced the sporadic clouds, illuminating the horrifying tableau spreading toward the Air Force base. The armored flesh of juveniles glowed in the light. The monsters galloped on all fours like a pride of starving lions.

Some of the beasts had already made it to the base's perimeter where they slammed into the chain-link fences tracing the border. HESCO bastions and guard towers provided another layer of defense. But the first line had already fallen.

Columns of smoke rose from fresh craters in the ground left by mines and other explosives. Hunks of shredded meat and bone smoldered in the dirt. Injured beasts crawled through the fields, some missing legs, others missing arms. None giving up on their pursuit.

Machine gun nests blasted sweeping waves of fire, and explosions bloomed across Fitz's view.

Specialist Justin Mendez crossed his chest in prayer. Sergeant Yas Dohi stared like a statue, his rifle cradled over his armor.

"How the hell are we supposed to stop that many?" Sergeant First Class Jenny Rico yelled.

Corporal Bobby Ace pulled at the bottom of his gray beard, looking over at Fitz for an answer.

"Doctor Lovato is gonna have to come up with another bioweapon," Ace said. "Might be the only cure for this outbreak of freaks."

"I got the cure right here!" Mendez shouted, patting his rifle.

Fitz had served with the Hispanic man long enough to know his brave words and Ace's dark humor masked the pain they carried and the fear seeping into their bones.

As much as Fitz didn't want to admit it, they couldn't wait on another miracle from Kate and her science team. The only way to stop these things was to kill them the old-fashioned way with bullets and blades.

Or at least slow them down… he thought.

The fresh ammunition and grenades the crew chief had distributed to Team Ghost would help.

"This mission is for Lincoln!" Fitz yelled.

Mendez crossed his chest again. The rest of the team simply uttered quiet acknowledgments as they looked out the open door at what they were about to face. They all had bags under their eyes and blood smeared on their clothing and flesh.

Only a few hours had passed since their extraction from Minneapolis, and they hadn't had a chance to recover mentally or physically.

On the deck behind them was the covered body of their deceased brother-in-arms, Specialist Will Lincoln.

The chopper had changed course after he had bled out. Instead of heading home, they had flown straight to Scott AFB to help save it from the Variant attack.

There was no time to grieve, no time to put Lincoln to rest, and no time for the team to rest.

It was straight back into the fray.

"Ghost," the primary pilot of the Black Hawk said over the comm channel. "I'm going to get you over the parking lot outside HQ."

Fitz identified the command building in the center of the base. The square structure stood out among the others around it with a white roof and a huge parking lot filled with Humvees and troop transports.

Speaking to his team, Fitz said, "We're assisting with the defense of Scott's command building. We got VIPs galore down there, civilian and military. They're organizing the evac."

Fitz gestured further out. Buses and transport vehicles rushed toward the runways where aircraft waited to take off.

"Our mission is two-fold. First, we ensure as many people get out of here as possible. We'll drop in between the evac lines and the Variants, buddy up and provide covering fire," Fitz said. "Second, we keep this base from falling under Variant control. Questions?"

Mendez lifted his hand. "If the whole point is preventing Scott from falling, why are we evacuating people like it's already lost?"

"Because the brass already thinks Scott *is* lost," Fitz said. "We're going to prove them wrong."

"All it takes is all we got!" Rico shouted.

The motto from their fallen brother Sergeant Jose Garcia continued to motivate the team through tough missions, and those words never felt so true.

The chopper lowered toward the parking lot, and the crew chief gave the signal for Ghost to jump out the open door.

Fitz looked one last time at Lincoln's body and the jacket over his face.

I'm sorry I couldn't save you, brother.

"Go, go, go!" yelled the crew chief, waving the team out.

Dohi went first, followed by Rico. They hopped out and took off in a crouch, heading for a row of Humvees and personnel vehicles. Just as Fitz went to jump out, the chopper jerked and pulled up. He lost his balance and crashed to the deck.

"What the hell!" he shouted.

Ace helped him up and Mendez shouted, "Tunnel!"

The chopper pulled up from a bulge in the parking lot. Asphalt broke away from an opening. From a cloud of dust and debris, emerged a huge beast with sinewy arms and bat-like ears. Long ropey tendrils jutted out of its back. It surveyed the surroundings with milky white eyes as it let out a high-pitched, clicking shriek that pierced the whoosh of the chopper rotors.

"Alpha!" Ace yelled.

Dohi and Rico took shelter behind a car, firing into the Alpha's flank. More Variants churned up from the fresh hole in the ground, spilling from one of the many tunnels the monsters must have used to invade the base.

"Get us back down there!" Fitz shouted.

"Hold on!" yelled one of the pilots.

The chopper lowered over a cluster of abandoned cars. Fitz jumped out, his blades hitting the roof of a van. Mendez and Ace leapt out after.

Fitz opened fire on the Variants climbing out of the tunnel, but had lost sight of the Alpha.

Tendrils of the red webbing stuck up from the tunnel like shredded blood vessels in a wound. Those bloody-looking vines were transmitting signals to the beasts now attacking Scott. Team Ghost had killed one of the masterminds in Minneapolis, but there were more.

Another Variant climbed those red ropes and stuck its ugly, wart-covered head out of the hole, tongue whipping against wormy lips.

Fitz squeezed the trigger and blasted its face off.

A horrifying shriek ripped through the air next to him. The Alpha suddenly slammed into the side of the van, knocking Fitz off. He crashed onto a car and hit the pavement hard.

Fitz rolled to his back and fired as the Alpha leapt to the van above him. The heavy beast crunched the roof of the van inward. Rounds lanced into its chest, punching through gray flesh.

It let out a series of clicks and jumped to the ground. Fitz emptied his magazine into the Alpha. Blood sprayed from the monster's wounds as it stumbled forward and reached toward him.

A shotgun blast boomed.

Part of the Alpha's shoulder blew off, painting Fitz with gore.

"Move it!" Ace yelled.

Fitz didn't waste time. He turned and scurried between the vehicles for cover. Another blast thundered behind him. When he finally got his legs under him and spun to face the Alpha, it had collapsed.

"Thanks!" Fitz yelled.

Ace pulled hunks of gore off his beard. Then they

both ran back to find the others. The Variants continued to pop out of the tunnel. Another beast's reptilian eyes caught Fitz's, and its lips curled back into a snarl, revealing a maw full of jagged teeth.

"Fire in the hole!" Mendez yelled.

He lobbed a grenade into the hole as the creature dragged itself out. It didn't make it far. The ground lifted up behind it, dirt and rock exploding. The blast blew the abomination in half.

Another rumble shook through the ground, and the asphalt around the tunnel cracked, dropping into the hole.

Dust billowed up as part of the tunnel collapsed in on itself.

"Hell yeah, boyyyyyy!" Mendez yelled.

The remaining Variants dropped from concerted fire as Team Ghost formed up.

More choppers descended toward the command building. Soldiers and Marines hopped out, quickly running for the front entrance.

Fitz gave the signal for his team to fall back to command as well. Setting off in combat intervals, they moved cautiously around the holes between them.

Closer to the building, another razor wire-topped fence surrounded command. Machine gun nests had been set up to cover zones of fire around the entrance.

On the roof, snipers perched, their barrels flashing with calculated shots. Beside them crouched men with AT-4s, concentrating their shots on the strongest of the monsters.

A .50 caliber machine gun blazed to life from a third-floor window.

Over the gunfire came a message on the comms.

Fitz strained to listen.

"All units in command vicinity respond," came the voice. "Variant tunnel identified directly on the west-side of command. Requesting immediate response. Over."

Fitz waved the rest of the team toward the road crossing and closed gate in front of the command building. The third-floor gunner fired on a stream of Variants coming from a hole in the street just beyond the fencing.

Already there was a pile of corpses—human and Variant—around a hole that had exploded inside the border.

Another hole swallowed the asphalt in the middle of a group of soldiers defending the southern side of the building. An Alpha lunged out right into a stream of gunfire. Rounds punched into its flesh until it collapsed in a heap of bloody limbs.

The ground rumbled again a moment later.

It didn't take long to see that the fences and thirty some soldiers holding back the hordes would be overrun. Fitz knew they had to do something drastic to keep command from falling, but the only thing he could think of was a long shot.

"Command, Ghost 1," he said over the public channel. "We need access to an R2TD system now!"

From past experience, they knew the rapid reaction tunnel detection system was perfect for hampering the Alpha's echolocation abilities and driving them mad. Sowing chaos among the Alphas would put the Variant attack in disarray.

The response was impossible to hear over the gunfire.

Fitz led the team to the gate on the eastern side of the building. Two Marines held sentry behind a secondary fence. They opened both gates to let the team inside the secure area.

"Go, go, go!" one of them yelled.

Fitz grabbed the guy's arm. "We need an R2TD unit!"

"The hell is that?" the man said.

Letting go of the man, Fitz marched toward the sealed off doors of the command building. Team Ghost followed him through a maze of sandbags. They ran toward the west side of the building where most of the soldiers and Marines were holding back the attacking beasts.

Fitz repeated his request for an R2TD system over the channel, and this time he heard the response.

"Copy that, Ghost 1. What's your location?"

"We're outside the west entrance of the command building!" he shouted.

"Copy, Ghost 1. Hold your position!"

Fitz and the rest of the team took up position behind a mound of sandbags. He spent two magazines on the incoming Variants before the sliding metal door opened behind them.

A soldier carrying an R2TD system hurried outside Ace slung his shotgun to take the unit.

"Plant that in one of the tunnels!" Fitz yelled.

"Let me take it," Rico said. "I'm faster."

"You sayin' what I think you're sayin?" Ace said as he started to turn on the device.

"Yes, you're too damn slow," Rico said.

Fitz didn't intend to see either Rico or Ace play martyr.

"We're all going out there," Fitz said.

He brought up his rifle as Ace primed the device. Hundreds of Variants had already reached the fences on the west side, climbing the leaning sides and reaching the top to tear off coils of razor wire.

Sending anyone out there sure looked like a death sentence.

But the beasts had ignored the area that Fitz and his team had entered. Instead of asking for covering fire from other soldiers, Fitz gave the advance signal to Team Ghost, hoping to go unnoticed.

They set off for the gate they had entered through.

One of the two Marines still standing sentry held up a hand.

"Where the hell you think you're going?" he asked.

"We have to get this device in one of those holes," Fitz said, pointing.

The Marines both followed his finger.

"You fucking crazy?" the other man said.

"Crazy will keep us alive, so move it," Ace said.

The Marines opened the gates without more protest, and Ace charged toward one of the holes with Team Ghost covering him along the way.

Variants had already emerged from another hole and rushed toward the gates, scaling the fences. Several made it over the top, dropping into the secure area, only to be cut down by gunfire.

A Black Hawk circled, raining fire from the sky at the devilish army.

Another hole burst open, unleashing more of the monsters and one of the larger blind Alphas. The beast let out its staccato shriek and twisted toward Team Ghost just as Ace lobbed the activated R2TD into a hole.

While the sound waves it emitted were too high for the human ear, they were perfectly suited for hammering the sensitive ears of the Alphas.

The creature let out a shriek, attracting the attention of the hordes attacking the western gate. Many of them turned away from the fences.

"Oh shit," Mendez stuttered.

An entire group peeled off, falling to all fours, some of them tripping and falling over each other as they changed directions.

At least forty beasts charged Team Ghost.

"RUN!" Fitz yelled.

The team bolted away from the hole back toward the gate where the Marines were shouting and waving. A hail of bullets chewed into the Variants pursuing Team Ghost, cutting some of them down, but the meat of the pack ran faster.

Fitz was the last one in the gate. The Marines sealed it behind them and everyone backed away. The wave of Variants slammed into it seconds after.

"Back!" Ace shouted.

Fitz retreated from the barrier, scanning for the Alphas. He finally spotted one lumbering toward the R2TD system.

Another Alpha climbed out of the newest hole and ran toward the abandoned R2TD equipment. Fitz waved at the soldiers with AT-4s on the rooftop.

"Hit those Alphas!" he shouted.

Fitz brought up his rifle and fired bursts at the Variants still slamming into the fences. A grenade sailed overhead and exploded behind one of the Alphas, smearing the beast across the asphalt. Another explosive round slammed into the parking lot between two vehicles. The fuel tanks ruptured, and the resulting inferno consumed the beasts.

But another Alpha pushed its way through the charred

corpses of its brethren, bullet holes weeping blood across its body. It reached the R2TD system, smashing the cylindrical machine with its clawed fists. The equipment broke into pieces, but not more than a second later, a rocket tore the Alpha into just as many chunks of bloody flesh.

"Wooooo!" Mendez wailed. "That's how we do this shit!"

The remaining Variants flagged in their assault, turning and squawking like disoriented beasts at the death of their monstrous leaders. They scattered as the soldiers and Marines fired into their fleeing ranks.

"Parking lot clear," came a voice over the public channel. "All units near the parking lot, fall back to command."

Fitz retreated with Team Ghost, listening to the rattle of gunfire. Some of it came from the airfield where people still rushed through nearby streets, streaming toward the planes waiting to evacuate them.

Two helicopters circled, their door gunners firing bursts to keep back the Variants.

An officer moved onto the landing of the command building.

"Fine work, everyone!" he yelled.

Several grunts and "Oorahs," roared from the men.

"Don't celebrate yet," the officer said. "We have another group pinned down. We need volunteers to extract them. The rest of us will stay here and hold this post."

"Where are they?" someone asked.

The officer pointed toward a cluster of buildings about a mile away from the command building.

"Damn," Mendez muttered.

Fitz looked at his team in turn. There was no way they could stand idly by while those families were stuck out there. But at the same time, they were needed here to help defend the command.

"Dohi, Rico…" Fitz said. His words trailed off. Could he really send his girlfriend out there? He hated doing it, but she was the second in command. When Ghost split into Alpha and Bravo teams, Bravo was always hers.

He had to trust her like she trusted him.

"We got this, Fitzie," she said, chewing on her gum. She jogged with Dohi toward a group of volunteers gathering in front of the officer, apparently not even thinking twice about heading behind enemy lines.

Fitz swallowed hard and looked out from the base wondering how long they could hold back the beasts. If the previous night's attack was just the beginning, the next time the Variant hordes returned, they would crash over the Allied States' defenses.

— 2 —

Marine One and Marine Two flew north to the USS *George Johnson*. The choppers hugged the eastern shore close enough that Captain Reed Beckham could see the fires on the horizon.

An inferno blazed in Outpost New Boston.

After eight years of peace and reconstruction, everything was falling apart. If they didn't stop this invasion soon, the Allied States would be nothing but ashes.

"Must be collaborators," said Master Sergeant Parker Horn.

"Yeah," Beckham agreed.

Variants didn't use guns, but the collaborators and their raiding parties were well versed in guerrilla warfare, utilizing everything from C4 to the acid produced by Variants.

Almost every face in Marine One was turned to the windows. Kate had Javier wrapped up in her arms next to Beckham, and Horn watched the fires next to Tasha and Jenny. An unlit cigarette wobbled between his lips as he cursed under his breath.

"We shouldn't have left Timothy," Tasha said, wiping her eyes.

"He's going to be okay," Horn replied.

Beckham nodded back. He wanted to believe they could stop the invading monsters and collaborators, but with the addition of juveniles in their army, he wasn't so sure.

Command didn't even know the Variants' strength anymore or where the masterminds controlling the hordes were located.

For a split-second back in the Presidential Emergency Operations Center (PEOC), Beckham had given some thought to Brigadier General Lucas Barnes's suggestion to nuke the cities where they suspected the masterminds might be. But even using low-yield nuclear weapons was no guarantee they would stop the masterminds, and it would guarantee the death of any human prisoners there along with the people in the surrounding outposts.

Evacuating those outposts by land would be nearly impossible now that the Variants were attacking and surrounding them. It would be almost as difficult by air, given the dearth of resources currently available to the Allied States and the sheer number of people who would need to be transported.

The numbers simply didn't add up, and places like Outpost Boston only had one option right now.

Stand their ground and fight.

"We should have evacuated before," Beckham said quietly.

"Do you think Portland is going to be okay?" Kate asked.

Javier glanced up to his dad for an answer.

"Portland is a long way from the main target cities and it's well-defended," Beckham said. "They should be fine."

He said it as much to reassure himself as the others.

"I'm worried about Donna, Bo, and Timothy." Javier's gaze flitted from Beckham to Kate and then back again. "They're going to get on another helicopter, right, Dad?"

"If we think they're in trouble, we'll get them out of there," Beckham said.

He exchanged a glance with Kate, seeing the extreme worry in her eyes.

"I'll be right back," he said.

"Where are you going?" Javier asked.

"To talk with the president."

Kate pulled Javier closer while Beckham made his way through the technicians, soldiers, and others occupying the troop hold between the leather seats. The helicopter was packed to the limit.

Standing between Beckham and the president was Doctor Jeff Carr and two lab technicians. The group was talking about the mastermind Variants and juveniles.

Beckham squeezed past them, more interested in what the president's team was talking about. They huddled in seats near the cockpit. Chief of Staff James Soprano and National Security Advisor Ben Nelson shared reports with President Ringgold and Vice President Dan Lemke, while Chief of Staff Elizabeth Cortez spoke on a satellite phone.

Judging by their dour looks, the reports coming in were anything but good.

Once he made it directly behind Nelson, Beckham picked up a few things from the conversation. Cortez said something about the US Bank Stadium in Minneapolis being destroyed and the hordes being pushed back from the walls of Outpost Chicago.

"Our forces have repelled the attack at the White House, too," said Lemke. "The area is being secured."

"Thank God," Ringgold said, breathing an audible sigh of relief.

"We dodged some bullets tonight, especially at Portland," Cortez said.

Ringgold spotted Beckham and waved him over.

"Captain Beckham, join me," she said. "How much of our situation did you overhear?"

"I heard the White House has been secured," Beckham said.

Ringgold nodded. Her expression softened. "Team Ghost made it to Scott AFB, and they've helped hold back the Variant hordes, but I'm afraid I have bad news about Outpost Portland."

Beckham's stomach curdled.

"An assault started a few minutes ago," Lemke said.

"Reports indicate the collaborators hit from the inside," Nelson said.

Beckham's mind raced with thoughts of Donna, Bo, Timothy, and everyone else.

He should never have left them.

He should have stayed to fight.

But once again, he had fled the fighting to protect his family.

"There must be a collaborator sleeper cell involved," Nelson said. "These assholes made it into the outpost far too easily."

"Based on what we're seeing, I wouldn't be surprised if that's true for many of the outposts," Lemke said.

"That would explain how the first raiders on Peaks Island knew where the lab was," Beckham said. No, he knew they weren't simple raiders.

They were collaborators.

In his mind's eye he saw the pair of would-be assassins back at the campaign rally. Before one had died, he had said, "Adios, Reed." He couldn't help wondering if there was something personal about this. Almost as if the collaborators and Variants held a grudge against him.

Couldn't be, though. Could it?

He tried to shake the idea, turning his thoughts back to who might be working with the collaborators inside Outpost Portland.

Was someone he called a friend actually a traitor?

Chances were good the culprits hadn't betrayed their neighbors purely out of evil. It was more likely the collaborators had threatened their family or held some kind of leverage over them. Maybe they had convinced them that a Variants victory was all but assured and the monsters would spare their lives if they cooperated.

Whatever they had done to seduce people within the outposts, Beckham knew one thing: It was all lies.

"How long until we land?" he asked.

Nelson peered at his watch. "About thirty minutes. Maybe a bit less."

Beckham looked over his shoulder at his family. He saw Big Horn leaning over to talk with Tasha and Jenny, too. Horn had to have identical thoughts as him—that returning to fight risked condemning their kids to the same fate as Timothy Temper.

Fatherless.

Just like Timothy, Tasha and Jenny would become orphans.

Beckham wasn't sure what to do. He couldn't bear the thought of Kate raising all three kids on her own. But they couldn't just abandon Bo, Donna, and Timothy to the monsters and collaborators. He would never be able to live with himself.

"Madam President, would you consider sending Marine One and Marine Two back to Portland to evacuate more people?" Beckham asked.

"Already planning on it," Ringgold said. She narrowed her eyes, studying Beckham. "I hope you're not thinking about going back with the helicopters though. We already have plenty of boots on the ground."

Beckham gathered his thoughts for a second.

"Outpost Portland is my home," Beckham said. "It wouldn't feel right if I didn't at least help manage the evacuation."

"I wish you would reconsider your position," Ringgold said. "There are others more than capable of helping your friends and neighbors."

Cortez finished up another call, then turned to the others, interrupting the conversation.

"I just received an update on the outposts around the target cities," Cortez said. "Our bombers are going back for another run."

No one said a word as Marine One curved away from the shoreline and headed farther out to sea. The dark gray shapes cutting through the water confirmed the rest of the 1st Fleet had gathered around the USS *George Johnson.*

Nelson broke the silence. "You sure it's safe out here?"

"Unless the collaborators have also commandeered a warship," Lemke said.

"It wouldn't be the first time one of our enemies have," Ringgold said.

Beckham guessed she was thinking about Resistance of Tyranny (ROT), and how Lieutenant Andrew Wood had managed to gain control of Navy warships to launch a coup against Ringgold's administration.

"Even if we think we've got control over all our ships," Beckham began, "what if a collaborator has infiltrated our ranks and made it on one?"

"That is highly unlikely," Lemke said. "Every sailor on the 1st Fleet has been thoroughly vetted."

"Highly unlikely is what we would have said two weeks ago about the attacks around our country," Ringgold said. "But Captain Beckham has a point. We underestimated the monsters and their collaborators. Now we're paying the price."

Lemke didn't look pleased, his lips curving into a frown. Finally he said, "You're right. I'll have General Souza dedicate a team to investigating everyone on those ships."

"I'd advise sending the USS *George Johnson* to a covert location, isolated from the other ships, until we can confirm there are no collaborators among the rest of the Fleet." Beckham said.

Ringgold looked at Lemke, prompting him to speak first.

"That doesn't sound like a half-bad idea," he replied.

"Then let's make it happen," Ringgold said.

She gestured at Nelson who took the satellite phone from Cortez to call in the order.

"Prepare for landing," said one of the pilots.

The bird dipped through the choppy air, preparing to touch down on the sternward helipad of the Zumwalt Class Destroyer. Beckham retreated to his family. Javier latched onto him as the chopper landed.

"It's okay, bud," Beckham said. "Everything's going to be okay."

A Marine opened the side door, and a cold wind blew inside. The passengers filtered out, starting with the president and vice president. Beckham glimpsed a scene of organized chaos on the decks of the ships flanking the stealth destroyer.

Groups of Marines and soldiers were gathered, waiting to board flights that would take them back to the land for missions around the country.

Several F-22 Raptors took off and rose into the sky from an aircraft carrier, their tails glowing as they tore across the horizon. They would join the bombers to pound the Variant hordes.

Beckham helped his family onto the deck and herded them toward a hatch where Marines were waving people inside.

"Civilians this way!" yelled one of the men.

"Science team follow me!" shouted another.

Kate and Beckham stopped inside the passage with Javier, letting others pass them.

"You have that look, Reed," Kate said. "What are you thinking?"

Horn paused beside them, stepping out of the flow of people. Tasha and Jenny stood beside him as they held the collars of their German Shepherds, Ginger and Spark.

"Are you going to save Donna, Bo, and Timothy?" Javier asked.

"Please," Tasha begged. "Please bring them here."

Beckham and Kate exchanged a look.

"Mom, you're going back to the lab to save people, right?" Javier asked. "Well, Dad's a soldier and he's got to go back to fight to save our friends."

"Yes, he does." Kate reached out and hugged Beckham. "I love you, Reed."

"I love you, too."

"You aren't doing this without me, brother," Horn said. "Plus, Tasha told me that she'll kick my ass if I don't get Timothy."

"I didn't say it like that." Tasha's face warmed, then looked sorrowful. "Please don't let anything happen to him, Dad."

"We won't," Horn said.

"You promise?"

"I promise." Horn kissed Tasha on the forehead and bent down to Jenny. "I love you both. When you see me next, I'll have Timothy, Donna, and Bo."

The girls joined Kate and Javier while Beckham and Horn took off for the chopper. A team of Marines joined them. A crew chief closed the doors behind them, and Beckham grabbed a handhold with his prosthetic.

Looking out the window, Beckham saw their families in the open. Tasha, Jenny, and Javier waved at them. Kate looked sternly up at the helicopter, her hair dancing about in the wind and rotor wash.

"You ready for this shit, boss?" Horn asked.

Beckham nodded. "It's about time we got back into this fight."

***

A man crawled forward over the dirt in the dark chamber, dragging two shredded legs behind him. Blood streaked away from the strands of muscle and grit hanging from where his feet should be. He reached up with a trembling hand for S.M. Fischer.

"Help… me…" the man stuttered through quivering lips.

Fischer recognized the man's face in the darkness. It was Aaron Galinsky, the former Israeli military soldier that he had hired to track down the Variants on his property.

A hulking Alpha emerged from the shadows beyond Galinsky.

Fischer raised his rifle and aimed.

He pulled the trigger, but the magazine was spent.

The beast grabbed Galinsky by the head and stabbed his eyeballs, popping them with a sickening squelch.

The scream that followed sounded inhuman. More animalistic than from a man.

Fischer pulled out a new magazine, his fingers shaking, and palmed it into the gun, pulling back on the charging handle. Then he aimed and pulled the trigger.

Another click.

The gun wouldn't fire.

Fischer fumbled to replace the magazine again. But when he looked down, all his magazines were empty.

What in the Sam Hill?

The monstrous Alpha tossed Galinsky aside and reached for Fischer. Claws wrapped around his head, squeezing his skull, pain blinding him.

He woke up in a dark bedroom.

A moment of paralyzing terror gripped him as he tried to remember how he had gotten here. The events over the prior few days surfaced in his mind. Those nightmares weren't just dreams. They were real. All those memories came crashing down over him: the attacks on his oil fields, the loss of his livestock, and the death of so many of his men.

He snatched his wristwatch off the bedside table. It was the morning after he had climbed out of those tunnels, and the events of the previous day still haunted his mind.

"Shit," he muttered.

He pulled on a pair of pants, put on a shirt, and

grabbed the .357 Magnum he had under his pillow. The M4 he had killed dozens of Variants with rested against the wall. He slung it over his back.

Descending the stairs, he entered the communications hub that had been set up in his living room. A group of soldiers worked at the tables with enough satellite phones and computers for a platoon of soldiers guarding his oilfields. The lieutenant in charge was following orders from General Cornelius to protect the oil fields.

He had effectively turned Fischer's ranch into a forward operating base (FOB) overnight. All of the soldiers wore normal fatigues and gear but one thing set them apart from the military Fischer was used to working with—blue armbands with the insignia of an Orca whale.

It wasn't surprising to Fischer that the General had picked the super intelligent predators to represent his army, and frankly, he was damn glad to have them on his property.

"Sir," came a familiar voice.

Tran waved from a desk. Chase was also there. Both men had on fresh clothes, their faces clean from the blood that had soaked them last night, but neither appeared rested.

"Sir, did you get some sleep?" Tran said.

"A few hours," Fischer replied. "You two are looking rough. Didn't you get any?"

Tran nodded. "I slept an hour."

"How's that injury?"

A shrug from Tran. "I'll be fine."

"And you?" Fischer asked Chase.

"I slept, and I'm fine, but I got to be honest; I'm ready for that private jet ride to a beach."

Fischer forced a grin, trying to ignore the nightmares

still playing across his mind. "You and me both, son."

Another voice boomed across the room.

Sergeant Ken Sharp made his way through the maze of metal tables and communication equipment with Lieutenant Marcus Dees, the man in charge of the platoon. Dees had a graying mustache that looked similar to Fischer's.

"Lieutenant," Fischer said. "Can I have a word?"

"I'll be with you in a moment," Dees said. He continued to another table.

Fischer wasn't used to being brushed off like that. Especially in his own home. But he did appreciate having the military here, finally, to protect his fields.

Sergeant Sharp emerged from another hall. He nodded a greeting at Fischer before joining Dees.

"Sir, it's worse than we thought out there," Sharp said. "Variants and collaborators attacked over half of our outposts."

"Half the outposts?" Fischer said. "I'm surprised General Cornelius sent us a full platoon with those numbers."

"Your oil is necessary to sustain the war effort," Sharp said.

War effort…

"So we're at full-blown war now?" Fischer muttered.

"The diseased freaks have been breeding underground," Sharp said. "Brass says they have these masterminds controlling the smaller monsters with some sort of network. The science jockeys think they use the webbing we saw in the tunnels like a freakish internet."

Fischer felt like he had woken from one nightmare into an even more terrifying one. The beasts organizing themselves like that was something he never could have fathomed before.

"We've cleared out most of the Variants from this area," Sharp continued. "They seem to be heading roughly southeast."

"Toward Outpost Houston?" Tran said.

"That's a lot of ground to cover," Fischer said. "Houston should have nearly a week before the Variants reach them."

"A shit ton of juveniles are already attacking there," Sharp said. "Not sure the forces can hold them back. Outpost Houston might be long gone before the other monsters even get there."

"Mr. Fischer," a female voice called out. Fischer turned to see his maid, Maddie, standing between a few tables in the center of the room, arms wrapped around her chest like she was giving herself a hug. Still, she trembled.

"I'll be right back," Fischer said.

He motioned for her to head back into the hallway.

"You okay?" he asked her.

"Mr. Fischer, pardon me, but I heard what you were talking about," she said. A wet sheen formed over her eyes. "My family is at Outpost Houston."

Shit that's right…

"I'd like to go there and be with them," she said. "Is there any way I can get on a flight?"

Fischer waved Sergeant Sharp over.

"Do you have any birds going to Outpost Houston anytime soon?"

"In the morning, sir," Sharp said. "Of course that's assuming it will be there in the morning."

Maddie put a hand over her mouth, tears flowing freely now.

"Shit, sorry, ma'am, didn't mean to upset you," Sharp said.

Fischer put a hand on her shoulder. "It's going to be okay."

Dees spoke up. "He's right, ma'am. We're evacuating everyone from the worst hit outposts. Chances are good your family is already being relocated. No need for you to go to Houston."

Maddie managed a slight smile through her tears. "That's good to know, sir."

"I'll try to squeeze out some information through our friends here," Fischer said. "If we find anything out about your family, I'll let you know."

She nodded. "Thank you, Mr. Fischer. I would greatly appreciate that."

"You bet. Now go get some rest."

She left to join the rest of the staff in the kitchen cooking meals for the soldiers. The aroma of barbecue drifted down the hall.

It was the last time he would smell it here for a while now that his livestock had all been slaughtered by the monsters.

Fischer returned to Dees. He needed to try a different tack to get the lieutenant to open up to him.

"Thank you for everything you're doing, sir," Fischer said. "I'm grateful your platoon showed up when they did."

"General Cornelius sees this real estate as very important, Mr. Fischer,"

"I certainly agree. This land is my life's work."

"Well, you're going to have to trust your life's work with me for a little while, then," Dees said. "General

Cornelius has requested your presence at Outpost Galveston."

Fischer paused before responding.

"All due respect, Lieutenant, but can't we do a meeting over the phone or radio?" he asked.

"General Cornelius wants to talk to you in person," the lieutenant said firmly.

"Sir, I don't think it's safe for you to be traveling all the way across Texas in the middle of this shit," Tran said.

Dees arched a brow at Tran before returning his gaze to Fischer. "This isn't a request, Mr. Fischer. It's an order from General Cornelius. Remember, he graciously sent me and my boys to protect your oil."

"My oil for you to use as you see fit," Fischer said, eyes narrowing.

"I expect you to be on the next flight to Galveston," Dees said before walking away.

Fischer waited a moment, then gestured for Tran and Chase to join him in his office. He shut the door.

"I don't like this," Tran said. "I have a bad feeling about that guy."

"You don't succeed in the oil and ranching industry through ignorance," Fischer said, taking a seat at his desk. "I've learned a thing or two over the years. I can handle men like Dees who think they own the place, swinging around their rank and ego like a hammer."

Fischer stroked his mustache. "To be honest, I'm more worried about the Variants right now than the military taking over my land. Long as they protect it, I can live with them shipping some oil to protect the country. If we're all dead, doesn't matter who the oil belongs to."

"So we're going to Galveston?" Tran asked.

Fischer nodded.

"Guess this means I'm going to that beach after all," Chase said.

"I'd settle for a warm shower and a long nap over the beach," Tran said.

"Screw that, I want my girlie drink and some babes to look at," Chase said with a shit-eating grin.

Fischer chuckled. He grabbed the whiskey bottle off his desk and poured them all a drink. "This ain't no margarita but it's the best I can do for now."

"Thank you, sir," Chase said.

The men all took their glasses and raised them toward one another.

"It's been wilder than a buckin' bronc'," Fischer said. "And it's going to get even wilder still."

They clanked their glasses together, and Fischer filled his gut with warm whiskey, wondering where this crazy rodeo was going to lead them next.

— 3 —

Dr. Kate Lovato stood at the entrance to a lab on the USS *George Johnson.* Tasha, Jenny, and Javier were off in their quarters, playing with the dogs and resting. Boxes of lab equipment lay in stacks against the bulkhead. A cylindrical plastic centrifuge tube had somehow gotten loose from one of those boxes. It rolled back and forth over the deck as the ocean swells rocked the ship.

"It's going to take some work to get up and running," she said to herself.

She would have liked nothing better than to sit back in their cramped cabin with the children and dogs. Her body demanded it, nearly sapped of energy, especially with her husband and Horn out in the field, and the fate of Donna, Bo, and Timothy uncertain.

Yet just like Beckham and Horn heading back to Portland, she had duties. Obligations to protect the ones they loved and their fellow man. Despite her emotional and physical exhaustion, she had to carry on.

For now, she had to compartmentalize. Focus on one thing at a time. She tried to push thoughts of her family and the war from her mind as she began unpacking lab equipment.

Her muscles and back protested. Maybe it was her exhaustion. Maybe it was something psychosomatic, telling her this was ridiculous to once again be setting up a lab on the high seas hoping that this time they would finally stop the Variants.

She had to wipe away the sheen of wetness forming over her eye.

"Doctor Lovato," a voice said. "Sorry I'm late. I slept a bit longer than I would have liked."

Kate straightened and looked at Doctor Carr with his greasy dark hair.

"At least you got some sleep," she said. "One of us needs to be rested."

He helped her lift a heavy box onto one of the lab benches. She could feel him studying her from the side.

"What?" she finally asked.

"Nothing, I just hope you're okay."

"I'm fine," she lied. "We've got a lot left to figure out. But it's tough to focus on science when I'm more concerned about all those people we had to leave behind."

"I know what you mean."

That surprised Kate. Carr was usually all about science and to hear him express emotions like that caught her off guard.

"Without as many lab techs, we're going to have more work to do ourselves," Carr said.

Oh, so is that it? Kate thought. *He's just concerned about not having enough help.*

She thought to ask him to clarify his statement but decided it would be better not to have a definitive answer. For now, she would rather assume he actually had concern for people's well-being.

They began unloading liquid reagents and pieces of equipment.

"I know we still have some work left to do to

understand the communication network and the masterminds," Kate said, "but I'm certain we're on the right track now."

"Yes, I'm pretty confident you're right." Carr paused, his hand atop a box. "One thing I don't quite understand is how the Variants were breeding all this time without us knowing."

"Nature always finds a way," Kate said. She had a difficult time trying to keep the *Jurassic Park* line from her mind. But the saying had never felt so appropriate.

"Right you are. Mother Nature can be a, shall we say, stubborn bitch."

Kate almost smirked.

"The juveniles must've been breeding in those tunnels and within the cities right out of reach from our surveillance," she said. "The masterminds and the collaborators probably took great pains to keep the Variants' offspring hidden."

"Most definitely. And if our theories are correct, the Alphas digging those tunnels between masterminds and Variant hives weren't just creating lines of attack."

"No," Kate said. "They're like an ant-colony. Masterminds as queen ants, and underground chambers for breeding, feeding, and transportation, kind of like what we saw in Europe with the mutations there."

"Indeed."

They worked in silence for a while. A knock at the hatch caught Kate's attention.

A tall, willowy man with a mop of shaggy blond hair held out a hand toward her. "I'm Sean McMasters. I'm one of the new lab techs."

"Good to meet you, Sean," Kate said. "We're just setting up."

Sean directed a cadre of other lab techs to help place some of the heavier equipment like PCR machines and microscopes in their new homes within the lab.

The space was crowded, even with only Sean and a few other lab techs. It couldn't have been more than 900 square feet, perhaps the smallest laboratory Kate had ever worked in.

Sean carted in another dolly full of supplies.

"Where should we put these?" he asked.

"What's in them?" Kate replied.

Sean examined one set of boxes. "Looks like some biopsy samples."

"They'll need to go in the freezer then," Kate said.

"It's already stuffed."

"Then figure out how to make more room. Consolidate samples. Whatever we've got to do."

Carr looked around at the space. "This is smaller than my first studio apartment in Boston during my post-doctoral study days. I don't know how we're going to get much work done within these confines."

"We don't really have a choice," Kate said.

The lab was beginning to look like a lab finally, but Kate didn't feel any more prepared to start their research.

She kept thinking about Beckham, Horn, Donna, Bo and Timothy and all the other thousands of people trapped on the mainland while she had the luxury of being far away from the most immediate danger drifting on a stealth US warship.

"Maybe you should get some rest," Carr suddenly said.

Kate glanced over.

"I don't mean to tell you what to do, but a good bit of honesty between lab mates makes the work easier. I can tell your mind and heart are back at Outpost Portland."

He was right about the latter.

"I won't be able to sleep," she said. "Trust me, I'll get my head in the game. I just need time. The way I get past my worries is busying myself with work."

"Well, yes but…"

Kate turned her back to him and flipped on their computers. She missed Doctor Pat Ellis more than ever. Carr wasn't just odd; he didn't seem to have normal human emotions.

Maybe that was a good thing, Kate said. He could work without worrying.

It took her a while, but with Carr and the other lab techs working beside her, she finally managed to lose herself in her work at one of the computers.

The goal of deciphering the language of the masterminds motivated her to forget the other worries outside of these secured bulkheads. Any advantage the Variants had would be nullified if they could win the battle inside the lab.

But, as always, time was not on their side. For the second time in a decade she was fighting against the doomsday clock, only this time the human race was much closer to eradication than before, and there were far fewer people to stop it.

***

Taloned footprints crossed front lawns of the Shiloh Housing neighborhood area on Scott AFB. They led away from cratered asphalt holes where Alphas had broken through the middle of the street.

Dohi crouched behind a Humvee with Rico, scanning the rows of nearly identical houses for any sign of survivors. Another dozen soldiers were spread out behind them. Brave men and women that volunteered to sneak behind enemy lines.

"That looks like it might be it," Rico said, pointing to a house down the block. It had blue shutters and beige siding, just like they'd been told by command. Bushes lined the front yard and stretched into the back.

They'd been forced to come out here on foot, so what normally would have been a five-minute drive had taken the better part of the morning. Vehicles would have attracted every Variant straggler that hadn't gone back underground.

There were still a good number prowling in the sunlight. The team of volunteers had engaged multiple packs through the blocks from command to the northwestern corner of the base, losing one soldier along the way to a Variant hiding under a car.

Dohi spotted a pair of beasts perched on rooftops ahead. He pointed them out to their snipers.

Two suppressed shots punched through the monsters' wart-covered skulls. Both corpses slid down the roofs and crashed to the grass.

Rico gave the advance signal, and the team snaked down the road between the houses.

Some had broken windows, and others had doors torn down. Smeared bloody handprints covered the driveway of the house to Dohi's left. Those streaks of blood led straight to a tunnel.

He took point again and the volunteer team set off for the target house, weapons roving for beasts. When he got to the front door, he slammed into it, knocking it inward.

Checking his near corner, he then ran down a hallway that led to a large carpeted living room. Glass shards sparkled on the carpet alongside muddy footprints. Two large windows in the living room were broken. Wind tugged at the curtains.

Rico signaled half the team to clear the first floor, then gestured for Dohi to lead the second team upstairs. He picked up the scent of rotting fruit on the first step.

Shit, we're too late…

Dohi quietly ascended the carpeted stairs. At the top, a gruesome sight awaited. Gore splattered the walls, ceiling, and carpet. He followed the bloody mess to a bedroom where the remains of two men and a woman lay spread behind a broken-down door.

Two Variants sat hunched over the corpses, peeling away muscle and flesh, and stuffing them into their mouths. They chewed noisily, lips smacking together as bloody ligaments hung around their necks and chests.

Dohi let his slung rifle sag, then pulled out his knife and hatchet. The starving creatures continued to feed, unaware of his presence.

He lunged forward and brought the hatchet down on the head of the larger creature, burying it deep in the beast's skull. Then he jammed the tip of his knife into the eye of the other.

Both monsters slumped to the ground with a dull thud. He wiped the blood off his weapons on the carpet and walked back into the hallway.

Several of the soldiers stared at him as he and Rico led the way to another room where they found more corpses, nearly picked to the bone.

"Down here," came a voice.

A soldier stood at the top of the stairwell waving at them. The team followed the man down the stairs.

"We found six kids in the basement," said one of the

men who had cleared the first floor.

Dohi's heart flipped at the sight of the children being led out of a doorway.

"Thank God," Rico whispered.

"How'd they survive?" Dohi asked.

"The adults must have hidden them," the soldier said.

Most of the kids appeared catatonic, but one girl around the age of eight broke into hysteric screams when she saw the blood covering the walls.

"Where are my parents?" she cried. "I want to see my parents!"

Rico tried to quiet her, but it was already too late.

An inhuman shriek sounded outside.

A soldier pulled back the drapes to look out over the lawn.

"We got company," he said.

Dohi's heart pounded as he surveyed the kids. There were two that weren't older than four. This wasn't going to be easy.

"You all have to be super quiet, okay?" Rico said to the children.

A couple nodded, eyes wide and faces pale, but most of the kids still seemed completely in shock.

"Hurry," Dohi said. He signaled a team of soldiers to guide the children, then led the way out the back door into a yard lined with bushes. Over the spindly branches he saw neighboring backyards.

The sounds of clicking joints and growls came from the street.

"Watch our six," someone called.

The soldiers holding rearguard aimed at the back door of the house they had just left. The armored flesh of a juvenile exploded out a moment later.

Gunfire rang out, punching into the armored coat around the Variant. The creature stumbled a few feet before collapsing like a turtle with a broken shell, blood oozing out of its wounds.

Two more juveniles bolted out, sheering off the frame and barreling into the gunfire from the four soldiers at the rear of the group. Their rounds fractured the monsters' armor, and both beasts crumpled into a pile of tangled, bleeding limbs before they could reach the children.

The distant cries of other hunting monsters rang out. Several more shrieks answered their call.

A soldier with a crooked nose shook his helmet. "We ain't going to make it back with these kids. Not without a ride."

Another soldier slung his rifle over his back and picked up a sobbing young girl. She clung to him with her arms wrapped around his neck.

"Jim's right," the man said. "No way we walk all the way back to command like this."

The group hunched down as another Variant cried from the street in front of the houses. The beasts were definitely searching for them.

"Rico, see if we can get air support," Dohi whispered.

A nod, and she bent down.

"Command, Ghost 2," she said. "We need exfil, ASAP. We have six kids at the target. Over."

"Copy, Ghost 2," a voice replied over the channel. "Hold tight. I'll try and get you a Black Hawk."

Dohi's gut twisted while they waited.

The chorus of Variants swirled around the neighborhood, each voice representing a beast calling its brethren to join the hunt for fresh prey. These were the stragglers, the ones that hadn't yet retreated into the tunnels and back into the darkness.

From what Dohi had seen, they were desperate and hungry enough to risk everything in the intense sunlight for a meal.

The operator came online a few moments later.

"Got two birds in the air for you, Ghost 2. On their way to your location, over."

"Hell yeah, thanks," Rico said.

She smirked and nodded at Dohi.

"We're in business," he said. "Everyone, keep the kids quiet and we might just make it back to command in one piece."

The beat of chopper blades thrummed somewhere to their east, rising above the din of the monsters. It wouldn't be long before the Black Hawks arrived. But their loud engines would also alert other Variants to their position.

"We can't wait here," Dohi said.

"No cover," another soldier carrying a boy said.

Dohi was also worried about a tunnel opening up.

"There," said the soldier with the crooked nose said. He pointed to another house directly across from them through the backyard. "That deck. It's not much, but it gives us some shelter and gets us off the ground."

Another Variant wail punctured the steady thrum of the choppers.

Dohi walked at a hunch, scanning their surroundings. Two other soldiers followed him on his flanks. The rest carried or helped the children. The frightened kids weren't old enough or aware enough to stay in line on their own.

Past a line of bushes that separated the two backyards,

Dohi followed a set of wooden stairs that led to a deck standing almost four feet off the sloping ground of the backyard.

The team brought up the children and set them down in the middle of the deck. He and two soldiers leading the group carefully moved the metal deck furniture against the wooden slats along the deck's perimeter.

The location wasn't ideal, offering little protection, but the raised position provided firing zones through neighboring backyards and houses—most importantly, a direct line of sight to the house they had come from only fifty yards away.

"Keep them away from the sides, but be ready to run as soon as the choppers touch down," Rico said.

Another howl exploded from the home where they had found the children.

A juvenile stuck its face out one of the windows, blood dripping from its putrid lips. Brown nostrils flared as it sniffed the stink of its dead brethren lying nearby in the grass.

Dohi lined up his sights and pulled the trigger. Crimson splashed from a fresh hole in the monster's forehead, and it slumped out of view.

For a moment there was complete silence, but Dohi kept his rifle steady, waiting. Something was coming.

He was right.

The quiet was shattered all at once with full-grown Variants bursting through the bushes lining the backyard. The sinewy beasts galloped over the grass. Several juveniles joined the mix.

Armor piercing rounds speared through the plates bulwarking their organs. Monster after monster fell, sliding over the lawn now wet with their own blood.

The beasts became more incensed, swarming toward the deck. One lunged from a bush and made it through the fire on Dohi's right. It got all the way to the handrail and slashed at a soldier trying to change his magazine.

Dohi turned to help, unleashing rounds that chiseled into the monster's side. It squawked in pain and tumbled backward, but the damage was already done.

The soldier dropped his rifle and magazine to hold his neck, arterial blood gushing between his fingers. Red bubbles popped out of his mouth as he tried to say something.

Screaming children snapped Dohi away from the horrific sight. Two of the soldiers had to retreat from their firing positions just to keep the kids from scattering.

"Son of a bitch," Dohi said.

He tried to reassure himself with those words Fitz so often repeated to them.

All it takes is all you got.

But this time it wasn't just his life or Team Ghost's he was trying to save. They had six children with them.

Another minute passed with straggling Variants hurtling through the wide-open yards and filtering out of houses. They came in spurts, drawn from every direction. Not like the relentless waves they had fought upon arriving at Scott AFB, but still with a ferocity that chilled Dohi to his core.

That minute dragged on into a small eternity until one of the soldiers, covered in blood, pointed to the sky. Two black silhouettes contrasted sharply against the sea of blue.

The thump of helicopter rotors and the bark of M240s rose over the Variants' cries. Rounds tore up the yards around the deck cutting down stray monsters.

"Gather up the kids, and get ready to move!" Rico yelled.

The first of the Black Hawks touched down, and the second circled to provide covering fire.

"Now!" Rico shouted.

She and a squad of surviving soldiers scooped up the children and ran for the bird.

A few remaining juveniles charged for their position, but a crew chief quickly picked them off with the mounted M240.

Dohi was the last one inside. As soon as his boots hit the deck, the chopper lifted off.

The Black Hawks climbed into the air, leaving the carnage-filled neighborhood behind. A handful of Variant latecomers gathered in the grass, staring up for a few seconds. They soon disappeared into the holes that scarred the neighborhood like pustules from hell.

The ride back to command provided a chilling view.

Towers of smoke rose across the base. Streaks of red and brown painted the sidewalks and driveways of houses with broken windows and busted-down doors.

Rico plucked the piece of gum she'd stowed in her helmet and began chewing nervously.

"Hey, look at that!" the soldier with the crooked nose. "There, on that rooftop!" He pointed at a square office building below. Blocky white letters had been haphazardly painted across its flat roof, reading HELP.

Dohi considered asking the pilots to set down, but as they flew closer, it was clear that whoever had painted that SOS was long gone. Variants in the street chewed on bodies they had pulled from the buildings. Others dragged corpses into a tunnel.

"Oh, shit!" yelled another soldier. "That guy's still alive!"

Dohi raised his rifle and zoomed in his Elcan SpecterDR optic on a man who was being pulled into one of the tunnels. He gripped his abdomen, but his hand fell away, revealing glistening exposed organs. This man wasn't long for the world, and he was suffering.

You can't save him, but you can end the torture.

Dohi lined up the sight, thinking back to the tunnel he had been a prisoner in, and what awaited this man.

Then he pulled the trigger.

The prisoner went limp in the grips of the Variants. Those monsters glanced up at the bird as it flew over, then went back to feeding. He lowered his rifle and turned away from their feast.

Several of the soldiers in the troop hold stared at Dohi.

Rico patted him on the shoulder, and then went back to helping the shell-shocked kids. Dohi was proud they had managed to save these children, but today sure as shit didn't feel anything close to a victory.

— 4 —

"I think we're getting close," Beckham said.

Next to him, Horn twisted to look out the window of the helicopter.

The bright light of the afternoon sun filled the cabin with a yellow glow as the chopper curved through the air. Marines sleeping in the leather seats stirred awake. Others were already alert, checking their weapons and gear.

Nearly sixteen hours had passed since the collaborators hit the White House, and in that time over half of the ninety-eight outposts had suffered devastating attacks. Outposts near the target cities were on the brink of falling.

Beckham had spent most of that time in the air. First traveling from the White House to Outpost Portland, then to the USS *George Johnson*, and now back to Outpost Portland.

He was anxious to get on the ground and join the battle, but feared he'd already lost his chance to make a difference.

The Marines looked ready to jump back into the fray as well. Their leader was an eager sergeant named Buck with big eyes and a thin mustache.

"What's the latest, Sergeant?" Beckham asked.

"There's still fighting on the ground according to aerial surveillance, sir," Buck replied. "I haven't heard from Lieutenant Niven's team for over an hour, so there's no telling how bad it really is."

Beckham stood and walked to the cockpit.

"How much longer?" he asked, hoping for more information.

"About ten minutes," said a pilot. "We're working on identifying a secure LZ. Sounds like command wants us to put down at the University of Southern Maine."

Beckham brought a hand to shield his eyes from the glare of the sun. He leaned forward for a better view as they closed in on the shoreline. Thick columns of black smoke billowed away from the center of the outpost. Most of that smoke rose from two specific locations within the city.

No flames chewed through Peaks Island, and Beckham didn't see any charcoaled buildings or pillars of smoke. The island might have been spared from the fires, but Beckham knew he wasn't returning home there anytime soon.

Radio chatter crackled from their contacts on the ground.

One of the pilots replied, "Roger that."

"Prepare for landing," the other pilot said over the internal channel.

Beckham returned to his seat. The bird lowered over an abandoned part of the city. Then they flew over the first line of defense: blocked off streets and a wall of razor-wire-tipped fences.

Soldiers manned machine guns in the guard towers. Other groups patrolled the FOB's perimeter, weapons in hand. One soldier raised a hand into the air as the chopper passed over.

"Get ready, everyone," Buck said. "We're headed straight to the FOB for assignments."

The Marines all finished their final preparations as the chopper descended toward the lawn of the university. It touched down with a slight jolt, and the crew chief opened the doors.

Beckham and Horn followed the Marines out and marched toward a group of soldiers holding a perimeter. Even from a distance Beckham could see the bags under their eyes and the glassy expressions of exhaustion they wore. Splotches of blood covered their fatigues.

Sergeant Candace Ruckley was one of them. She limped over with a bandage covering her right arm and another wrapped around her thigh.

"Good to see you, Sergeant," Beckham said.

Horn looked her up and down. "Looks like you took a hell of a beating."

"Never thought I'd see the sun again," she said. "Also didn't think I would see you two back here so fast."

"We came to help and get our friends," Horn grunted.

"Kind of late for the fighting," Ruckley said. "A few collaborators are pinned down toward the southeastern edge of the city, but they won't last another hour."

She jerked her helmet, indicating for them to follow her. "I'll take you to the information tent first. We can check on the location of your friends while our teams mop up the rest of those animals."

"What the hell happened last night?" Beckham asked.

"The collaborators hit us from inside the outpost, sir. Not long after you took off," Ruckley said.

She pointed to the plumes of dark smoke.

"The sons of bitches blew up the water tower, took out the power station, and tore through our checkpoints," she said. "All right behind our backs. Someone in here was definitely coordinating with them."

The guilt of not seeing this coming ate at him. He could stomach their failure to predict the monsters breeding and scheming beneath the cities, but this?

The collaborators had been under his nose the entire damn time.

"Do we know who yet?" Horn asked.

Ruckley shook her head. "Unless we got a good forensic analyst in town we're not going to."

"What do you mean?" Horn asked. "They escaped?"

"Blew themselves to bits," Ruckley said sourly.

Beckham halted. "It was a suicide bomber?"

"The one in the power station was," she replied. "That set everything off. The rest of the damage was from LAWs and AT-4s."

Horn's lip curled into a snarl. Beckham felt the same surge of anger.

"Don't worry," Ruckley said. "Most of the people are fine, just a bit frightened."

Hearing that helped quell the rage a little, but *most* didn't mean *all*. Beckham wouldn't be satisfied until he knew that Donna, Bo, and Timothy were among the safe ones.

"I have a hard time believing someone we know could've helped the collaborators last night," Horn said. "I can't think of anyone that would do something like this."

"What's hard to believe is how they could have access to such powerful weapons," Ruckley said.

"Is it though?" Beckham asked. "We thought the Variants were dying off under the cities, and seeing as how they were thriving, it makes sense the collaborators were too."

"He's right, and there could be a lot more of the

assholes," Horn said. "We have to start searching."

"Already working on it," Ruckley said. "We've been interviewing witnesses, tracking down anyone who is remotely suspicious, and reinforcing checkpoints to prevent more collaborators from sneaking into our borders."

"Good," Beckham replied. "We've got to focus on stomping out any final collaborators and securing the outpost before the next wave."

Ruckley stopped in her tracks and winced as she rotated her injured body. "Next wave?"

"This looks like it's just the beginning to me," Horn said. "They're trying to destroy our resources and infrastructure while they probe our defenses to prepare for the real attack."

"Let them come." Ruckley spat on the ground. "We'll be ready."

Beckham had other thoughts on the matter but kept them private for now. He wanted to evaluate the situation first.

The trio crossed the dry brown grass between the university buildings to the information tent.

A young woman with curly hair sat behind a folding table. She looked up from an open ledger.

"How can I help you?" she asked.

"We're looking for Donna and Bo Tufo, and Timothy Temper," Beckham said.

"Going to take a bit to locate them," she replied. "We moved a lot of people around today. Come back in twenty or thirty minutes, and we'll have better information."

"Thanks," Ruckley said, then turned to Beckham. "I'll take you to the roof of Corthell Hall. It has the best views of this area. You can see the damage from there."

Beckham followed her with Horn through the campus. They entered the hall that was now serving as makeshift barracks for the soldiers deployed to protect the outpost.

When they made it upstairs, three snipers were camped out on the roof. Sleeping bags, MRE wrappers, and gear littered the space.

Ruckley pulled out her radio. She called her platoon officer, Lieutenant David Niven, as they walked over to the ledge. "Sir, I have Captain Beckham here if you have updates for him. We're on top of Corthell."

"Hold tight up there," Niven replied. "I'll be there soon."

"Copy that, sir," she replied.

Horn sidled up near one of the snipers. "Where are the collaborators?"

They all pointed toward a building across the interstate near West Bayside, not far from the hotel where Beckham had spent several days with his family after the first attack.

Ruckley handed Beckham a pair of binoculars. He took them and zoomed in on M-ATVs and Humvees surrounding the structure. A group of soldiers hugged the eastern façade, waiting to storm the building.

Beckham had wanted back in the action, but here he was again, watching from a distance. Still, there were other things he could do to help.

"Where are the checkpoints the collaborators hit?" he asked.

Ruckley pointed toward the northwestern side of the city.

"They tried to take out another checkpoint there, but we stopped them," she said.

He centered his sights on a blackened vehicle on a road leading west. Concrete barriers blocked off the road, and a team of soldiers stood behind sandbags.

"Captain Beckham, Master Sergeant Horn," came a voice.

Lieutenant Niven joined them at the edge of the rooftop.

"LT," Horn said.

They exchanged formalities.

"Hell of a night. Day wasn't much better. But we stopped them and are in the process of relocating most of our resources," Niven said. "Still got about half of our people in West Bayside, but the area will be secured soon."

Beckham moved the binos back to the building surrounded by armored vehicles. Soldiers were already walking out of it, carrying bodies between them.

"Who's in charge of the outpost now?" Beckham asked.

"That would be me," Niven replied.

"Good. As native to this place, I've got some suggestions."

"I'm all ears."

"I'd recommend moving everyone from West Bayside to the campus," Beckham said. "We were telling Ruckley that we think the attacks on those checkpoints were just the enemy testing our defenses."

"They cut the power, took out the water tower," Horn said. "They're going to be back. Maybe it'll be tonight. Maybe tomorrow night. They'll hit harder, and I'll bet you dollars to donuts they come back with Variants, too."

Niven looked out over the campus. "Pulling the non-combatants here might not be a bad idea. It would at least cut down on the real estate I need to protect. But this thing about Variants. You really think they'd come all the way out here?"

"Based off the experience of other outposts, I wouldn't be surprised if the beasts show up sooner rather than later," Beckham said. "How many troops are stationed here?"

"One hundred and fifty, plus the two hundred strong local militia," Niven said.

"Sounds like a lot, but not against hundreds of Variants," Beckham said. "Not to mention we've gotten reports across the Allied States that armored juveniles are joining in the assaults."

"Then we've got to move fast," Niven said. "Sergeant Ruckley, give the order."

Ruckley started relaying the command over her radio.

Niven turned back to Horn and Beckham. "I take it you two didn't come all the way back here just to offer a little advice. What brings you back?"

"We came to finish the fight, but it looks like things are under control," Beckham said. "We should've stayed last night."

"It's still good to have you here now," Niven said. "And besides, the President needs you more than I do. Your families need you, too. Time to let people like me and Ruckley do our share."

Ruckley cracked a grin. "Everything's taken care of. We're going to start the evac. Permission to check on their friends, sir?"

"Go," Niven said.

Beckham and Horn followed Ruckley back down to the campus grounds. The young woman at the information tent was still looking over the ledger when they got there.

Her eyes caught Beckham's on their approach. "I found Donna and Bo Tufo, but Timothy Temper has left the outpost."

"What?" Beckham said, narrowing his eyes.

"I'm still trying to figure out where the militia group he's with went," she said.

"Hold on. Militia?" Beckham asked, heart pounding.

"That's got to be wrong," Horn said. "Timothy's no militia soldier. Check again."

The girl looked back down and then back up again. "Timothy Temper?"

"Yeah…" Horn said.

"He went out with a group of militia soldiers." She jabbed her finger on the ledger. "Says so right here."

"Can you tell us where they went?" Beckham asked.

"Not exactly. All I know is they're out west hunting a truck of those collaborators."

"That's Variant territory!" Horn said, face turning red.

Beckham couldn't imagine what would have compelled the militia to head out there when the outpost was in jeopardy like this, but he did know what had compelled Timothy to go with them.

A memory surfaced of Timothy's father, Jake, bleeding out back on Peaks Island after the raider attack—no doubt the same group affiliated with these collaborators.

Timothy wanted revenge.

"What should we do, boss?" Horn asked.

"Timothy's not ready for this. He has no idea what he's getting himself into."

"You're not actually considering going after them, are you?" Ruckley asked.

"That's exactly what I'm considering," Beckham said.

"*We're* considering," Horn corrected. "You ain't going out there alone."

***

Timothy thought back to the hunting trips he had taken with his dad when he was younger. In a way, this wasn't that different, aside from the prey they were tracking.

At least that's what he kept telling himself.

But deep down he knew that was a lie.

This was *very* different.

And the farther away they went from Portland, the more he felt like the prey.

He marched with a group of twelve militia soldiers carrying M-16s down a dirt road about twenty miles away from the outpost. Two trucks trailed them.

They had chased a Jeep Cherokee until the vehicle had run out of gas and the collaborators inside disappeared into the forest.

The militia soldiers had lost the trail and were back on the road on foot. Timothy was in the middle of the group, his father's Remington 870 Wingmaster twelve-gauge shotgun cradled in his arms.

Several of these men had known his father, but none of them seemed to know who Timothy was. The group leader was a guy named Stephen Rhodes, a guy about as old as Timothy's dad. Stephen was in good shape. He wore green fatigues with a baseball cap and scarf to match. He hadn't even questioned Timothy when he claimed he was eighteen years old and wanted to join the militia right there and then.

"Get in the truck if you're coming," Stephen had said.

Timothy had hopped into the pickup's bed, and they

had raced out of the city. The only regret he had was not dressing a bit warmer, especially now with the late afternoon sun behind the trees.

He shifted the weight of his shotgun and scanned the forest. They were on the border of Variant territory now. Maybe even inside it for all he knew. In his mind's eye, he could picture his dad yelling at him about how dangerous this mission was.

Beckham and Horn would have something to say about it too, but Timothy didn't care. He didn't want to sit back in the outpost, scared and crying. He wasn't afraid of dying.

Without his father, he was already dead.

The dread returned, filling his chest and gut. Anger replaced it from time to time, but right now he just felt… empty.

His dad had been his world.

Stephen balled his fist, and the group halted.

The trucks behind them crunched over the dirt road before coming to a stop. Silence passed over the road. The two drivers stepped out of the trucks, joining the huddled group.

"We definitely lost the trail," Stephen said in a gruff voice. "We can turn back or head into these woods to try and pick up a new one."

The men around Timothy looked at each other as if gauging what their comrades wanted to do.

Timothy raised his chin, trying not to show any fear. "I say we keep going."

"Me too," said another.

"I won't lie to you: the sun sets early and night will be here before we know it," Stephen said. "We aren't prepared to hunt in the dark and we could very well run into a pack of Variants."

He shrugged. "On the other hand, if you're like me, I'm guessing most everyone in this group lost someone to those bastards or you wouldn't have volunteered. This could be our best chance of catching up to them."

Timothy thought back to what Big Horn and Beckham had told them about the Army Rangers giving up the chase when they literally had the collaborators in sight.

"Military sure as hell ain't going to do it," Timothy said. "They had their chance once, and let them get away."

"How about this," Stephen said. "Half of us will continue on, the rest will head back to the outpost just in case we need backup."

Six of the militia soldiers climbed into a truck with one driver, and the engine rumbled back to life. The departing truck did a U-turn and headed back. The remaining five soldiers, including Stephen, fanned out into the forest as the driver of the second truck waited in the cab for their return.

Timothy walked into the weeds along the side of the road, following the other men into the woods. He was definitely the youngest here. Several of these guys were old dudes. Too old to join the military even with their relaxed requirements.

They set off, and Timothy scanned the hilly woods, breaking the area down into a two-dimensional canvas just like his dad had taught him. Surveying it from left to right, and then back again, looking for any sign of movement.

The beasts could easily camouflage themselves to blend in with the terrain, but they were easier to spot when they moved.

Leaves and twigs crunched under the weight of their boots as they marched deeper into the forest, the trees swallowing the group. Timothy made his way closer to Stephen, trying not to make too much noise.

"You're a brave kid," Stephen said quietly.

"Not a kid," Timothy whispered back.

Stephen's mouth curled into a smirk. "Bullshit. I knew your dad. You aren't eighteen. I just figured if you're anything like your old man, we could use your help."

So he did know…

Timothy simply nodded.

They walked for the next thirty minutes into the forest, searching for any sign of buildings, tracks, or a trail. He wasn't the best tracker, but he could have spotted human footprints had they come across any.

Stephen halted and pulled out a compass. Then he put it away and pulled out a bottle of water. He handed it to Timothy.

Timothy brought the bottle to his lips and downed a third of it. His stomach growled. They hadn't come prepared for being out here so long. This was supposed to be quick.

"Thanks," Timothy said, handing it back.

An older man with glasses stood and pointed. "I think I see something."

Timothy brought up his shotgun, but he didn't have a scope to zoom in on whatever it was this guy was pointing at.

"I don't see shit," Stephen said.

The older man looked away with a frown. "I'm sorry, my old eyes must be playing tricks on me."

Stephen slowly lowered his rifle and picked the bottle of water off the ground.

"Let's keep moving," he said. "If we don't—"

Crows burst from the trees to the east, filling the late afternoon with their caws. The men all aimed their rifles in that direction.

Timothy moved his finger to the trigger. After blinking away the sting of sweat in his eyes, he searched the carpet of leaves littering the forest floor for movement and then the phalanx of trees around them.

He saw nothing out there but skeletal branches shedding more leaves.

The crows flapped away, silhouetted against the blue sky, their cries fading.

Silence again shrouded the group.

They remained frozen for what felt like an hour. One of the men tried to keep his rifle up, but it wobbled in his grip, the weight too much for his old muscles to support.

Stephen took a few steps, his boots making a faint crunch over the leaves.

He gave the advance signal toward where the birds had taken off. Timothy fell in next to him. They walked slowly toward a cluster of massive trees that towered into the sky. The older man with glasses turned to wait.

A flash of movement in the branches far above the man's head caught Timothy's attention. The few remaining leaves rustled on one particularly large branch. This one looked different than the others, like it had something clinging to it.

Two reptilian eyes suddenly focused on him. Before he could raise his shotgun, the camouflaged Variant let go of the branch and pounced.

The beast slammed into the guy with the glasses. Leaves and dirt exploded into the air. Timothy aimed his shotgun, but before he could get a clean shot the beast dragged the man around a tree.

"Help me!" he wailed.

A second militia soldier slammed into the ground with a thud, a Variant standing atop his chest. He fired off a burst, but the rounds hit the dirt.

All at once, a dozen beasts poured from between the tree trunks. They had all taken on the colors of the forest. Timothy fired on the beast straddling the second downed soldier just as it slashed the guy's throat open.

The shotgun pellets hit the creature in the chest, punching into vital organs.

The crack of automatic gunfire came from both sides as Stephen and the two remaining militia soldiers fired on the encroaching monsters. Timothy pumped his shotgun and fired at the creatures.

Stephen dropped several beasts with headshots. Timothy's aim wasn't as good. His shots harmlessly hit trees and dirt. In less than a minute, he was out of shells. He back pedaled as he struggled to pull more from his sweatshirt and load them into the shotgun.

He dropped one in the grass, fingers trembling, but managed to load the next two.

"Run!" Stephen yelled over the gunfire.

Timothy took off with the other two soldiers. Stephen led them, turning every few moments to shoot off a burst or two.

Turning, Timothy did the same, firing the two shells.

"I'm out!" Stephen said, grabbing a new magazine.

Timothy was out, too. He reached into his sweatshirt pocket. There were no more shells there. He threw his shotgun away and snatched his pistol from his holster. He twisted to fire wildly behind him while Stephen reloaded.

In the seconds it took to fire, Timothy glimpsed at

least a dozen of the sinewy beasts moving between the trees. They were on all fours, but they were slinking in and out of cover rather than running straight into the gunfire at full speed.

A hidden Variant lunged and took down the soldier running behind Timothy and Stephen. The talons slashed his face off. His screams faded as the beast dragged him away.

"Come on!" Stephen yelled.

Timothy bolted after him. The man paused and fired until his bolt locked back, and he was forced to replace the magazine.

They ran like that for almost ten minutes, covering each other to hold the beasts at bay. The Variants grew more desperate, their screeches closing in.

Stephen and Timothy let loose a flurry of gunfire. The rounds dropped some of the creatures still pursuing them.

"Move it, kid!" Stephen shouted.

They couldn't be far from the road now. Timothy spotted two hills he thought he recognized. The road was just on the other side.

Stephen stopped again to lay down more covering fire before leading them down the first of the two hills. Timothy kept his balance, but Stephen tripped and fell. He got right back up and kept running.

Timothy charged ahead, trying not to slide, and then ran across a creek, his boots splashing up muddy water. He bolted up the next slope with Stephen close behind. Halfway up, a shriek sounded from the crest of the first bluff.

"Keep going!" Stephen shouted. He turned to fire, giving Timothy time to get to the top. When he reached the crest, Timothy turned with his pistol, aiming at a pack of Variants loping down toward the creek. Three of the creatures jumped into the water with a splash.

Stephen stood his ground, firing bursts with his rifle. Timothy squeezed his trigger as fast as he could. Most of the wild shots missed, but a few made their mark.

The creatures that were brought down were replaced by more barreling down the hill. They were no longer held back by caution now that it was only Timothy and Stephen left.

Stephen turned and locked eyes with Timothy just as the beasts swarmed him.

"Run!" he screamed. "RUN, KID!"

The beasts pulled him to the ground, ripping through his clothing and flesh with their claws. Timothy took a step backward, nearly frozen by fear. It wasn't until one of the beast's locked eyes with him that he snapped out of it.

Turning, he ran onto the road, looking left and then right. The truck was still there.

"Help!" he shouted.

Waving his hands, he ran toward it.

A Variant screeched behind him, bursting onto the road. It dropped to all fours and bounded toward him. There was no way he would make it to the truck in time.

Halting, he closed one eye and then fired at the beast.

The first two shots missed, but the third and fourth clipped the monster in the upper chest. The fifth shot punched into the skull, finishing it off. It crashed to the ground, kicking up a cloud of dust.

Timothy ran, not stopping until he got to the passenger side of the pickup. He opened the door and jumped into the cab.

It was empty. The driver was gone.

Blood soiled the driver's seat. The window was broken, pebbles of safety glass spread over the floor. Timothy climbed into the driver's seat and reached down to start the engine, but the key was missing.

He looked up as two Variants skittered onto the road in front of the truck.

Heart pounding, Timothy ejected the magazine of his pistol and slapped another one home. It was his last. Not nearly enough for the rest of the Variants that would be on him shortly.

Without the keys, he was going to die.

He thought he wasn't afraid of death, but the icy grip of fear washed over his muscles as the Variants charged.

Timothy raised the gun in a shaky hand and pulled the trigger.

— 5 —

The USS *George Johnson* sailed farther away from the 1st Fleet, putting distance between President Ringgold and the majority of their remaining Navy. Everything she had worked so hard to achieve had become an inferno back on the mainland, and this time she feared she couldn't put out the flames.

She sat in her new office that doubled as what would be her quarters for the foreseeable future. The small space had belonged to a dead officer, and the evidence of his life still haunted every corner. An empty picture frame that read, *Dad*, was adhered to the bulkhead, and a Bible with dog-eared pages rested in one of the drawers.

It hadn't felt right to remove those little memorials to the man's life.

The dimly lit, cold room felt more like a prison cell than home, but it still beat being underground.

You're safe here, she thought.

Repeating those words didn't relieve her anxiety. In fact, the more she reminded herself of her own safety, the more guilty she felt. Hundreds, if not thousands of people had perished over the past twenty-four hours, and she had fled just like she had done during the first war.

The country—and the world—had already lost so much to the monsters. Almost an entire generation wiped out, and the youngest generation of adults that had survived the first war now faced another.

She dreaded the thought of sending youth out there to fight the monsters or to eradicate American history by destroying what was left of their cities with bombs.

But now she wasn't sure she had any other options.

One thing was certain…

We have to fight.

She took a moment to look at herself in the mirror before setting off for her next strategy meeting. Her dark skin had more wrinkles than she remembered, and deep bags hung under her eyes. It wasn't exactly a surprise. She had only slept a few hours.

A splash of water on her face helped snap her alert. She repeated something she had said to Doctor Kate Lovato near the end of the first war.

"There is always hope…"

She drew in a deep breath, straightened her back, and pushed open the hatch. Marines posted outside threw up salutes. She returned the salutes and hurried through the passages to the Combat Information Center (CIC). Most of her staff and the officers were already there. Some looked like they had been there since the night before.

They all rose from their chairs and stations to salute and greet her.

"Good morning, President Ringgold; I hope you got a few hours of sleep," Vice President Lemke said.

"Madam President," said General Souza.

Judging by the glassiness in his eyes, he hadn't slept in *days.* His LNO, Lieutenant Festa, also looked equally exhausted.

"Lay it on me," she said.

"The good news is that we haven't lost any more outposts," Souza said. "Even the ones around Minneapolis, Chicago, Lincoln, Kansas City, Indianapolis, and Columbus survived last night."

He passed her a briefing folder.

"Casualties at those outposts, however, are very high. In some cases, over half the defense forces were wiped out," Festa said.

Cortez crossed her chest in silent prayer, and Soprano looked at the deck.

"We're in the process of evacuating people by air and pulling them to more protected places, including locations where it will be more difficult for the Variants to tunnel under our defenses," Souza said. "I have a list of outposts for you to review later."

Festa handed a second folder across the table. She took it but didn't want to look right now; she was having a hard enough time keeping it together.

This all felt like a bad dream.

"Do we know enemy numbers yet?" she asked.

"Early estimates project somewhere in the hundreds of thousands with the addition of the juveniles," Festa said. "We gave them a good pounding last night, but most returned to their hives before we could get accurate estimates."

"That could make sending in any teams to find the remaining masterminds a suicide mission," Souza said, clenching his square jaw. "But we did it before, and we can do it again. We have teams on standby, waiting for your orders."

She glanced at Lemke. "What do you think, Dan?"

"We're trying to come up with other ways to find the mastermind Variants," he replied. "I'm hoping Dr. Lovato and Dr. Carr will eventually help us locate them through the webbing in all those tunnels, but so far they haven't come up with anything we can use."

Souza cleared his throat. "All due respect to Dr. Lovato and her team, but we're running out of time for science. And something tells me we haven't even seen the full power of the Variant army yet. Last night was merely the vanguard to what I expect will be a more powerful assault than we've seen before."

The implications chilled Ringgold to her core. She couldn't shake the fact they hadn't seen this coming over the past eight years. While she partially blamed her advisors and generals, she also felt the heavy burden of failure herself.

"How did we miss this?" she said, exasperated. "We monitored all six target cities and sent missions into Variant territory. We didn't see any evidence of juveniles or the masterminds."

No one had an answer.

"I'm sorry," General Souza said. "If you would like my resignation, I have already drafted it."

She thought on it, but shook her head. "We can't dwell on failure; we have to focus on saving our people."

"We're already fortifying all of our outposts," Souza said. "We're withdrawing from those around the target cities to concentrate our forces. That will also give you the option of nuking them if you so choose. And finally, we're requesting armed support from Europe."

"They aren't experiencing attacks like this?" she asked.

"Not yet," Nelson said. "All our requests for support have been received lukewarm at best. They fear helping us will leave them vulnerable."

"Has *anyone* promised anything?"

"The French, Russians, and Brits have sent us a few aircraft," Nelson said.

"How many?"

The National Security Advisor tightened his red tie.

"How many, Nelson?" Ringgold repeated.

"A total of ten planes, Madam President..." He swallowed. "Not fighter jets, these are jumbo jets to help evacuate people."

She sighed. "I'll talk to my counterparts directly today. You keep pressing your contacts."

"Yes, Ma'am. I will."

Ringgold didn't expect much but they needed more than ten extra planes to repel this invasion. She had opened the doors to refugees from other countries, feeling responsible for the virus that the military had unleashed on the world. But she wasn't exactly surprised the leaders of other countries were reluctant to help the Allied States now.

"What else do you all have for me?" Ringgold asked.

"By sunset, we hope to have most fortifications complete," Souza said. "We've also got a fleet of private planes and helicopters that have been serviced and put back into commission. But even with those, it won't be enough to complete the evacuations from the worst hit outposts by then, and if the Variants do attack again..."

Another shiver coursed through Ringgold's body.

"What about evacuations by land?" she asked. "We could try to pull people back in convoys."

"That's already happening in some places, but anyone that leaves in a convoy risks being attacked on the road," Festa said. "People are too afraid of driving in Variant country."

"We really need more help to win this fight and get everyone to safety," Lemke said. He raised his chin slightly. "If our international allies can't offer that support, I suggest turning inward."

He paused, and then said, "Madam President, I think we should consider reaching out to General Cornelius. He's got two thousand men and a load of aircraft and vehicles at his disposal. Plus, he's already arrived at Fischer Fields to secure the petroleum supply."

Ringgold looked at the man who she had hoped would succeed her as president. He was suggesting she ask his political opponent for help, which wasn't all that shocking considering their situation, but it still took her slightly off guard.

"The election doesn't matter now," Lemke continued. "Saving our country and our people is all that I care about. If Cornelius can help us, I say it's worth setting aside differences."

"You're talking about negotiating with your opponent," Ringgold reminded her vice president. "If we ask him for help, he will in turn ask for favors, some that we're not going to like, and some that I can't accept, like nuking the cities and conscripting our young people."

Lemke nodded. "I know, but we might have to negotiate if we want to save what's left of the Allied States."

She used a moment to think. Lemke was right about needing Cornelius. She just hoped the general was more reasonable than he had been in the past.

"Okay, Dan, talk to General Cornelius and inform him that we're officially putting the election on hold," Ringgold said. "It's time to try and work together."

***

Fischer would have preferred his private jet and the luxuries that came with it, including a cold brew and fresh steak from his ranch. Rare, of course.

But those days were over.

He sat in the belly of a V-22 Osprey. It was certainly a fine piece of machinery, though "luxurious" was definitely not the word he would use to describe it or the flight from his ranch to Galveston.

The thrum of the engines reverberated straight into his bones. He was strapped into a seat along the bulkhead of the tiltrotor aircraft beside his most loyal men, Tran and Chase. Sergeant Sharp sat close by. He had insisted on coming even though he wasn't assigned to Cornelius's private army.

The six soldiers that wore Orca badges didn't seem to trust Sergeant Sharp or appreciate his presence. But Fisher sure trusted him, especially after Sharp had risked his life to protect Fischer Fields.

Their priority had changed overnight from saving the fields to saving what remained of the Allied States. From the reports still coming in, salvaging what was left of the country was going to take more than oil from his fields.

They needed a bigger army.

Fischer's stomach twisted as the Osprey began to bank slightly northeast. He tried to focus on the purpose of this meeting, and although he had his suspicions, he wasn't sure why they needed to meet face-to-face.

Being in the oil business and defending his fields against the Variants, he had come to expect all kinds of nasty surprises in life. He wouldn't be shocked if this upcoming meeting with the general was one of them.

"Got about twenty minutes before we touch down," Sharp said.

"Any hostiles we should worry about?" Tran asked.

"Nope, and once you see this place you'll understand why."

It didn't take long before Fischer saw for himself.

Galveston Island stretched below them, basking in sunlight. Murky brown waters lapped against yellow sandy shores on the eastern side and piers to the west. The long land mass trailed south, but most of the activity was contained within the northern city limits of Galveston.

The Osprey curved through the sky, providing a closer view of the outpost. Thick concrete walls traced the perimeter. Guard towers crested multiple positions, giving sweeping views over the water and the rest of the island.

On the eastern shore, walls overlooked beaches of razor wire. Fischer had once heard of Variants that had evolved gills and were capable of amphibious assaults. Cornelius clearly had seen the intel and was not taking any chances with his defenses.

Another group of soldiers piled corpses on a pier at the end of the beach past a ruined Ferris wheel.

The only way to the island by foot was via the heavily garrisoned port or the long bridge connecting Galveston to the mainland. Concrete barriers and mounds of sandbags were set in various locations to slow attackers, providing ample opportunity for the machine gun nests to riddle hostiles with bullets.

Heavily armed patrols and armored vehicles were posted along the docks. Another set of gates there would thwart any waterborne invaders mistakenly looking for an easy entry.

"Impressive," Fischer said.

"Yeah, but I see a big problem, sir," Chase said.

"What would you have added?" Fischer asked.

"I would have left a small section of beach for laying out, but with all that razor wire, it doesn't look like soaking in the sun with any babes is in the cards."

"Galveston's fun in the sun days are over for now," said one of the soldiers across the seats.

The guy sitting next to him joined in and said, "There used to be an Ironman triathlon here. I finished it once, but the only swimming, biking, and running people are doing here now is to get away from the monsters. Not exactly the kind of stuff that makes you want to lounge around."

"Man, you're killing me," Chase said. "Can I at least find a place that serves cerveza?"

The Osprey's engines roared as the tiltrotors turned vertical. They descended toward a makeshift heliport on a large parking lot abutting the wall overlooking the beach.

A jolt shuddered through the aircraft when the wheels touched asphalt. The crew chief lowered the rear ramp, and Sharp led the group out into the salty breeze that also carried the acrid scent of petroleum. Vacation homes on stilts and restaurants surrounded the parking lot.

Most of the homes had been transformed into barracks or offices now, but the restaurants appeared active—or at least the kitchens were. Lines of soldiers and civilians stretched out the front of a few seafood joints that had busy patios.

Across the parking lot, two Black Hawks had set down. These didn't look like the military craft Fischer had seen at other outposts. Graffiti covered the hulls with call signs.

The troops milling around the choppers all wore blue armbands with the Orca insignia that Dees had worn. Flapping in the wind high above the parking lot was a flag with the same logo.

"Welcome to Outpost Galveston," said the triathlete soldier. "We got a limo waiting. Follow me."

Fischer let out a low chuckle when he saw a Humvee parked nearby.

The ride took them through a residential area with a view of the beach. Most of the people out here were soldiers. He saw very few civilians.

From their hurried actions and constant arrival and departure of aircraft, Fischer got the feeling that this place operated like a well-oiled machine. There was no hemming and hawing, politicking or bickering.

There was a singular mission here, and everyone on Galveston shared in it: defend the outpost from the monsters.

But it hadn't always been this way. Fischer had heard Outpost Galveston was a slum four years before General Cornelius arrived.

"Cornelius built all this?" Fischer asked the driver.

"Yes, sir. He brought this place back to life and managed the construction of the fortifications himself. If it weren't for him, no one here would have survived."

"I see," Fischer said, fidgeting with his mustache.

He was beginning to respect Cornelius more and more.

The streets passed by in a blur of motion. Everyone had a job ranging from putting up fresh razor wire to cleaning weapons.

It struck Fischer then.

This was the future of the Allied States.

The Humvee ground to a halt in front of what once had been a fancy hotel neighboring the port. A pair of guards opened the door to the Humvee and gestured for

Fischer and his men to follow. Sharp went with them into the lobby of the hotel.

Desks had been set up around the ornate space. Chandeliers cast white light over men and women carrying on trenchant conversations at scattered tables.

"This way," said a guard. He led them to the back of the room where two double doors were shut.

Tran and Chase stepped up, but the guard shook his head. "Only Mr. Fischer is allowed inside."

Fischer exchanged a glance with his men and then nodded.

"I'm with Mr. Fischer," Sharp said.

Fischer took off his ten-gallon hat.

The guard nodded and let them into the room.

General Cornelius sat behind the table talking with two officers. As soon as the doors opened, he rose from his seat and walked briskly from behind the table.

"Mr. Fischer, so glad to have you join us," Cornelius said, clasping his hand. "I appreciate you making the journey."

"And I appreciate you saving my oil fields," Fischer replied. "You got quite an operation set up here."

"All the better to prepare for the next stage of war." Cornelius glanced over to Sharp. "And you are?"

"Sergeant Ken Sharp, United States Army, sir," Sharp said, snapping to attention.

"He's with me," Fischer said. "Sharp gave a lot to protect my fields before your men showed up. Lost all but one of his own, too."

"Thank you for your service, Sergeant," Cornelius said. "Please, make yourself comfortable. We've got a lot to discuss."

Fischer and Sharp sat down as the general went to the

other side of the table.

"I take it you didn't bring me here just to convince me to support you for the election," Fischer said.

Cornelius smirked. "No, Mr. Fischer. If we don't act soon, we won't have a country left. And without a country, I see no point in having an election."

"No thanks to President Ringgold," Sharp muttered.

Cornelius didn't respond to the comment.

Realization hit Fischer. He got the sense Sharp hadn't come here to help; he had come here to switch sides.

"I've asked you here for your support, but not the political kind," Cornelius said. "Earlier, in fact, I got off a call with Vice President Lemke. We've come to an agreement that we'll work together for the better good of the country. The election is on hold."

Fischer wasn't completely shocked to hear that, but the agreement did take him by surprise. He guessed there was some intense negotiations going on to get a guy like Cornelius to team up with the president and vice president.

"You saw our defenses," Cornelius said.

Fischer nodded.

"All have been effective against the Variants until now… monsters that tunnel underground and appear beneath and behind walls that have kept them out for eight years have changed the game."

"Indeed."

"Our scouts can't find them. Even our choppers and drones can't spot them before they hit us."

"Right, and that makes this outpost a damn fine choice," Fischer said. "The Gulf on one side and bay on the other will ensure this place is hard to hit. The sandy soil on the neighboring mainland makes it hard for beasts to maintain the tunnels' structural integrity, too."

"Exactly. I figured you would notice. Any man worth his salt in the oil and gas industry has at least a basic understanding of geology."

"More than just a basic one."

"You and your engineers are some of the best petroleum producers in this country and we need you for more than that now."

Fischer braced himself.

"I could use someone like you for a special project that could change the tide of this new war," Cornelius said. "Someone with your experience with all the gizmos and gadgets used to find oil deposits to help us identify Variant tunnels on a large-scale basis."

Fischer stroked his mustache, listening.

"We've reached somewhat of an impasse. Our R2TD systems work well at identifying Variant tunnels. But their range is extremely limited, and they can't cover much area effectively."

"You're looking for something more efficient," Fischer said. "Something that can defend a whole outpost. You're talking about seismic vibrations, aren't you?"

"Precisely, and here's the deal. We've located a few vibroseis trucks from some defunct oil and gas companies outside Houston. They've already been moved out to El Paso. But what I really need are men that know how to work this equipment. Men like yours."

Fischer's mind swam back to the destruction of his fields and the casualties he endured. Before he'd been swept away to Galveston, his staff was still tallying up the dead and missing.

"How many you reckon you'll need?" he asked.

"Just one team to start. Maybe eight or nine engineers."

"Last count I made, we might only have twenty left. That's barely enough to run and repair the oil fields."

"I have a feeling you're a man who knows how to make limited resources work. Can you spare even a handful?"

"For this project, I'll find a way to make it happen," Fischer replied.

"Well then if you agree, I'll call in an airlift to move your engineers from Fischer Fields to El Paso right now. They can be there before you arrive tonight."

Fischer wasn't sure he had a choice in the matter.

"We need to prove that this tunnel identifying technology works," Cornelius said. "I'm counting on you and your team to make that happen."

"Point of clarification, sir."

"Go ahead."

"When you talk about the entire Allied States, I do want to be clear that my handful of engineers and whatever equipment you've moved to El Paso isn't going to be enough to take care of a hundred other outposts."

"Of course not. I've got a plan for that, Mr. Fischer. One that involves some technology that we've neglected for far too many years. But you don't need to worry about that for now. Think of El Paso as a trial run. An experiment to show this strategy is worth pursuing. If all goes well, we will change the tide, like I said earlier."

An end to those vile beasts that had taken so much from him and his men was an opportunity Fischer simply would never pass up. He stood and reached across the table to shake Cornelius's hand.

"Sir, you've got yourself a deal. Fischer Fields is up for the challenge."

"Glad to hear you say that, because this work in El Paso isn't exactly going to be safe." Cornelius sat back down in his chair. "You will be well protected, but you might have to get up close and personal with the Variants for this to be a success."

— 6 —

The exodus into the University of Southern Maine was well underway by late afternoon, and Timothy still wasn't back. Beckham and Horn stood in the back of a parked pickup truck outside the campus.

People streamed by on their way to the garrisoned campus in preparation for what Lieutenant Niven and Beckham believed could be an imminent Variant attack. Beckham couldn't help but wonder if any of these people were collaborators.

Paranoia set in as they passed. Some glanced up, but most kept their gaze downward, trudging along like so many refugees Beckham had seen in war-torn countries trying to escape bloodshed. They carried suitcases, backpacks, and rolled up sleeping bags.

He didn't see collaborators here—he saw innocents looking for refuge.

For now, all he could do was trust Ruckley and Niven had the situation under control and find his friends.

He searched the slow-moving group of hundreds for Donna and Bo. Horn nursed his last cigarette. For the first time in a while, Beckham felt like taking a drag. He needed something to take the edge off. He was trying not to worry about Timothy. That proved difficult considering the kid had taken off after the collaborators straight into Variant territory.

For now, there wasn't anything Beckham and Horn

could do but wait. They'd asked Lieutenant Niven for help, but Niven wouldn't commit any forces to going out into the field.

Frankly, Beckham didn't blame him for not wanting to send out any spare men. In truth, there weren't any spare men. They needed every person that could hold a weapon to stay stationed at the campus for whenever the collaborators and Variants struck next.

If the monsters' behavior in the past was any indication, the beasts would send everything they had in the next attack and it would come soon.

Come nightfall, Beckham worried they would face an army no one even knew existed until recently—an army that had hidden in the shadows, biding its time as it grew to horrific numbers.

"Hurry up, folks," a Ranger said.

"Almost there. Keep moving," said another.

Sergeant Ruckley and her twelve-person team of Rangers from the Iron Hogs helped keep the mess of people moving. They patrolled the sidewalk, keeping an eye on the masses and encouraging them to keep going forward.

Beckham scanned the dreary faces again, but still didn't see Donna and Bo. All he knew was that they had hunkered down at a hotel with the other survivors of Peaks Island the night before.

The plan was to get them back to the USS *George Johnson*, and this time Beckham vowed not to leave them behind. He figured he and Horn could stay in the field to help for at least a few more hours. No way they were going to abandon the outpost this time, especially without knowing Timothy's fate.

"Yo, boss," Horn suddenly said.

Beckham glanced over. "Do you see Donna and Bo?"

"Nah, but I was thinking… You know what the good news is about the world falling apart again?"

"I have a feeling you're going to tell me."

"I don't have to listen to you giving some silly ass campaign speech."

Beckham couldn't help but smirk. "True. You know what else is good news?"

Horn blew smoke skyward and shrugged.

"I don't have to see your donkey ass try and squeeze into a suit."

"Donkey ass?" Horn spat onto the pavement. "You haven't called me that for a really long time."

"That's what Panda used to call you, isn't it?"

"Man, I miss that big son of a bitch."

"Me, too."

"And the kid."

Beckham thought of Alex Riley, the Delta Force Operator that had become wheelchair bound after breaking both legs in New York City. He had later lost his life to the Bone Collector Alpha on Plum Island. It was one of the deaths that had sent Beckham close to the edge.

If it weren't for Kate and Horn, he would have lost it back then and probably gotten himself killed. But people like them and Fitz had kept him sane. They had motivated him to keep his head on his shoulders instead of doing something rash. Something like what Beckham feared Timothy was doing.

"There they are," Horn said, pointing with his smoldering cigarette.

Donna winced with each step as she leaned on her son. Both had their eyes on the road.

"Come on," Horn said.

He hopped out of the pickup bed to the street. Beckham wasn't as agile with his prosthetic leg. He sat down on the liftgate and slid down.

"Reed!" came a voice.

Bo worked his way through the throng, helping his mom. She hobbled on a bandaged ankle, but her eyes brightened when she saw them.

"You came back," she said.

"We shouldn't have left without you," Beckham said. "I'm sorry. It was chaos last night."

"You had no choice," Bo said. "But I almost punched one of those soldiers holding me back."

"Good thing you didn't or we'd be bailing you out of the stockade," Horn said.

"Have you guys seen Timothy?" Donna asked. "He took off after the helicopters left, and we haven't seen him since."

"We heard he went out with the militia," Horn said. "We've been waiting for him to come back, but…"

Beckham glanced at his watch, and then looked at the skyline.

They only had a couple of hours of light left. If Timothy didn't come back before then, the chances of him coming back at all would be close to zero.

"Hey, you found your friends?" came a voice.

Ruckley made her way over the sidewalk and stopped near the pickup.

"This is Bo and Donna Tufo," Beckham said.

"Nice to meet you," Ruckley said. "Hate to break this up, but you really should get moving so we can assign you a room or a tent…" She eyed Bo. "You should have a weapon."

"Aren't we leaving with you?" Donna asked Beckham.

"Soon enough, but we might stay the night yet," Beckham said. "I wanted to wait and see if—"

"I say we stay here and fight," Bo interrupted.

Donna looked at her son. "What?"

"I don't want to run," Bo said. "We did that eight years ago, and look where that got us. The monsters are back. It's time to fight, Mom."

"We're survivors, not fighters. Your dad tried to fight and died as a result. *So* many other people did too. I can't lose you now Bo."

"She's right, kid," Horn said. "You don't have any combat training."

"I'll learn," Bo said.

"You sound like Timothy," Donna said, her face growing red. "Where do you think he is now?"

The words silenced all of them.

Even Ruckley looked at the ground until her radio buzzed and she held up a hand, excusing herself. She walked away for some privacy.

"Bo, I'm begging you, please don't do this right now," Donna said. "Let's just get to the campus for now. We can talk more later."

Bo held his mom's gaze.

"All right," he said finally.

Beckham placed a hand on Bo's shoulder. "You're making the right choice." Then he looked to Donna. "Come on. We'll give you guys a ride."

Donna wrapped her arm around Bo's shoulder. He helped her into the passenger seat of the single cab pickup. Horn took the wheel, and Beckham climbed in the bed with Bo.

"Hold up," Ruckley called out.

By the look on her face, Beckham could tell she had news for him.

"What is it?" he asked.

"I told my team to keep an ear out for word on Timothy. A corporal just found out one of the two militia trucks returned to campus an hour ago," Ruckley said. "From what the militia told us, your friend Timothy is part of another group that stayed out there to hunt down the collaborators."

Beckham growled out a curse.

"Did they say where Timothy's group was last seen?" Horn asked.

"No," Ruckley said. "But they're still at the staging area. You can ask them yourselves if you want."

A loud voice called out behind her. One of the other Rangers was arguing with the straggling crowds.

"Keep moving," he said in a tone just shy of a shout.

"We need a ride too," a woman said, pointing at the truck. "Why do they get one?"

"I better handle this," Ruckley said. "The staging area is between Woodbury Campus Center and Masterton Hall. I'll meet you there."

Beckham nodded and tapped the side of the pickup. Horn pulled onto the curb and over the grass to another road curving through a residential area. Then he turned onto Bedford Street and headed for the checkpoints.

Ahead, soldiers and civilians worked together to create sandbag fortifications for machine gunners, and forklifts moved concrete barriers. Razor wire torn down from other areas of the outpost was being redistributed. Snipers and machine gunners perched on the top of the buildings.

The university was quickly transforming into a fortress.

Horn parked in the lot between Masterton Hall and the Woodbury Campus Center. Lines of people snaked away from tents set up in the lawn for temporary housing assignments.

More lines had formed outside a shipping container on the back of a flatbed truck. Soldiers handed out weapons and ammunition to anyone that appeared capable of fighting.

Bo jumped out of the pickup and helped Donna down from the cab.

"You guys go get your temporary assignment for now," Beckham said. "We're going to find these militia guys. I'll come back for you later, okay?"

Donna hesitated, uncertainty crossing her face.

"We promise," Horn said.

Beckham jerked his chin, and Horn followed him toward a cluster of pickup trucks and Jeeps where about a dozen men in camouflaged fatigues had gathered. They were clearly militia judging by their shotguns, non-military clothing, and unkempt beards.

"Were you the ones chasing the collaborators?" Horn called out.

The men turned from their conversation to look at Beckham and Big Horn. A heavyset bald man with a long goatee hanging to his chest walked over.

"I was part of that group," he said. "You got a problem?"

"Yeah, we got a problem," Horn started.

Beckham put a hand on Horn's arm, trying to coax the man's burly aggression down a notch. "Problem is we need to know what happened to the other truck. One of our friends was with them."

"They ain't back yet," the militiaman said.

"No shit," Horn said. "Show us on a map where they went."

"I can do y'all one better," the man said. "I can take you there."

Horn and Beckham exchanged a glance.

"Just a thirty-five-minute drive," the man said. "My boys and I were thinking about going back out there in the morning. How about we wait until then?"

"We were thinking today," Beckham said.

The man looked at the sky, eyes narrowed. "We can manage a short trip, but we got to move fast if we want to be back before we lose the light."

"What do you think, boss?" Horn asked.

"I think this is our best chance," Beckham said. "Niven made it clear he isn't sending anyone anytime soon."

"Better stop wasting time then," Horn said. He pointed at the man with the goatee. "You driving or you want me to?"

"I'll drive," the guy said. "Anyone else coming?"

The other men avoided his gaze.

"The rest of you boys scared of the dark?" the man said, then shrugged. "Guess it's just us three. Name's Sam, by the way."

"Captain Reed Beckham, and Master Sergeant Parker Horn," Beckham said.

"Nice to meet you, fellas," Sam said, shaking both their hands. He led them to a single cab Toyota pickup with a mounted M240 in the rusted bed. Beckham went for the passenger side door, and Horn climbed into the back.

The diesel engine of a Humvee roared behind them, and the vehicle pulled up alongside them.

"What the hell do you think you're doing?" Ruckley growled.

"Timothy was our responsibility," Horn said. "We promised his dad we would look after him. That's what we're going to do."

"Team Ghost does not break promises," Beckham added.

"That lady back there—Donna, right?—she was right about Timothy," Ruckley said. "I hate saying it, but we all know he's probably already dead."

"Probably doesn't mean one-hundred percent," Horn said.

"Sergeant, I know you regret letting the collaborators get away during that first attack," Beckham said. "This is your chance to get revenge."

"Vicariously, through us," Horn said, leaning on the pickup's cab.

Ruckley clenched her jaw, fists trembling for a second. "God dammit. You're putting me in a really shitty position here. If Niven finds out I let you go at this hour, my ass is toast."

"We'll be back before he even knows," Horn said.

"You fucking better be, Master Sergeant," she said. "All due respect, and all that other crap."

"Can't hear you," Horn said. "Because you were never here and didn't see me leave." He grabbed the machine gun and tapped the top of the cab.

Sam started the engine, and Beckham closed the door. He kept his window rolled down and charged his rifle as Sam drove out of the lot and through the city. The soldiers manning checkpoints all gave them the same look as if to say, *You guys crazy*?

It wasn't the best of plans, but Beckham and Horn couldn't just leave Timothy out there.

The sun continued to lower in the sky on the ride. Sam didn't talk much and Beckham kept quiet. They both clearly had one thing on their mind—finding the militia soldiers.

Thirty minutes later they pulled onto a gravel and dirt road.

"There," Sam said, pointing.

He eased off the gas as they approached an idle truck.

"Stay here and keep it running," Beckham said. He opened his door and motioned for Horn to stay on the mounted machine gun.

Beckham shouldered his M4A1 as he approached the truck. Bullet holes had fractured the windshield, and the driver side window was shattered, revealing torn seats covered in blood that gave him a pretty clear mental image of what had happened.

He halted when he saw long scratches marred the door.

It wasn't the collaborators that had attacked the militia.

Variants had done this.

He cautiously opened the truck door to look inside. A pistol with a bloody grip rested on a floor mat, surrounded by empty bullet casings.

Beckham picked the familiar gun up, confirming it was the same pistol Jake Temper gave his son for his sixteenth birthday by the engraving on the barrel.

Never Stop Fighting.

He remembered Kate insisting on holding the party at their house. The memories sparked a wave of dread that washed over Beckham, deflating him like a punctured tire. He wiped the pistol handle against his pants to clean off the blood, then stuffed the gun in his waistband.

As he made his way back to the pickup, he scanned the woods. The autumn colors glowed in the final hours of sunlight in what might have been considered a divine view before the age of monsters.

But Beckham knew evil dwelled in those woods and wouldn't hesitate to show itself once they'd turned dark.

Ruckley was probably right. By all odds, Timothy was likely dead. But there was a chance, however small, that the young man was still alive. If he was, then he was almost certainly a prisoner to the beasts. A fate even worse than a quick slash of a claw to the throat.

He walked over to the side of the truck and looked up at Horn, then pulled out the pistol. "It was his."

"I could tell by the look on your face," Horn said quietly. He clenched his jaw, face turning red as he looked out over the forest.

They stood in silence for a moment before Beckham gave an order that almost physically hurt. Timothy's trail ended here. Coming out here had been a big enough risk. Searching for Timothy now would be suicide.

"We have to get back to the outpost for now," he said.

Horn didn't protest. The brash man knew they had no choice. Instead his eyes went low, and he kicked at the pickup bed, muttering a stream of curses.

Beckham got back into the cab.

"Either the guys that stayed out here are all dead or they're prisoners now," he told Sam.

The old militia soldier didn't seem too surprised. "I see. We calling off the search then?"

"I'm afraid so."

Sam put the vehicle into drive. Beckham kept his rifle on his lap as they drove away. They wound back down the road, surrounded by the hilly forest rising on either side. Shadows enveloped them as the sun began its descent beyond the trees.

"Lost some good men out there," Sam said, nose twitching. "Men I called friends. Stephen was one of the best I ever had."

"I'm sorry," Beckham said.

"Me—"

The M240 barked the same second Beckham saw the men emerge from the woods. Muzzle flashes came from the foliage, rounds peppering the passenger door and shattering the window.

"Floor it!" Beckham yelled. He leaned down, barely avoiding a volley of bullets meant for his head. They sliced past him, but still found a target.

Hot blood splattered his neck as he remained hunched. Beckham glanced to the side. Sam had been hit across his shoulders and chest. Despite the injuries he kept his hands on the wheel and foot on the pedal.

Sam tried to open his mouth to talk, but only blood came out.

The crack of the M240 exploded again.

Return fire punched through the passenger door, letting in rays of light. Another bullet clipped Sam in the neck, blood spraying out. He reached up to staunch the wound, and Beckham grabbed the wheel.

Sam slumped forward onto the wheel, breaking Beckham's grip.

The truck swerved into the ditch and down an embankment that ended at a cluster of large trees. Beckham sat up. In the side mirror, he saw Horn jump out of the bed and roll into the foliage. The pickup jolted violently at the bottom of the ditch.

There was no time for Beckham to brace himself. Crunching metal and shattering glass sounded when the hood of the truck crumpled against a tree. Beckham's head snapped into the dashboard. There was pain, but then only darkness.

A voice stirred him awake some time later.

Beckham groaned, his head pounding.

He opened his eyes to a view of overhead branches. Leaves fluttered down behind over a blurred face.

"Boss, you got to wake up," Horn said.

Beckham's vision cleared enough to see Horn, a cigarette sticking out from the corner of his mouth.

"There you are, brother," Horn said. "Can you sit up?"

He grabbed Beckham under the arm and helped him up. Beckham reached up to touch a tender gash on his head, blood still trickling from it.

"Reed, say something," Horn said.

"Where are the fuckers that ambushed us?"

Horn grinned. "Dead. All four of 'em; I fucked 'em up good. We got to move before more come."

Beckham saw Horn had already gathered their weapons and added a backpack to the mix. He guessed that's where the new cigarette came from too.

"Can you walk?" Horn asked.

"I think so. You got the radio?"

"Yeah… but it's broke dick," Horn said. "We're on our own, boss."

— 7 —

Spotlights snapped on around Scott AFB as the horizon swallowed the last drop of sunlight. They flitted back and forth over the terrain as the soldiers prepared to defend the base for a second night.

Beyond the defenses, smoke still drifted away from smoldering buildings and houses. The crack of gunfire echoed through the early evening as the final hunter-killer teams finished picking off the rogue Variants still prowling for food.

Fitz carried a box of explosives out of the command building. The rest of Team Ghost was working to put up a third fence surrounding the building. The front gate to the first layer of defenses opened as the armored vehicles returned from their missions.

About one hundred soldiers had remained behind to protect the command building from the Variants now that most of the non-combatants had been evacuated. The sounds of hammers and shouting voices echoed over the parking lot.

Fitz was glad that command had decided to try and hold this position.

"Hurry up!" someone shouted.

The urgency was shared by every soldier and Marine working near the command building. They were all exhausted, and Fitz wasn't sure when any of them would get to rest.

He handed his crate of explosives off to a Marine and then joined Rico who was working on piling up sandbags in the glow of portable lights.

She dropped another onto a small pile and wiped the sweat from her forehead. Both dimples widened when she saw him, but quickly turned to a frown. "You doing all right, Fitzie?"

"Yeah, I'm good, how about you?"

"Glad we saved those kids but worried about what the night brings." She turned to look out over the defenses. "I got a bad feeling we might have just been delaying the inevitable."

"I know what you mean," Fitz said.

She gave him another sideways glance. "Seriously, you sure you're good? If you need to grab thirty minutes of shuteye, I can pull double duty."

Fitz nearly laughed. That was one thing he could never fault Rico for. She would look out for everyone else at the sacrifice of her own needs.

"No way," he said, almost calling her babe. If his teammates heard him call Rico that he would get more shit than a Kandahar porta potty.

Ace, Dohi, and Mendez were working on another mound of sandbags nearby but they didn't seem to be listening.

"What I would do for a few hours of sleep," she said. Then she playfully hit him in the arm. "And a little of you know what…"

"Get a room, kids," Ace said.

Fitz's cheeks warmed. Apparently they were listening.

"I wish," Rico chuckled.

Mendez joined in. "Does fucking up Variants get you all as hot as it gets me?"

"Christ, man," Ace said. "You're a nut."

Dohi didn't react. The stoic man grabbed another sandbag and placed it on top of the mound.

"How you doin', brother?" Fitz asked him.

Dohi shrugged. He always had a way of keeping his emotions and thoughts close. Trying to get at them was like prying at a crate with a plastic shovel to see what was inside.

"I heard what you did in that chopper," Ace said. "You did the right thing."

Fitz recalled what Rico had said—that Dohi had shot a man being torn to shreds by the Variants. His silence made even more sense.

"Pops always taught me to put an animal out of its misery, and the same goes for humans," Ace said. "He also told me to always know more than the name of the guy on your left in the assembly line."

"I track things and I shoot things, what else do you want to know?" Dohi asked.

Ace looked like he was about to try again when a Marine jogged over from an M-ATV holding another rocket-launcher-shaped R2TD device.

"Master Sergeant Fitzgerald!" the man called out. "We've got new orders for you."

Fitz had been waiting on those words, and for the R2TD. Several other teams were already using the surviving devices command had on hand to mark tunnels around base.

Now Fitz had a feeling Team Ghost was going to help beyond the walls again.

They had danced with death too much lately, and although Rico was a skilled soldier, he couldn't help the anxiety that coursed through him when she was out there on her own.

Of course that was the life they had both chosen, but the past few days were different than the past few years of missions. This wasn't just hunting down an errant Variant or two. This was all out war.

"Any word on enemy movement?" Fitz asked the Marine as he took the R2TD unit.

"The only activity in this area are the rogue Variants still scrounging for food, but most of them have been eliminated by our hunter killer teams."

"So no indication that they might attack again tonight?"

"And no sign of the hordes?" Ace asked.

"Not yet," said the Marine.

Fitz stamped the ground with one of his blades. "They're still down there. They have to be."

"Guess it's a good thing we still have a couple R2TD systems," Rico said.

"No kidding," the Marine said. "We're lucky we got this one. It was on the chopper dropping off those kids y'all rescued."

"Glad to hear they were evacuated," Rico said.

"Them, and the rest of the people here. Just us jarheads and our brothers… and sisters left now." The Marine unslung a pack and handed it to Rico. "These will help the demo teams collapse any tunnels you locate."

"Thanks," Fitz said.

The Marine nodded and jogged back to command.

Inside the pack was a jumble of stake flags—plastic flags on small metal posts that looked like they could be used for marking electrical lines under a lawn.

"Not the most sophisticated way to do this," Rico said.

Dohi shrugged. "Sometimes sophistication is just unnecessary complication."

Ace flicked on the R2TD system, and the equipment buzzed to life.

"Let's get this over with," Fitz said.

He led the group through the soldiers working overtime to make final preparations. Most of the men and women didn't even look up.

Spotlights guided the way to the fences. The fact snipers and machine gun nests had their backs reassured Fitz as he made his way beyond the secure zone. But despite the firepower, stepping outside the wire sent a chill through Fitz.

He battled his fatigue and kept his rifle at the ready.

Not long after leaving the barriers, Ace signaled he'd found part of a Variant tunnel beneath their feet. Rico placed a flag in the soil.

They moved on and Fitz watched the scanner for contacts. "Still no signs of life down there?" he asked Ace.

"Nothing heading towards us," Ace replied.

"Probably running away 'cause they smell your sweaty fat ass," Mendez said.

"If that's true, then you're welcome," Ace replied.

Dohi smirked for the first time in… Fitz wasn't sure how long.

But all trace of jocularity vanished at the sound of an explosion from a grenade. Dust bloomed across the parking lot to the east where Army engineers had detonated C-4 in a tunnel, closing it off so the Variants couldn't reuse it.

In his mind's eye, Fitz couldn't help seeing that horrific theater at the University of Minnesota and the explosions that had taken Lincoln's life.

He would never forget that moment. It was always like that when you lost a brother or sister. The death playing like a nightmare on a loop that you can't stop.

Fitz turned at the sound of footsteps pounding the pavement.

A team of Rangers fanned out across the lot. "We're here to relieve you all from R2TD duty," said a Sergeant in command of the group.

"Already?" Mendez asked. "We were just getting started, and I'm ready to do some damn work!"

The sergeant nodded. "Command says they've got something else for you. Didn't tell me what it was, but they said to tell you all to get ready to ship out. You're going back out in the field."

Rico gave Fitz that look, the forlorn one that said rest and whatever else would have to wait. Their job at command was done; the place was secure, and ready for the next Variant assault. But for some reason, Fitz had a feeling wherever they were heading was going to be far worse than another attack on Scott AFB.

***

It was going to be a long night, and thanks to her advisors' input, President Ringgold feared it would be a deadly one. Across the Allied States the outposts had spent all day refortifying their defenses to prepare for the next phase of Variant attacks that they believed was imminent. A few furtive warnings had been sent to outpost leaders that collaborators may have infiltrated their ranks, just as they had in Outpost Manchester. So far, Ringgold hadn't heard of any traitors that the military had identified or captured. She wasn't sure if that was a good sign or if these human monsters were waiting in the shadows like the Variants had for eight years.

"Last night was a test…" she kept hearing.

If that were true, then tonight could be the worst night of her administration. Everything and everyone in the Allied States was at risk.

She took a short, but necessary shower, then finished getting ready for her next briefing. Leaving her private quarters, she found Chief of Staff Soprano waiting outside her hatch with a cup of warm coffee.

"Thought you might need some caffeine," he said.

"You know me too well," she said.

Two Secret Service Agents led them through the bowels of the stealth warship. Sailors backed against the bulkhead as they passed, saluting.

She saluted and tried to nod at each one, but her mind was a tangled mess as she pieced together her next steps.

Ringgold was doing everything she could to keep it together.

Plan. Organize. Achieve goals.

"And never lose hope…" she whispered.

By the time she arrived at the CIC, she had focused her mind and was ready to face whatever reports awaited her inside.

A Marine opened the hatch. The space buzzed with activity. Officers worked at stations monitoring everything from troop movements and evacuation routes to the arrival of support from other countries.

"This way, Madam President," Soprano said.

She followed him into a briefing room already filled

with staff. LNO Festa, General Souza, NSA Nelson, and Vice President Lemke, among others helping strategize the war efforts.

Soprano handed Ringgold a briefing folder and then joined Cortez near a bulkhead. She sat at the head of the table. She took a sip of coffee, set the cup down, folded her hands, and nodded.

"Outposts outside the primary target cities of Minneapolis, Chicago, Lincoln, Kansas City, Indianapolis, and Columbus are all bracing for attack," Souza said. "We're still sending air support to help evac the civilian populations, but we're losing daylight quickly."

Souza gestured toward a wall-mounted monitor. "These are the remaining outposts across the Allied States."

Ringgold already knew how many were left.

Eighty-four.

Eighty-four of the ninety-eight that the country had labored over for almost a decade, struggling against setback after setback to create a new, safe civilization after the Great War. She was relieved to see that number hadn't dropped since she had taken a shower.

But night hadn't even begun.

"What about other countries? Did your calls or mine help?" she asked Nelson. He had helped arrange most of the support and aid after Ringgold talked to her counterparts in each country.

"Page twenty summarizes our current levels of support, Madam President," Nelson said. "We just updated the responses."

She opened up to page twenty and scanned the report. "This is…"

"Afraid so, Madam President," Nelson said. "The

European Union, Mexico and the Central American Coalition, the Southeast Asia States, and most of our other strongest allies seem to be sitting on the sidelines to see how bad this is."

"French President Morain promised me he would send us more than this," Ringgold said. "Am I reading this correctly?"

"Yes, Madam President. Instead of sending troops, he has sent one hundred consultants that will help with the detection of tunnels. They come from private sector, government, and military roles with experience combating those worm Variants that dug underground in Europe."

Ringgold managed her disappointment with a breath. "That's good, but we don't just need help finding tunnels. We need help destroying them. That means more than just sending people over."

"We can win this fight without them, especially with the help of General Cornelius," Lemke said.

"He called not long ago with an idea he wants to discuss," Soprano said. "I said you would call him back as soon as you had some free time."

Ringgold nodded. "Get him on the phone now."

Cortez left the room with Soprano.

In the meantime, General Souza went over other updates.

"Doctor Lovato and Doctor Carr are still figuring out how this webbing network works," Souza said. "We've got multiple Special Op teams preparing to track down new masterminds. Team Ghost is on standby for a mission to New Orleans where we've identified one. At your orders, we'll deploy them."

She thought on it a moment. They had no choice. The masterminds had to be destroyed.

"Permission to proceed," she said.

Souza nodded at Festa who left the room to give the order.

"We've done everything we can to prepare with the time and resources we have," Lemke said. "If the Variants do come tonight… our outposts are as ready as they can be."

Ringgold noticed Cortez making the sign of the cross. Praying was one of the only things they had left at this point, although with the way things had gone lately, God didn't seem to intervene in their affairs as much as the devil did.

The hatch opened and Soprano walked back in with a satellite phone. "Madam President, I have General Cornelius on the phone."

Ringgold took the phone to another office where she could speak in private.

"This is Jan," she answered.

"President Ringgold, it's good to get ahold of you. I want to discuss something beyond my initial conversation with Vice President Lemke."

"If it's nuking the outposts, then I don't have the time."

"No, it's something else that doesn't require nuclear weapons."

"Then I'm all ears, General, go ahead."

"You know S.M. Fischer from Fischer Fields?"

"I do."

"He has agreed to help me test some equipment to detect Variant tunnels as they form in El Paso," Cornelius said. "If it works, then we can not only locate them, but destroy them before the Variants surface."

"That sounds like a winning proposition."

"Exactly," Cornelius said. "Problem is we don't have the people to run the equipment. I may have some ideas on how to get more and better equipment that the military abandoned out west, but first and foremost, we need the manpower."

"Do you know if it even works?"

"We're testing it tonight, Madam President."

Ringgold thought about the consultants from France. Perhaps they would be more useful than she had originally thought, but first she wanted to ensure Fischer could do what Cornelius hoped he would.

"If the test is successful, then we'll help get you whatever you need," she said. "In the meantime, while I've got you, I could use your assistance with something else."

"What's that?"

"You have two thousand soldiers at your disposal, and I respectfully would ask if you would deploy some of them to the outposts," she said. "We think last night's attacks may only be the beginning of something bigger."

"So do I, but I'm curious if you can share any intel?"

"Let's just say we believe collaborators have attempted to infiltrate more than a few outposts and we might be dealing with sleeper cells."

"I see… And how many troops do you need?"

"As many as you can spare to bolster our defenses."

"Madam President, with all due respect, I don't think being on the defensive constantly is going to win this war."

"Of course not," she said. "We've got plans to launch a counter strike and we have a team of scientists working on ways to locate the masterminds and tap into their network. If they are successful, it will lead us right to them."

There was a brief pause on the other line.

"I may not agree with the way you've protected our country, Madam President, but we're in this together now," he said. "I'll coordinate with your people to send some of my troops where they're needed the most."

Ringgold almost breathed a sigh of relief.

"Thank you, General."

"I'll let you know how our test goes."

"Good luck."

"And to you as well."

She hung up and almost smiled for the first time in days. Hearing the general was willing to commit some of his personal troops was great, but hearing he was also working on testing out equipment that could help was even better.

When she got back to the CIC, Souza was on a call with the commander of Outpost Kansas City.

Soprano pulled Ringgold aside and whispered, "We just got a call from Lieutenant Niven at Outpost Portland."

"What now?"

"Apparently Captain Beckham and Master Sergeant Horn went on a manhunt for one of their friends, and now they're missing, Madam President."

All the optimism she'd felt after getting off the phone with Cornelius evaporated.

"What? How?" she stammered.

"They went to find Timothy Temper and some militia that went missing but never returned," Soprano said.

"Does Kate know?"

"Not yet, we just got this report." Soprano scrunched

his brow together and paused. "There's a lot riding on her work. Maybe we should wait to tell her when we know more."

Telling Kate that Beckham and Horn were missing could throw off everything, but this wasn't something she could keep from the doctor for long.

"Wait until we know more," she said reluctantly.

Souza raised his voice at the table as Soprano walked away.

"Give 'em hell," said the general.

"Wilco," came the reply from the speaker.

Ringgold walked over. Souza palmed the table and kept his head bowed as if in defeat. When he looked up to meet her gaze, she saw a cold look of fear that she had never seen in the SOCOM chief before.

"That was the Commander at Outpost Kansas City," he said. "The second wave of the attack has begun, Madam President…"

— 8 —

Timothy woke to the sound of dripping water. He cracked an eye open. His head pounded, confusion muddling his thoughts. Most everything was bathed in darkness, but a single shaft of moonlight streamed through a hole in the ceiling to reveal he was in some kind of round, concrete structure.

Something that looked like veins hung from the opening above.

Where the hell am I?

It took him a few moments to realize he was actually in a standing position against a wall. He tried to move his arms, but something pressed against them. When he tried to look down, something pulled against his forehead.

Whatever had him pinned to the wall was out of view.

He strained to remember something, anything, but his brain wouldn't work normally. All his thoughts felt just out of reach, like he was stuck in a pit of tar reaching for purchase.

One thing was certain…

He wasn't alone.

Several other people were against the wall across from him, slightly off to his left and right. He could barely see their blurred figures in the pervasive dark beyond the moonlight.

"Help…" he tried to say.

The word came out muffled, trapped in his mouth. Something sticky covered his lips when he tried to open them. Cold panic gripped his body as he took in another breath through his nostrils.

He squirmed in the restraints, trying to twist and turn, fueled by adrenaline. His frantic movements did nothing to break his bonds. If anything, it just made things worse. His skin tore under the rope, tape, or whatever had him stuck to this wall.

He snorted, frustrated and terrified.

A squawk answered the noise.

Timothy froze.

Memories flooded his brain of the ambush in the forest. He had made it to the truck, only to be pulled out and dragged here by a pack of camouflaged Variants.

But they hadn't killed him like the other men.

For some reason he was still alive.

Popping joints commanded his gaze across the chamber. A shadowed figure moved on all fours across the floor, stopping in the beam of moonlight.

The sinewy Variant snarled in the eerie glow. Blue veins webbed across its pale and hairless flesh. The beast reeked of sour, decaying meat.

Wormy sucker lips smacked as it studied him with reptilian eyes. It let out a low growl and took another couple of steps closer.

Timothy fought violently to get free; turning, twisting, and pulling up with his chin. He winced in pain from the struggle, as more skin and hair pulled away under his restraints.

The Variant stood and the yellow-slotted eyes met his. Timothy winced as swollen lips peeled back to expose jagged, chipped teeth. It tilted its head, showing a hardy black collar wrapped around its neck.

Leaning in, the beast sniffed him, nostrils flaring. He closed his eyes as the monster's rancid breath rolled over him.

The Variant shrieked into his face, splattering him with saliva.

Timothy knew what was coming next.

Unable to scream, he gritted his teeth and waited for the beast to tear open his guts and feed on his intestines. It was their favorite part of their prey.

The beast noisily ground its teeth together.

Timothy forced his eyes open when the creature didn't immediately sink its claws into his flesh. He could see every pulsating blood vessel in the creature's eyes. Something compelled him to watch, like this was a nightmare that might end if he willed himself to wake.

But this wasn't a figment of his imagination.

This was real.

He was about to join his dad.

The monster's mouth opened wide to release another long shriek.

Timothy's muscles locked up like a boxer preparing for a punch. The animalistic cry echoed through the chamber, but another sound rose above it.

A human shout.

Timothy snapped his eyelids open to the sight of three figures striding into the chamber. An electronic click sounded, almost like a buzz.

The beast wailed in pain and reached up with a clawed hand to grab at the black collar around its neck.

"Back you, filthy shit!" a man called out.

Three men appeared in view, all carrying rifles.

Timothy's heart flipped. The militia had come back for him after all!

The Variant bolted away, passing the men, frightened like a dog with its tail tucked between its legs. It curved far around the militia soldiers, and none of them gave chase. They stopped in the center of the chamber, directly under the moonlight.

Timothy didn't recognize any of the dirt and grime-covered faces. Their camouflaged clothes appeared no cleaner.

Stark reality struck Timothy like a claw to his guts.

These weren't militia… they were collaborators.

The smallest of the three stepped out in front. He was in his fifties and had a thick head of gray shaggy hair pulled back with a black bandana. Dark eyes drilled into Timothy.

The other two were both muscular and about six feet tall. They were younger than the leader. The man on the left wore a stocking cap, and the guy on the right had a thick beard and wore a Boston Red Sox hat with a frayed bill.

Timothy gritted his teeth again, rage boiling inside of his veins. He bucked against his restraints, desperate to get free.

The men all laughed.

"Got a real squirmer," said the short guy in a Brooklyn accent.

"I'll kill you!" Timothy tried to scream. "I'll kill all of you!"

The trapped words came out an indecipherable gargle, prompting more guffaws from the collaborators.

Timothy thrashed harder, fueled by the cruel laughter. This time part of his shoulder ripped free and the restraint on his forehead came loose, allowing him to move his neck. He saw then what had trapped his body.

White glue cocooned him from the chin down.

He had once heard about these Variant excretions used to keep human and animal prisoners like a spider with its prey.

Now he was one of them.

The men stopped laughing as Timothy craned his neck enough to get a good look at the other prisoners. His heart caught in his chest at the gruesome sights.

The man to his left didn't look human anymore. A Variant had chewed off most of the face, including the nose, eyes, and lips. Long bangs hung over what was left of his cheeks.

Past the hanging corpse, two women hadn't fared much better, their features erased by claws and teeth. Flags of red flesh hung from their torn skin. One of them still had her eyes, and Timothy sucked down a horrified breath when he realized they were focused on him.

No… she can't be still alive, he thought.

He forced his gaze back to the collaborators.

"Damn," said the guy with the Red Sox hat. "Never seen one break free like that."

The short guy walked over to Timothy and then reached out with a knife. He angled the blade toward Timothy's eyes, but Timothy kept them open, glaring at the abominable man.

Using the curved blade, the collaborator punched a hole in the glue covering Timothy's lips. Timothy let out a scream as the knife cut through his upper lip.

"Oops, sorry about that, kid," the man said. He stepped back and studied Timothy like the Variant had earlier.

Blood gushed from the cut in his lip and into Timothy's mouth.

"You are one lucky son of a bitch," the short man said. "Everyone else ended up as snacks. Wouldn't have been long before you became one, too."

He looked from left to right before focusing back on Timothy.

"I would've liked to keep the others around, but it's okay," the man continued. "Our pets need the energy for tonight."

Timothy glared, resisting the urge to spit in his face.

"Not going to say anything, huh?" asked the short man. "No?"

He raised a remote in his hand. Timothy figured that was what had set off the shock in the Variant's collar.

"Soon as I press this button, I send that monster into shark mode," he said.

The man in the Red Sox hat chuckled, his beard parting over his lips. "And you know who the chum is, don't you, pal?"

The man in front of Timothy stepped closer. His lips spread in a lop-sided smirk, exposing yellow and rotting teeth that smelled as bad as they looked.

"I'm not afraid of dying," Timothy said. "Go ahead. Kill me. You'll be doing me a favor if I don't have to smell your rotten breath anymore."

The guy chuckled and then looked over his shoulder at his men. Timothy used the opportunity to throw a head butt that almost connected. He strained, his neck extending as he spat and snarled.

"Well shit, you are a rabid little fucker, aren't you?"

"Maybe he could come in handy," said the guy with the stocking cap. "Tough guys are hard to find."

The short man held up the remote so Timothy could see it.

"Maybe," he said. "Or maybe he'll end up bait, all depends on tonight."

"What's happening tonight?" Timothy asked.

"You'll see," the man with the stocking cap said.

Then the collaborators filed out of the room, leaving Timothy in the darkness with the dead and dying prisoners. His pounding heart slowed and after a few minutes he finally relaxed in his restraints, saving his strength for later.

A screech broke the silence, and another answered the first.

The chamber darkened as a cloud passed over the moon.

All at once, many shrieks sounded outside, rising into a chorus like a pack of werewolves howling at the moon.

Only it sounded like an army.

***

Beckham's head still pounded with a fiery agony. He figured he was suffering a concussion.

Two hours had passed since the ambush. They were still another fifteen minutes from the outpost by car, and probably two hours or more on foot. At this rate, they wouldn't be back until midnight.

Not only had they failed to find Timothy, they might not return in time to defend the outpost from another attack. Kate was probably worried sick, if she even knew he was out here, and he had no way of telling her what was going on.

You really screwed things up this time, Reed, he thought.

Night had fallen, and Beckham and Horn weren't prepared to fight in the dark. With the radio broken, they couldn't even call for help.

They were on their own, but they had plenty of ammunition. Beckham carried an M4A1 and a vest full of magazines, plus his sidearm. Horn grabbed the M240 from the pickup truck and two belts of rounds, now draped over his chest. His primary rifle was also slung over his back, and he had a pistol if it came down to it.

Beckham also carried Timothy's pistol.

They salvaged grenades and a backpack of explosives from the dead collaborators. Even more importantly, they had snagged FLIR thermal binoculars off one of the assholes.

Beckham had a feeling the explosives he carried were intended for Outpost Portland.

"How you doin', boss?" Horn whispered over his shoulder. "Want to stop and rest?"

"I'm fine. We need to keep moving."

Grogginess clouded Beckham's head, but he did his best to stay alert. Collaborators lurked out there. Variants too.

They crept through the trees and light foliage at the edge of the road. Beckham stopped every now and then to scan the forest with the thermal binos. The monsters could camouflage their bodies and mask their heat signal a little, but the optics were still better than his naked eyes.

Crickets chirped in the underbrush, and the caw of crows echoed through the forests. Beckham searched the darkness for moving shapes, but could hardly see anything. If not for the moon, he would be blind.

For the second time, he tripped and fell to the dirt.

Horn helped him up, and they kept walking. With his

head aching, Beckham felt like a drunk. He did his best not to stumble on roots or rocks.

An hour later they made it back to the main road.

They crossed over the intersection to survey the muddy field framing the paved road. A crunching in the distance drew Beckham's gaze to the woods at the edge of the field.

"If we're lucky, that was just an animal," Horn whispered.

"Maybe." But Beckham didn't believe in good luck anymore. "Let's pick up the pace and keep to the shoulder."

If they encountered any hostiles they could always veer off and find cover, but this way he could run without worrying about falling on his face.

They jogged for half an hour before finally stopping to rest.

Beckham took a sip of water, and listened. He half expected to hear the distant sound of gunfire and explosions, but the night was still as the surface of a frozen lake.

"How far are we now?" Horn asked.

"At least another hour if we keep up this speed," Beckham said. "Hard to say."

"I hope my girls don't know we're out here."

"Same with Kate and Javier. Chances are good they think we're still at the outpost, unless Ruckley got in contact with them."

"Ruckley probably thinks we're dead. Hate saying it, but maybe she was right about coming out here."

"At least we killed some collaborators," Beckham said. "Four less assholes with explosives to use on the outpost or elsewhere."

"True… I lit those fuckers *up*, man. Wish you could have seen it."

"I wish I could have helped."

"All that matters is you're alive."

Beckham took in more water before pressing onward. The moon climbed higher into the sky, a carpet of white pushing the shadows away.

He was thankful for the brightening glow. If it had been overcast, or even a half moon, they would have had to hunker down for the night.

Fatigue really set in over the next two miles of the journey. Lactic acid built up in Beckham's muscles, his stomach growled, and his head felt like it was inside a slowly closing vice.

Horn was slowing down too, the heavy machine gun definitely taking a toll.

It was pure luck that Beckham glimpsed the movement of diseased flesh in the woods to their left. Freezing, he watched a group of Variants sneaking through the tree line.

Horn saw them too and went low as he followed Beckham into the ditch on the right side of the road. They ran into the woods until they were safely positioned on the crest of a small hill overlooking the road.

"Did they spot us?" Horn whispered.

Beckham stared into the forest where he had seen the pack of Variants. These creatures weren't camouflaged and their sallow flesh almost glimmered in the moonlight.

He counted six but when he raised the thermal optics to his eye he saw there were many, many more.

Most were camouflaged after all.

"Holy shit, there's a small army," he said.

A hulking figure strode along the smaller beasts.

Beckham couldn't see it well, but knew enough about the Alphas to identify them.

Horn reached out, and Beckham handed the binos over.

"Judas Priest," Horn mumbled. "There's got to be more than a hundred and is that a…"

"An Alpha, the new kind, I think. They're going in for round two tonight."

"We have to do something," Horn said, handing the binos back. "Warn LT Niven somehow."

"How? Even if we open fire we're too far away. No one will hear our shots."

"Yeah, but they might hear those," Horn said, pointing to the pack of explosives Beckham wore.

He considered their options as he looked out with his thermal optics again. The beasts were moving fast, but not as fast as Beckham and Horn could move if they really hauled ass.

All the pain in his skull was nothing compared to imagining what those Variants would do to the outpost if they made it in unannounced. If he and Horn could get ahead of them, maybe they could lay an ambush and take most of them down.

An explosion and fire might also attract attention from the outpost. Hell, maybe Niven would even send a team to figure out what was going on.

Or maybe it's suicide, Beckham thought.

He explained his idea to Horn, and the big guy agreed.

"Sounds like a Kamikaze mission, but you know I'm always down for some fireworks, boss."

"Good, then let's move."

Beckham followed Horn this time, hoping the bigger man would be better able to carve a path through the woods. Even with Horn ahead, Beckham fell several times. He pushed himself up each time, unwilling to fall behind.

Within fifteen minutes they had put themselves a good distance ahead of the Variant horde. They found another embankment overlooking the road protected by trees. From there, Beckham spotted the perfect place for the ambush: an abandoned van.

He told Horn to plant C4 on the gas tank, set off the car alarm if possible, and then retreat back to a hill where Beckham would be camped out with his rifle.

Once the horde came, they would detonate the C4, toss their grenades, and open fire before retreating to the road toward the outpost.

"It really is full blown Kamikaze mode," Horn said. He set up his M240 and laid out the belts of ammunition. Then he unslung his rifle, ready to go.

Beckham brought up his thermal binos again to make sure the path was clear.

"Ready when you are." He patted Horn on the shoulder. "Be careful."

Horn sprinted down the side of the hill and then bolted for the van. When he got to the road he kept low, but fast.

Beckham continued surveying the area. He still saw nothing nearby but his friend's heat signature. Horn bent down to setup the C4.

Across the road, in the woods, the Variants were advancing. Horn's estimate of a little over a hundred seemed about right. Trying to take them all on at once would be difficult. He hoped their explosives would be enough to thin their ranks.

Horn was now at the van's driver side door and was

working on setting off the alarm. The wail sounded a beat later.

An animalistic shriek answered, different than a normal Variant.

This had to be the Alpha.

"Run, Big Horn," Beckham whispered. He picked up his rifle and pressed the butt against his shoulder as he settled into a prone position. The beasts were on the open road now, their pale, almost translucent skin captured by the rays of moonlight.

They streamed out toward the screaming vehicle. Horn made it back up the hill and got down on his belly. He handed Beckham the C4 detonator and then prepared the grenades.

Beckham waited until the front of the horde had reached the van. Several of the beasts broke the windows and tore at the car's interior.

"Barbecue time," Horn whispered.

Beckham clicked the remote, then grabbed his rifle again.

The explosion lifted the van off the ground, metal and glass bursting outward in the fiery blast. Hunks of shrapnel peppered the surrounding Variants that weren't immediately consumed by the inferno.

Horn raised a hand to shield his face and then stood to toss the grenades one at a time. They were close enough that both men hit the dirt again to avoid shrapnel. The explosions rocked the road and the ditch. From his prone position, Beckham glimpsed the mangled beasts cartwheeling and flying into the air.

Body parts thumped back to the ground while Beckham opened fire with his suppressed rifle, picking off the ones that had escaped the flying debris and flames. He worried they would find his position anyway, but the beasts were too disoriented to figure out what was happening.

It wasn't until the throaty wallop of Horn's M240 joined the fight that the creatures homed in on their position. Horn raked the weapon back and forth, cutting down the abominations with bursts of gunfire as they scaled the embankment.

"Changing," Beckham said. He heard the shriek of the Alpha and finally saw the beast lumbering behind a pack of others across the road, beyond the blazing van.

Horn covered both of their firing zones as Beckham reloaded. By the time he brought the rifle back up, the Variants had started to scatter to flank their position and the Alpha had vanished.

"Let's go," Horn said.

They left the hill, leaving a surprise behind.

After sliding down the other side of the embankment, Horn led them into the forest. Beckham could hear the snap of joints and shrieking of furious monsters as they closed in. The dying wails of others faded away as Beckham and Horn added distance between them and the battlefield.

The first of the creatures reached their former sniping position a minute later. The fuse on the small chunk of C4 Beckham had left behind went off, detonating the explosive, and erasing more of the monsters.

They ran harder, headed toward the road. A glance over his shoulder and Beckham confirmed the creatures were on the pavement too, running like wild animals on all fours.

He halted and shouldered his rifle, firing off a couple of bursts. Horn did the same thing, taking down five of the beasts. They crumpled in bleeding tangles of limbs and claws.

"Go, go, go!" Beckham shouted.

They ran like that for the next ten minutes, stopping only to take down the creatures drawing too close. But it was the hostiles bolting through the woods on both sides of the road and the missing Alpha that had Beckham worried.

Horn switched back to his M240 to finish off the rest of the ammo while Beckham took a knee by his side and reloaded his M4.

Rounds lanced across the road and into the ditches as dozens of Variants exploded out of the trees toward their position.

Beckham was on magazine three of six now.

Horn's M240 went dry a few minutes later. He switched to his M4A1 and turned to keep running.

This wasn't the first time the two men had fought off overwhelming numbers. Back at Fort Bragg they had been down to just their knives as Variants closed in.

As they slowly burned through their ammo, it seemed like they were heading for the same fate.

There were still at least twenty or thirty Variants pursuing and the Alpha still held back. Waiting to make its move.

Beckham turned and ran again, seeing a single light spearing through the dark in the distance. The spotlight glowed like a beacon, but it was still impossibly far.

A high-pitched screech erupted through the chorus of the monsters. The beasts all stopped their pursuit, but Beckham kept firing calculated shots, killing three before they darted away and vanished into the night.

Horn, panting, stepped over to Beckham, pistol in hand.

"Sounds like the Alpha," he said. "Maybe it's calling a retreat."

"Or reorganizing. I don't want to wait here to find out."

They fought against the exhaustion choking their muscles, running with all the vigor they could muster until more lights blazed across the road ahead. Horn pulled Beckham to the shoulder out of view as an armada of vehicles sped toward them from Outpost Portland.

"Think those are our friends?" Horn asked.

Beckham squinted, but couldn't tell. "Don't want to chance it in case they're not. Get in the ditch."

They lunged for cover as the growl of diesel engines grew louder.

The vehicles ground to a halt and a spotlight clicked on, sweeping over the ditch until it hit the two men.

"Fuck," Horn muttered, holding up his hand to keep the light out of his eyes.

"Get up!" someone yelled. "We know you're out there."

Beckham squinted into the beam.

A familiar voice called out. "Captain Beckham, Master Sergeant Horn!"

Beckham started up the side of the ditch with Horn. At the top, Ruckley stood looking down with a scowl.

"You two got more lives than a pack of feral cats," she said.

Horn laughed and helped Beckham up the ditch. Something shot high above them like missiles. They both spun to look as a rumbling sounded.

"What the…" Beckham began to say.

The scream of fighter jets roared through the night. A second later, explosions boomed in the woods miles away, lighting up the sky in an apocalyptic glow.

They dropped payloads on more targets beyond that, the ground trembling with each impact. The jets came back for a second run, raining more bombs in brilliant explosions.

As the vibrations and noise of the aircraft faded away Ruckley clapped Beckham and then Horn.

"Thanks to you two, we were able to go on the offensive tonight," she said. "The explosion on the road helped us ID exactly where those Variants were with a drone."

Horn grinned proudly.

"Thermal vision identified the location of several other hordes, and we called in those F-35s from an aircraft carrier off the coast. If you hadn't set off those explosives, that drone would still be going around in circles searching all the wrong areas for those things."

"Glad our crazy plan paid off," Horn said.

Beckham stared at the flames raging in the distance. He didn't hear any cries or wails from the beasts. Not even the Alpha had survived.

He wanted to feel the same joy as the others celebrating the victory, but he couldn't help thinking that, if he was still alive, Timothy might have been in the path of these bombs.

— 9 —

The abandoned cup rolled back and forth on the mess hall deck of the USS *George Johnson*. White light flooded the space, belying the black night that had settled outside the stealth warship. Kate marched through the mess and scooped up the cup while Carr kept walking.

They had been working in the laboratory almost nonstop. Now that they had an idea of what the webbing in the Variant tunnels was used for, they had changed gears to focus on experiments to uncover the molecular mechanisms by which the webbing worked.

So far, none of it had been helpful in translating the signals passing through the webbing into information that they could interpret and understand.

They had reached an impasse and needed a new revelation. A breakthrough to push them beyond what they already knew. Being confined to that claustrophobic laboratory with a half-dozen technicians working shoulder-to-shoulder had been suffocating Kate's mind.

Sometimes a brief break from her routine allowed her to think outside of the box. Coffee didn't hurt, either.

"Back in my MIT lab, I told my graduate students that if they left their lab benches a mess, I would expel them from the program," Carr said.

Kate deposited the cup in a sink filled with other dirty dishes soaking in soapy water.

"Did you ever have to follow through?" she asked.

Carr let out a chuckle. "No, thankfully they always kept everything clean. I'm pretty sure they assumed I was serious."

"Were you?" Kate asked.

"Of course not," Carr said. "But I didn't mind that they thought I was."

He reached up to a cabinet and pulled out a tin of coffee. From another drawer, he took out a spoon and scooped a pile of the grounds from the tin into the coffee maker.

"I'm surprised they bought that," Kate said. "It would've been an extreme response."

"Very true. Not to mention replacing a graduate student isn't easy or cheap when you're trying to secure new grant funding."

Kate chuckled at Carr's dry humor. The man was finally beginning to seem a bit more human around her despite his rough edges. She still didn't envy any of the former students that had studied under him.

The gurgle of the coffee maker filled the silence between them, along with the aroma of the fresh brew. Once the pot was full, Carr removed it and poured a mug for each of them.

Kate took a cup, closing her eyes and breathing in the aroma.

"Pulling all these long shifts is getting to me," Kate said. "Pretty soon all the coffee in the world isn't going to keep me awake."

"Me, too." Carr took a sip. "It doesn't help that we've only got access to subpar beans. I miss good coffee. Colombian used to be my favorite."

"Ethiopian for me."

"The things we've lost…"

"I wish coffee was the least of our worries."

Kate motioned for him to follow her back to the tables in the mess. They slumped into seats across from each other in the otherwise empty room. A sudden smack of an opening hatch caught their attention.

The lanky form of technician Sean McMaster came through the opening.

"Hey, Sean," Kate said. "We just brewed some coffee. Would you like some?"

He nodded almost sheepishly, shuffling off to the mess, then joined them at the table with a mug.

"We've got caffeine now, and a new location," she said. "Is it enough yet to inspire any new ideas on how we can tap into the Variant webbing network?"

Sean took a sip, watching them both, but he didn't reply.

Carr furrowed his brow in concentration, the steam from his coffee swirling up toward his face.

"It might take all day running chromatography and fluorescence spectroscopy tests," Carr said. "But we'll identify every single molecule that passes through the webbing."

"That'll take a lot of time," Sean said. "I'm not sure how helpful it'll be. What do you think, Dr. Lovato?"

"I agree. None of that will help us understand what those masterminds are telling the Alphas and other Variants. It's like having a whole pyramid of hieroglyphics in front of us with no Rosetta Stone." Kate traced a finger around the lip of her coffee mug. "Might as well be a bunch of gibberish."

"Gibberish," Sean repeated. "Maybe it's just not something we're supposed to figure out. Maybe we're barking up the wrong tree?"

Carr shot him a bemused look. "What do you suggest?"

"I don't know," Sean said.

Kate's thoughts drifted again, and she looked through one of the portholes. A river of white stars studded the night sky, unobstructed by light pollution or clouds out here.

Beckham was still at Outpost Portland, with Donna and Bo waiting at the University of Southern Maine campus. She hadn't heard anything from him since he left this morning, and she was starting to worry.

If there was another wave of attacks, Outpost Portland would likely be one of the targets, putting her husband and her friends in danger.

"I guess we're truly stuck," Carr said, snapping Kate out of her thoughts.

"There must be a way…" she said.

"If only I was back in Cambridge, I could just send an email off to my students and"—Carr snapped his fingers—"by the end of the day, I would have a new report in my hands just in time to cross the Charles River and go into Boston for happy hour."

"We've got plenty of help here," Sean said.

"Yes, you're certainly talented, and so are the others, but the students and post-docs in my MIT lab were top-notch."

"Oh, did you say you used to work at MIT?" Kate asked, getting slightly annoyed by his repeated mention of the institute.

"Did I not say that before?"

"I heard you say it several times," Sean said.

Kate let out a laugh.

Carr shook his head. "Oh, I'm sorry. I missed the

joke." He sighed, staring at his coffee. "Used to be that academic pedigree was as important in science as was having a good microscope. But now, none of that really matters, does it?"

"No, not as much as it used to," Kate said. She studied Carr. He really was a tough son of a gun when it came to the techs, but…

Then it hit her.

Kate leaned forward in her seat. "That thing you said earlier… the emails…"

"What about it?" Carr asked.

Kate stood suddenly, her coffee splashing onto the table.

"The computers from Virginia," she said. "The ones Beckham and Horn recovered. From what I heard, Ringgold has intel experts poring over them. Computer scientists. But they're not the ones that should be doing it."

"They seem to me to be the most qualified," Sean said.

A puzzled looked crossed Carr's face. "Hold on a second. I want to hear what she has in mind. Who should be looking at them?"

"*We* should."

"I have a PhD in Bioengineering," Carr said. "Not in Computer Engineering."

"I know, but hear me out. We can solve all of this much faster." She took her coffee mug to the galley and left it there without refilling the mug. She didn't need more caffeine to help her focus.

Work. She needed to work.

Carr and Sean followed.

"What are you thinking?" Sean asked.

"The Variants were communicating with human

collaborators. And we're presuming those computers have all the information the collaborators sent. If we can hook those computers up to the webbing we have in the lab, we might be able to simulate those signals and decode how the webbing-computer interfaces work."

"That sounds like it might be out of our wheelhouse," Sean said. "Maybe we should just let the computer people do their thing."

But Carr's eyes lit up as they left the mess and marched through the passages. "You're right, Dr. Lovato. The computer scientists might miss something that we could see, especially if there's a strong biological connection between the nerve cells in the webbing and the computers."

"Exactly, and this neural-computer interface technology is nothing new," she replied. "Not by a longshot."

She took a turn in the corridors than started up a set of ladders.

"Not new?" Sean asked. "What do you mean?"

"I think it was 2004 or 2005 when researchers connected rat brain cells in a plastic culture dish to a flight simulator. The cells were actually trained to carry out basic maneuvers." She stopped to look at him on the landing. "And think of all the more recent advancements in computer-nerve interfaces for advanced prosthetics."

Sean simply nodded.

"Good Lord," Carr said. "This could all be explained away by existing technology." An incredulous expression crossed his features. He took off his glasses.

"That's even more disturbing if you consider the implications," Sean said.

"Computer-brain or computer-nerve interfaces make

sense," Kate said. "It's technologically possible. But just because it's possible doesn't mean it's easy. Are you thinking what I'm thinking?"

Carr rubbed his eyes before putting his glasses back on. "These interfaces take a lot of scientific know-how. In other words, there are some very smart collaborators out there."

"So the Variants don't just have mindless collaborators working for them as grunts," Sean said.

"It might be the opposite," Kate replied after a swallow. "What if the monsters are working for the collaborators and scientists, and what if these collaborators are every bit as intelligent as the people on this ship?"

Sean shrugged but Carr shook his head.

"You really think that could be true, do you?" he said.

Kate hadn't even considered the notion earlier, but the thought chilled her to the core.

"If it is true, then we've got to hurry and connect those computers to the webbing samples in our lab," Carr said. "If we can decode the messages they're sending, we can unravel everything."

***

Night dragged on over Scott AFB. Team Ghost waited on the tarmac as the cold fingers of the late autumn breeze brushed over them. Stacks of ammo cans formed a fort around Dohi and the others waiting for a V-22 Osprey.

A pair of loadmasters waited beside them, ready to prepare the bird for Team Ghost's departure as soon as it landed.

So far, all Team Ghost knew was that the aircraft would take them to New Orleans where they were tasked with destroying a mastermind suspected of organizing some of the Variant and collaborator activities. Beyond that, they didn't know much about this new mission.

A distant pop like the sound of gunfire rattled somewhere far from the command building. Dohi tensed, waiting for the chorus of gunfire and Variant shrieks to erupt in response. Beside him, Mendez and Rico both readied their suppressed M4A1s.

"Maybe just another straggler," Fitz said.

Ace lowered his shotgun and tightened the strap on the M4A1 slung over his back. "All this waiting has me on edge, man. And I need to take a damn shit."

"Makes two of us," Mendez said. He smirked. "I mean, on edge. Took care of my business earlier, old man."

The team turned as soldiers rushed out of command between the razor wire and fences surrounding the building. Some lugged heavy machine guns into new positions; others carried ammo cans and crates of supplies to defensive positions. The patter of boots against pavement drilled the ground around them like a rainstorm.

"Better clench your cheeks," Mendez told Ace. "Shit's about to go down."

"Ghost!" a voice called over the tarmac.

Lieutenant Mark Forster jogged toward them, a glowing tablet cradled in one arm. Two men flanked the officer.

"The Osprey is en route, ETA ten minutes," Forster said.

He was out of breath, and Dohi didn't think it was

because of the run.

"The Variants are beginning their assault, mostly concentrated around the target cities," Forster added. "Most aircraft were diverted to evac missions."

Dohi thought of all the innocents in harm's way, and the man he had put out of his misery. The image wouldn't leave his mind.

"Three additional teams are already on their way to other mastermind locations," the lieutenant continued. "With any luck, their success and yours will disrupt the Variants' communication networks enough to hold back the hordes so more people can reach safety."

The staccato burst of automatic weapons filled the night. Forster turned toward the direction of the gunfire. Once again, it settled without resulting in wailing alarms announcing a true attack.

Forster held out his tablet. "Gather around. We've got a lot to cover and not a lot of time to do it."

The screen showed an aerial view of New Orleans. Most of the city looked flooded, each block and building its own island in a sea of muck-strewn water. At the center of the image was a large white dome, its roof fractured and missing in places.

"Earlier today, one of our drones captured an image of the mastermind in the French Quarter of the city."

He showed the screen to the members of Team Ghost in turn. They all knew what they were looking at from their experience in Minneapolis.

Huge folds of tissue hung from a monstrosity with a face that looked like it had been melted in a nuclear explosion. Long tendrils of red webbing stretched from its flesh as it navigated between ruined hotels and restaurants.

"Why the hell didn't you destroy it already?" Dohi asked.

"We tried, but the damn things are faster than they look," Forster replied. "Still, we have reason to believe it isn't far from the French Quarter. That's why we're sending you."

"We'll burn this bastard to a crisp, sir," Mendez said.

Rico nodded while chewing her gum.

Forster's radio buzzed and a voice came in clear after a burst of static. He pressed it to his ear to hear above the din of soldiers preparing the base for attack.

"Osprey's on its descent," he reported.

Dohi scanned the night, looking for a glimpse of the aircraft in the moon-soaked sky. He heard the roar of the craft's engines before he saw it.

As soon as he began to point the Osprey out to the rest of the team, another chorus of gunfire blazed from a pair of machine gun nests and a guard tower not more than a mile north of their position.

This time the gunfire settled into a constant flurry.

Spotlights lanced through the darkness, illuminating wide swathes of the base outside the defensive barriers.

Forster stared for a beat, and in that moment Dohi almost felt bad for the man. In a few minutes, the terror from the night before would commence again.

The two soldiers accompanying Forster aimed their rifles toward the sounds of war, and the lieutenant drew his Sig Sauer M17.

"Form a defensive perimeter around the LZ!" he ordered. "Keep this area clear until Team Ghost is away."

One of the two loadmasters trembled near the stack of ammo cans. He looked over at the Delta Force

Operators, his lip quivering at the sound of the advancing monsters.

Dohi shared that fear though he worked to repress it. He couldn't help but think of a quote that his father had told him.

A brave man dies but once, a coward many times.

"Look out!" a voice cried from one of the barricades.

A rocket streamed from somewhere beyond the fence. It slammed into one of the guard towers. A soldier flew backward from the tower, his limbs separating from his torso. Another fell out, fire coursing over his body.

"Collaborators!" Ace yelled.

More howls and screams erupted between the waves of gunfire.

The ground rumbled beneath their feet. One of the ammo cans fell from the stack, clinking to the tarmac with a metallic ring. A loadmaster bent to recover it.

Behind him, a hole appeared in the ground, asphalt and dirt giving away. An Alpha clawed itself up, its bat-like ears twitching, nostrils flaring, body covered in soil. The monster let out a roar followed by rapid clicking.

"Open fire!" Fitz yelled.

Rounds lanced into the Alpha's flesh. It let out a screech as it dragged itself toward the loadmaster, blood spraying out of the bullet holes. Despite the storm of gunfire, it lifted a claw into the air, ready to slash down across the loadmaster's chest.

Dohi aimed for the creature's face and fired a burst, shattering bone. Blood gurgled out of the beast's nostrils and mouth, and it finally collapsed.

"Osprey incoming!" Forster yelled. "Ghost, get ready!"

The aircraft came into view, lights glowing from the

fuselage. It made a vertical descent toward them, the rear ramp already opening to allow a quick getaway.

Smaller beasts began climbing from the hole the Alpha had broken through. Their joints clicked, and their teeth gnashed together. Everything blurred around Dohi as Team Ghost sent a fusillade of rounds tearing into their ranks.

This was not the only hole that had opened up behind the defensive lines.

Others appeared across the airfield, swallowing asphalt and even people rushing to new positions. Alphas emerged from the earthen craters, shaking off dirt from the long tendrils snaking over their bodies. Legions of armored juvenile Variants followed behind them.

A loud thump sounded as the Osprey's wheels touched down.

"Good luck, Ghost! Kill that motherfucker for all of us!" Forster roared.

The loadmasters and Ghost rushed onto the aircraft, carrying their supplies. A pair of crew chiefs helped throw the ammo cans onto the deck. The activity attracted the Variants like bugs to a light.

Even with the gunfire resounding from other units scattered around the airfield, the beasts were almost within striking distance. Forster fired his M17 into two of the monsters that came bounding on all fours. His guards continued to flank him, their rifles blazing to keep the monsters at bay and buy Ghost time.

One of the loadmasters ran back to the stack of supplies for another crate. Before he made it, a lunging Variant tackled him and sunk its claws between his ribs.

Dohi killed the beast, firing from within the Osprey, but the damage was done. The loadmaster took a final breath before going limp.

The other man hefted on a final ammo can. As soon as he did, a Variant wrapped its claws around him, pulling him backward.

"No!" Dohi yelled. He tried to get a shot but it was too late. The beast sunk its teeth into the man's neck and ripped out a chunk of flesh and artery. Blood sprayed across the interior of the Osprey.

The aircraft lifted off as a swarm of the beasts consumed the dying loadmasters while Forster and his men retreated. Team Ghost continued to fire at the advancing beasts from the troop hold next to a crew chief on a mounted M240.

Creatures threw themselves at the tiltrotor craft, raking their claws along the outside. Dohi trained his fire on the diseased beasts now surrounding the lieutenant and his two soldiers. One of the men went to change his magazine and was shredded by a pair of deadly claws.

Forster and the other two men disappeared under a wave of gray flesh.

Dohi choked out a breath, watching again from the sky while men died below. Once again, there was nothing he could do to save them. He couldn't even end their misery with a bullet.

Fitz bowed his head, and Rico put a hand on his shoulder as they retreated into the Osprey with Ace. Mendez remained at the rear lift gate with the crew chief, raining fire into the hordes.

Dohi brought his rifle back up with a new magazine and joined them. He fired where he had last seen the three brave soldiers that had given their lives for Team Ghost.

"Incoming!" one of the pilots yelled.

Dohi spotted the cloud of smoke from a launched LAW rocket. With a lurch, the craft suddenly decelerated hard and then descended just enough for the rocket to careen overhead.

The rear ramp was almost closed as the pilot started to pull them back into the sky. But now they were within an arm's distance of the monsters again.

A juvenile leapt and thrust itself through the gap between the rear ramp and the fuselage. It bristled with claws and flesh covered in tough armor. Slotted yellow eyes fixed on the crew chief as it let loose a screech and slammed into the man.

Wild gunfire in a space like this was far too risky, but Dohi refused to let another man die for them tonight. He drew his hatchet and slammed it into the armored skull. The monster crashed against the bulkhead.

Dohi ripped the blade out and brought it down again. Bone split, flesh peeled, and blood poured from the gaping skull wounds. It still managed to snap at him, and he brought the hatchet down again, and again, until he had opened up a red canyon in the skull.

Brain matter sloshed out over the deck.

"Ace, Rico, help him," Fitz said.

The duo began tending to the crew chief's lacerations. The man writhed on the deck. None of his wounds appeared fatal, but he was definitely hurting.

All things considered, he was lucky to be alive.

Team Ghost was just as lucky.

Dohi stepped back to a window for a view of command. The base had quickly transformed into a war zone, leaving the soldiers in the path of the monsters.

Through a window, Dohi saw the flicker of dozens of rifles around command.

One by one, the glimmer of muzzle flashes disappeared.

A few sparks of gunfire cut out from a final guard tower, but it too vanished in a bright explosion from a LAW rocket. The resulting fireball illuminated a landscape covered in crumpled bodies.

Variants stormed the base, skittering up the main building and consuming the final defenses like an angry colony of ants.

Dohi tried to comfort himself with more words that his grandfather had passed onto him from their tribe.

There is no death, only a change of worlds.

But from what Dohi had seen in the tunnels, from what he had seen down there, he could not find solace in those souls "changing worlds" when the transition looked so terrifyingly horrible.

Accompanied by the collaborators, the horde of monsters had easily overrun the final defenses of the base and consumed the command building.

"Lord have Mercy on their souls," Ace said.

"They didn't stand a chance," Rico said.

"I hope their sacrifice was worth it," Mendez said.

"That depends on us now," Fitz replied. "I just hope the other outposts and bases fare better than this one did."

— 10 —

Fischer never got the opportunity to share a drink with Tran and Chase in Galveston. Instead, they were already on their way to work to Outpost El Paso in a C-23 Sherpa with Sergeant Sharp and a few of Cornelius' soldiers. The propellers buzzed as they began their descent.

Coming in at the dead of night, Fischer was thankful he had grabbed a couple hours of shuteye on the flight. He had a feeling he was going to need it with this new mission. General Cornelius had given him no easy task.

Moonlight illuminated the craggy Texas landscape, nearly silhouetting the Franklin mountains overlooking the Briggs Army Airfield within the outpost.

"Almost there," Sharp said. He rotated for a better view, his new blue armband showing.

Fischer valued loyalty. Chase and Tran had proven their fealty to him time and again. Usually he would be skeptical of a man like Sharp who so quickly abandoned his post to join another's army. But as the Sherpa's wheels touched down on the runway, he couldn't blame the sergeant for joining up with Cornelius.

The retired general knew how to get things done and might be one of the best hopes the Allied States had of surviving the Variants.

The plane's prop engines wound down, and it taxied

to a stop. As soon as the side door opened, the chilling night air flooded the plane's interior. Fischer stood, following Sharp and the soldiers out.

A large man in military fatigues waited on the tarmac.

"Welcome to El Paso," he said in a gravelly voice.

The soldier offered a hand to Fischer as he spoke with a strong northwest Texas drawl that might've been shared by one of Fischer's neighbors.

"Pleased to have y'all here. I'm Lieutenant Riggs, in charge of organizing defensive operations. Born and bred right here in El Paso."

"Good to meet a fellow local," Fischer said.

"I know the city and the land around it like the back of my hand. Still, I can't tell you how glad we are to have your boys working with us."

"Honored to help with the war efforts," Fischer said. "Anything I can do to kill some Variants is all right by me. Have my men already setup the prospecting equipment?"

"Yes, sir. Follow me." Riggs motioned to a pair of Humvees idling near the airstrip.

The two-vehicle convoy took off, racing away from the airfield. They passed through darkened city streets; their headlights illuminated craters in the ground. Those craters looked like Variant tunnels that had recently been filled in. Scree piled up next to broken adobe houses, and bullet-hole pocked cars lined many of the streets.

"We took a beating last night," Riggs said without turning.

"We did too," Fischer said. "Lost a lot of good men myself."

"Cornelius warned me you didn't have enough to adequately outfit these trucks. But he promised you'd make do. Seems like your men have done just that."

Spotlights from guard towers probed the darkness. Banks of floodlights hooked up to rumbling diesel generators provided a wall of light over the huge concrete ramparts topped with razor wire looping around the outpost.

"We're headed straight into Variant country at the foot of the mountains," Riggs said.

"With all these tunnels, seems to me like everything's become Variant country now," Fischer said.

"If this works tonight, we can start reclaiming what's rightfully ours." Riggs held up his radio. "Bravo 1, Echo 1 actual. We're approaching the gate now."

The radio crackled with a reply. "Copy, Echo 1. You're clear to proceed. Good luck out there."

A huge steel gate rolled back with the assistance of a growling motor. Heavily armed guards stood outside the entrance.

"Lost about a quarter of our men last night," Riggs said.

"But no contacts yet tonight?" Tran asked.

"Not out here," Riggs replied. "As late as 1800 we were still dealing with a few stragglers that hadn't retreated. They were mostly hanging around the mountains."

"How are the other outposts faring?" Chase asked.

"We're receiving reports the Variants have launched attacks," Riggs said. "Size and scope vary, but safe to say, if that's any indication, we've got to be ready for anything. This will be the ultimate testing ground for the equipment."

"From the sounds of it, we don't have time for testing and we need to get this tech deployed around the outposts ASAP," Chase said.

"Ain't that the truth." Riggs rubbed the stubble on his cheek. "Got to prove it works though, and to do that, we got to go where the beasts are."

"Trial by fire," Fischer said.

A rooster tail of dirt kicked up from the first vehicle as it tore over the dusty terrain beyond the walls. The Humvee bucked as they rumbled off-road and the headlights captured dried tumbleweeds and prickly cacti.

Farther ahead a series of mobile light posts had been setup. Beside them was a truck that looked like a militarized RV with long arrays of netted cables stretching across the ground.

"Ah, the geophone truck," Fischer said.

While most of the netted cables stretched into the darkness, he knew sensors were scattered along them, capable of picking up vibrating seismic waves coursing through the ground.

Five men were already stationed around the vehicle with weapons, patrolling the rock-strewn landscape. A machine gunner lay prone atop the truck.

The two Humvees filed in next to the mobile unit. Fischer opened the door to let himself out. Tran and Chase trailed him into the rocky landscape with Riggs.

"We've also got scouts posted with NVGs and thermal binos around each of the trucks," Riggs said.

He gestured to another three trucks scattered in the distance, each with their own set of floodlights. They appeared to be a cross between a lunar buggy and a Soviet-style Katyusha multiple rocket launcher truck. Those were the vibroseis trucks, each equipped with a large piston-driven shaker capable of generating seismic waves.

"You think one squad per truck is going to be enough to protect them when those monsters attack?" Fischer asked.

"It'll have to be," Riggs said. "We can't divert more manpower from base given the reports of attacks elsewhere."

"Seems pretty risky for valuable equipment like this," Chase said, eyes narrowed. "Especially if you're expecting an attack."

"Worst case, we call in air support and hightail it out," Riggs. "I'd rather lose equipment than men. It's not ideal, but it's what we've got to work with."

"Then let's not waste any time huffing about it," Fischer said. He set off for the geophone truck, spotting familiar faces working at the instruments inside the back cabin. He raised a hand in greeting, and they waved back.

Green screens glowed in front of each. Soon those monitors would come to life when the thumper trucks activated, generating vibrations deep into the ground.

Depending on how those seismic waves bounced toward the geophone truck's sensors, the engineers could identify the density of rock and earth beneath their feet. That meant it could also detect the hollow cavities where there was no rock. Exactly the kind of signal they expected from tunnels dug by the Variants.

"If we can prove this system works, then we can save a lot of lives by tracking Variant tunnels before they burrow under our walls," Riggs said.

"And when we detect burrowing Variants, I'm assuming you have the means to deal with them?" Fischer asked.

Riggs cracked a cocky grin. "We've had the past few decades to perfect bunker-busting bombs. You sure as hell bet that if we find the monsters underground, we can blow them sky high."

"That's what I like to hear," Tran said.

Fischer grabbed a metal bar on the back of the geophone truck and hoisted himself into the open back door. He slid in beside the two engineers, and Riggs climbed in with him. Sharp, Tran, Chase, and the others formed a perimeter around the vehicle to reinforce the meager security forces.

"Good to see you all made it out here safely," Fischer said to the engineers.

"Likewise. We're glad to have you with us, sir," the nearest engineer said, a portly man in his early fifties with a crown of graying hair. "Everything is ready to go when you are."

"Time's already ticking by, so tell the thumpers to start pounding ground."

"Yes, sir," the engineer said. He relayed Fischer's commands to the other trucks, and the burble of their engines echoed over the bleak landscape. Each time the thumpers slammed against the ground, Fischer could feel the tremor pass up through the geophone truck and into his bones.

"Strange sensation," Riggs said. "I feel like a T-Rex is running at us."

The thumping continued as if the trucks were playing the Earth like a bass drum. Fischer looked over the engineers' shoulders, watching the resulting signals passing to the geophone truck.

"What can you see?" Riggs asked, squinting at the screens.

"Sure ain't any oil down here," Fischer said. "No natural gas deposits, if I'm reading it right."

"Yes, sir," the graying engineer said. "Nothing so far. No aberrations to indicate tunnels."

"Better not be," Riggs said. "We collapsed the ones we found earlier. Took more effort than I'd like to admit since we relied solely on the holes the Alphas left behind. If Variants are coming back to attack El Paso tonight, they'll still have to pass back this way."

"Your men did a damn fine job then—" Fisher stopped, spotting something on the screen.

Lines bounced around, indicating varying depths and densities of the ground. One of those lines had suddenly dropped. That meant there was a void there. A sure sign of a natural gas deposit if it had been hundreds of feet deeper.

But at only a few feet beneath the earth's surface, he knew better.

"Is that one of them?" Fischer asked.

"It's an anomaly, certainly," the engineer said. "But there are also a few small caverns around these parts. Nothing unusual."

The thumper trucks continued sending seismic waves coursing through the Earth. Fischer blinked at the lines zig-zagging across the engineers' screens. The shapes became mesmerizing, almost hypnotic as the engineers surveyed the land.

He thought he heard a howl break through the night air. But the diesel engines and thumping from the machines made it difficult to tell whether it was real or not. He looked around at the others. Their attention remained on the screens.

Maybe his mind was playing tricks on him. His exhaustion was getting the better of him, like it did in the tunnels back under his fields. He could still hear his wife's voice now, warning him danger was at hand.

"Keep an eye on that so-called cavern," Fischer said.

Their efforts continued for another thirty minutes as they identified potential sites to investigate, but nothing that leapt out as Variant activity.

Then the first engineer leaned back, mouth open, his fingers frozen at his keyboard. "Sir, the anomaly. It's growing… and… and it's headed straight toward us."

Riggs started barking orders into his radio, telling his men to be on alert.

"We've detected the formation of what looks like five tunnels in total. The Variants must be burrowing as we speak."

Fischer turned to Riggs. "We got the tunnel locations you wanted. Now how about sending them all to a fiery hell like you promised?"

"You give me the coordinates, I'll send the bombs," Riggs said.

"We're tracking them now," the engineer said.

Riggs called in the coordinates as the engineer relayed them. The tunnels crawled forward, drawing ever closer to the trucks and Outpost El Paso. Fischer couldn't help but wonder if this was happening across the country.

"Where's that fire support?" he snapped.

Riggs twisted his wrist and looked at his watch. "Thirty seconds."

Those seconds passed by agonizingly slowly. Fischer waited for the ground to open before them, Alphas pushing out followed by a horde of wart-covered Variants clawing for fresh meat.

A voice sprang in his mind.

Leave! Now! Go!

It was his wife's voice again. More adamant now. He

had failed to heed her warning back in the tunnels under Fischer Fields, and it had nearly gotten everyone on his team killed.

You can't stay here.

The tunnels grew slowly. Fischer's heart thundered. To him, watching the screens was like witnessing the mushroom cloud of a distant atomic bomb, seeing the devastation that would soon overcome them. But he was unable to do anything to stop it except to pray.

Leave!

He considered telling his men to stop. To retreat, but he held steady.

Another few seconds passed, and a sonic boom tore overhead. Fischer nearly jumped at the roar. Somewhere above them, like dragons in the night, the fighter jets tore through the sky.

A flash of light exploded over the horizon.

Another four followed in quick succession, more blinding than any of the floodlights around the trucks. The ground rumbled violently.

The relentless sound blasted over the truck, assaulting Fischer's eardrums. He stood tall, watching the screens. The vibrations from the bunker buster bombs sent a crash of signals through the ground and into the geophone truck, throwing off their tunnel detection abilities.

Fischer waited for the signals to settle. The engineers stared at the monitor, neither of them blinking.

Ten seconds passed before the seismic waves from the bombs dissipated, leaving only the heavy smack of the thumper trucks to shake the ground. On the screens, the five tunnels appeared again.

But this time they were much larger.

Fischer stroked his mustache nervously, anticipating movement from those new caverns in the ground. But the earth beneath them remained lifeless.

"Sir, I think we're clear," said one of the engineers, in a surprised voice as if he didn't believe it himself. "No indications of anomalies. No expansion of the original tunnels."

"I'd presume them Variants are all crispy critters now," Fischer said.

"You're sure?" Riggs said.

Fischer leaned over the engineer's shoulder to study the screen. "Dead as door nails, Lieutenant."

"Ho-*ly* shit," Riggs said, looking away from the screen. "Sir, I have a feeling you and your men are going to find yourselves very busy over the next few weeks. If this technology works this good all the time, it could very well be the thing we need to win this war."

"Maybe," Fischer said. "I sure hope you got a big supply of those bunker busters, 'cause we're going to need a hell of a lot of them."

***

"Our F-35s have eliminated the targets outside of Outpost Portland," reported General Souza.

Victorious cheers and applause filled the briefing room. President Ringgold wanted to share in the celebration with her staff and the officers, but the leaden weight of dread held her back.

For every victory, they had ten more setbacks, and she still hadn't heard anything new about Beckham and Horn since their disappearance.

Not to mention the reports of new Variant attacks at

other outposts. The news kept hitting like a relentless hailstorm.

Scott AFB was already gone. Wiped off the map just hours earlier.

Her eyes darted back to the wall-mounted monitor where a digital map of the Allied States displayed the now remaining eighty-three outposts. The six main target cities of Minneapolis, Chicago, Lincoln, Kansas City, Indianapolis, and Columbus were again under full-scale attack.

But at least Team Ghost had escaped Scott's collapse. By now they would be closing in on their new target to find another mastermind.

She had to keep reminding herself that while the Variants were on the offensive, so were the brave men and women of the military.

Tonight she felt a desire to be out there, fighting alongside those who placed themselves in harm's way.

"Sometimes it's better to craft a strong strategy for the troops on the ground rather than standing there with them and pulling a trigger. A good leader knows the difference," Beckham had told her during the first war.

Remembering those words helped assuage the guilt she felt. After all, she had a plan. She had a way that humanity could survive this mess.

The science team just needed to tap into the network of the masterminds. If Kate and Carr achieved that and if the tunnel detecting equipment worked for Fischer and his men, then they had a chance at stopping this madness before it consumed the Allied States. Especially if General Cornelius pulled through on his somewhat mysterious promise of potentially having access to even more powerful technology to bolster their defenses.

"Madam President, I just got a report that the final defenses of Outpost Kansas City have fallen," announced General Souza. "We've got live footage from one of our teams in the air."

The words made Ringgold's stomach knot.

Lieutenant Festa turned on a wall-mounted monitor. The view came on screen with an image of the interstate. Hundreds of headlights from evacuating vehicles glimmered on the road. The footage turned dark as the pilots circled for a better vantage point.

They had established this outpost six years ago after the military cleaned up the area. Its strategic location on the Missouri River made transportation of resources easier. The vast network of sheltered limestone caverns also proved useful for storage for so many local businesses.

By almost all measures, it was the biggest outpost in the Allied States with multiple districts, including clearly demarcated residential, business, and industrial zones. The river and roadways provided multiple convenient routes to transport resources.

"Please tell me we got everyone into the caves," Ringgold said.

"Most of them, and the outpost commander has dedicated a good chunk of forces to protect the caves," Festa said. "We'll evacuate more of them tomorrow when daylight drives the beasts back."

"Tomorrow…" Ringgold whispered.

For much of the country there wouldn't be a tomorrow.

"Who has a SITREP on the other outposts? I want to know if we have identified or captured collaborators," she said.

Festa held up a marked-up map. He was helping oversee the prioritizing of outpost defenses and evacuations.

"The few that have been captured have committed suicide, and we haven't identified any new cells," he said. "But we're working hard on this, Madam President, I assure you."

"Redouble your efforts on that front," Ringgold said, holding back a sigh. "Now how about the physical threat of an attack?"

"As you know, we're moving more of the survivors east as the outposts around the western target cities are overrun," he said. "While the current attacks are mostly centered around these six targets, there are smaller Variant hordes that seem to be working alongside collaborators to hit places like Outpost Portland, Outpost Boston, etc."

"The safest places to move these people are locations with geographical or geological attributes that make it difficult for Variants to tunnel under," Lemke said.

The vice president noted outposts including Norfolk, Kent Island, and Manchester.

"We're going to start evacuating more people to these areas and concentrating our defenses there as a last resort," he said.

The aerial footage came back online. This time, the helicopter was flying over the outer defenses along the banks of the river. The fences and walls had collapsed, and the minefields were nothing but smoking craters. Dark holes with halos of fresh dirt and rock marred the inside of the outpost where Variants had burst through the ground.

The chopper turned back to the interstate. Muzzle

flashes sparked from people abandoning their vehicles and trying to hold back the hordes of beasts.

Cortez put her hand over her mouth.

Armored juveniles raced down the road, chasing helpless people fleeing the devastation. Suddenly a section of the interstate burst with the bright glow of explosions. Fighter jets had dropped their payloads to buy the survivors time. For those already captured by the juveniles, it was a swift and merciful end to their suffering.

Another round of bombs burst across the interstate and then the chopper turned away from the view.

As the hours passed, the other six outposts around the target cities crumbled, their defenses failing, and the Variants spreading like a virus.

The irony wasn't lost on her.

Festa and other officers worked to keep the map updated, but by two in the morning, almost every outpost in the Allied States was under some degree of attack.

A surprise call came just when Ringgold felt her brain boiling with frustration and fear.

Soprano handed her a satellite phone.

"Ringgold here," she said.

"Madam President, it's General Cornelius. I have an update on our work in El Paso."

"I could use some good news. What's going on, General?"

"It is good, ma'am. The technology works. Fischer and his men were able to not only detect tunnels, but we also used that data to destroy them before the monsters could even surface."

"You have no idea how glad I am to hear this. How soon before we can start deploying these measures?"

"I'm going to need help getting this equipment to the outposts where it's needed most. I think we can also locate better technology to augment these defenses from some old Department of Defense laboratories in California."

"Whatever you need."

"Time is what I need most, and I'm afraid we don't have that." The General paused and then said, "I've got five hundred of my troops ready to deploy where you see fit. What I don't have is the aircraft to make all this happen."

"I think we can handle that," she said. "Let me speak to my team. I'll call you later when we've decided on our course of action."

"Okay. Thank you, Madam President."

"Talk soon," Ringgold said. She set the phone down and described the request to everyone in the room.

"I won't be able to identify the outposts where we need those troops the most until sunrise," Festa said.

"Not until we know which ones are left…" Ringgold said, realization hitting her like a brick.

"If this strategy works as well as General Cornelius claims, then we need to make that a priority mission," Lemke said.

"That will require rearranging our resources and aircraft," Souza interjected. "Which means pulling some off evacuations."

Being president for almost eight years had taught her she often had to choose the greater good over individuals, but in this case they were talking about leaving thousands of people stranded in order to save tens of thousands.

"If we don't get that equipment where we need it, then all we're doing is prolonging the inevitable by evacuating people," Lemke said. "I'm afraid we have no choice but to resource aircraft for this new mission."

Ringgold knew the guilt would crush her later, but for now, there was no other choice in her mind.

Lemke gave her a hard nod of approval.

"Authorized," she said.

The room broke into a bustle of activity as the staff and officers erupted in conversation. Ringgold sat watching in silence, considering the implications of her orders.

"Ma'am," came a voice.

Cortez bent down next to Ringgold. "We just got word that Captain Beckham and Master Sergeant Horn have made it back to Outpost Portland safely."

"Thank God," Ringgold said. She welcomed the additional good news.

"Lieutenant Niven said they took on an entire horde of Variants…" Cortez said. "That's how the Iron Hogs knew where to call in the air support."

Ringgold twisted to look back at the younger woman.

"Guess those two aren't so retired anymore," Cortez said, flashing a smile.

Ringgold smiled back and then got out of her chair. She walked over to the hatch, a voice calling out after her when she reached it.

"Madam President, where are you going?" Soprano asked.

"To see Doctor Lovato to let her know her husband is safe. At the way things are turning out, hopefully she'll have some good news for us."

"All the science in the world won't save us if there are more collaborators out there ready to unleash hell," Lemke said.

The vice president was right, and Ringgold knew it. At this point, she wasn't sure there was anything that could save the Allied States, but she would rather die than hand it over to the monsters.

— 11 —

The thuds from the not so distant explosions had passed over an hour ago, maybe longer, but the group of collaborators were still fuming across the chamber from Timothy.

They stood near piles of collapsed ceiling. Several of the pieces had landed on human prisoners, tearing them from the wall and crushing them to pulp on the concrete floor.

It was a mercy, Timothy thought.

"He's going to be furious…" said the short man in his Brooklyn accent. "We got to blame someone for this. Pete seems like the logical choice. You boys got to back that up, okay?"

He paced in front of the passage that the men had entered through. The other two collaborators, one with a Red Sox hat, and the other wearing a stocking cap both sat on crates.

A radio crackled across the space, but Timothy couldn't make out the transmission. He strained to listen, but he was still groggy. He had passed out earlier, and had been jolted awake by those explosions. All he heard was the response from the short collaborator.

"Oh man, this is *so* fucked up," he said. "Everything has gone to shit, and someone is going to have to answer for this… one of us… one of us is going to be fed to *them*…"

The other two men got off their crates and paced nervously. From what Timothy had gathered so far, a group of their soldiers had engaged a truck back on the same road he was kidnapped.

But those collaborators had never returned. Someone had killed them and apparently taken off with explosives meant to be used on the outpost.

Not only that, but the Variant hordes they had deployed to attack Outpost Portland, had been destroyed—probably by whatever had caused those explosions Timothy had heard.

Someone had severely messed up the collaborators' battle plan, and Timothy couldn't be happier. He held back a grin.

In the past he might have thought something like this was Beckham and Horn's doing. But they had abandoned him, Bo, Donna, and everyone else they had sworn to protect.

Someone else… someone with real balls was responsible for the badass attack that had killed those raiders and resulted in the utter demolition of the Variant horde.

Another man suddenly walked into the chamber wearing camouflage and a black ski mask. He stripped the mask off, and long dreadlocked hair fell over his shoulders.

The other three collaborators all took a step backward.

This must be the real leader, Timothy thought.

The man they all feared.

"The attack on the outpost failed," said the new man, almost calmly. "We lost one wave of beasts and two demo crews. I've called back the other teams, and the rest of the beasts are safe for now."

He looked away from his soldiers to scan the crushed prisoners.

"What a fucking disaster," he said. Anger rose in his voice in his next words. "The master's wrath is going to come down hard."

"Master will want a head," the short man said in his Brooklyn accent. "It'll be one of us, won't it?"

"Don't be such a pussy, Vin," said the man with dreadlocks. "The only way our heads don't end up on pikes is if we show strength."

"I'm no pussy, Pete," said Vin.

"You're sure acting like one," Pete said. He flipped his dreadlocks over his back and looked to the other two collaborators. "With tonight's fuckup, we got to show we still have plenty of meat to draw from at the outpost."

Vin looked across the room, and Pete followed his gaze to Timothy. The dreadlocked man took a step forward.

Timothy squirmed in the restraints, sensing whatever happened next wasn't going to be good.

"Check the others," Pete instructed.

The four collaborators fanned across the space but Pete stopped a few feet in front of Timothy.

"He's a real wiggler," Vin said. "Like a worm."

"Only one to survive the Variants in the forest," said Red Sox hat.

"So he's a fighter," said Pete. He leaned forward. Once again, Timothy was being studied and scrutinized by a monster in the chamber.

Judging by the way the collaborators kept their distance from Pete, even they were scared of him. This guy was not someone Timothy would want to be in a room alone with. He exuded confidence and terror.

Maybe he was the one that had led the attack on Peaks Island.

Maybe he killed my father.

Rage warmed his chest. A spike of adrenaline helped him fight harder against the glue holding him in place.

"Yeah… he's a fighter," Pete said.

"That's right, and I'll kill that wannabe gangster over there if you let me go," Timothy said.

For a moment Pete simply glared at Timothy, but then his face twisted into a grim smirk. "You got balls, kid."

"Not a kid," Timothy said. He directed his eyes at Vin. "And that guy is a real fucking coward if you ask me."

He raised his voice and added, "You should have heard what he said before you got here."

"What the fuck!" Vin yelled, his voice echoing.

He ran over, clearly caught off guard. Before he could get to Timothy, Pete stuck out his arm to hold Vin back.

"He's lying, Pete," Vin said. He spat on Timothy. "He' just a lyin' little rat."

Pete pressed his arm harder against Vin's chest.

"Get back," Pete growled. "I want to hear what he has to say."

"He was going to throw you under the bus for whatever is happening out there," Timothy said.

"That's a fucking lie," Vin protested in a nasally voice.

Timothy would have shrugged if he could have. "Just ask the other two guys if you don't believe me."

Pete looked over at Red Sox and Stocking Cap. "Well, boys? Kid telling the truth?"

Neither made a move.

"I find out you are lying to me too, all three of you are being fed to our fanged friends. So again, the kid telling the truth?"

They both nodded, nearly cowering as they did.

Vin looked at them both, and then turned back to Pete who had drawn a knife. Before he could so much as mutter a word of protest, Pete sliced Vin's neck from ear to ear.

Blood gushed from the wound. Vin reached up to stop the flow, mouth opening like a fish on land, and dropped to his knees, eyes pinned on Timothy.

Timothy smirked at the dying collaborator, hoping he suffered as he crumpled to the floor. Blood spread around him like a broken shadow as he writhed.

Pete leaned in close to Timothy.

"So you are part of the militia at Portland?" he asked.

A nod.

"You *were* part of it," Pete corrected. "You're the type of dumb kid thinks he's invincible, aren't you?"

Timothy didn't reply.

"That's why the military has always had an age limit and recruits from high schools. I know. I was one of them kids…" Pete snorted. "Somehow you got lucky to survive this far… Or, maybe not, maybe you can fight and know how to stay alive."

Timothy raised his chin slightly. He didn't want this guy's compliments. He wanted to kill the fucker. But if sucking up gave him an opportunity to do just that, he'd take it.

"I respect that, but I don't like rats," Pete said. "Still, some rats are bigger than others. Especially the kind that try to stab you in the back."

He again looked at Vin. The man was twitching, his face bleach white as the final seconds of life faded away.

"Guess our team has a new opening." Pete returned his gaze to Timothy. "You might be lucky enough to join our army if you play your cards right."

The guy with the Red Sox hat took it off. "The most powerful in all of history—the army that the military only dreamed of when they created VX-99."

"An army of super soldiers and genetically superior beings," said Pete. "Come over here, Alfred."

The man with the stocking cap joined Pete. He took it off, exposing a balding head with long thin hair. He pushed the cap to his chest, and reached out with his other hand to Timothy's forehead like a priest might during a blessing.

"You've been saved to help with the great reckoning," Alfred said in an almost soothing voice. "To help fight for the Land of the New Gods."

He let his hand fall away from Timothy's forehead but held his gaze for several long beats before stepping away.

"Get him down from there, Whiskey," Pete said.

The man with the Red Sox hat put it back on and moved over with a knife. He used the blade to start cutting Timothy out of the glue prison.

"My name's Nick," he said. "They call me Whiskey sometimes."

The man's breath sure smelled like his nickname.

When Timothy was free, his numb body fell forward. He crashed to the ground in front of Vin's corpse, the man's dead eyes staring up at him.

In time, Timothy knew all the collaborators would be doing the exact same thing. This was his chance to get in his enemy's head. He would have his revenge, and he would become the soldier his father would be proud of.

The men surrounded him and dragged him up to his feet. He staggered but kept his balance as his vision cleared. Nick pulled out a water bottle and handed it over.

Timothy didn't want their charity, but he needed it to survive. He snatched the bottle and gulped it down until he choked. When he finished coughing, he took another sip, this time slower.

"Easy, kid," Nick mumbled in a deep voice.

Wiping droplets off his chin, Timothy handed the bottle back.

"Let's go," Pete said.

The dreadlocked man led them from the chamber.

Timothy stumbled several times, his muscles weak from neglect and his legs numb, but he managed to keep going. As he passed the crushed and mangled prisoners, he kept his eyes forward.

The circular room emptied into a long passage way. Candle wax bled from sconces along the concrete walls and pooled on the floor.

Pete led the way with Alfred and Nick following Timothy.

They passed multiple steel doors, all of them rusty. Several were open, and Timothy glimpsed living quarters, pantries, and supply rooms.

Finally, they came to the entrance of another chamber, sealed off with mesh wire. Pete flipped on a flashlight. The beam penetrated the inky black beyond the wiring and hit a concrete wall covered in dark stains.

"Come here," Pete said, jerking his chin.

Timothy stepped up to look into the chamber. This one was deeper, like a silo that plunged so far into the Earth he couldn't see the bottom, even with the light angled downward. Pete pulled out a remote that looked like the one the men had used to control the Variant that had nearly eaten Timothy's face.

A rustling sounded, followed by what sounded like

gusting wind. A shiver coursed through Timothy's flesh. He wanted to back away but a hand on his back kept him in front of the mesh wire.

Pete clicked a button on the remote.

A shriek exploded up the silo, echoing loudly. It faded away, replaced by the rustling that quickly grew to a strong din like a tornado rising up through the chamber.

Timothy couldn't remember ever hearing anything like it.

All at once, hundreds of birds surged upward, flocking around the exterior of the mesh, some of them flapping into the wire.

Timothy flinched, but the collaborator's hand kept him where he was. Pete tilted the flashlight to illuminate the creatures. The glow revealed these weren't birds.

They were bats.

Both Nick and Pete laughed, but Alfred remained silent.

"This… this is your army?" Timothy asked.

"Not exactly," Pete said.

He pushed Timothy against the wire.

"Have a good look, kid," he said.

Bats screeched in his face, their wings beating the air.

"Cross me, and I promise I won't slit your neck like Vin," Pete said.

Pete removed his hand from Timothy's back. Timothy staggered back a few feet to put distance between him and the wire, watching the colony of twisted creatures rattling the mesh wall.

"Ever seen hundreds of starving bats infected with VX-99 swarm a human?" Nick asked.

Timothy shook his head.

"Cross me, and you'll find yourself on the other side

of this wire, kid," Pete said. He turned away and nodded at Nick.

"Get our rabid little friends ready, Whiskey, it's time for round two," Pete said.

***

Beckham and Horn sat in lawn chairs outside of Corthell Hall at the University of Southern Maine. At four in the morning, they were both exhausted, but Beckham couldn't manage a wink of sleep. His head pounded from his injury, making it all the more difficult.

Knowing Timothy was still out there, or more likely dead, dragged heavily on his mind. He had failed in his promise to Jake that he would look after his son. He had failed Timothy.

Those thoughts haunted him. When he had made a call to the USS *George Johnson*, he was almost glad that Kate had been in the middle of an experiment. As much as he wanted to talk to her, he didn't want to admit he had let Timothy down. Instead, he'd just made sure that someone would tell her that he and Horn were okay.

"His sacrifice helped protect the city, at least," Horn had said earlier. "If it weren't for us going after him, those Variants might have made it to the outpost."

Horn was right, but that didn't make Beckham feel better.

He massaged the knot on his scalp and looked at the tents spread out across the campus lawn. Somewhere in one of those tents, Bo and Donna were sleeping.

While Beckham couldn't see them, there were snipers on every rooftop watching over these people like angels in the night—angels with M107A1 fifty caliber rifles and a few M72 LAW rockets.

Snoring that sounded like chainsaws chewing wood distracted him from his thoughts, ensuring he wasn't going to sleep anytime soon. He glanced over at Horn. The big man had finally managed to drift off.

It wasn't surprising. Big Horn could sleep through a firefight.

Beckham closed his eyes, hoping for some sleep too, but it simply wouldn't come. Besides the snoring, he was too worried about things outside of his control, including Kate. He worried about what he would say to her when he returned and what their next steps would be.

He got up from his chair, deciding to head back up to the rooftop of Corthell Hall. That's where he would find Ruckley.

When he got there, she was standing near the edge of the roof with a pair of FLIR BN-10 thermal binoculars scanning the city. One of the snipers glanced back at him as he approached, but then turned back to his scope.

"How's it look out there?" Beckham asked.

He approached Ruckley as she lowered the binos.

"So far no sign of another attack," she replied. "We're lucky. Sounds like outposts are still being hit hard."

Another voice came behind Beckham.

"You trying to sneak away from me, boss," Horn grumbled, rubbing sleep from his eyes.

"Sorry, didn't want to wake you," Beckham said.

Horn shrugged and walked over to the edge with him.

"At least it's quiet now," Beckham said.

"I'd say we got lucky for tonight being quiet," Ruckley said, "but luck has nothing to with it. That was all thanks to you two."

"Wish Lieutenant Niven would have sent scouts out to

look for the collaborators after those airstrikes," Beckham said. "Now is the perfect time to hunt those assholes and look for their rat nests."

Ruckley frowned. "Look, I want to find the collaborators as much as you guys do, but we're on defense right now. We simply don't have enough people to risk missions without better intel."

She was right, and while Beckham knew that, he also remembered the risks they took during the first war against the Variants. Some were stupid, but others paid off. Tonight was stupid and had paid off.

Ruckley sighed. "Glad you guys came up here, because I got some news."

"Good, I hope," Horn said.

"Afraid not," Ruckley replied.

Beckham braced himself.

"Scott AFB fell a few hours ago," she said. "The Variants hit them hard and fast, overwhelming the command building in less than an hour."

"What about Team Ghost?" Beckham stammered.

"They made it out. They were launching a new mission when the attack came."

Hearing Fitz and the remaining team members were alive was a relief, but finding out they were being tossed into the fray again was another gut punch.

"Where?" Horn asked.

Ruckley shrugged. "Not sure. It's classified."

Horn cursed and muttered under his breath.

"I'm sorry…" Ruckley said.

With everything going on tonight, the chances of Team Ghost surviving this new war weren't good.

Then again, the chances of the Allied States surviving weren't good either.

"I hope wherever they're going will help put an end to all of this," Ruckley said. "Someone far above my paygrade better have a plan, because sitting here waiting for the bastards to attack again feels like we're waiting for a bomb to drop on us."

Beckham knew all too well that part of the plan would include Team Ghost, but he didn't reply.

"So what's *your* plan?" Ruckley asked. "I sure hope it doesn't include pulling any more stunts like tonight."

"No more stunts," Beckham agreed. "I think we'll get Bo and Donna back to command tomorrow, and then figure out how we can help with the war effort."

"What are your orders?" Horn asked Ruckley.

She looked out over the city. "For now, the Iron Hogs are digging in and holding this outpost. Portland has been designated one of the safer zones. We're supposed to get refugees from places that were hit harder than us. Like Kansas City, maybe Houston."

The sniper Beckham had noticed earlier got up and walked over. "Sorry to interrupt, Sergeant," he said in a timid voice. "But I overheard you say something about Kansas City. My sister is there. Do you know how they're holding out?"

The sniper was young, probably only nineteen or twenty, with a baby face and scared blue eyes. He reminded Beckham of Alex Riley.

"Things aren't good, Johnson," Ruckley replied. "I'm sorry but last I heard their defenses had fallen and people were being evacuated into the nearby caverns for shelter."

Johnson's eyes dropped in despair.

"We've been written off a lot of times, brother," Horn said. "And we've made it back each time."

"You just got to have a little faith," Beckham added.

"Damn straight," Ruckley said. "Hell, I thought you were both dead tonight, and you ended up taking on a horde of Variants one hundred strong. Alone."

Johnson let out a light huff. "Yeah, but you guys are legends."

"Nah, we're just normal guys that don't give up when shit hits the fan," Horn said. "Try not to worry too much, and focus on taking each day one at a time."

"Thanks," Johnson said. He returned to his post not looking convinced.

An eerie quiet hung over them for a few minutes. If Beckham closed his eyes and forgot about the past several hours, he could almost be at peace, listening to the chirp of a few nocturnal animals and feeling the gentle caress of the breeze.

But even if he tried to forget it all, the world seemed intent on reminding him this was no time for letting down his guard.

The handset radio crackled on Ruckley's vest.

"Iron Hog 2, go ahead, over," she said.

"Iron Hog 2, Raptor Eye 3, we're picking up movement on the north edge of—"

A blinding explosion suddenly erupted in the distance.

It had come from Peaks Island.

The Raptor recon team was camped out there to watch for collaborators, and something had just blown them to pieces.

Horn readied his rifle.

"Raptor Eye 3, do you copy?" Ruckley said.

She tried again and again, receiving only static.

Another flash lit up the island. One by one, blasts rocked the terrain, geysers of smoke and fire gushing up from the impacts.

"Is that artillery?" Horn said.

A siren wailed, and people emerged from the tents, dazed, and groggy. Soldiers ran out to escort them into the buildings, but chaos quickly broke out, people tripping and falling in the darkness. Frightened screams carried through the makeshift campgrounds as people stampeded for shelter.

"What the hell is that?" Johnson said. The sniper lowered his rifle from the skyline and pointed.

Ruckley brought up her thermal binos.

"Looks like birds," she said. "The blasts must have scared them."

"Let me see," Beckham said. Ruckley handed him the binos. He used his good eye to focus on the red dots flocking across the view. There were hundreds of the creatures, a dark undulating cloud traversing over the horizon.

But they weren't scattering like Beckham would've expected a flock of frightened birds to do. They were heading right for the campus.

He lowered the binos to look at the fires now dancing across Peaks Island.

These weren't just birds.

When strange things like this happened, Beckham didn't believe in coincidences. Something about those birds hurtling toward them set his nerves on fire.

"We have to get everyone inside now!" he yelled.

Then he pointed to the unmanned spotlight on the rooftop next to Johnson.

"Get that light on those birds!" he commanded.

Johnson did as ordered.

Ruckley brought her radio to her lips. "Turn all spotlights to the sky. Target those birds."

The spotlights on the other roofs turned skyward to the formation of black. The creatures didn't soar, but zigzagged and swooped through the sky, their wings moving in a blur.

"Ho-ly shit," Horn said, drawing out the syllables. "Those aren't birds. They're bats, and they're coming straight at us!"

"Shoot them!" Beckham yelled. He didn't know why the little flying mammals would be coming at them, but he knew it wasn't for anything good.

He raised his rifle and flicked off the safety.

Muzzle flashes came from the other rooftops as the order passed over the comm channels. The bats dipped lower, some diving and flapping through the rounds. They were nearly impossible to hit, flickering through the gunfire. An explosion rocked the first building across the campus, sending soldiers cartwheeling away from the roof.

Beckham changed his magazine and watched in horror as the creatures dove for the tents and the fleeing innocents. Something detonated, spitting up fire so bright he had to shield his eyes from the glow. Even from the rooftop, he could feel the heat.

More bats crashed into the ground and surrounding buildings, blowing up upon impact. Beckham might have brought down a couple, but he could quickly see they weren't going to stop this destructive force of suicidal creatures.

A formation broke off and flew toward their location.

"Run!" Ruckley shouted.

The team retreated back inside the building, as blasts shook the rooftop. Retreating soldiers tumbled from the concussive force, falling against the stairs. Heavy booms rattled the structure, and ceiling panels collapsed, breaking over the floor.

Beckham tripped on a landing and fell, only to be yanked up by Horn.

When they got to the bottom of Corthell Hall, the thunderstorm of explosions ceased, replaced by the agonized screams of the injured and dying. Beckham saw the surviving creatures peeling away, disappearing almost as fast they had attacked.

Civilians flooded through the doors. Some of them had devastating burns and bleeding shrapnel wounds. One man had lost an arm and staggered, eyes staring blankly ahead with shock. Another man's face was partially burned away, his ear and nose darkened into crisped flakes.

Soldiers helped carry in the injured. The shouts and cries of horror filled the night. Beckham looked for Bo and Donna in the masses of panicked people, wading through with Horn.

"Bo! Donna!" Beckham cried. Smoke burned his eyes, and the scent of charred flesh filled his nostrils.

Horn coughed, deep and hard.

Dark columns of smoke rose from dozens of craters. Bodies lay strewn across the field of destruction.

Beckham only knew they had reached Bo and Donna's tent because it was the center of the camp, and strips of burned red plastic had survived the inferno.

He didn't see any bodies in the remains, but corpses lay twisted in one of the nearby craters. Most were mangled and burned beyond recognition, but one of the victims was still moving.

Beckham ran over and bent down next to the man. He was hurt bad, his legs charred. Most of his hair had been singed away, leaving a glossy, red and black scalp.

"Medic!" Beckham yelled. He put a hand on the man's shoulder hoping it wasn't Bo. The man turned, but he had no eyes left to look at Beckham.

My God…

Beckham felt guilty when he felt a wave of momentary relief that it wasn't Bo.

"Hold on, man, help is coming," Beckham said. "Just stay still, okay?"

A soldier came running over with a medical bag and crouched next to the injured man. Beckham nodded at the medic and then ran to Horn.

He knelt next to a victim draped over another body.

The big guy looked up at Beckham, tears running down his eyes.

"Bo…" Beckham said quietly.

The teenager had valiantly shielded his mom's body with his own. But his heroic efforts had been futile. A touch to her burned neck confirmed they were both gone.

— 12 —

Kate walked side by side with Carr and Sean down a passage of the USS *George Johnson.* Accompanying them now was a computer engineer named Sammy Tibalt, a former military contractor specializing in cyberwarfare and technology. The war had brought her back to helping the Allied States. She was whip-smart and had helped with testing their neural network hypothesis.

Sammy had a tangle of tattoos, dragons, phoenixes, and lions interwoven in a colorful tapestry along her arms. Kate didn't bat an eye at the ink, but Sammy's long dreadlocks did catch her attention.

A bit unconventional, Kate thought. *But she knows what she's doing.*

Carr, Kate, and Sean had spent the night locked away and working in the lab with Sammy, oblivious to what was happening outside the airtight fish bowl until Ringgold had come to check on them earlier.

The president had informed Kate that her husband and Horn had gone out on a mission, and had returned.

"I'm sorry for not telling you sooner, but I wanted to wait until I had better intel," Ringgold had said.

Kate's first reaction was anger, but that had passed. All she cared about was that Reed and Horn were okay. Knowing that had helped get her through the early morning hours. Aside from that, she had no idea how the other outposts had fared during the night.

Exhaustion and worry weighed on her, but the knowledge she carried with her after a night of experiments was enough to keep her going. They now better understood the role the red webbing in the Variants' tunnel played in their communications with the collaborators. It had also led them to an insurmountable roadblock and they needed the president's help.

Sailors and other crew members flowed past them until they reached a hatch with two Marines standing guard.

"Dr. Lovato, Dr. Carr, Sammy Tibalt, and Sean McMasters," Kate said, holding up an ID card. "We're here to meet with President Ringgold."

One of the Marines squinted at her ID before locking eyes with her. He then opened the hatch. They stepped into a space with a U-shaped table. Chairs lined each side, and a large monitor was mounted to the bulkhead.

Already seated were President Ringgold, Vice President Lemke, General Souza, and Lieutenant Festa. Chief of Staff James Soprano stood in a corner with his arms folded.

The dark circles under Ringgold and Souza's eyes showed Kate she wasn't the only one who had missed out on some shuteye. No doubt, the attacks last night had kept them occupied.

"Did you bring me some hope?" Ringgold asked.

"Yes, but we need your help, Madam President," Kate said. "Starting with some coffee."

Soprano disappeared out of the briefing room.

"Have a seat, please," Ringgold said.

Kate suspected she was about to get some very bad news as Sammy, Sean, and Carr dropped into seats beside her.

"There was another attack on Outpost Portland after I saw you," Ringgold said. "Beckham and Horn are still okay, but we lost a lot of people."

"No," Kate stammered. "How? I thought…"

"The collaborators used bats strapped with explosives to attack the outpost," Souza said.

"Bats?" Kate was taken completely off guard.

"How in the world could they control them?" Sean asked, face going pale.

"It could be any number of things," Sammy said. "Some kind of implanted micro-electrodes. Radio-telemetry systems that deliver microcurrent pulses, maybe. There's so much documented research in this area to draw from."

"If they can control bats, think about what else they can control," Carr said. "The scientific implications… they're frightening."

"The result was certainly devastating," Festa said. "Whoever was responsible might've been inspired by the experimental bat bombs developing in World War II."

"I wouldn't be surprised," Kate said. "More alarming is that these bats could be mutated by VX-99."

Carr put a hand on his chin, deep in thought. "That would explain how those animals could carry payloads with such catastrophic effects."

"Every time we take one step forward, the Variants and collaborators push us one step backward," Lemke said with a shake of his head.

"How about the other outposts?" Kate asked.

Souza looked to Festa for a report.

"It was a tough night," said the lieutenant. "Three of the six outposts around the target cities have fallen completely. I'm still going through all the data to figure out which are the safest outposts to evacuate survivors to."

"This is why your work is so crucial," Ringgold said, her eyes looking between each of the researchers. "We need to intercept the messages being sent on the webbing network if we have any hope of organizing our defenses appropriately."

"Right now, we're just evacuating people toward the Atlantic coast and hoping we can stop the advance of the creatures," Lemke added.

"I think we're close to a breakthrough." Kate set up her laptop and synced it with the briefing room monitor.

She clicked on her touchpad. An image of the red webbing within a beer can-sized bioreactor appeared on the screen. Next to it was one of the computers that had been recovered from the collaborators at the Luray Caverns in Virginia.

"What are we looking at now?" Lemke asked.

"We successfully recreated the webbing network," Carr said.

"The connection between the computer and the neural cells was made with a flexible microelectric array." Sammy swept her dreads over a shoulder. "It's very similar to a design documented as early as 2006 by Dr. Simon Wong at the University of Florida."

"Without getting into specifics," Kate said.

"Right," Sammy said. "Bottom line, Dr. Wong showed that a group of rat neurons could be successfully paired with a fighter jet simulator program."

"I remember that," General Souza said. "The DOD discussed investigating these topics to create better artificial intelligence for drones."

"Did they?" Sean asked, leaning over the table.

"Yes, in fact," Souza replied. "The DOD picked up many of the researchers involved in these efforts and hired them to continue their work on these subjects."

"By chance, are any of these scientists still employed by the Allied States?" Kate asked.

Sean nodded. "If we knew who they were and had their help, they might be very useful."

"I'll look into it," Souza said. "But I can't promise anything."

"For now, let's assume you are the best minds we have left. Please continue," Ringgold said.

Soprano returned and passed out hot cups of coffee as Kate moved on to the next slide. A graph showed the electrical output from the webbing. Next to it were screen captures from the collaborators' computers that displayed a jumble of words.

"We connected the wires from the collaborator's computer to the neural network contained within the webbing," Kate said. "Sammy's help was instrumental in this part."

"By stimulating the cells, I recorded output signals from the webbing that were translated into inputs readable by the computers," Sammy added.

Carr motioned at the screen with his coffee cup. "As you can see, while the computers could detect a signal, we couldn't produce anything that made a lick of sense."

Sammy agreed with a nod. "I've got the best computer scientists on my team, but even we can't do anything to turn these messages into something understandable. It's all just a bunch of gobbledygook."

"How long do you need to decipher this?" Ringgold asked.

"What we have now is a slate full of hieroglyphics,"

Sammy explained. "The symbols and the words are there. The message is there. But it's hidden. We need our Rosetta Stone to translate this."

Ringgold raised an eyebrow. "Tell me, then… What is your Rosetta Stone?"

Carr glanced at Kate while Sean rocked a leg.

They all knew what the request meant.

More soldiers were going to die.

"It's a mastermind," Kate said. "We need to connect the computers and neural network to one of those monsters in order to get a proper input signal. With that, we might get what we need."

"You *might*?" Souza asked.

"Our team agrees this is the best option," Sammy said. "This should be enough to complete the circuit, so to speak, and decode this language the Variants are using."

"There's really no other way," Sean said emphatically. "No intel could be better than working directly with a mastermind."

Lemke shook his head. "I don't like the uncertainty, especially if you're asking what I think you're asking."

"This information will be invaluable to predicting their movements and tapping into their networks." Kate tapped on her laptop, and the monitor showed the collaborators' computer systems again. "With it, we could even send signals of our own through the webbing. We could weaponize the enemy against themselves."

Ringgold looked to Souza. "That's something our troops could use. Imagine the possibilities."

"Our job would be a lot easier if we knew the Variants' plans," Festa said.

"Think about the lives we could save," Sean said.

"I don't disagree," Souza said. "But this requires us to

locate a mastermind, secure the area, and connect your computer contraption up to it."

"That would be one method," Carr said. "But not what we'd recommend. Science is best done in a controlled environment. In a place where we can modulate all the external stimuli to ensure that the language we decode is uncorrupted."

"You want us to capture a mastermind and bring it in?" Souza asked.

"I know it sounds insane," Kate replied. "But we've done this before to study the Variants and Alphas. There's nothing like having that kind of research subject to ensure we succeed."

"We suggest isolating and moving a mastermind to a defensible location with a large-scale laboratory infrastructure," Carr said.

"Have you identified a place?" Ringgold asked.

Sammy leaned forward in her seat, her tattoos peeking out from her cuffs. "That's where we were hoping you all might come in."

Festa nodded right away. "I think I know a place. Outpost Manchester in New Hampshire might work. There's a cluster of manufacturing buildings there where they used to research and produce tissue engineered organs. This is exactly the type of facility we could reuse for the mastermind."

"That sounds ideal," Carr said.

"They have had zero successful Variant attacks due to their defenses," Festa continued. "It's protected by bodies of water, rocky outcrops, and water-logged topsoil that is nearly impossible for the beasts to tunnel into. The commander is a decorated veteran from the Great War of Extinction."

The room was silent for moment.

"I know what you all might think. Capturing a mastermind, relocating it, hooking it up to a bunch of machines in some outpost," Kate said. "It's a huge commitment with resources we are desperately low on."

"We understand what we're asking sounds ambitious," Carr said. "Even foolhardy. But if we want to win this war against an enemy like this, we need to take big risks."

Ringgold stared at the computer monitor with the garbled message. "If we do this, if we can actually figure out how to bring in a mastermind and tap into their network, you truly believe we can not only intercept their messages but also send signals to disrupt their communications?"

"Yes," Sammy said. "Working firsthand with a mastermind will tell us what we need to know from a data perspective."

Kate sat straighter. "With these revelations, we can eliminate the advantages the Variants have over us."

Sean continued rocking his leg and nodded enthusiastically.

"And with the new equipment S.M. Fischer and General Cornelius are bringing to the table we can add a stronger layer of defenses to the outposts still standing," Ringgold said.

Kate thought of Beckham and Horn and their children. In her mind's eye, she saw all the other people they had left behind in Outpost Portland, like Donna and Bo and Timothy. All who could be dead now. They were among tens of thousands of people driven from their homes across the Allied States or dying at the claws of Variants.

"This plan might not be perfect, but it's the best we

have, and we have to do whatever it takes to stop these monsters," Ringgold said.

"I can get behind it," Lemke added.

General Souza sat quietly, seeming to contemplate all they had presented. He finally stood and let out a brief sigh.

"It's a risky plan, but you're right; it's the best we have and fortunately for us, Team Ghost is already on their way to kill a mastermind. Lieutenant Festa, contact them and tell them their orders have changed from kill to locate and secure."

***

Team Ghost trekked through the outskirts of a flooded New Orleans. A chopper had dropped them off the night before under the cover of darkness. Since then, they had moved slowly to avoid enemy contacts.

Fitz held point, listening for hostiles in Louis Armstrong Park as they approached the large white arch marking the entrance. The sun hid behind a blanket of dark gray clouds, and the city was quiet.

Somewhere in the city a lone rogue beast screeched, and a flock of birds exploded into the sky. Judging by the distance, they were out of the monster's scent range. Hopefully, the rub Team Ghost had used to mask their scent would protect them.

Fitz gave the order to halt in front of the white arch that had "Armstrong" welded to it in big, blocky letters. His blades creaked as he stopped in front of a thin film of murky, brown water.

The levees had failed years ago, and swamplands had reclaimed most of the terrain. He looked at Rico. Stains climbed up from her boots to her knees showing the depth of the waters they'd had to pass. Soon they would have to cross more.

"The French Quarter is only a block away. Keep your eyes peeled for any sign of the mastermind," Fitz said. "Once we find it, we keep an eye on it and stay hidden until air support and backup arrives. When they do, we'll help hogtie that bastard and get it out of here for the scientists."

"Hogtie," Mendez said. "Personally, I'd prefer to barbecue the damn thing and turn it into Carne Asada."

"Don't disrespect Carne Asada, brother; that shit is good," Ace said.

"True," Mendez smirked. "I still can't believe they want us to capture this thing."

"We won't be alone," Rico said in a low voice.

"This should be easier than killing it, actually," Fitz said.

"Nothing involving Variants is ever easy," Dohi said, eyes narrowed and tone gravely serious.

"You're right about that, amigo," Mendez said.

Fitz pictured the last time they had come face-to-face with a mastermind. It had only been a couple days, yet it felt like eons ago. In that time, they had lost Lincoln and watched hundreds of good men and women die at Scott AFB.

Snap out of it, he thought. *You've got a mission to complete.*

"You good, Fitzie?" Rico asked in a whisper, as if she could sense his thoughts.

"As good as I could be after wading through polluted floodwater in the middle of Variant territory," he said. "You?"

"Fine, but I sure as hell wish Variants didn't know

how to swim."

She stared out over the rippling brown water filling the streets between the park and the French Quarter.

"I always wanted to come to New Orleans," she said. "Thought it would be romantic, like Paris or some shit."

"Someday we'll go somewhere nice," he said. "A beach, or the mountains. Wherever you want."

Ace snorted. "All right kids, let's focus."

Fitz nodded and scanned the terrain one last time.

To avoid ambushes from the floodwaters, they had picked routes over higher ground, staying to decaying houses, restaurants, and bars as much as they could. The buildings were set nearly half-a-foot higher than the street, meaning that while the streets were flooded, there was usually no more than a couple inches of water in the buildings.

"Dohi, you're on point," Fitz said. "Keep us on dry ground or shallow water as much as possible. Find us a trail to that monster, and from here on out, cut the chatter."

The team set off through ankle-deep waters to cross the street from the park. Then Dohi led them through a cemetery with raised stone graves. A crumbling angel statue with outstretched wings shadowed them, its head long gone as tendrils of green and brown vines grew over it. Water flowed around the graves, running toward the southern exit of the wrought-iron fence tracing the cemetery's perimeter.

Fitz took every step slowly, probing beneath the water with his blades to ensure he didn't trip on some tangle of trash concealed by the murkiness.

Caught against the fence were coffins that had been freed by the floodwaters. They had popped open like ruptured boils. Their skeletal contents were picked bare, all the leathery or decayed flesh had been snacks for desperate monsters.

Dohi held up a fist, and the rest of the team froze. He used two fingers to indicate he had spotted a potential contact toward the west.

Through his Leupold Mark 8 optic, Fitz scoped in on the movement. Near the stone steps leading to a mold-covered house with broken windows, the water rippled as if something swam just beneath the surface.

He held his sights on the movement and waited.

The creature was drawing near, but Fitz gave the order to hold fire, not wanting to draw attention unless absolutely necessary.

An elongated skull surfaced, and two beady black eyes surveyed the cityscape for prey. Those eyes sat atop a long maw full of needle-sharp teeth.

Fitz lowered his rifle.

It was just an alligator, far less dangerous than a Variant with gills. Never in his life had he been so thankful to see the huge predator this close.

He signaled for the team to stay put as the alligator propelled itself lazily down the street-turned-river, its tail slowly undulating. Once it had moved out of sight in the opposite direction, they advanced again.

Their route took them between buildings disintegrating from the unforgiving humidity and water lapping at their baseboards. Piles of debris lay strewn at the foot of the structures.

They passed through the shadow of a hotel with wraparound cast-iron balconies, looking for any sign of the mastermind's presence. In the distance, the cries of hunting Variants wailed through the city again.

Dohi thrust his fist into the air.

A chorus of clicking joints sounded to their south. Fitz strained to see the source of the noise, but saw nothing.

The chatter and squawk of Variants erupted again from a different direction. This time a scream—all too human—pierced the din.

The agonizing cries continued for a few seconds before going silent. It had definitely come from the center of the French Quarter.

Maybe there were still people alive. People they could save with the airlift. Fitz found new motivation to find their target. If they could secure the area, they might be helping more than just the science team today.

Dohi waved them onward. He guided the team through a series of restaurants and into a bar. At the back exit, Fitz gave him the order, and Dohi opened the door to a flooded alleyway.

This time Fitz stepped down a short set of stairs and waded into water that came up to his naval. Dohi suddenly grabbed him and yanked him back up the stairs and into the door as a splash exploded from behind a mostly submerged dumpster. The scaled body of an alligator shot through the water, headed toward the two men like a living torpedo.

Dohi aimed his rifle right at the animal's center of mass as Fitz scrambled back inside, dripping wet. Before Dohi could squeeze the trigger, another creature burst from the water behind the gator. The yellow eyes of a Variant glowed as the creature wrapped its sinewy arms around the alligator and chomped into the beast's armored neck.

The animal rolled in the water, writhing desperately to shake itself loose from the Alpha predator.

Fitz and Dohi moved back into the shadows as a second Variant surfaced, water sluiced down pale, veiny flesh. It waded over, claws extended, waiting to strike.

Shrieks called out from a nearby shop.

Fitz held the team there, waiting with his rifle aimed at the creatures in the flooded alley. The alligator finally stopped thrashing and a circle of water turned an even darker shade of brown.

The two Variants ripped the alligator apart. Seeing no other beasts, Fitz ordered Dohi to take the two monsters down with his hatchet.

Fitz pulled out his knife. They moved into position and then tossed the sharp blades. The hatchet found a home in one of the Variant's skulls, but Fitz hit his target in the back.

Dohi threw his own knife before the creature could let out a shriek. Both monsters slumped into the water, floating next to the disemboweled remains of the gator.

Fitz waited another moment, then gave the advance. They moved out into the water, retrieved their weapons and pushed on until they reached a street that had been spared from the floods.

Red webbing plastered the sides of buildings framing the road. The organic ropes imprisoned the bodies of enough creatures to make Noah's Arc seem like a miniscule collection. All evidence of food that the mastermind would need to create its organic central command of the webbing network.

"We're getting close," Fitz whispered.

Suddenly Dohi took shelter behind the charcoaled husk of a delivery truck. The others sheltered behind the wall of a nearby building.

Fitz tried to settle his thumping heart.

A horde of Variants surged through a water-filled street ahead. Fitz counted their numbers, watching them hurtle by. Some ran, splashing through the street, on their way to the alley the team had just left behind.

"Go, go, go!" Fitz whispered after the monsters passed.

Team Ghost ran across the street, fighting through deeper water.

Clicks from snapping joints and far off screams of prowling Variants haunted the city.

Fitz's blade suddenly snagged on something before he made it to the other side of the street, stopping him in the middle of the open water. Rico halted and reached out to help.

Mendez, still on rearguard, paused beside them, scanning the water.

Fitz twisted his blade, bending down to remove it from whatever garbage it had gotten jabbed into. As he did, something burst from the water to his right.

The armored flesh of a juvenile barreled toward Fitz. He couldn't move out of its way with his blade caught, and there wasn't time or space for a clear shot.

Rico swung the butt of her rifle into the creature's face, then delivered a heavy kick into the monster's side that knocked it off course again.

Blood gushed from the monster's crushed nose.

Fitz swung his rifle up as the Variant turned on Rico. It raised its claws as bullets lanced through the creature's chest, chewing through the bone and organs at near point-blank range.

The *choof-choof-choof* of the suppressed rifle reverberated over the water, but the splash the dead monster made was even louder. It sank in front of Rico.

If the rest of the Variants hadn't known more than alligators were in their midst, they did now.

Rico bent down, reaching into the water, to help Fitz pry his blade loose. As soon as he was free the shrieks of a dozen monsters rang out.

They poured from the darkened buildings to the north and south.

"Run!" he ordered.

The team sprinted onto another soaked street as the monsters pursued them. A half-crumbling spire of the St. Louis Cathedral speared the gray sky nearby. Dohi pointed to a museum across from Jackson Square in the center of the French Quarter.

The team stormed past, rifles up as they moved into the lobby of the building. Rotting furniture and broken display cases lay in the water.

The team splashed across the room toward the ticket counter where they took shelter. Red webbing grew across the walls, even denser here than when they'd seen it before outside. He crouched next to a pile of brown bones loosely wrapped in tendrils of red tissue.

They were close. Fitz could feel it in his gut.

Outside, the clamor of the Variants went on for what felt like an eternity.

But slowly the monsters scattered, their wails becoming more sporadic, more distant, and their clicking joints fading as they searched for their lost prey.

Fitz waited, letting the furor of the Variants die down. Their angry voices were replaced by the drone of human voices in agony, sounding all too similar to the pained cries and moans the team had heard in other Variant tunnels and Minneapolis.

He had a feeling that those voices would lead them to

the mastermind—or, if not the beast directly, then at least to its lair.

Fitz signaled for the team to move back out toward Jackson Square. There, Dohi pointed out a path that led into the St. Louis Cathedral where the water began to recede.

More red vines of tissue stretched out of the thin layer of water along the streets and grass up to the steeples of the church and into half-broken stained-glass windows.

The team skirted between the overgrown trees and bushes of the square, making their way to the former place of worship. As they closed in on the cathedral, moans traveled out of the broken windows.

Fitz indicated for everyone to stay put except for Dohi.

Together, the two men climbed a short set of stairs and clung to the shadows until they made it into the nave.

The missing roof allowed shafts of light that played across puddles of water between rotting pews covered in red webbing. Tendrils rose to the pillars in the middle of the space and clung to the stained-glass windows.

Cocoons of the red tissue pasted decaying corpses along the walls. Many were nothing but skeletons and flags of leathery brown flesh. The bodies of different native wildlife were there; fish, birds, even a gator.

Other long strands of tissue dangled from the ceiling like bloody icicles. At the bottom of those macabre vines hung more bodies; these were all human, wrapped up like a spider's prey.

Dozens of Variants climbed up and down those growths, picking at the animals and people suspended in them. Many of the victims moaned in agony.

At the rear of the cathedral, past the sanctuary and

altar was a massive creature that stood nearly four times Fitz's height. Large, pink folds of skin covered the beast, and its stygian eyes peered around at its surroundings.

It stuck to the shadows, apparently wary of the light plunging in through the massive holes in the ceiling.

Fitz slowly backed away with Dohi. They hurried down the stairs and joined the team back on Jackson Square.

"Rico," Fitz whispered. "Radio command. We found the ugly son of a bitch."

— 13 —

The cool morning air reeked of death and suffering. Beckham and Horn waited outside the maintenance warehouse on the University of Southern Maine campus. Lawn mowers and equipment sat outside to make room for body bags.

The inside had been turned into a makeshift morgue for the victims of the attack. Like so often before, Beckham wondered why fate had chosen to take Bo and Donna. So many other innocent men, women, and children had perished, gone in an instant or cursed to horrific burn injuries, their moans still haunting the campus.

And somehow he had once again been spared. Left alive to watch all these people suffer.

Beckham looked up to the sky, but he didn't curse God nor did he question why God might allow atrocities like last night. He had always believed that if there was a God, he had nothing to do with what happened on Earth.

Humans had to live with the consequences of their actions, good or bad. Lately, Beckham had seen too much of the bad.

Especially this morning.

Soldiers and volunteers continued to carry body bags into the warehouse.

In some cases, the bags looked light. Not much remained of the deceased. The real weight was on the minds and hearts of the survivors.

Another pickup truck pulled up. Civilian volunteers lowered the lift gate to reveal more bodies, these ones without the luxury of body bags. People who had likely died in triage.

In the past, with the proper treatment, some of them might have survived. But out here, the medical staff simply didn't have the supplies or equipment needed to treat them.

Beckham still didn't know how the collaborators had controlled the bats or what type of explosives they were rigged with, but he had a feeling this was just one of many tricks they would use to win the new war. Between those new weapons and the conspirators within their ranks, he feared the enemy was far stronger than anyone realized.

"Fucking *animals*," Beckham growled.

First Jake, then Timothy, and now Donna, and Bo.

All killed by the collaborators. Those people were worse than terrorists. They were demons. He gritted his teeth and punched the side of the metal siding, denting it with his fist. Blood filled the cracked skin over his knuckles.

It wasn't his hand that hurt the worst though. His head still throbbed from the truck wreck. He closed his eyes and drew in a breath to manage the pain until it passed.

Horn didn't say anything. The two men had barely slept in twenty-four hours of hellish insanity, and they were at their wits' end.

A side door to the maintenance building opened and a soldier stepped out, gesturing for them.

"Captain, Master Sergeant, the bodies are ready for you to identify," said the young man.

Beckham and Horn followed him inside. The door clicked behind them a moment later, sealing them in the long space. Eighty some corpses lay on the concrete floor in zipped up black body bags.

Another soldier with a clipboard walked up and down the aisles, checking off names on his list.

"Captain Beckham and Master Sergeant Horn are here to confirm the identity of the deceased, Donna and Bo Tufo," their escort said to the soldier with the clipboard.

He glanced at his board, and then looked across the room. "Please, come with me, sir. Master Sergeant."

Beckham and Horn followed the soldier until he stopped at two body bags.

"These are them," he said.

Horn bent down and unzipped the bag on the left, the odor of charred flesh exploding out.

"Christ have mercy," he muttered, covering his face with his wrist.

Bo Tufo's face was hardly recognizable. Scorched and disfigured, his features had melted into a hideous sight.

Beckham pictured the young boy he had rescued during Operation Liberty. He had survived the monsters and grown up into a young man only to die at the hands of humans.

Bile rose in Beckham's throat.

"This is Bo Tufo," Horn managed to mumble.

The soldier with the clipboard nodded, and Horn unzipped the second body bag.

Donna didn't look as bad as her son. Partly due to the

fact Bo had shielded her from the blasts. Despite his sacrifice, he hadn't saved her.

And maybe that was for the best, Beckham thought. The two were so close that they wouldn't have survived without each other.

Beckham stood, his blade creaking.

"This is Donna Tufo," Horn said.

"Thank you," said the soldier. "From my records, they don't have any other kin here, is that correct, sir?"

"Yes," Beckham said.

"Would you like us to take care of the burial or…"

"We'll do it," Beckham said. Donna and Bo deserved to be buried together on Peaks Island where they had enjoyed a hiatus of peace in the middle of this endless war.

The soldier nodded and stepped away.

Beckham began the short walk to the exit of the maintenance building. Each step felt like a mile. His head spun. The black body bags stretched in all directions.

It was too much, even for him; when he got outside, he vomited into a bush.

Horn patted him on a shoulder, but didn't say anything.

"I'm good," Beckham said, wiping his lips. He drew in a breath and started back to the campus with Horn.

Chimneys of smoke rose from the damaged rooftops where suicidal bats had flapped into the sides. Soldiers had reclaimed some of the positions, but what could they do against another attack like that?

Beckham started the march to the command tent on campus.

"Are we going to head back to the *George Johnson* after we bury our friends, or do you want to keep looking for

Timothy?" Horn asked.

Beckham drew in a breath. They both knew the odds of finding the young man alive were slim to zero. "If we go back out there looking for him, we're not comin' back, Big Horn."

Horn rubbed his neck, wincing at the reality. They fell into silence until they got back to the command tent. Beckham pushed past the flap to go inside where Lieutenant Niven was going over maps with Sergeant Ruckley. They both stood at the table.

There were no good mornings or salutes. Only the hard looks of soldiers that had just gotten their asses handed to them and fully expected more.

"Have you heard anything from SOCOM?" Beckham asked.

"We spoke to Lieutenant Festa, but our orders have not changed," Niven said. "We are to hold this post at all costs."

Ruckley raised her chin a bit, clearly wanting to say something. If Beckham had to guess she didn't like those orders.

"People are being evacuated across the Allied States, and we're expecting to receive over a hundred refugees by tonight," Niven continued. "We've been marked high on the safe list."

"How the hell did that happen?" Horn muttered.

"I guess command thinks since we don't have issues with tunneling Variants we're safer than other outposts."

"Yeah, but those bats might be worse," Horn said. "Plus, we got sleeper cells wreaking havoc inside our borders. Tunneling Variants aren't the only damn issue we should be worried about!"

"All I know is that I'm staying put until command says otherwise," Niven replied.

"How about you two?" Ruckley asked. "What's your next move?"

"We're going to bury our friends on Peaks Island and then return to command," Beckham said.

"We'll see if we can get you some extra support," Horn said.

"The Iron Hogs are grateful for whatever we can get," Niven said. "I'll get a bird ready for you after you're finished with the burial."

"Sir, permission to accompany them to Peaks Island," Ruckley said.

Niven paused, seeming to think on it.

"It won't take long, sir," Ruckley said. "They'll need some help. And besides, it's the least we can do."

"Approved, Sergeant, but make it fast, okay?" Niven said.

"Yes, sir," Ruckley said.

"Thank you," Beckham said.

"I'll meet you in the staging area," Ruckley said. "Give me ten minutes."

"I'm very sorry about your friends," Niven said.

"Me too," Beckham said. He walked away with Horn while Ruckley made a call over to the morgue requesting Bo and Donna's bodies be prepared for their arrival.

"You want to call Kate about Bo and Donna?" Horn asked.

"I don't want to give her the bad news until I can do it in person. Besides, she's got so much on her plate already, and Niven already informed SOCOM last night we're okay."

"Good point…" Horn wagged his head. "Man, Tasha

is going to be a wreck when she hears about Timothy. I promised her I would…"

Beckham put a hand on his friend's shoulder.

On their walk to the staging area between Woodbury Campus Center and Masterton Hall, a line of military transport trucks passed by. The beds were filled with equipment and soldiers. Many of them looked no older than Timothy had been.

The staging area, too, was a flurry of activity between stacks of shipping containers. Militia and soldiers listened to orders from their leads. People in civilian clothing lined up, too, joining the call to arms after witnessing yesterday's events.

"Jesus, that kid looks like he's ten," Beckham said nodding toward one.

The cost of the war was never more evident. While he and Horn had saved Tasha and Jenny from the fighting, Bo had lost his life and Timothy had almost certainly lost his against the collaborators and Variants. Now kids younger than eighteen were joining up to fight.

That was something Ringgold had fought so hard against. And now they had no other choice as those men and women of fighting age perished in the Variants' attack.

Ruckley showed up with a truck a few minutes later. Two body bags were in the bed, along with shovels.

They took the truck to the shoreline where a speedboat was tethered to a dock. Four soldiers standing guard ran over to help them unload the body bags and joined them in the boat.

The ride to Peaks Island was quiet. Horn and Beckham watched the horizon in a trance. They had both dreamed of returning home, but doing so like this was more nightmare than dream.

The island loomed ahead of them, and Ruckley looked back from the wheel.

"Which way?" she called out over the motor.

Horn pointed toward the shoreline where they had all lived. The boat curved over the water, thumping against the waves.

Beckham's heart accelerated with the engine when he saw his home.

Or at least what was left of it.

Charred skeletal boards and a brick foundation were all that remained.

Beckham grabbed handholds on the gunwale as he climbed toward the bow for a better view. The boat passed houses on the shore, none of which had been hit. The only destroyed home was the one Beckham had shared with his family. He was too upset to consider the implications.

"Damn, boss," Horn said.

"Is that your house, Captain?" Ruckley asked as they pulled up to the dock.

"It is… was my house," Beckham said.

The four soldier escorts jumped out and tied the boat off on the dock's pilings. Then they got the body bags out and hauled them to the shore with Horn and Beckham.

"Where to?" one of the soldiers asked.

"This way," Beckham said, leading them to the tree where a stone marked Apollo's grave and the grave of his female companion. The branches creaked in the breeze, saved, thankfully, from the flames.

"Here is good," Beckham said.

Ruckley instructed the four soldiers to start digging with her while Beckham trudged over to look at the remains of his house.

"I'm so sorry, man," Horn said.

Beckham stopped just outside where the back door had been. A metal picture frame had melted on the remains of a metal bedside table, the picture erased into ash.

They walked around the crumbled side of the house together to the front when Horn suddenly halted.

"FUCK!" Horn yelled.

The soldiers all came running, shovels discarded, and rifles shouldered.

"What? What's wrong?" Ruckley said.

Horn stared across the street at the remains of the house where he had raised Tasha and Jenny for the past eight years.

For a moment no one said anything, but realization hit Beckham when he scanned the rest of the road. The other houses on the block were spared from the explosions and flames.

"This isn't a coincidence," Ruckley said.

"We were targeted," Beckham said.

Beckham thought back to the collaborator in Boston that knew his name, and then the attack on the lab that nearly killed Kate.

There was no doubt in his mind now.

"Someone in Portland is compromised," Beckham said. "And this was a message."

"Why not just shoot us?" Horn growled. "Least then I could see the slimy fuck's face and fight back."

Beckham grabbed his rifle, a chill running up his spine. The other soldiers raised their weapons again, slowly turning.

"It's not safe here," Ruckley said.

"Fuck this, I'm going to skin the little prick alive," Horn said. "Or pricks. Hell, I'll take on an entire fucking ARMY!"

"Calm down," Beckham said.

Horn kicked a burned board.

"This is our goddamn home, boss," he said. "They killed our friends, destroyed our houses. They're after our whole damn country. I want to find the motherfuckers and kill them all."

Ruckley spat on the ground. "You're welcome to stay here and help me find them."

Beckham tried to bite back his own fury. Revenge could wait. There were more important matters at hand.

"First we bury our friends so they can rest in peace," he said.

***

Hours ago Fischer had left El Paso, Texas. He and his men had left Sergeant Sharp behind with Lieutenant Riggs to guard the seismic detection trucks. Sharp would then oversee the deployment of a seismic detection truck near Outpost Galveston. But what they needed now was a way to deploy this technology across the Allied States.

Cornelius had requested Fischer to come to Outpost Manchester in New Hampshire to focus on a new mission implementing seismic detection defenses.

Fischer wasn't sure yet how they were going to do it with limited manpower, and the equipment they had scrounged up wasn't enough for more than a few outposts. The trucks were already being deployed, but simply couldn't cover the ground they needed to adequately defend the Allied States.

Apparently, Cornelius had something else in mind for Manchester.

The town had once been a mill town bisected by the Merrimack River and later evolved into a center for high-tech startups and niche businesses. The place appeared to Fischer as if it was on the next stage of its life, currently occupied and defended by a combination of General Cornelius' army and the Allied States' military.

At Cornelius' behest, Fischer had gone with Chase and Tran to an office building overlooking the Merrimack for a meeting and call with the president. He entered a conference room with his two guards.

"Mr. Fischer, it's good to see you again." General Cornelius said. He was polite but he remained seated behind a long mahogany table, a laptop resting in front of him. Not rising was a reminder who was in charge here.

Four officers wearing the Orca badge and blue armband of his private army also remained seated in brown leather chairs. Three empty fabric-covered chairs stood nearby, looking out of place. Fischer shook hands with Cornelius across the table and then took a seat with Tran and Chase.

"You all outperformed my expectations in El Paso," Cornelius said. "We'll deploy this strategy across the Allied States as soon as possible. Hopefully this will buy us the time to destroy the brains of the Variant network. But unfortunately we are running out of time."

"Some outposts have already ran out," Fischer said. "I heard we lost eight last night."

"Actually, ten," Cornelius said.

Tran and Chase exchanged a look but Fischer remained stern-faced. The losses were hard to stomach, but he couldn't let himself dwell on them. They had to focus on preventing further damage.

"Our enemies unleashed a new weapon," Cornelius added. "Somehow, they rigged bats with explosives and set the damn things loose on Outpost Portland."

"Good God," Fischer said, unable to contain himself.

"We thought by moving to places like Manchester we would be safe from the tunneling Variants, but the bats have added another threat into the mix," Cornelius said. "Fortunately, we have a secret weapon of our own."

Fischer leaned forward, curious.

"SOCOM is helping organize the evacuation and defense of strategic bases around the Allied States, and we've been asked to help with Manchester's defenses," Cornelius said. "This city was once the site of advanced biotechnological research. It will make a perfect research space for Dr. Lovato and her team."

"Research space for what, exactly?"

"As we speak, teams are working to capture a mastermind and bring it here for the scientists to study."

Chase laughed. "You can't be serious."

Cornelius didn't laugh.

"Wait, you're really not joking?" Chase asked.

"Not at all," said the general. "They have the beast surrounded right now."

Fischer stroked his mustache nervously. Then realized what he was doing and stopped. "What in the Sam Hill are they thinking bringing one of those creatures here?"

"The scientists think it will allow us to tap into the Variant communications network. Needless to say, we have reason to believe the Variants are going to want it back. It's up to us to ensure that doesn't happen."

Cornelius rotated his wrist to check his watch.

"It's about time to call President Ringgold." He turned

to one of the officers next to him, who in turn used a satellite phone.

"What I've been investigating will provide us unparalleled defenses in Manchester and the rest of the country," Cornelius said. "Better than the trucks you used in El Paso."

Fischer was anxious to hear what that might be when a voice came over the phone's speaker.

"President Ringgold here."

"Madam President, this is General Cornelius. I have S.M. Fischer with me in Manchester."

"Hello, gentleman, I'm with Vice President Lemke, General Souza and Lieutenant Festa."

"Before I begin, I just want to express my sympathy for everyone and everything we lost last night," Cornelius said.

There was a pause on the other end of the line.

"Thank you, and frankly, we're running out of time to save everyone else," Ringgold said.

Fischer thought he detected Ringgold's voice shaking slightly. He had once thought that she was a coward running off to a ship, far from land, but he knew she cared deeply for the people of this country.

"I'll get right to it," Cornelius said. "Mr. Fischer has proved seismic detection allows us to accurately detect and locate Variant tunneling activities in El Paso. I've identified a location with technology even more advanced than what Mr. Fischer used. When I was involved with the Department of Defense, one project I encountered consisted of advanced detection systems for tsunami and earthquake activity."

General Souza came back on the line. "I vaguely remember that. Wasn't that one of the DARPA-funded environmental warfare projects near Stanford?"

"Yes, it was called Project Rolling Stone. Researchers at the National Accelerator Laboratories were devising a system to detect seismic aberrations that might lead to a catastrophic environmental event. But that wasn't the only use they saw fit for this program."

Fischer raised a brow, intrigued by where this was going.

"North Korea has a long history of attempting to tunnel under the Demilitarized Zone," Cornelius explained. "South Korea needed something to detect those tunnels before they hit Seoul, and they reached out to us. Hence Project Rolling Stone took on a new goal."

"Pardon me, but if this project already exists, what did you need the vibroseis equipment for in El Paso?" Fischer asked.

Cornelius gave Fischer a knowing nod.

"The answer is two-fold. First, the technology developed in Project Rolling Stone is still out in California, deep in the heart of Variant-controlled territory. Second, if I was going to even suggest we consider retrieving it, we needed to show that seismic detection and location works."

"We don't have nearly enough of those vibroseis trucks for every outpost. How will we guarantee there's enough of this Project Rolling Stone equipment? And even if we have the equipment, how do we find the people to help run it?" Ringgold asked.

"When I retired, we had enough equipment to deploy all over the DMZ, plus surplus to detect environmental seismic events across the Pacific Northwest," Cornelius replied.

Fischer was impressed with the idea so far and listened anxiously.

"We can deploy this new technology in Manchester as soon as it arrives with Mr. Fischer's help, but in the meantime we will deploy the few vibroseis trucks we have at outposts they are needed the most," Cornelius said. "Then we'll roll out these Rolling Stone technologies to outposts all around the country."

"General," said a new voice. "This is Lieutenant Festa. France has sent us 100 consultants—engineers, soldiers, and more—with experience finding and fighting the monsters that dug through the ground in Europe. I believe that should help with the manpower issue."

"Then we have the people and enough equipment to cover far more ground than the vibroseis truck setups we used last night," Cornelius said. "One Seismic Detection System—or SDS—from Project Rolling Stone can cover a radius of approximately 200 to 500 square miles depending on geological factors. In other words, it will be more than enough for the outposts you decide to…"

"To save," Souza cut in. "We're abandoning outposts in the Midwest and continuing to pull people back east."

Festa spoke up again. "That's great that we might be able to scrounge up this equipment, but our aircraft are at their limits of use right now. What exactly does this SDS stuff look like? Is it hard to transport?"

Cornelius unfolded the laptop in front of him. "I'm sending you schematics of what this is so you know what to expect. Goes without saying, this was a highly classified project beforehand, and I think we need to keep this intel amongst ourselves for the time being."

The general twisted the laptop enough so that Fischer could get a look at the images on the screen. On it,

Fischer saw an array of metal-encased sensors, all of which looked similar to the small coin-sized sensors civil engineers used on bridges to detect stability issues and potential damage from traffic and floods. Each sensor could easily fit in the palm of his hand.

"As you can see, the sensors are quite small. It's no problem to scatter these around an outpost." Cornelius opened another image. "This is our signal processing unit."

A backpack-sized metallic device with a computer screen and an array of antenna came on the screen.

"Remember, these were only meant to be passive detection systems—not active like the equipment we used in El Paso," Cornelius said. "All they've got to do is receive even the most minute of signals from tunneling activity, and you can get an accurate read on any tunnel-making. Like I said, perfect for the DMZ between North and South Korea."

"That certainly exceeds my expectations if it works how you promised," Fischer said.

"Me, too," Ringgold said. "This sounds like something we can't pass up. Let's get it done."

"It's not that easy," Cornelius replied.

"Tell me what you need."

"My troops are made up of mercenaries, retired soldiers, and a lot of brave men and women, but these are not Special Op soldiers, and that's what I need to help locate the tech before our people can get it out of there."

Hushed chatter came over the other line.

"Anything could have happened to the SDS equipment since I last heard about it. The facility may have been inadvertently destroyed in the bombing campaigns in the war or marauders may have sacked the

National Accelerator Labs," Cornelius said. "We need a team with the experience of working behind enemy lines."

"I know of just the one," Ringgold said. "Unfortunately, they're busy trying to secure a mastermind."

"A mission to locate and retrieve this technology is imperative to protect the mastermind while the scientists research it," Cornelius replied. "This location is one of the hardest to get at, but that doesn't mean it can't be done if the Variants try."

There was silence on the phone for a few seconds.

Fischer had made some tough decisions in his time, but he did not envy the president's position now. Every soldier they had left was a valuable asset from a dwindling pool of resources.

"General Cornelius, I want you to send myself and General Souza all the intel you have on Project Rolling Stone," Ringgold said. "We'll need it if we're going to send a team out looking for it."

"Uploading now," Cornelius said.

"Thank you, we will be in touch shortly. Until then, stay safe."

"You too, Madam President."

The call ended and Cornelius stood.

"I'm counting on you now, Mr. Fischer," he said. "As soon as the SDS equipment arrives, I want your men ready to deploy it. In the meantime, I'll be heading back to Galveston." He crossed around the table closer to Fischer. "There's something else I want to warn you about."

"What?" Fischer asked.

"We have good reason to believe most of these attacks

have been aided by collaborators within and outside of the outposts."

Fischer furrowed his brow. "You're telling me there are traitors in our midst?"

A firm nod. "What you and the rest of the people are doing in this base is extremely important. Between the mastermind and the SDS equipment, these are perhaps the most crucial missions if we're going to beat the Variants and their allies."

"I'm all too aware of it."

"There very well could be people at this outpost that are compromised. You might run into some of these collaborators here on base and not even realize it. I want you to be vigilant, and I trust you can make sure the SDS equipment is safe when it's brought here."

Fischer swallowed. "I'm a good judge of character, but…"

"Stay frosty at all times and keep all classified intel quiet. The collaborators might be planning something even more sinister, and we can't afford any of our plans to fall into their hands.

"That sounds like you don't think our military and its scientists can keep a secret," Fischer said.

"Unfortunately from what I've heard and seen, it sure as hell seems like we've got compromised people who have sufficient security clearance to intercept classified data."

"Then who do I trust out here?" Fischer asked.

Cornelius drew in a breath. "Wish I could tell you exactly who to trust and who not to. But if we'd figured that out already, I wouldn't have to give you this warning, would I?"

Fischer swallowed even harder.

"All I can say is use your brain, use your gut, and trust basically no one," Cornelius said. He gave Fischer a nod and then exited with his team behind him.

— 14 —

"Ghost, Falcon 1, ETA five minutes," came a voice over the channel.

Dohi and the rest of Team Ghost had been patiently waiting for this moment, all of them spread out and hidden in vantage points covering Jackson Square around the St. Louis Cathedral in New Orleans.

After calling in the mastermind's location, they had retreated to observe the beast through the cracked and broken stained-glass windows. Dohi watched the abomination with a growing dread. He had grown up listening to Navajo folklore about many different demons, and had always believed them to be more fantasy than fact, but this beast proved his ancestors were right.

"Eyes on target," Fitz responded over the channel. "Awaiting orders."

"Four birds incoming, two to touch down," Falcon 1 called back. "Confirm LZ clear?"

The channel went quiet. Dohi scanned the flooded terrain filled with debris and charcoaled vehicles around Jackson Square.

"Negative," Fitz finally replied. "Not enough room to land you, Falcon 1."

"Understood, Ghost 1. We'll find an alternative."

The distant whir of the helicopters rose over the clicking of joints and the moans of the monsters' captives inside the cathedral. A howl burst over the din—the Variant version of an air-raid siren sounding the alarm over the helicopters.

From his position, Dohi could see the beasts cease feeding their master. Several of the smaller monsters skittered over the webbing toward the broken windows and doors.

"Eyes on movement," Fitz said over the private channel.

"Six… no, seven hostiles from the south," Rico reported.

Next came Mendez. "Got a pack of juvies streaming out of the apartments to our east."

"Four more around the museums to the northwest," Ace chimed in.

The whoop of the chopper blades cut them off. Dark silhouettes appeared in the rolling gray clouds.

"We're drawing heat," Falcon 1 said over the comms. "Got a horde growing in our wake. Ghost, you'll need to clear the pickup zone."

"Wilco," Fitz said. "All right, boys and girls, you heard him. We keep this square clear, then move inside and secure the cathedral. On my mark."

There was tension in his voice.

Dohi was nervous too. They were about to attempt something no other team had tried and he had a feeling it wasn't going to be easy, even with the air support en route.

The other members of the team shouldered their rifles, standing amid the overgrown bushes and masses of webbing. Dohi spotted an armored juvenile Variant with roving, saucer-shaped eyes.

"Execute," Fitz ordered on the comms.

Dohi pulled the trigger and suppressed rifle shots *choofed* all around the square. Their targets crumpled, red holes weeping from heads and chests.

The next volley punched through the flanks of the Variants drawn out of the cathedral by the noise.

Through the gaping holes in the windows of the cathedral, Dohi saw the mastermind go mad behind the altar where it stood. The hulking red form shook, the vibrations traveling through the folds of tissue that covered the monster. It reached out with huge, glistening claws and yanked on the tissue vines attached to its body like it was orchestrating a sickening puppet performance. Multiple cocooned bodies were slashed open by the raging beast, dumping the contents to the floor.

"South square clear," Rico said.

"North clear," Ace said.

Fitz gave the advance signal.

Dohi got up and walked at a hunch past the foliage and webbing he'd sheltered behind, moving across the lawn toward the cathedral. A clearing in the clouds let sunlight wash over the choppers. Their shadows surged over the hellish cityscape.

Screaming Variants chased after them on all fours. It wouldn't be long before the reinforcements arrived. Team Ghost had to move fast.

Keeping low, Dohi took point with Fitz and Ace converging on him at the Cathedral. At the south entrance, Rico and Mendez had joined up.

One of the stained-glass windows suddenly burst into rainbow shards. Dohi brought an arm up to shield himself from the hailstorm of glass as a Variant lunged through.

A suppressed burst took it down, and Fitz patted Dohi

on the back.

"You good?" he asked.

Dohi wiped fresh blood off his cheek where a shard had opened his flesh. He managed a nod and followed Fitz and Ace into the nave of the cathedral. The mastermind thrashed around, knocking into the webbing-wrapped bodies dangling from the ceiling as it tried to separate itself from the organic netting in an effort to escape.

The few remaining Variants in the cathedral launched themselves off the rafters and webbing-covered walls. Calculated shots dropped them all before they could get within striking distance.

Rico and Mendez joined the team in the nave, and they slowly surrounded the writhing beast.

"Falcon 1, Ghost 1," Fitz said into his headset. "We're inside. Mastermind is alone now, but trying to escape."

More webbing snapped from the mastermind. A gaping maw opened as it let out a roar so powerful its breath hit Dohi like gale force wind.

Fitz flashed hand signals for the team to spread out and cover the entries and exits. The team spread out behind the pews, facing the mastermind as if the creature was a demonic priest and they had come to worship.

Rotor wash cascaded through the missing chunks of the cathedral's roof. The Chinook blocked the sunlight as it managed a dangerous hover. Ropes uncoiled, and Marines fast-roped down. The men landed amid the puddles of water between the pews.

"Move, move, move!" a sergeant shouted as they rushed into positions, scattering among the pews, and securing the entryways throughout the cathedral.

One skinny Marine slid next to Dohi, carrying a

tranquilizer rifle fit for taking down an elephant.

The sound of the horde increased, the ground rumbling from what sounded like hundreds of clawed feet and hands pounding the concrete outside.

The Marine with the tranq rifle didn't waste time. He aimed and fired at the mastermind. Several other Marines did the same. The feathered metal rounds plunged into the folds of the mastermind's tissue.

Explosions boomed outside as Hydra 70 rockets from the Apache helicopters slammed into the advancing beasts. The chainsaw growl of the Apaches' 30 mm M230E1 chain gun burst to life next, spewing rounds into the onrushing horde.

Another deafening shriek escaped the mastermind. It lashed out at the nearest Marines, tearing away more of the webbing. The Marines backed away, letting loose a second volley of darts.

The mastermind recoiled; its movements were clumsier, slower.

A pair of Marines cautiously approached it.

"How much longer is this going to take?" Dohi asked the Marine next to him.

"Don't know," the man said, sounding a bit desperate. He loaded in another tranquilizer round. "We've never done this before. They don't work instantly either!"

The resonating blasts of bursting rockets shook the walls. Several of the red vines snapped, releasing shriveled corpses that crashed to the ground.

"Falcon, requesting a SITREP," the Chinook pilot said.

Dohi heard the worry in his quivering voice. Things must not be looking so good from the air. The machinegun fire continued, and another blast from a rocket thumped into the concrete.

Over the noises, came the angry shrieks of beasts.

They were getting closer.

But finally, the mastermind grew still, its eyes rolling in its gargantuan skull. It slumped against the back wall, knocking a lopsided crucifix from the wall.

"Falcon 1, slings now!" the Marine sergeant shouted.

Slings and nets unfurled from the Chinook, hanging like tentacles in front of the mastermind.

The sergeant stood from his hiding spot behind a pew and waved for his men to follow. "Move it, Marines!"

The men rushed the giant monster as it blinked slowly like it was struggling to stay awake. Teams of the Marines threw the heavy slings and nets around the creature's limbs, securing its bulbous feet and clawed hands.

A door suddenly exploded off the hinges and the first Variant staggered into the cathedral with a missing arm and blood cascading from multiple shrapnel wounds across its chest. It sucked in one last breath and then slumped to the ground.

But more creatures stormed over the corpse.

Dohi swiveled and squeezed the trigger, releasing a burst that blew off an armored hunk of a juvenile's head. His bolt locked back after taking out three more of them that had climbed through windows.

The Apaches circled outside, their chain guns still cutting through the mass of beasts. Survivors bounded through the open door where they were cut down by Team Ghost and the Marines.

Within minutes a wall of the dead had formed.

And still they came, trying to save the mastermind. The Marines worked fast and Team Ghost provided covering fire, but the Variants had made it into the nave.

A sinewy female launched herself into the air and careened down the aisle, headed toward the men struggling to secure the mastermind.

The beast turned toward Fitz, ducking under his fire. Magazine dry, Dohi pulled out his hatchet and let it fly. The blade landed squarely in the middle of the creature's face, splitting its nose.

"Step away from it! Step back!" someone yelled.

When Dohi looked, the mastermind's eyes had opened and bloody red lips peeled back into a snarl. The cornered animal, desperate, thrashed against its restraints as men threw the slings around its limbs like lassoes.

It fell again, pulling on the slack sling roped around its limbs. Panicked screams rang out. The creature fell on three of the Marines trying to secure the slings, silencing their screams with a loud crunch.

Dohi rushed over with Ace and Mendez while Fitz and Rico continued to lay down covering fire.

The beast got up again, revealing the mangled, broken limbs of the crushed Marines. One of them was still alive, but his legs were twisted beneath him.

Dohi helped pull the groaning man to safety.

Ace and Mendez helped the other Marines. While they worked to secure the monster, a transmission fired over the channel. "Ghost 1, we got a problem," the Chinook pilot said. "More hostiles headed our way."

"You got a count?" Fitz asked.

"A few dozen Variants and what looks like two fan boats full of collaborators," replied the pilot.

"Send an Apache to intercept and eliminate," Fitz ordered.

Dohi got the injured Marine to safety. "Hang on man, we're going to get you out of here."

One of his eyes bulged from the socket, but despite his injuries, he still pulled out his pistol.

A massive hole in the side of the church provided a window to the skyline. Dohi saw the Apache fly to take out the fan boats. He went to turn away when he noticed a stream of white smoke in his peripheral. Before he could turn, an explosion bloomed across the sky.

The chopper went into a spin and vanished from view.

"Gun bird down!" cried the Chinook pilot.

Now it was all too clear what the mastermind had been doing when it tugged on the vines and thrashed around. It was calling for reinforcements, buying time for itself as its Variant and collaborator allies descended on the unwary Marines and Team Ghost.

It had sprung a trap.

The surviving twelve Marines and Team Ghost all exchanged looks, each of them knowing the implications.

"Keep working!" Fitz yelled.

The Marine Sergeant barked at his men, and they went back to securing the beast again. The creature's eyes fluttered closed again from a new round of darts sticking out of its pink folds.

Dohi knew what was at stake, and the rest of the team would, too. Even if the team finished securing it, there was no guarantee of their success if the collaborators brought the other Apache down before they could leave New Orleans with their catch.

"We have to go back outside and take out those collaborators," Dohi said.

"Let's go, bro!" Mendez yelled. "I'll fuck 'em all up!"

"You'll get yourselves killed," Ace grumbled.

"Dohi and Mendez are right," Fitz said. "We have to buy these Marines time to get the target out of here."

"Good luck!" yelled the skinny Marine.

Dohi nodded at the young man and took lead back into Jackson square.

From there, they rushed eastward past the vine-covered bushes and wall, then around the square, and back to the flooded streets. He navigated through the water-filled craters left from the Apache's rockets and dodged past the red and crispy corpses of Variants. Smoke still shifted off their smoldering bodies.

Dohi paused at a street corner as the howl of Variants wailed over the square behind them. Another thunderous storm of Variant shrieks erupted from near the cathedral. The beasts were closing in around Jackson Square.

Geysers of dirt and water exploded around the monsters as the single remaining Apache struggled to keep them back. Chain gun fire cut through their ranks, but they gushed forward.

The monsters were mostly coming in from the north, where they had followed the choppers. Their attention was almost entirely on the carnage around the cathedral as they rushed to the mastermind's rescue.

If Team Ghost had delayed another minute, they wouldn't have made it out of Jackson Square.

Ahead in the flooded street, the glint of the abandoned fan boats caught Dohi's eyes. The burning wreckage of the Apache sizzled on top of a mountain of debris, sending up a column of oily black smoke, not far from the boats. A few Variants prowled, but these were the diseased, starving beasts, the ones too timid to charge into battle.

Dohi ignored them and searched for the collaborators. He saw no clear trail here except for their boats.

Another thump of rockets against the ground drew his

eyes back westward where the cathedral was.

One of the Chinooks hovered with it slings hanging through the open hole in the cathedral's roof. A crew chief on the other big bird manned an M240 on the open rear gate and two door-gunners unleashed hell from the M60s mounted on the side doors.

Despite their air superiority, the choppers were sitting ducks to the collaborators' rockets. The traitorous shits were definitely preparing another shot. They would be looking for the best spot to bring the birds down, and that's exactly where Dohi had to search, too.

He searched the roofs that weren't yet covered in flames from the burning Apache. Most of the apartments, restaurants, and bars had collapsed in on themselves.

He spotted a three-story nightclub covered in red webbing. At the top floor was a railing around an open-air bar.

It was the optimal location to launch a couple of rockets at a vulnerable Chinook.

Dohi pointed toward it.

Fitz nodded, signaling for them to head into the nightclub.

Inside, they navigated a floor littered with broken glasses and upturned tables. Footsteps led through the muck and grime coating the floor leading to a stairwell.

Dohi's pulse accelerated with each step.

"Ghost, Falcon 1, the mastermind is almost secure," said the pilot. "We're nearly ready to go, but—"

Something cut off the transmission. Dohi ran up the rest of the stairwell until he made it to the top, outdoor level. After opening the door, he sheltered in an alcove on the rooftop patio overlooking the street and Jackson Square beyond.

A violent storm of fire and noise bloomed from above the cathedral.

"Second bird down!" the Chinook pilot said.

Frantic cries surged over the channels, about Variants invading the cathedral.

Dohi tuned them out, focusing only on the world directly in front of him.

Laughing came across the rooftop patio.

The sounds fueled Dohi's anger. Thoughts of the people buried in tunnels, of Lincoln dying in the chopper, of all the children now orphaned because of these bastards.

Rico, Mendez, Fitz, and Ace all fell into line, their chests heaving with the rushed charge they had made to get here. With a hand signal, Fitz gestured forward.

Dohi went first, keeping low as he moved between chairs and tables. Then he hurdled over a bar covered in black mold.

Six collaborators were positioned on the other side of the roof, stabilizing their LAW rockets on the railing. Three handled the launchers as the other three prepped the next set of weapons.

One of the collaborators looked over his shoulder with a mangy beard dangling from his mud-covered face. Dohi halted and aimed his rifle as the man reached for a sidearm.

A squeeze of the trigger dropped the man with a round punching between his widening eyes. Dohi kept moving, firing as he did.

The others started to turn, scrambling for weapons. More shots lanced into their flesh. Only the sixth collaborator managed to let loose a final rocket. It was a Hail Mary that punched wide through the air, slamming harmlessly into the cathedral, sending bricks tumbling from a cloud of gray.

Dohi let his rifle sag and threw his hatchet. It found purchase in the man's back, sinking deep. He screamed in pain, dropping the launcher, and reaching behind him to try and grab the blade. Then he fell to his knees, still screeching.

"Falcon 1, Ghost 1, collaborators are down," Fitz reported on the comm.

"Copy, Ghost, good work out there," the Chinook pilot said.

The big bird with the sling-loader lifted into the air with the red, listless form of the huge mastermind dangling in its nets. The second Chinook flew into position, the rear ramp still open. The crew chiefs had exchanged the fast-ropes for rope ladders to load the Marines back inside.

Hundreds of Variants swarmed the streets below, shrieking in a desperate din that chilled Dohi to the core.

The M240 and M60s from the lead Chinook rattled, beating back the crowd that finally scattered in defeat.

Rotor wash blasted Team Ghost as the second Chinook came to a hover above them. Fitz got Rico up first, and then the rest of the team climbed to the safety of the troop hold. Only then did Dohi collapse against the bulkhead of the aircraft, sweat pouring down his forehead.

"We did it," Mendez huffed. "We actually pulled that loco shit off, man."

Ace clapped his shoulder, slumping beside him. "Nice work, amigo."

"Gracias, hombre."

Dohi surveyed the Marines around them.

Many hadn't made it back, including the man with crushed legs that Dohi had pulled to safety. He walked over to the skinny Marine who trembled. He balled his fists as Dohi approached, trying to hide his fear, or perhaps, his anger.

"Good job, kid," Dohi said. He took a seat next to him, resting his back on the bulkhead. The Marine Sergeant walked through the troop hold, checking his remaining men.

Fitz went over to the man, wiping blood from his face.

"I'm sorry about your losses, Sergeant," Fitz said. "Their sacrifices might have changed the direction of the war in our favor."

— 15 —

The conference room in the packed quarters aboard the USS *George Johnson* broke into applause as soon as General Souza finished speaking.

"The mastermind is secure and en route to Outpost Manchester," he said.

President Ringgold nodded, but didn't allow herself to celebrate.

"That was the easy part," she said. "Now the real mission begins."

"Indeed," Souza replied.

He continued debriefing, and when it finished, she marched straight to the lab. There she found the science team busy working behind glass windows on what looked like a lump of bulbous brain matter inside a clear plastic drum the scientists had called a bioreactor.

She jabbed the intercom, letting it buzz, and the scientists all looked up.

Kate hurried over, pressing a button to return the call.

"Is everything okay? Are Reed and Parker back?" she asked, her voice slightly muffled behind her clear face mask.

"They're fine and should be here soon," she replied.

Kate deflated, the anxiety draining from her.

"Would you like to join me on the deck for some fresh air while we wait?" Ringgold asked. "I do have some good news."

"Fresh air sounds great, and so does good news, just give me a second."

After Kate changed, she met the president in the narrow passage outside the lab. Several sailors walked past, so Ringgold stayed quiet, not wanting a single word of the classified information to find itself in prying ears.

At this point, leaked classified information spread like wildfire across the ship and it was imperative for morale to keep some things as tight as an airlock.

"Madam President, you have my curiosity piqued, what's the news?" Kate asked.

Ringgold looked up and down the passage as they strolled on. "I just want to make sure we're alone first."

They halted outside an exit hatch to the small flight deck. Two Marines standing sentry saluted, and Ringgold returned the gesture.

"It's a little cold out there today, Madam President." One of the Marines motioned toward the general use parkas kept by the exit.

"Thank you." Ringgold took one, slipping it on. "Let my agents know I'm about to go above deck. I have feeling they wouldn't be happy if I met the incoming chopper without them."

"Yes, Ma'am," one of the Marines said, before picking up a handset for intraship comms.

Her security escort team arrived a few minutes later. The group of Secret Service agents and Marines accompanied the two women onto the sternward deck.

Gusting wind beat against them outside, chilling Ringgold despite her layers of clothing. Bulky clouds rolled across the darkening horizon.

A scan of the vast sea dotted with white caps confirmed they were alone.

Marines and Secret Service agents fanned out across the deck nonetheless, prepared to defend her against any unforeseen enemies.

While the men spread out, she and Kate waited anxiously for the first view of the helicopter carrying the heroes that had helped save them during the last war.

Both women were worried for different reasons.

For Ringgold, she waited to hear more about the strange bat attack that had claimed the lives of so many in Outpost Portland, fearing this was yet another weapon that they weren't prepared to fight.

For Kate, she likely knew the reunion after days of being apart from her husband would be short-lived.

She would be right.

The same chopper would be taking Kate away from the stealth warship on a new mission, very soon.

Now that Ringgold was alone with Kate and out of earshot from the security team, she broke the news.

"The good news is that Team Ghost secured the mastermind in New Orleans, and it's on its way to Outpost Manchester," Ringgold said.

"Is everyone okay?"

Her response was typical Kate, always concerned about the men and women of the mission.

"Everyone on Team Ghost survived, but there were multiple casualties," Ringgold said. "Their sacrifices won't be in vain, and I know you're going to make sure of that."

Kate narrowed her blue eyes. "I take it that means I'm going to Manchester right now, too."

"I'm sorry, I know you're just about to see Reed—"

Kate drew in a breath and looked back to the ocean, determined. "I have to finish what we started. The future of the Allied States and, for that matter, the entire world might depend on our work."

The irony wasn't lost on Ringgold. Once again, the fate of the world rested on the shoulders of Kate Lovato and a handful of scientists.

"We're taking every precaution to keep your work and Outpost Manchester secure, but General Souza warned the Variants might try to recapture their leader," Ringgold said.

"We better work quickly then."

Ringgold had a feeling Beckham wouldn't want Kate to go to Manchester alone. She didn't plan on standing in their way, either.

"An advance team arrived at the facility earlier today and will be preparing the lab for your research," Ringgold said.

"Great. With the team we've got, I'm sure we'll crack the webbing's code in no time."

"Incoming!" shouted a Marine.

The man pointed at a black aircraft lowering through the cloud cover.

Another Marine with a handset confirmed the incoming Bell UH-1Y Venom was cleared to land. From what Ringgold had been told it was one of only four the military had left.

She backed away with Kate from the flight deck until they were safely against the bulkhead. The pilots put down in the center of the helipad, and the side door slid open.

Horn jumped out first, followed by Beckham, who held a hand to a bandage on his head. Even from a distance Ringgold could tell they were exhausted.

Rotor wash whipped their blood-soiled fatigues as they trundled over.

Kate ran to Beckham, and they embraced while Horn stood watching. He glanced at Ringgold almost with a rueful gaze.

As the rotors slowed to a stop, Kate pulled away and Ringgold joined them.

Beckham nodded at Ringgold. "Madam President."

"Good to see you both," she said.

Horn offered a brief, but pained smile.

Kate looked back at the helicopter.

"Where are Donna and Bo?" she asked. "I thought you were bringing them…"

Her words trailed off when she saw the troop hold was empty save for a crew chief. Beckham didn't respond right away, and when Kate looked to Horn, his eyes glazed with tears.

Their friends weren't coming home, Ringgold realized.

"Timothy?" Kate asked.

Beckham shook his head. Kate covered her mouth with a palm to hold back a gasp. She took a step back, and he reached out to her.

"The collaborators killed them," Beckham said. "They destroyed our home last night, too."

Ringgold stepped forward, unsure if she had heard the last part right.

"The collaborators used some kind of explosives on Peaks Island before the attack on the outpost," he continued. "Might've been the bats there, too, for all we know."

"Hit my house too," Horn said. "From everything we heard, they've infiltrated Outpost Portland."

"I don't understand," Kate said. She shook her head like she couldn't believe it, and Beckham wrapped her up in another hug.

Ringgold was equally dismayed. She had underestimated the Variant enemy. Everyone had. But it was the collaborators that the military had really underestimated.

The underground group was far more organized than she could have fathomed. In some ways, they were worse than the mutated monsters.

"Let's go inside," Ringgold suggested.

They went back into a passage, and she told the security detail to wait at the exit hatch. Then she took the others deeper into the passage where they could speak alone. She explained what she had told Kate about the mastermind being transferred to Manchester.

"And Team Ghost?" Beckham asked. "What are their new orders?"

"They're going to assist in finding some technology in California that can better protect our outposts," Ringgold said.

"*What*?" Horn blurted.

"The frontier?" Beckham said, sounding equally as shocked. "That's no-man's land."

"Worse," Horn said. "It's *Variant* land."

"We have no choice," Ringgold said.

Beckham and Horn exchanged a look, and Beckham shook his head.

"We've got so much to talk about with everything going on, and I want to see the kids," he said.

"We don't have much time," Kate said. "My team is heading to Manchester ASAP to begin studying the mastermind."

Ringgold wished she could let them take their time, but time, as always, was not on their side. Every minute they waited was another minute that the enemy drove humanity closer to extinction.

"No need to say goodbye," Beckham said after a brief hesitation. "We bring Javier and the girls with."

"You sure about that, boss?" Horn asked.

"I sure as hell ain't letting my wife go out there alone," Beckham said. "If you'd prefer to stay—"

"I go where you go, boss."

Beckham checked with Ringgold for her approval.

"Of course, you have my blessing."

She knew them all well enough to know there was no debating this. And deep down, she agreed it was best if they were all together. She just wished she could join them. These people were the closest thing to a family she had left in this world.

***

Timothy had spent the past twenty-four hours watching, listening, and learning. Those three words were all things his dad had taught him when he was growing up to survive in a world of monsters.

The collaborators had confined him to a small holding cell with a sink, toilet, and bed. It was disgusting and claustrophobic, but it beat being plastered to a wall.

He wasn't the only one here.

This wing of the makeshift prison held other people. Women mostly, at least he thought so. They all looked haggard and moved like they were drugged.

A young woman occupied the cell across from him. Since he'd noticed her, she hadn't moved from her position, lying face-down on the concrete floor. He guessed she was in her thirties, but it was hard to tell with the deep bags under her eyes and the way her nearly translucent skin clung to her bones.

He wanted to ask one of the other prisoners what in the hell was going on, but he didn't want to piss off the guards stationed nearby.

So he simply listened and waited.

As time wore on, he tried to distract himself with hopeful thoughts. Daydreams that would transport him from this misery.

He recalled afternoons hiking with his dad, and stories about his mother. Days at the beach with Tasha, throwing sticks into the rolling tides for Ginger and Spark to fetch.

He longed for those moments again, and he hated the collaborators for taking them from him.

They were talking again and he pushed his thoughts away to listen.

The guards discussed payback on Outpost Portland for the death of their comrades and the loss of so many 'thrall' Variants.

None of what they said helped much. Timothy still didn't know where the compound was, nor how many collaborators and Variants it held.

The guards had said something earlier that sounded important—something about a secret weapon that Pete had been saving. They had decided to use it early after so many of the Variants and the raider demolition parties had been killed.

Timothy prayed that secret weapon hadn't hurt any of his friends. Donna and Bo were still at the outpost.

At some point, Timothy finally succumbed to his exhaustion and fell asleep in his cell. He awoke to the sounds of a key jingling against the iron bars.

A man stood in the hallway outside, with his back to Timothy. He opened the door to the woman's cell across from him. Her eyes opened slightly, and she tried to squirm away. She raised a trembling hand and moaned when the man bent down with a syringe in his hand.

He made a cooing sound, like he was trying to get a child to relax. But the woman resisted, struggling sluggishly as he poked a needle into her arm.

"No," she mumbled. "No…"

"It's okay," he said, reassuringly.

The man remained crouched while her body relaxed. Moments later, her head slumped back to the floor and drool slid down her chin.

When the man turned, Timothy saw the Red Sox baseball cap and the dirty smirk of Nick, the collaborator his friends called Whiskey. He slipped the dirty needle back in a pocket of his black vest. Then he put his hand on the grip of a holstered pistol and turned.

"What did you do to her?" Timothy asked.

"She's one of the special ones," Nick said. "Pete likes to keep them quiet until they're ready for the great awakening. The New Gods will want them to help us propagate our lands."

He shut the gate, locked it, and then crossed over to Timothy. For a moment he just stood there stroking his beard.

Then he reached down to his vest. Timothy feared it was for another needle, but instead, he held out a plastic bag.

"Better eat somethin'. You'll need your energy for later." Nick ripped open the bag and handed it through the bars. Timothy reached out for what smelled like beef smothered in gravy, but then Nick held it back.

"That was quite the performance last night in front of Pete," he said. "You got Vin killed, and while I was no fan of that douche, he deserved better than getting a new pair of gills like a stupid perch."

"Then he shouldn't have…" Timothy let his words trail off.

"Shouldn't have what?" Nick pulled the bag containing a still warm meal away from the bars. "Finish what you want to say."

Timothy considered his words carefully, reminding himself that his goal was to get these men to trust him. His opportunity for vengeance would come only then.

"Vin would have thrown you under the bus next," Timothy said. "I heard what he was saying about pinning whatever happened on that Pete guy. You can't trust a guy like that."

Nick furrowed his bushy black eyebrows.

"I did you a favor, man," Timothy said.

"Favor." Nick chuckled while scratching his beard. "A favor is giving me a bottle of aged whiskey."

Timothy eyed the bag, his stomach growling.

"You know… before all this?" Nick said. "Before the monsters, the war… you know what I did?"

You were a drug dealer or an ambulance chaser? Timothy thought.

"I was a dentist with a wife I adored and two kids that would be your age now," Nick said. "I lost everything. You want to know why?"

Timothy stayed quiet. It was hard to believe this man could be anything but a traitorous animal.

"Because of our corrupt government and some fringe scientists that created the monsters," Nick said. "So I decided, you know what… why fight *them*?"

He raised his lip, exposing a rotted tooth.

You sure you were a dentist? Timothy wanted to say.

"Why not use those beasts against the government that created them?" Nick continued. "Why not take down the cog that keeps this war turning?"

"Maybe because the beasts will kill *all* of us if we don't stop them," Timothy said, trying not to sound too sarcastic. He managed his tone. "They aren't pets to be controlled. They're apex predators designed for the single purpose of killing."

Nick snorted. "Figured you'd say that, kid. You've got a lot to learn if you want to survive the reign of the New Gods."

Again, he reached into his pocket.

Nick pulled out a key chain and unlocked the cell. Then he handed Timothy the plastic bag full of mushed food. "Eat and come with me."

Timothy took it before Nick could change his mind again. They set off down the passage side by side. He was so hungry that he didn't bother looking at the people in the other cells while he downed what tasted like leathery roast beef and gravy. The lukewarm food filled his gut, and for the first time he felt a flood of relief.

By the time they arrived in the lobby of the prison wing, he had finished off the last of the food and was digging inside with his fingers to get the last drops of gravy.

Two guards sat at a card table with mugs of coffee and eggs over easy. They glared at Timothy while he passed.

The exit door of the lobby opened to a passage lined with closed doors. Nick kept his hand on the grip of a pistol while they walked.

Timothy wanted to ask where they were or what this place was, but he didn't want to sound like a cop. He let his eyes do the investigative work.

There were no windows. Everything was basically concrete and steel, which told him it might be some sort of old military bunker.

But that didn't quite explain the first chamber where he was pasted to a wall or the silo where the bats were stored to feed the beasts.

He got another look at that silo a moment later. The hallway came to an intersection. The passage on the right ended with the mesh wire that held back the bats.

This time he didn't hear any of their fluttering wings.

Nick went left, toward the sound of footsteps. Several guards with slung rifles walked toward them. Both men nodded at Nick who dipped his baseball cap.

Two more intersections later, and he stopped outside a door with a rusted radiation sign on it.

"Go inside," Nick said, opening the door.

Hanging lights guided the way up a steep ladder of rungs built into the wall. Another radiation sign marked a hatch at the top.

By the time Timothy got to the top he was out of breath.

"Open the hatch," Nick said.

Timothy hesitated, then twisted the wheel handle until it popped open. Another long hallway greeted them with a single door at the end.

When Timothy turned for orders, Nick had his pistol pulled and pointed at him.

"Walk," he said in a completely different tone. His features hardened as he pulled the hammer back.

Timothy's stomach dropped.

"What's going on?"

"Kid, I see right through you. You think you're smarter than us. Thought you were smarter than Vin, too." Nick jabbed the pistol forward. "But I ain't Vin, now move it."

Timothy set off down the passage toward the rusted door at the end with a third radiation sign. Each step felt more like his last, and he braced himself for the bullet to the back of the head. He cursed himself for not making a move earlier when he had noticed the gun. It could have been his way out.

But how could he take down Nick with a gun aimed at his head?

There was no way he could fight back. He had to try and talk Nick down.

"I can help you guys," Timothy said. "You need me."

Nick didn't reply, and Timothy kept walking all the way to the door.

"Open it," Nick said.

"I…"

"Open the goddamn door."

Timothy grabbed the wheel handle and twisted it, expecting to see a room full of starved Variants that would eat his corpse after a bullet blew out his brains.

But there were no Variants inside.

He walked onto a platform overlooking a massive room with a high ceiling that reminded him of a hangar. Huge banks of lights illuminated the concrete walls ribbed with iron beams.

"Look," Nick said.

"What?"

"Look below you."

Timothy drew closer to the platform's edge. Dozens of tents and other temporary shelters were pitched on the ground below. People, many of them women and children, walked about casually, some of them talking.

At first, he thought the people were prisoners like him, but most seemed happy, and a few even shared smiles as they went about their day. Some ate off plastic plates gathered around crates serving as makeshift tables. Others waited in a line for food outside a shack centered in the large hangar style room.

Nick grabbed the back of Timothy's neck, forcing his head down over the edge of the platform. Timothy's palms sweated as he knelt at the platform's end, his fingers gripping it tightly.

"You see those people?" Nick said.

Timothy nodded.

"I lied before… my family didn't die during the war," Nick said. "My family is here, *protected* from the new corrupt government and military."

"And you're not afraid of the Variants?"

"Fear isn't the word I would use to describe it," Nick said. "You were right, kid. The monsters will take over everything if we don't join them."

He eased the gun back a little. "The New Gods want the same thing as us. To end the very government responsible for their miserable existence, and I'm one of the warriors that will help them achieve victory on the battlefield. You can be too…"

Footsteps sounded behind Timothy and Nick lowered the gun.

"There you are," someone called out.

Timothy turned as two men with weapons slung over their shoulders walked through the hatch out onto the platform.

"Want to tell me why you brought him up here?" asked Pete. "We've got a briefing to get to."

Alfred stood next to him, staring at Timothy and

sizing him up.

"I wanted him to see the truth," Nick said.

"You sure he's ready?" Alfred asked.

"I'm the one that gets to make that determination," Pete said.

Nick fidgeted, like he had done something wrong.

Timothy already knew Pete was the leader, and Nick seemed to be the second in command. Alfred… Timothy wasn't sure what the hell his job was. He acted like a religious freak the way he'd offered Timothy that strange blessing the night before.

After a moment of silence Pete shrugged. "Guess now is as good a time as any to introduce Vin's replacement to the others."

Nick pushed Timothy toward a ladder leading to the ground.

Once they were on the ground-level with the tents, the three collaborators flanked Timothy. Women and children watched them go, and one kid no older than eight waved.

The kid actually looked happy.

Nick stopped and rustled the kid's hair, and then reached into his pocket and pulled out a chocolate bar. The kid grabbed it, a grin spreading across his face.

Timothy tried staring straight ahead until they got to a door that opened to another vast room like the one with the tents. Inside, were all sorts of vehicles and equipment, but most of them looked old, maybe Cold War era.

Only a few lights glowed over the space, but it was enough to see they were heading toward another door.

Two guards waited there, cradling rifles. Both came to attention.

The next room was smaller with a flag hanging over an

entire wall. A symbol resembling a misshapen skull was emblazoned on it.

It looked almost alien.

Metal tables furnished the center of the room and lockers lined a wall. About twenty men wearing military-style clothing sat in chairs facing a podium.

Pete walked in front of them and they all abruptly stood. Their eyes flitted to Timothy; scrutinizing him, some sneering, others with clenched jaws.

"Everyone, I want you to meet Timothy," Pete said. "He's going to help us get back into Outpost Portland."

— 16 —

Four Outpost Manchester soldiers headed toward a red-brick building that had been converted into apartments long before the war. Behind them, trailed Kate and her family, along with Horn and his girls.

"Don't give them too much leash," Horn kept saying.

Tasha and Jenny tugged against Ginger and Spark as the dogs pulled on their leashes, sniffing the new ground curiously.

The entire area was guarded by men wearing uniforms. Kate noticed a white Raven stitched onto the breast of each uniform, the symbol of the outpost. Few outposts had made the effort to give themselves an identity people could unite under. That kind of tactic, though seemingly minimal, was a surefire way to give people a sense of belonging and stoke their loyalty.

Sometimes winning hearts and minds was just as powerful as providing people with weapons.

Of course weapons were crucial, and Manchester had plenty.

Razor wire fences surrounded the streets. Armored vehicles passed by with soldiers in the turrets. Outpost Manchester was the most protected place Kate had seen yet, which was another reason why it was selected for researching the mastermind.

The soldiers were taking them to the new home they'd all been promised. It stood a little way down from a similar building that housed the laboratory Kate would be working in.

"This is it," the security guard said. "I'll take you in."

The other guards stopped outside as the guard took Kate, Beckham, Horn, and their children inside.

Their footsteps echoed eerily down empty, tiled hallways to a set of creaky wood stairs. They climbed these to a landing in a dimly lit hallway with antique sconces glowing over exposed brick walls.

"I don't like this building," Javier said.

Ginger and Spark both stopped, letting out low growls.

"Apparently they don't either," Kate said.

"This place is definitely on the creepy-side," Tasha said. "I wish Timothy was here; when is he going to join us?"

Kate and Beckham shared a quick look. They still hadn't told the kids what had happened.

"I don't know," Horn replied when Beckham and Kate didn't.

Jenny stopped to look at a cobweb. "I'd be surprised if it isn't infested with roaches," she said.

"Spiders aren't cockroaches," Javier said. "But I agree, this place is nasty."

"We're not going to be here that long, but at least we're going to be together," Beckham said. "Try to make the best of that, okay, buddy?"

Javier shrugged.

Kate was glad to have them together again, but she dreaded telling the kids about everything that had happened. She and Reed had decided to wait until they could all have some quiet time together. And that hadn't happened since the rush of packing and leaving the USS

George Johnson to travel here.

In truth, she wasn't sure when they would ever find enough downtime to have those tough conversations. They had arrived only an hour earlier, and as soon as they got settled, she would be off to the lab to see the beast Team Ghost had captured.

"This is it," said the security guard. He pulled out a key and unlocked the door. "I'll wait in the hallway for you, Doctor Lovato."

"Thanks…" Kate said.

"Oh, and ma'am, I don't mean to rush you, but I've been ordered to get you to the lab as soon as possible," said the guard.

"She'll be just a few minutes," Beckham said.

The man nodded and said, "Yes, sir." He stood against the hallway wall while Kate followed her family and Horn's inside. The dogs took off, probing the place with their noses and taking in all the new scents.

Kate followed Jenny and Tasha through while Horn and Beckham rested their cleared rifles against the wall.

The apartment was covered in dust. Cobwebs clung to the corners. A wide kitchen opened into what had been a plush living space. Panes of sunlight filtered in through windows to illuminate the dust motes floating in the air.

"This place *has* to be haunted," Javier said. "I mean, look at it!"

He swiped a hand through one of the cobwebs.

"It's not haunted," Beckham said. "This used to be the penthouse suite of the whole building. Five bedrooms, more than enough to go around. Just needs some cleaning up. I'd say we're pretty lucky."

Ginger and Spark barked at a corner and then jumped back as a cockroach skittered away.

"Gross!" Tasha yelled.

"What did I tell you?" Jenny said, turning around toward Horn.

Horn smashed the insect with a boot, then picked it up and dropped it into a trash can while the dogs sniffed the ground.

"Ain't haunted, just got a few bugs," Horn said.

Jenny wrinkle her nose. She sneezed and wiped her face with her sleeve. "Dad, I really wish we could just go home."

"Yeah, when do you think we can go back home?" Tasha asked. "I really miss Timothy and all our other friends."

Horn winced at the question. That was another thing they hadn't told the kids about. Kate still couldn't believe the collaborators had destroyed their houses.

She pushed aside the depressing thoughts and toured the apartment. Back when this place was new, it probably cost nearly a million dollars. The expensive furniture was now coated in dust, but at least the place didn't smell moldy like so many other abandoned homes.

The kids all moved to the windows with the dogs to look at the Merrimack River, but Beckham directed them to get back.

Kate recalled the bats from Outpost Portland, and suddenly didn't feel safe at all.

"Exactly how long do we have to stay here? One week? One month? A year?" Tasha asked, looking back at her dad.

"We won't be here that long," Kate said.

"All that matters is we're together again," Horn said.

Jenny hugged her dad's side. "I missed you, Dad."

Javier plopped down on a couch, dust puffing out.

"Well that's just great," Beckham said.

"Sorry…" Javier said.

Kate pulled Beckham aside into the kitchen. "I've got to get to the lab, and I know you have a meeting with the outpost commander. Who's going to stay with the kids?"

Beckham gestured for Horn.

"You're on babysitting duty first, Big Horn," Beckham said. "Keep the kids away from the windows, okay?"

"Why?" Javier asked.

"Just do what I say, please," Beckham said.

Tasha looked to him and then Kate.

"You're leaving already?" she asked.

"Kate and I have work to do," Beckham said.

"Horn, see if you can find some cleaning supplies in the closest," Kate said. "Girls, Javier, maybe you can help him?"

They groaned, and Horn grumbled.

Kate and Beckham said their goodbyes. He grabbed his rifle and opened the door. The guard led them down the hall and stairwell back to the ground level.

It felt almost odd being with her husband again. Kate wanted to take his hand in her own, but he was distracted. Probably with the same worries and heartaches about everything they had lost and everything that was still at stake.

"Let's try to meet up for dinner," Kate said.

Beckham nodded. "Nothing short of a Variant attack is going to stop me from sharing a meal with the family. Let's plan on eight o'clock."

They headed outside where they were greeted by the growls of vehicle engines and barking orders of soldiers rushing to reinforce the barricades and weapons around the wall protecting the outpost.

People in civilian clothes walked around, but there weren't many of them. The biggest group was a line gathered outside a building where recruits were being processed for the military.

Weeks ago, there might have been a farmer's market set up there. Kate could almost picture the smiles, the laughs, and the peace of mind. The Allied States of America under the Ringgold Administration had been, for a while, a place of hope.

So much had changed in such a short amount of time.

"Captain, command is that building," said the guard, pointing. "Doctor, if you would follow me, I'll take you to the lab."

"Sure you'll be all right?" Beckham asked Kate.

"There are plenty of people to keep the lab secure," she replied. "You go meet with the commander."

He nodded and planted a kiss on her lips. Then he pulled her into a tight hug, and she lingered there for a second, wishing they could stay like that longer, letting the world around them fade.

But duty called. For both of them.

She let Beckham go and then followed the guard. They navigated through the busy groups of mostly uniformed men and women working to set up defenses and help refugees move into their new homes.

Kate followed the guard toward a long parking lot between all the converted, red-bricked buildings that lined the river. They didn't stop until they reached a sign that read, *Organ Innovation Technologies.*

That company had disappeared during the war, but the facility remained standing.

Two more soldiers in black fatigues waited outside.

"These men will take you to the lab," said her guard escort.

"Thank you," Kate replied. She showed her identification to the soldiers standing at attention.

One of them looked it over, eyes narrowed as he scrutinized it. He then used a keycard to open the front door.

"This way, Doctor Lovato," he said.

The halls inside were nearly empty with only a few laboratory techs milling about the place. Overhead fluorescent lights lent the place a sterile, bureaucratic feel with plain white walls and laminate floors that creaked when she walked. Smaller offices furnished with desks lined the passage.

The accompanying soldier took her to the manufacturing room once used in the nascent fabrication of artificial organs made from live cells. It was hard to believe the space had gone from being used to create life-saving medical treatments to housing a creature designed to help eradicate the human race.

The soldier used his keycard to open a door to the large chamber. He gestured for her to enter but she hesitated, a breath held in her lungs at the monstrosity inside.

Giant squid-sized eyes closed as nostrils flared with each huffing breath. Wrinkled pink flesh covered muscular limbs, and tendrils of red webbing hung off its bulbous shape.

The enormous beast was secured by chains to iron columns erected specifically to keep it imprisoned. They stretched from the grated stainless-steel flooring all the way up to the high ceiling where air ducts and filtration systems wormed through the air.

Despite the expensive system, she was still struck by a stench like an unearthed landfill and the sour rot of lemons.

"Don't worry, Doctor," the guard said. "That thing isn't going anywhere."

A dozen other soldiers with automatic weapons patrolled the area. But she still didn't feel safe. The monster was well over four times the size of a man, and its bulk looked like it could take plenty of damage.

She set off into the vast space cautiously, guided by the hanging banks of fluorescent lights. In the white glow, the monster's gigantic chest rose and fell in deep heaves. It was still fast asleep.

Kate searched for Carr among the technicians preparing an arsenal of equipment to run the analyses they would perform. Huge silver bioreactors lined both sides of the chamber behind the laboratory benches.

She spotted Carr supervising a pair of lab techs hooking IV lines the size of garden hoses into the creature's arm.

"Don't worry. It doesn't bite," someone called out.

Sammy walked over in a white bunny suit.

"How are things going?" Kate asked.

"Good so far… did you get your family settled?"

"Yes, and I'm ready to get to work."

"Follow me," Sammy said. She crossed the room toward a lab bench on the other side of the mastermind. Kate stopped about ten feet away, still struck with awe by the monster.

"It's okay," Sammy said. "We have it completely sedated."

They walked in a wide arc around the creature to lab benches where Carr worked quietly.

"Good to see you, Dr. Lovato," he said. "Are you ready to get started on this beauty?"

"Absolutely," Kate said, trying to disguise her trepidation.

Another lab technician stepped up next to Carr, his hands behind his back. It was Sean, but Kate almost didn't recognize him at first. He was so thin, he looked like a broom wearing a tarp in his bunny suit.

Sean welcomed her and then gestured to a clear, aquarium-like chamber that had a mess of red webbing growing in it. Wires and a microelectrode array connected the webbing to a nearby computer on one end.

"This is our setup," Sean said, excitedly. "Exactly what our team requested."

At the other end of the bioreactor chamber, tendrils of webbing still attached to the mastermind stretched from the monster and were secured by clamps to the tissue within the chamber.

"Looks good," Kate said.

She grabbed a pair of nitrile gloves from a box beside the computer. She slipped them snugly over her hands, then walked toward the behemoth, determined now that she had buried her fear.

"All right you ugly son of a bitch, time to figure out how you work," she said.

***

The four-story command building was a former library retrofitted into a modern-day fortress. Two guards stood at the white pillars of the colonial brick building. On the roof, machine gun barrels and even flamethrowers protruded out.

Beckham stood in the sunshine observing the defenses on the other rooftops.

So far, not a single clawed foot or hand had touched this place.

But that didn't guarantee the base would remain safe. Beckham had lived through attacks where the Variants managed to get into top-secret and well-guarded facilities deep underground. He had also seen how the collaborators could infiltrate safe zones and if they had sleeper cells in Manchester, then it could already be too late.

Eventually an attack would happen.

The enemy proved they were adaptable and smarter than Beckham could have ever predicted. His only hope was that they didn't know the mastermind had been taken here. If they did, he had no doubt the Variants would send an army to rescue the beast, especially if it was as important as Kate and Dr. Carr insisted.

The doors behind the pillars of the command building finally opened. The two guards came to attention as an officer in black fatigues walked out. He wore a Raven symbol and a colonel's rank insignia. The dark-skinned man had a neatly trimmed mustache and salt and pepper hair.

"Captain Reed Beckham," he said in a deep voice.

The man instantly reminded him of Lieutenant Colonel Ray Jensen, one of the best men he had ever known. A man who had sacrificed himself for his country. Beckham had carried the lieutenant colonel's pistol, a gift, for many years before regretfully losing it on a mission that had nearly claimed his life.

"I'm Colonel Presley," the officer said. "Honored to have you at Outpost Manchester, Captain. Last time I saw you was during Operation Liberty."

Beckham paused for a moment, not remembering the man at all.

"Sorry, sir, but you were in New York?"

"Yes, Captain, I was one of the few that made it out before the bombing began. I'll never forget you staying behind."

More painful memories surfaced, but Beckham pushed them aside.

He shook the colonel's hand. "Looks like you learned from the mistakes we made since. You've done a great job securing this place, sir."

"We've certainly done our best," Presley said. He gestured for Beckham to follow him through the open front doors. The click of boots from officers and staff down the tiled floor echoed through the hallway.

Presley led them to a stairwell that took them to a second floor of open space. The bookshelves had all been removed, replaced with tables and storage for equipment along with a few cots.

Another stairwell took them to a hall of offices. Presley's was the last one on the left. Two men in black fatigues stood guard outside. They looked oddly familiar, but Beckham couldn't figure out where he had seen them before. Neither wore a Raven badge or an Orca badge, making it difficult for Beckham to guess where their allegiance lay.

He walked through the open door of the office. A man sat in a chair in front of his desk, holding a cowboy hat. He turned to reveal a bushy-mustached face and grinned.

"Ah, Captain Beckham, we meet again," the man said in a southern drawl, standing.

Beckham recognized S.M. Fischer, the oil tycoon he had met at the White House. The men in the hallway must be his bodyguards.

"You're a long way from Texas," Beckham said.

"A lot has changed since we last met," he said. "Fischer Fields' operations have expanded more than I expected."

Presley gestured to the two chairs in front of his desk. Beckham took a seat and Fischer sat back in his, placing his ten-gallon hat on a crossed leg.

"When I was told you were coming here, I kept thinking about how small the world really is," Fischer said. "But then I realized it's not as small as we think."

"How do you mean?" Beckham asked.

"We were just talking about Team Ghost," Fischer said.

Presley leaned forward on his desk.

"You must already know that Ghost is headed to California to locate equipment from Project Rolling Stone," he said.

"Our world is expanding even as our country is shrinking," Fischer explained. "It's been a long time since anyone dared venture west again."

"The trek will be worth it," Presley said. "Mr. Fischer and his men are going to set that equipment up once it's retrieved to help protect outposts and refugees while buying time for SOCOM to mount an offensive."

Fischer gave a short briefing on Project Rolling Stone and how the SDS equipment would locate Variant tunnels that the military could then destroy before the beasts surfaced. This, he argued, would protect the base from all underground attacks.

It sounded great, but none of that addressed a key problem.

"Those machines won't do shit against attacks like the one I lived through last night," Beckham said. "The collaborators aren't just using the Variants now. They're using bats, rigged with explosives. God only knows what they'll roll out next."

"We're well aware, and we're preparing for aerial attacks," Presley said.

"With flamethrowers?" Beckham asked.

Presley stood and walked to the window, hands behind his back as he scanned the rooftops for a few seconds.

"You can't see the other defenses, but the flamethrowers are just part of our overall strategy," he said, returning to his desk. "You might have seen the snipers from the street earlier. We also have scouts with FLIR MilSight T90 thermal scopes to watch for anything in the air miles out. Not only will we know if bats or other airborne threats are coming, we have M134 Miniguns on the rooftops to eliminate them before they get close."

Beckham hadn't seen all of those defenses on his way in, and if someone of his experience hadn't seen them, it was a good sign. The Variants and collaborators wouldn't see them either.

"Part of what makes this place easy to defend is the terrain," Presley said. "We have bedrock called granodiorite not too far below the topsoil. That has prevented the Variants from tunneling deep into the safe zone."

"Outpost Manchester is situated with a river on one side, and a lake on the other," Fischer added.

"The beasts aren't tunneling under the water or through the rock, I promise you that," Presley said.

"All due respect, I already know that," Beckham said. "It's not just the monsters I'm worried about getting in, sir."

"You're worried about collaborators?"

"Worried?" Beckham with a snort. "Sir, I'm *more* than worried after what I've seen in the past few weeks. We might have an underground network of collaborators working to destroy the Allied States. For all we know, we could have a mole or an entire network of moles in our midst, and I'm afraid we've just seen the tip of the iceberg when it comes to these lunatics."

Presley opened his mouth to speak but Beckham kept going.

"They have attacked our outposts, tried to kill President Ringgold and Vice President Lemke, and are working with the monsters in a way I don't think anyone has fully realized yet," Beckham added. "So yeah, I'm *damn* worried about the collaborators."

"We don't have any collaborator problems here. Trust me." Presley stood again. "I want you to see something."

He got up and motioned for Fischer and Beckham to follow him out of the office.

"Stay here," Fischer instructed his guards. Tran and Chase remained outside the office while Presley took Beckham and Fischer down the hall to a stairwell that led to the rooftop.

Snipers and soldiers manned positions across the vantage point.

Presley went to a wall that overlooked a parking lot lined with black M-ATVs and other armored vehicles.

"We have a dozen hunter killer teams like that one

strategically located across the outpost. They'll respond to any collaborator attack, and while you can't see it, we also have two Apache helicopters and some damn fine pilots," Presley said. "If the collaborators do try some shit here, they will find themselves up against some of the best trained and best equipped soldiers the Allied States has left."

The group crossed the roof to a railing overlooking a lake in the distance.

"We have mines in the water and on the shores," Presley said. "If the Variants or collaborators make it through that, then they have thousands of rounds of ammunition in their way before they can get close to our fences."

"This is all to buy us time," Fischer said. "Once Team Ghost finds that equipment, we'll expand our borders, bringing in more refugees to protect while General Souza will be free to go after whoever or whatever is behind this."

Beckham took in the sights, impressed.

"You run a tight ship here, sir," he said. "But if the monsters and collaborators find out what Team Ghost dropped off to the science team, we can expect more than some rogue attacks."

"We're ready for a full-scale assault," Presley said.

"I appreciate you taking the time to show me," Beckham said. "But how do you know you don't have a problem with collaborators that might have already infiltrated Manchester?"

"We've gone to great lengths to ensure that isn't possible," Presley said. "Besides, if we did, don't you think we would have had an attack by now?"

Beckham raised a brow. In war, sometimes silence wasn't a good thing. Sometimes it meant the enemy was scheming, like the Variants and their human allies had done for the past eight years.

"Captain, you aren't a guest here. You're a partner," Presley said. "If you have anything else on your mind, just let me know. I'll be as transparent as possible."

Beckham smiled kindly at that. He liked this man already, and not just because he reminded him of Lieutenant Colonel Jensen. Presley was truly an intelligent leader.

"You mentioned scouts earlier. Do you have any outside the walls right now?" Beckham asked.

"Drones in the sky and my best men on the ground at all times," Presley replied.

"Good, that's the one thing we really failed at back in Portland, but resources were also a lot tighter." Beckham stepped to the side of the rooftop. "If the Variants do come, we need plenty of warning to get people into shelters."

"Agreed," Presley said. "I'll see if we can widen our scouts' range."

Beckham nodded again. For the first time in weeks, he felt like his family was relatively safe. Even with the mastermind here.

"If you'll accept a compliment from a company grade officer, this is good work, sir," Beckham said. Presley clapped him on the shoulder and smiled.

"Anything else, Captain?"

Beckham glanced at his watch. It was already late afternoon. "If you'd excuse me, sir, I'd like to go see how my wife and the science team are doing."

"Let me know if there is anything we can do for your

family while you're here," Presley said.

"Likewise, sir," Beckham said. "I'm here to help."

He gave a nod to Fischer, but Fischer followed him away from the railing.

"Mind if I join you, Captain?" Fischer asked. "I want another look at that ugly bastard."

Beckham didn't really want company, but he also didn't want to disrespect a person so crucial to the war effort.

"Sure," he replied.

They went to the street and walked to the lab building, accompanied by the two guards that Fischer had brought with them, Tran and Chase. Neither of the men spoke other than to say hello to Beckham. They scanned the streets and people for threats, clearly taking their job protecting Fischer very seriously.

"Your family is here?" Fischer asked.

"Yes, we decided to bring them along. I worry less when they're close, and President Ringgold assured me this is one of the safest outposts."

Fischer put on his cowboy hat. "General Cornelius did a good job making Outpost Galveston pretty damn secure, too. I was there not long ago."

"That's good to hear, and especially since he's working with President Ringgold, even though he's retired—"

"He's not retired. General Cornelius is doing more to save the Allied States than you might know."

"I'm aware of his commitments—"

"I need to be honest with you," Fischer interrupted again. "A war hero like you probably has a better perspective on this than me, but I was always taught to back the best horse in a race, and that is, without a doubt, the general."

Beckham halted and faced Fischer. The two guards moved away to give them some space.

"The only race right now is the one for survival, Mr. Fischer," Beckham said. "I'm not interested in talking politics or who to support now that the election is on hold. I'm interested in saving our country, so that maybe someday we *can* have that conversation."

"Fair enough, but I urge you to make some time to talk with General Cornelius. Your talents might be better spent keeping a closer dialogue going with him than you'd expect."

"I work for the president."

"Of course. I mean no disrespect."

Beckham kept walking, slightly frustrated. Fischer kept up and his guards closed back in around them. The sound of diesel engines provided a welcome distraction to the awkward silence that passed between them on the rest of the journey to the lab.

People walking on the street moved to the side as a convoy of armored vehicles turned down the road and raced past Beckham and Fischer. Soldiers gripped machine guns in the turrets of Humvees.

Beckham looked toward where they were heading, and a dark pit formed in his stomach. The first Humvee had already stopped right in front of the lab, and soldiers had piled out.

Tran and Chase both cradled their rifles, looking around, clearly nervous by the commotion. They weren't the only ones caught off guard.

The security Beckham felt slipped away at the sight of a strike team speeding to the location where his wife was working.

It reminded him that the biggest threat from an enemy wasn't always from the outside; sometimes it came from within.

— 17 —

Team Ghost had slept on the C-130H flight to Palo Alto, California, refueling their energy reserves after their successful mission to New Orleans. Eight hours ago, Dohi and the team had changed aircraft at an FOB in Alabama.

Now Dohi sat in one of the mesh jumper seats against the plane's sand-colored fuselage beside Ace, who was still snoring on his left with his arms folded over his chest and belly. Mendez was another seat down, clutching a rosary. Rico and Fitz were on his right, talking quietly amongst themselves.

She smiled, dimples forming at something he said.

Dohi usually envied them, but not today—today he needed the silence.

He surveyed the Orca soldiers across the tracks and bolts of the deck. The Wolfhounds, a platoon-sized group of twenty soldiers led by Lieutenant Singh were all seated along the opposite bulkhead.

The team was a hodgepodge of former mercenaries and militia who had joined General Cornelius's private army. Another group of soldiers with Orca badges sat near the cockpit, but they would be staying back to guard the plane during the mission.

Dohi had listened to them talk on the long trip across the country. From what he gathered, the Wolfhounds had spent most of the past eight years working in the field on missions hunting collaborators and Variants outside of Galveston.

But this mission had pushed them out of their element, and Lieutenant Singh had made it clear Fitz was in charge. Their rank meant nothing because the Orca soldiers weren't part of the Allied States army. And so long as they were out in Variant territory, the Wolfhounds would defer to Team Ghost.

Dohi just hoped their new friends lived up to their namesake, but he wasn't impressed. The nervous tap of boots echoed in the aircraft while the soldiers looked out the windows.

They were beginning their descent over the coast of California. A low-lying fog blanketed most of the landscape. A few skeletal skyscrapers pierced the gray like broken bones through flesh, some of their upper levels sheared off.

"It's a graveyard down there," said one Singh's men.

Ace stirred awake, pulling his folded arms away from his chest.

"Is that… is that San Jose we just passed?" asked one of the Wolfhounds.

"Yeah, I think so," answered the first soldier.

"We haven't seen anything yet," said a Wolfhound soldier with a spider neck tattoo. "The shit at the ground level is the really bad stuff. I heard there are mutant animals out here with the Variants."

"Martin, what did I tell you about sharing conspiracy shit?" Singh asked.

"LT, it ain't conspiracy shit," Martin replied. He toyed with a gold chain that had a gold AK-47 pendant on it.

The young man was another example of a former merc turned soldier.

A man with a scraggly beard and deep-set green eyes chuckled. His name-tape read Hopkins. "You got to learn the difference between reality and your damn nightmares."

"Shit is real, brah," Martin added. "I heard 'bout a guy that saw some dogs that looked half-zombie. That VX-99 stuff can make animals crazy."

"That was just a rabid dog," Hopkins said. "Not VX-99. You do know the difference, don't you? The shit doesn't work on animals."

"You sure about that?" Martin asked, one eyebrow raised.

Ace leaned over to Dohi and whispered, "These guys are like puppies at a fireworks show. Nervous as hell."

Dohi gave a half nod.

Truth was, the Wolfhounds weren't the only nervous ones.

The difference between Ghost and these guys was that Dohi and his teammates knew how to control the fear. Countless missions behind enemy lines had taught them to handle their fear and use it to their advantage.

Newbies like Martin and Hopkins didn't.

And that's what made Dohi really nervous.

"*Mios dios*, if this is Cornelius' best, we're fucked," Mendez said quietly. He slipped his rosary back in his chest pocket.

Rico narrowed her eyes, leaning in so the Wolfhounds wouldn't overhear. "Come on, amigo. You don't remember your first drop into uncharted territory?"

Ace chuckled again. "I heard you pissed yourself."

"That's a damn lie," Mendez said. "Stepped into a creek. Sure smelled like piss though."

"Whatever you say, man," Rico said.

Fitz shook his head. "Guys, come on."

San Jose disappeared into the distance, and Dohi turned back to the troop hold as the plane descended toward the coastline. Dark waves lapped over a wide, pebbly beach beneath sheer cliffs.

"All right, listen up," Fitz said. "Our mission is to infiltrate the National Accelerator Laboratories and retrieve all the SDS equipment and available intel on Project Rolling Stone…"

He paused a moment. "We'll move in two units, with members of Team Ghost leading both. Lieutenant Singh has command of the Wolfhounds, but for the purposes of this mission, I'm top dog. We get in, find the material we need, bring it back to the plane, and we're out of here. If you listen to orders, stay frosty, and keep your eyes open, we'll all go home. Understood?"

Most of the soldiers nodded. It was clear they looked up to Team Ghost, which was good, because that hopefully meant they would listen to them in the field. But there were a few that didn't seem to appreciate the ad hoc rank structure.

"What about enemies?" Martin asked. "You going to tell us what to expect down there?"

"SOCOM doesn't have much intel on this area," Fitz said.

"What's that mean?" Hopkins asked. "They have to know something."

Rico plucked a piece of chewed gum from her helmet.

"There could be collaborators. Could be Variants. Could even be some invaders from another country looking to take some land when we're not looking," Fitz said. "We're prepared to face any threat. Anything with a weapon should be considered hostile, but you do not engage unless fired upon. Stealth is our primary weapon here."

"I heard all the collaborators moved east," Martin said. "Same with the Variants. After all, that's where all the food is."

"Martin, shut your trap and listen," Singh said.

"For all we know, Variants have been camping out here underground for the past eight years just like they were back east," Fitz said. "Maybe breeding too."

Dohi was prepared mentally for anything. After all, the one thing he had learned in the apocalypse was that unpreparedness was the worst enemy.

"Once we reach the freeway outside the National Accelerator Campus, we split up to cover more ground," Fitz said. "Lieutenant, you and ten men are with me, Rico and Ace. Dohi and Mendez, you take the other ten."

Fitz finished his orders as the plane dipped. There were no other questions, just solemn looks, and whispered prayers.

One of the Wolfhounds leaned down, and Dohi thought he was going to puke, but he managed to keep all of the food in his gut.

"Get ready!" Fitz yelled.

The big airplane touched down, the troop hold rattling. When it eased to a stop, the crew chief lowered the rear ramp.

"Go, go, go!" Fitz yelled.

Dohi immediately took point at Fitz's signal, spearheading the group as they charged out into the sand, rifles at the ready to set up a perimeter.

As soon as the last soldier was out, Dohi took point. He found the remnants of a trail that had once been a hiking path marked with rusted signs. It was now overgrown with weeds and brambles, but it would be no problem for him to find his way through, even with the fog.

It took an hour of hiking in silence through the muck and tall grass shadowed by trees before Dohi paused at the crest of a wooded hill. The higher ground, too, was suffocated by the ominous fog.

He was unable to see more than the trees clawing through the gray a few dozen yards in front of him. The other members of Team Ghost gathered beside him to figure out their next move. Several of the Wolfhounds trailed behind them, all organized into combat intervals.

The chirp of birds was reassuring. It meant there probably weren't Variants in the area. For now, Dohi would take this as a good omen. But he didn't like the fog.

Fitz didn't either. "We're only a few miles out from our target, but we could be walking into an ambush set by anything or anyone that saw the plane," he said.

"You want to hold here a bit and see if the fog clears?" Singh asked.

Fitz thought on it, shooting Dohi a glance first.

"We need to keep moving," Fitz said. "Dohi will make sure we don't wander into a trap. Tell your men to keep frosty and report anything suspicious."

"You got it," Singh said, before turning back to his platoon.

Fitz signaled to move out.

A cold wind blowing in from the west sent chills up Dohi's flesh. He kept his ears perked for the singing birds, letting them know that they were safe.

But he knew they weren't safe by any means—they were in Variant country now. The deepest anyone had been in years, and the question wasn't if they would encounter the beasts. It was when.

Coyote is always out there waiting, and Coyote is always hungry.

More words from his grandfather haunted his thoughts.

The soldiers speared through the fog behind Dohi, and he guided them deeper into a field blackened by fire. Skeletal trees twisted out of the ash covered dirt.

The birds had stopped chirping, but he saw no tracks from animals, Variants, or humans. Nothing living at all.

Fitz gestured for Dohi to keep pushing forward, and Dohi brought his rifle back up to his shoulder, scanning the haze for hostiles. His boots crunched over branches that fell away into dust.

Somewhere a crow cawed.

A breeze rustled over the crisped plants. The hair on the back of his neck stood straight.

From the tendrils of gray fog emerged a cluster of living trees. Not much grass grew along the ground, but leaves covered it as densely as the fog choked the landscape.

Something about those leaves looked wrong to Dohi. Kind of like he was looking at a forged one-hundred-dollar bill.

He stopped and thrust his fist in the air, trusting his gut.

"What's up?" Fitz whispered.

Dohi jerked his chin toward the leaves.

Fitz gave him a cockeyed gaze at first, seeming to be confused. Then realization dawned over him, too.

The leaves only rustled a little when the wind blew over them, but never flew away. They were too perfectly dispersed along the ground. Dohi knelt and peeled back some that were stuck to the ground.

Instead of coming up separately, they came up in one big carpet, exposing a pit nearly six-feet deep. Punji spikes jutted up from the dark soil at the bottom. The chamber spread along to the north and south, bordering the burned down woods, nearly twenty feet in length.

A rotten odor drifted up from the freshly revealed booby trap; they hadn't been the first to discover it. But those that came before had seen it when it was too late.

Dohi crouched for a better look at the bodies impaled by the spikes. Two of them had grown leathery and dry. A fresher corpse was covered in white maggots crawling out of a misshapen skull.

It took him a moment to realize they weren't humans.

The corpses were Variants.

Someone had set a trap for the monsters.

Dohi rose to his feet.

The enemy of my enemy is my friend, he thought. Maybe the adage would prove true. But something told him these people, whoever they were, could be just as big of a threat as the monsters.

***

Two guards wearing black fatigues with the Raven logo stood outside another entrance to the laboratory. A line of armored vehicles and Humvees were parked in a semi-circle in the parking lot, providing a second line of defense around the building housing the mastermind.

Fischer and his guards had waited outside with Beckham for over an hour, trying to figure out what was going on. But even after telling them who they were, the heavily armed guards would not grant them access to the lab.

Every minute that passed, Beckham grew angrier. Fischer had a feeling things were about to get heated.

"This is such fucking bullshit," Beckham said.

Tran and Chase looked at Fischer, but he shook his head to keep them from getting involved.

"Screw this," Beckham said. He set off for the vehicles.

The soldier in the closest turret shouted, "This is authorized access only!"

"My wife is inside!" Beckham yelled. He marched toward the line of armored vehicles; gun barrels rotated toward him.

"Stop, sir!" yelled the same soldier in the turret.

"Ah, horse shit," Fischer said. He walked after Beckham despite protests from Tran and Chase.

"I said halt!" the soldier yelled.

"You're going to have to shoot me!" Beckham shouted back.

Fischer twisted toward the sound of squealing tires. A Humvee came to an abrupt stop in front of the parked M-ATVs and other armored vehicles forming a barrier in front of the lab facility.

The soldiers in turrets pushed their barrels up as the passenger side door opened. Colonel Presley got out and hurried over to the entrance.

"What the hell is going on?" Beckham asked. "If my wife is in danger, I…"

"She's not," Presley said. "My men are just following strict orders to keep this place secure. Your wife is safer in there than out here, Captain. I need you to come with me."

Fischer wasn't sure what in the Sam Hill was happening now.

The sun was already going down on the horizon. Soon darkness would swallow them, bringing with it the evil monstrosities it concealed. His fingers caressed the handle of his holstered pistol.

Tran and Chase picked up on his worry, shifting their rifles up out of relaxed mode.

"Captain, let's go with the colonel," Fischer suggested. "Assuming, that is, my men and I may also join. I have enough manners to bow out of a dinner party I'm not invited to."

"Of course." Presley nodded. "You're free to come with us, Mr. Fischer, as are your men."

Beckham looked back at the lab entrance and then reluctantly walked over to the Humvee with Fischer and his guards.

"You need to promise me the lab is safe," Beckham said.

"Safest place here with all this security," Presley said gesturing. "Now, you coming with me or not?" He hopped into the front passenger seat, not waiting for an answer.

Fischer got in the back with Beckham and his men.

"Our scouts spotted packs of juveniles on the outskirts of the outpost," Presley said as the truck pulled away. "About two clicks out from the main wall. They're small packs, the equivalent of a recon unit."

"How many of these packs have you spotted in the past?" Beckham asked.

"None. This is the first time we've seen Variants so close."

"They know the mastermind is here, don't they?"

Fischer asked, cold realization hitting him like an unexpected blizzard in Texas.

Beckham cursed. "That's what I was afraid of."

"I'm hoping that's not the case, but either way I'm not taking any chances and don't believe in coincidences any more than you do," Presley said. "I've got all hands on deck, and we're moving civilians into the shelters for the night."

"My family," Beckham said. "That apartment had glass windows, if we're hit with bats—"

"The building has a shelter in the basement," Presley reassured him. "There are guards on the roof; the street is completely blocked off; and our aerial defenses are locked, cocked, and ready for any threat."

Fischer could tell Beckham wasn't convinced.

"Sir, all due respect, but are you sure you don't have any collaborators in your midst?" Beckham asked. "How else could the Variants know about the mastermind?"

Presley didn't hesitate even a second in his answer. "Captain, I told you that we do not have a collaborator problem here."

"That's what we thought in Portland." Beckham ran a hand through his hair, pulling it back. "We underestimated them… I underestimated them, and I've lost a lot of friends and my home because of it."

"I'm sorry for your losses, but this isn't Outpost Portland," Presley said.

Fischer turned to look out the windows on the drive. They sped through empty streets in silence, the fiery glow of a sunset retreating on the horizon. He re-positioned his holstered .357 Magnum, fearing that the silence was about to be shattered by the screech of monsters.

He had listened quietly back at the command building

while Presley explained how safe this place was to Beckham, and all of the things they had done to ensure it never fell.

And while Fischer wanted to believe the defenses were as good as Presley kept saying, he remembered Cornelius's ominous warning about not trusting anyone.

The driver steered the Humvee toward a cluster of tents at the far reaches of the walls. Soldiers hurried back and forth, carrying equipment from a stack of crates being unloaded from the back of a flatbed.

Others worked at tables under a camouflage tent that shielded computers and electronic equipment from view and rain. Swollen clouds rolled in from the west across the purple skyline, threatening storms.

"This is it," Presley said. "Won't take more than fifteen minutes."

Fischer put on his hat and stepped out of the vehicle. He followed Beckham and Presley into a tent furnished with metal tables with computer monitors. A young female officer with short hair and blue eyes stood to attention, then backed away to give them all room.

"Colonel, this is live footage from our scouts," she said.

Fischer leaned down to look with Beckham and Presley.

At first glance, Fischer didn't see anything. That wasn't entirely surprising. The beasts were probably camouflaged.

The officer that had brought up the live feed used a finger to point at the hilltop. There the weeds moved back and forth, and Fischer glimpsed a flash of gray armored flesh.

"They've just been sitting there for the past hour," she said. "And we've picked up more units like this at two other locations."

She went to a mobile board with a map of the outpost. Using a pen, she noted spots on all sides of the perimeter.

"We're being surrounded," Presley said.

Beckham stiffened and wiped sweat from his brow. "They're definitely scoping out the defenses."

Fischer had personal experience with the depths of their organized intellect but this was on an entirely new level.

"Colonel, we have more movement," said another officer. The man walked over with a handset. "Just got word some of the juvies are taking off."

"Follow them with a drone or a recon team… your best team," Beckham said. "We need to know where they're going. If we can, then we locate the horde or hive, or whatever is out there."

Presley acted slightly annoyed by what sounded like orders, but he agreed and nodded at the officer with the handset.

"Anything else I should know?" Beckham asked. "I'd like to personally make sure my family is safe before shit hits the fan."

"No, Captain, thank you," Presley said.

"Keep me updated on things, please."

"Of course, I'll get you a radio before we have someone drive you back to the building so you don't find yourself waiting again." Presley looked Beckham in the eye. "Sorry about what happened outside the lab; it was a misunderstanding."

Beckham nodded and left the tent.

"Thanks for the updates," Fischer said. He followed

Beckham and joined his men outside, feeling completely useless. Waiting on Team Ghost and the SDS equipment was really starting to make his visit here a drag. He hoped whatever was taking Ghost so long would be resolved soon.

"Mr. Fischer, I'd suggest going to one of those shelters, if you want a ride," Beckham said. He walked toward a pickup truck where a soldier waited.

"I have a feeling tonight is going to be a long one," Beckham added.

Fischer tipped his leather hat. "I appreciate the advice, Captain. But I'm not the kind of buck that goes scampering at the first sign of danger."

"Suit yourself," Beckham said. He got inside the truck and the driver pulled away.

Fischer watched him go, hoping the Captain was wrong. One thing was certain, Fischer wasn't going to cower in some shelter.

He was done hiding a long time ago.

— 18 —

Timothy sat quietly in an exam room that looked like it had been pulled straight from the doctor's office he used to visit as a kid. It was even furnished with a table that had bedding on it.

But there weren't serene pictures of mountains or rivers on the walls. The only decoration was a banner hanging over the closed door with a misshapen skull. The same banner he had seen in the briefing room.

Alfred had brought him here and told him to get into the green scrubs he wore now. According to the tag, the scrubs were supposed to be size medium. A size that had once fit snugly on Timothy's frame. Now it hung as loose as a sail.

His stomach growled. He was hungry again.

No… he was *starving.*

He had hardly eaten in the past few days.

Food wasn't the only thing on his mind. He had sat there for hours with nothing to do but worry and try to figure out why the hell they had brought him down here. Thoughts of his father, of Tasha, and all the people back in Portland haunted his mind. He tried to conjure happy memories, anything to assuage the ball of dread growing in his stomach, but he failed every time.

All he could do was stare at that strange skull on the banner.

Now he was more sure than ever that he knew what it was.

The thing was a damn Variant. It had to be, and it made sense after his conversation with Nick. The man had sold his soul to the monsters. Everyone down here had.

While he had figured that much out, there was still so much that didn't make sense.

Normally, at least from what he had heard, collaborators worked *for* the monsters. But the ones here controlled them. The shock collar… the concerted attacks…

Timothy didn't see how that could be possible. There had to be something he was missing. The collaborators his dad had told him about worked for powerful Alpha Variants. Monsters that were both twisted and intelligent in their own strange ways. Maybe there was an even more intelligent Variant out there working with the collaborators now.

Some beast that Nick, Alfred, and Pete had sworn loyalty to.

Timothy grew more anxious as he waited for the men to return. He got off the table and walked over to the door, trying the knob. It twisted, but a click confirmed it was still locked from the outside.

Was this some kind of test? Were they watching him through a hidden camera, seeing if he was smart enough to escape—or loyal enough to listen?

He glanced at the banner again as he stood in front of the door. These men must have some awfully good reasons to swear fealty to monsters that wanted to kill so many people. Or maybe everyone down here was just batshit insane.

But there was an even bigger question that Timothy couldn't bury. One that emerged from the emotions roiling in his chest.

A question he wondered every time he looked at Nick, Alfred, and Pete.

Had they been there the night his father died on Peaks Island? Had one of them pulled the trigger?

In time, he would know. That was what mattered most. Once he figured that out, he would happily return the favor and put a bullet in that man's brain, then everyone else loyal to the monsters.

He returned to the table, fists clenched. Maybe they were watching him. He wouldn't give them the satisfaction of going nuts.

Taking long, deep breaths, he tried to force himself to remain calm. But the longer he sat there, the more he boiled over, until he found himself pressing his fingers into his palms with his filthy overgrown nails.

You're going to get yourself killed, he thought to himself.

The only way he was going to get revenge was if he played it cool. If he did that, then he had a chance to bring down this entire shadowy organization.

Watch, listen, learn.

The words his dad had taught him echoed in his mind.

Timothy let his hands relax and closed his eyes, counting to ten.

When he hit ten, he took a deep breath, then counted to ten again. Over and over, a silent meditation. He tried to think of good thoughts. Like what it had been like to be back on Peaks Island. The trees and water surrounding him. Being able to spend time with Tasha, running off together with their friends to go hiking and explore the landscape, spending long nights on the shores.

He had no idea how much time had passed when the door finally clicked and slowly creaked open. Timothy tensed, sitting as straight as he could.

A balding doctor, maybe fifty years of age, walked into the room wearing a white lab coat and holding a clipboard. Behind him, two bearded men wearing fatigues stood guard with machine guns.

They remained in the hallway, and the doctor kept the door open.

"State your full name," he said.

His eyes may as well have been pools of darkness, not the kind that Timothy remembered on his doctor at home. This man had seen too much death.

"Your full name," the doctor entreated.

"Timothy Lance," he lied.

The doctor looked down at his clipboard and scribbled something onto the paper. Then he moved over toward the table.

Timothy flinched when he reached out for him.

"Relax. I'm going to do some basic tests to make sure you're healthy."

Timothy wasn't sure if he believed that, but he decided it didn't matter. The two guys with machine guns in the hall gave him no choice but to obey.

For the next thirty minutes, Timothy endured many of the same tests he remembered from his normal physicals with his physician. The doctor took his blood pressure, listened to his heart and lungs. He even made him stick his tongue out, using a wooden depressor to see the back of his throat.

When he finished, he scribbled some more on his clipboard and left without saying another word, closing the door behind him.

Timothy tried to relax on the cold seat. All he could do was wonder what the hell all that had been about.

When the door opened again, the doctor returned and gestured for Timothy to follow him into the hall.

The two guards accompanied them down the narrow passage with a tiled floor and white walls. The air carried a sterile smell, like a laboratory.

They took a right at an intersection and entered a hall with glass windows. More armed guards stood outside a set of doors with biohazard signs.

On the other side of the glass windows, scientists in bulky hazmat suits worked inside an open laboratory with metal tables. Several of the workers surrounded a clear plastic container with some sort of rodent inside.

Timothy slowed to get a better view.

"Move it," said one of the escort guards.

They passed another lab where a monkey with bandaged legs screeched inside a cage, rattling the bars with its hands while a scientist watched.

What the hell were they doing down here?

His mind raced…

He had assumed they were checking his health, like the doctor said. Now he wondered if he was about to become a test subject.

They continued past more labs, but these were empty and dark inside.

Not completely dark, Timothy realized.

He stopped, squinting to try and make out what looked like glowing eyes. The eyes belonged to a bulky animal that trotted on four legs, moving toward the window.

"What in God's…" Timothy whispered.

The doctor turned and walked back to Timothy while

one of the guards laughed.

"You aren't afraid of dogs, are you?" he asked.

This was no dog inside the dark room. Not anymore. The beast was a monster with thick muscles and a spiky back. Veins bulged from light brown skin.

"Let's go," said the other guard. He elbowed Timothy hard in the back, pushing him forward. They didn't stop again until they got to another wing of labs. The doctor stopped at a door and opened it with the flash of a keycard.

"Come with me," he said to Timothy.

They walked into a white laboratory, the guards staying outside.

At the center of the room was a single person in a white coat. He had his back turned and was working on something on a metal cart next to a chair with leather straps.

Timothy's eyes turned to the cart, inspiring a pang of nausea. On the top sat two long needles, a black collar, and an open tool kit.

"Sir, I've brought the recruit," said the doctor.

"Ah, Timothy," said a familiar voice, as the man in the white coat turned.

Dread snaked its way through Timothy's insides.

It was Nick.

"Have a seat," he said, gesturing toward a chair.

Timothy hesitated at the sight of the open leather straps on the arm rests.

"What are you going to do?" Timothy asked. He shivered, unable to hold back his fear or his thoughts. "You going to turn me into one of those creatures?"

"Wow, you must really think I'm the monster, huh?"

Timothy didn't reply, and Nick followed his gaze to

the metal cart with the tools and the needles.

"Oh, those…" Nick said. "Well, you didn't think we were going to induct you into our army without some insurance, did you?"

He laughed.

The doctor picked up the collar.

"We didn't live in the shadows all this time because we're stupid," Nick said. "We've planned every move."

"You'll wear this until you can be trusted," the doctor said.

"Now have a seat," Nick said, his voice deeper.

Timothy did as instructed. His mind whirled trying to figure a way out of this. But he came up with nothing. The doctor walked around the chair and started tightening the leather straps around his arms and legs.

"This one's a healthy young man," he said.

Nick nodded and patted Timothy on the shoulder. "That's good, because you, my friend, are going to be very important to our master. I've been told he has special plans for you."

"Master?" Timothy asked.

"In time, you'll learn more," Nick said. He grabbed a syringe with a long needle and held it up toward a light.

Timothy recoiled.

"Don't worry." Nick flicked the syringe, loosening a couple bubbles. "I didn't just lie about my family being dead. I also lied about being a dentist. I was actually a lab technician. Something that's come in very handy for our plans."

Timothy swallowed hard, wondering what else Nick had lied about.

There was one thing he knew for sure.

The collaborators were far better organized than

anyone on the outside had imagined.

Nick stuck him in the arm with the needle, and a wave of heat rushed through his veins. Then came a feeling of cool relief and exhaustion.

Timothy tried to keep his eyelids open, but they grew heavier by the second. His vision started to blur as he watched the two men prepare the collar and what looked like a small microchip.

Any illusions he had about escaping vanished.

As he drifted off, he thought of his dad. He knew in his heart that his father would have wanted him to forget about revenge and focus on stopping whatever these men had planned.

You are the only one that can stop them now, he heard his father say. *I trained you for this.*

And then there was only darkness.

***

"I'm moving the kids to a shelter just in case," Beckham said through the intercom.

Kate stood on the other side of a glass window in the laboratory trying to make sense of what he had just told her about the juvenile scouts. She was alone in an antechamber to the larger lab, trying to keep calm.

All of a sudden, she felt trapped, like the mastermind in the main chamber. And the thought of Javier and the kids hiding in a basement shelter in a place she told them would be safe sent a pang of regret through her.

"Don't worry, Kate," Beckham said as if he could read her thoughts. "Horn and I'll make sure the kids are okay. You just focus on your work."

"I'm trying but..."

"Really, everything will be fine, I promise."

She wanted to believe that, but if the Variants really knew the mastermind was here, there would be hell to pay. Her husband helped make her feel a little better, but still there was the burning question about the juveniles and how they would have known the beast had been brought here.

They hadn't connected the creature to the external webbing network, and the top-secret landing during the dead of night had only been known by the science team and trusted military members.

She hit the intercom button. "Do you think Colonel Presley has taken care of any collaborators here?"

"The colonel is confident we have nothing to fear."

"But you aren't."

Beckham hesitated. "No, I'm not."

Sammy entered the room behind her and said, "Doctor Lovato, we need you back in the lab."

"Just a moment," Kate said.

Sammy nodded and exited back to the main lab.

"Go," Beckham said. "I'll take care of things. The kids, collaborators. I can handle it."

She looked at the clock. It was seven thirty-five.

"I still plan on taking my break to see you all if I can," she said.

He put a hand on the glass and she matched it with her gloved hand.

Kate returned to the lab, trying to manage her heartbeat. She was shaken up by the news that juvenile scouts had been spotted around the outpost, but decided to keep it to herself for now. Saying anything could throw off her team, and she trusted they would be alerted if it was absolutely necessary, by staff or by her husband.

Focus, Kate, you have to focus.

She and Carr had to unravel the mystery of the mastermind network. There was no room for failure. As soon as she reentered the chamber, she spotted Carr hunched over a lab table. By him was Sammy and another computer engineer engrossed in their work.

All around, she noticed the same determination in the other scientists, engineers, and lab technicians. Dressed in white cleanroom suits and masks, they worked hurriedly at the banks of computer terminals and filtered between the huge iron columns in the center of the three-story room. Others carted supplies and samples to different lab benches.

The twenty-person team was a significant upgrade from when it was just her and Dr. Pat Ellis in the early days of the war. But while she had not grown as close to Dr. Carr as she had been with Ellis, at least she respected the man's work and drive. It would be people like him, intelligent and steadfast, that enabled them to survive the coming days and weeks, the crucial tipping point of the war that they were currently losing.

Kate crossed the lab to Doctor Carr and Sammy, navigating the maze of lab stations and bustling staff.

While she had grown accustomed to working with this large group and this enormous space, there was one thing she would never get used to. The constant odor of rot and sour trash that her bunny suit couldn't mitigate.

The beast responsible for that smell lumbered in the middle of the room like a huge lump of crumpled red tissue. Snores that sounded like horrifying growls echoed through the room.

Long red tendrils, some as thick as anchor chains and others as thin as spaghetti, hung off the creature. Those were the remnants of the webbing network that had secured the monster to the cathedral back in New Orleans. Steel chains held it in place, attached to iron columns stretching from floor to ceiling.

"How are we looking?" Kate asked when she reached Carr.

He turned in his full white bunny-suit and facemask. "I think we're about ready to bring you in. Follow me."

Sammy joined them as they went to a bench filled with computer terminals and sat about six-feet from the creature's restrained claws. Two other computer engineers worked at the keyboards.

Next to them was a clear bioreactor about the size of a football. A series of micro-electric arrays connected the blob of red webbing tissue growing inside the bioreactor.

Sammy gestured to the bioreactor. "The connections are complete."

"Good, then the last thing we have to do is connect the webbing to the mastermind," Kate said.

Carr stood next to the bioreactor with another micro-electric array in hand. The device looked to be nothing more than a series of circuits and metal prongs that Kate didn't know much about. She certainly wasn't the expert in brain-neural interfaces, but people on the team around her were.

Sean joined them with his arms folded across his chest.

"We've prepped the connection tendril," he said.

"Bring it over, please," Kate said.

Sean walked over to the beast's open palm, approaching fearlessly. Kate was a bit shocked to see him acting with such confidence. It was almost like the imminent threat from outside had sparked new courage in the young tech. From the mastermind's hand, he dragged a red vine of tissue.

It looked like an enormous piece of stringy, chewed bubble gum.

Sean clamped the tissue into a vice on the table right next to the bioreactor. Carr then connected the micro-electric array.

Next, Sean moved a large surgical lens into place above the vice gripped-tendril.

"Okay," Sean said.

Carr bent down and peered through the lens to help him surgically attach the probes from the array into the tendril. Connecting nerve bundles one-at-a-time required expert precision.

To an outsider, what they were doing might have looked like nothing more than connecting some wires to a few chunks of meat. Kate's nerves were alive with coursing electricity, adrenaline pumping through her vessels.

This was the ultimate experiment, connecting a mastermind to computers loaded with the programs the collaborators had been using to communicate.

No one in the Allied States had ever done this—and it could change the course of the war in their favor.

Carr pulled away from the tendril and nodded. "It's connected."

Sammy leaned toward the monitor on her bench. A moment later she looked up. "Holy shit, I'm already getting something," she said. "An electrical pulse."

A long groan escaped the monster's bulbous lips.

The click of weapons being shouldered echoed around the room from the soldiers standing guard.

Kate tensed up, but the monster quieted once more.

"What else are you seeing?" she asked.

"I'm getting a constant pulse," Sammy said. "It looks to me just like a repeated signal to let the collaborator software know that the beast is connected."

"Hmm," Carr said, twisting to look at the beast. "Nothing in English yet?"

"Not yet." Sammy typed something on the keyboard. "Let me adjust something on our end."

Text scrolled on her screen. A series of 1s repeated over and over. Like they were appearing at the beat of the drum.

"I think I've got this tuned right." Sammy pointed to the screen excitedly. "The '1s' appear in the collaborator program when the mastermind is present, but not actively communicating. Kind of a neutral state."

"So how do we get it to a non-neutral state?" Kate said.

Sammy gulped, locking her gaze with Kate. "I think it's waiting for an input. We need to experiment with it."

"You can type a query that'll be translated through the webbing to the beast, right?" Kate asked.

Sammy nodded.

"Ask it: What are our commands?"

Sammy typed the words onto the computer terminal and hit the enter button. Everyone moved closer to the screen.

For a second, nothing happened. Just a series of more 1s and the low rumble of the comatose mastermind's breathing. Then the beast started twitching. Some of the severed tendrils draping off its body whipped like live electrical wires fallen from a power line.

The lab technicians retreated behind the iron columns. The soldiers around the perimeter advanced toward the center, their weapons trained on the monster. The giant's eyes fluttered open, and its yellow reptilian pupils flicked back and forth, surveilling its surroundings.

The soldiers closed in while the science team backed away.

Kate held up a hand, hoping to keep the soldiers from acting too hastily. "Don't fire!"

"Increase the anesthesia!" Carr ordered.

The beast pulled its legs and arms toward its body. Then it started to stand. Metal protested as the columns and chains resisted the strength of the monster. Pops like rivets breaking loose sounded from where the columns met the ceiling.

"We're losing it!" Sean yelled.

The soldiers moved closer, weapons up.

"Hold your fire!" Kate yelled.

"More anesthesia!" Carr snapped at Sean.

Kate watched Sean work quickly to increase the dose. She could feel the tension striking like lightning between the soldiers and the research team.

If the beast broke free, it could kill everyone here. But if they killed it, they would lose everything they had fought for. This was their only chance at uncovering how the Variants and collaborators were coordinating their attacks.

The beast took a faltering step, fully upright now. It let out a bellow that shook the ceiling, releasing dust. A few bolts fell free and clanged on the floor.

Researchers scattered as it took another step, dragging the huge IV lines attached to its body.

Kate moved away from the beast, stumbling into a lab station.

"What do we do?!" one of the soldiers yelled.

"Light this motherfucker up," replied one of the men.

"NO!" Kate shouted.

The soldiers moved closer, hunched, weapons aimed at the head.

"Not yet! You can't!" Sean cried, adjusting the dosage on the IV. He moved slightly to obstruct the target.

"Out of the way," said one of the soldiers.

Defiant, Sean remained in place.

Kate started to walk toward him when the creature staggered. The guards moved for a better vantage, but all halted as it slumped to the ground between the iron posts with a thud.

The rifles remained aimed at the beast, but the soldiers calmed down.

"Dr. Lovato, I think…" Sammy said in a quiet voice. "I think it worked."

Kate went back to look at the screen, her nerves still frayed. Words scrolled across the monitor.

Command? Command? Where am I? What is happening? Who are you? What is this place? You are my enemy!

The mastermind had spoken through that neural-computer interface, and they had been able to listen. Kate found herself smiling, such a rare reaction she hardly recognized it.

They finally had their key. Soon they would have full access to the Variant-collaborator network.

This was the beginning of the end for the Variants.

— 19 —

Fitz had prepared mentally for a lot of different things, but finding traps built for Variants was the last on his list. Coupled with the heavy fog, the traps and terrain made their advance extremely dangerous.

Fitz was grateful now more than ever they had Dohi to guide them. If it weren't for the Navajo tracker, half of Team Ghost and the Wolfhounds following them would have been impaled by now.

Dohi bent down to look at a snare trap they had just discovered. He glanced up at the tree and raised a brow.

"These guys are good," he whispered.

Fitz relayed the location of the trap to the others and then gave the advance.

For the next hour Dohi navigated the terrain expertly, uncovering more pits. The putrid odor of Variants drifted out of some, but others were empty. They found a skeletal Variant dangling from a snare in the trees, and another beast whose leg had been clamped nearly in two by a bear trap.

Most of the fog had thankfully lifted, replaced by pale moonlight when they finally made it to a tree line. An unobstructed highway appeared before them. Beyond it were the scattered buildings of the National Accelerator Laboratory campus.

Weeds had grown through the cracks in the broken asphalt of the road. Fitz crouched out of view to scope the area, searching for hostiles, human or monster.

He didn't see anything alive, but he did see evidence of life. The roads had been cleared of charred and rusted vehicles.

But when?

His stomach dropped. If the pits were any indication, the people out here were organized and intelligent. They'd made this place their home and defended it.

The real question was whether these would be the type of people who invited their guests in to share a meal or the kind that made their guests into the meal.

Dohi pointed to something a few hundred meters away. Fitz used his NVGs to search the darkness. In the green hue, he saw a tall fence barricading part of the town. Atop each post was something that confirmed these weren't collaborators.

Collaborators didn't mount Variant skulls on fence posts, and trap the beasts in pits.

But Fitz still didn't know if these people were allies or hostile, and there was only one way to find out.

He gave the advance signal.

As they crept through the overgrown grass leading up to the fence around the facilities, Fitz halted to scan parking lots containing rusted vehicles and shipping containers.

It was a huge area to cover and he split the team up with more hand signals. Normally he would have sent Rico off with another team, but this time he sent Dohi and Mendez. He wanted that group to focus on tracking down the equipment while he surveyed what they were up against with his team.

The men nodded back and set off with ten Wolfhounds around the north side. They headed toward a series of warehouses and neighborhoods that had mostly been taken back by nature.

Singh took the remaining ten men and followed Fitz, Ace and Rico southward.

If anything went wrong, they were to meet back near the freeway, their designated rally point. It was always hard seeing his team split off, but this was worse than normal. They were being dragged down by inexperienced soldiers.

A harsh wind carrying the faint scent of a bonfire pulled him from his thoughts. The scent vanished as quick as it had emerged.

He moved along the fence until they came to a corner concealed by a thicket of trees. Even here, among the foliage, the metal post sticking above them had a Variant skull stuck on it.

Fitz crouched down beside the fence and signaled to one of Singh's men. The one called Hopkins moved over with a pair of bolt-cutters. He went to work snipping through the chain-links. Then a pair of Wolfhounds pulled the puckered chain-link fence back.

Rico ducked through, followed by Fitz. Then came Ace and Hopkins.

A wall of trees demarcated the end of a parking lot and Rico took them past those trunks. She halted on the other side, crouching. Fitz held his fist up to the Wolfhounds and then joined Rico and Ace.

Rows of white buildings with tinted windows towered above a cracked asphalt parking lot. Through those fractures grew a mess of plants taking back the land. Shipping containers rose like small houses out of those tangled yellow weeds.

Rico pointed at the west end where tarps and tents

rippled in the wind. Clotheslines were hung between the containers with clothing flapping like tattered flags.

Fitz gazed through his rifle's optics, glassing the makeshift village. In areas cleared of weeds, he spotted empty chairs and tables with plates and cups.

It all looked recent, but where were the people?

Everyone had just disappeared.

He wondered if they would find Variant tunnels or the site of a massacre on the other side of those big white buildings. If only they had been here a few hours earlier, maybe a few days, they might have been welcomed into this place.

They could've entreated these people to help them with their mission and even bring them back into the fold of the Allied States.

Rico and Ace waited for orders. As much as Fitz hated sending them straight into this eerie setting, he had no other choice.

Fitz took point with Hopkins, leading the team into the camp.

New scents danced on the air like the charcoaled smell of grilled meat along with something more putrid. An odor he had long grown used to. The scent of decaying flesh.

They passed a shipping container with a door ajar. Fitz signaled Hopkins to open it and allow Ace inside. He aimed his weapon at the container, and with a gesture from Fitz, Hopkins pulled open the steel door.

Before Ace could go inside, a wave of bones rolled out, rattling noisily against the patchwork pavement.

Fitz flinched at the noise, anticipating a howling Variant to call out.

But it appeared most of the beasts around here were

dead or too far away to hear the noise.

He counted off twenty seconds in his mind before examining the bones.

"Something is wrong with these," Rico whispered.

She was right. The ribs were thick. Some even looked plated. The finger bones he saw were elongated, as were the femurs and arm bones. All the skulls looked smashed and malformed, but not because they had been damaged.

"Sweet Jesus! Those are Variants!" Hopkins said in a raised voice.

Fitz whipped around. Singh was already staring daggers at Hopkins.

The lack of discipline made Fitz worry about stepping another foot into this gruesome place, but he had no choice.

He gestured for Rico and the others to get back in formation and waited a few minutes to allow everyone to have a breath. The smell of death was more potent, and Fitz fought to contain the disgust welling up in his stomach.

Another open shipping container lay ahead, one door open.

An incessant droning buzzed from inside.

Clouds of black flies swarmed the place.

Fitz held in a breath and flicked on his infrared illuminator and laser designator to check the inside. He almost let out a gasp at the ghastly tableau.

Meat hooks hung from the ceiling. Beastly carcasses dangled from those hooks, chunks of meat missing from their haunches and ribs.

There was no mistaking it: the monsters had been slaughtered and were in the middle of being butchered.

Fitz didn't want the Wolfhounds to see this, especially

Hopkins. He closed the door slightly and whispered to Rico.

"Over here," came a voice.

Singh pointed around the container.

Fitz rushed over with Rico to see a firepit and a spit roast. The embers beneath the roast were still glowing slightly. All around the firepit were abandoned bowls and silverware.

The source of the scent he had smelled earlier.

If those past couple of sights hadn't already confirmed Fitz's suspicions, this one did. The Variant being barbecued on the spit roast had been cut like a tender hog.

A chill shot down his spine. The chances of these people being friendly and hospitable were dying with each gristly find.

He brought up his mini-mic, deciding this was worth breaking radio contact.

"Ghost 3, Ghost 1. Do you copy?" he whispered over the comm.

He was met only with the constant sizzle of static.

"Ghost 3, Ghost 1. Do you copy?"

Again, nothing.

Three more times, and still no response.

When Singh tried to ping his men, none of them replied.

"I can't get through," he said.

Fitz's guts tangled as he studied the charred Variant.

If these people ate monsters, then what would they do with humans?

He prayed to God the other team wasn't in danger of finding out, but with the lack of radio response, he couldn't help but wonder if they were next on the menu.

***

"Boss, this is some *bull*shit," Horn said.

"Relax, Big Horn," Beckham said. He eyed the children and their dogs clustered around cots with folded blankets. They had gone from a luxury apartment to the damp, claustrophobic ancient bomb shelter. Ironically, the shelter was cleaner than the apartment, despite the dust.

There were dozens of people here. Families. Single people. Most were either too young or old to fight. Those that weren't were supervising gaggles of children.

"I thought this place would be safer," Horn said. "And now we're in a Cold War bunker with a bunch of civvies that are lookin' at me like I've got a Variant head growing from my stomach."

Beckham turned to see if he was exaggerating, but a quick scan of the wide room proved he was telling the truth. Everyone around the shelter snuck furtive glances their way—some were far more obvious, openly gawking at them.

His eyes gravitated to a middle-aged man in a wheelchair wearing an Army Veteran hat. He held a shotgun and watched the steel door that was guarded by two outpost soldiers.

"I don't like feeling like a zoo animal, boss," Horn growled.

"You're definitely not helping matters by glaring back, man," Beckham said. "They're probably worried you're going crazy in here. Now calm down, and let's talk to the kids."

Tasha and Jenny were each reading a book, but Javier

was tapping his foot; he was bored and anxious. Beckham knew it wouldn't be long until the boy started asking more questions about why they were down here.

Tasha surprised Beckham and beat Javier to it.

"Dad, you going to tell us what's *really* going on?" she asked. "This isn't just a safety drill, is it?"

Jenny looked up from her book. Her freckled nose twitched as she prepared to sneeze. It came out in a blast of snot.

"Come on, Jenny, you're not a little girl!" Tasha said. "Cover your nose!"

Jenny dabbed at her nose with a handkerchief Horn gave her.

"I can't help it," Jenny said. "There's so much dust down here. It's probably my allergies kicking in."

Another person sneezed across the room, and a cough followed, the sounds echoing off the concrete walls and low ceiling like a chain reaction.

A conversation broke out near a column where a family sat.

"Why'd they bring us down here?" asked a woman holding a baby. She rocked it back and forth. "Are we in danger?"

"I heard they spotted Variants," replied another woman.

"Just a matter of time before they hit us," someone called out.

"It's because of those scientists," said a husky woman with a rough smoker's voice. "They brought something in during the dead of night. I heard the commotion. Whatever they're doing is probably not something the monsters like."

The first woman with the baby spoke again. "We were

fine before. Now we have all these scientists and… these guys," she said, nodding her head in Beckham and Horn's direction.

A man with a hunched back walked over to Horn and Beckham. A woman with braided red hair stood by his side, one arm tucked through his to help him stand.

"You all know something about that?" she asked them.

The man in the chair wheeled over, readjusting his shotgun when he arrived alongside the other two.

"You're new here," she said. "You know what they brought in, don't you?"

"Ma'am, we're sheltering down here just like you," Horn said. "Why don't you go sit down with your, uh, entourage?"

"Don't try and dismiss me," she snapped. "I've had enough of that. I want some damn answers."

"And I'm telling you we don't have them," Horn said in a deeper voice.

Some of the people got up from their cots and chairs, forming a tight circle around Beckham and Horn. Those that remained sitting turned their attention on the group.

"Great," Horn muttered.

Beckham considered telling a lie to get them off his back and make them relax, but these people weren't stupid. Plus, that would only come to bite him in the ass later. Better to be honest, but sparing in the details.

"It's true." Beckham held out his hands in a placating gesture. "A few Variants were spotted far outside the outpost perimeter. We're just taking a precaution, but there's no sign of any immediate attacks."

Hushed voices broke out. A couple of loud curses, too.

Javier, Jenny, and Tasha didn't seem disturbed by his raised voice or the news. Spark and Ginger moved closer to the gathering crowd, curiously. They were a welcome distraction to some of the spooked children that came to pet them.

"I promise we're safe here," Beckham said.

The promise didn't seem to help the red-haired woman to relax. She shook her head and muttered something to the old man leaning against her for support.

"We haven't had a beast set foot in this outpost for eight years," said the veteran in the wheelchair. He narrowed his eyes, looking between Beckham and Horn like he was studying them. "Seems awfully strange that you all show up and that happens now, doesn't it?"

Beckham got the feeling the man was trying to place them in some memory.

"These fine gentlemen are here to make sure the beasts don't get inside," said a voice in a refined Texas drawl.

Beckham turned to see Fischer entering the shelter with his two guards. The two soldiers standing guard parted to let them through.

"If I were y'all, I'd be thanking these two war heroes. They're trying to keep you and their families safe," Fischer said as he approached. "The reason everyone here is still alive is because of the sacrifices they made in the Great War."

"This dude again," Horn whispered to Beckham.

Beckham nudged his friend discreetly to indicate he needed to be polite.

Fischer took his cowboy hat off and exchanged a nod with Beckham and then Horn.

"You can all go back to your seats," Fischer said. "You're safe down here."

Everyone turned away except the woman and the two older men.

"Come on, Sally," said the guy with the hunched back.

Sally held her ground. "My father fought in the Great War too, when he was sixty years old. He spent his golden years fighting the beasts and knows a thing or two about sacrifice."

Beckham gave the guy a once over again. He didn't look a day younger than eighty with wrinkles, liver spots on his bald head, and thin, wispy hair. Maybe her math was off.

"Honey," said the man. "Please…"

"My father's name is Lieutenant Frank Rodman," she said. "He has stage three bone cancer from the chemicals he was exposed to in the war, so maybe you should be thanking him."

The retired Lieutenant waved a hand. "Sally, dammit."

"And this is Sergeant Christian Brown, also a veteran of the Great War who broke his back and lost his family," Sally said, gesturing to the man in the wheelchair.

Brown took off his baseball cap, revealing a bald skull with scars across the top that looked to be from Variant talons.

"Nice to meet you," Beckham said to them in turn. He reached out and shook the lieutenant's hand, then the sergeant's.

"Sally, you're absolutely right. These men do deserve our thanks and respect," Beckham said. "Without men like them, none of us would have been able to start our lives over after the war."

"We should be thanking you," Rodman said. He

squinted at the fatigues Beckham and Horn both wore. "I thought I recognized you both. Sally, I'd like to introduce you to Captain Beckham, and Master Sergeant Horn. True heroes."

"Wait, you know them?" Sally asked, skepticism clear in her voice when she looked at Brown.

Both men nodded.

Sally pursed her lips, looking between Beckham and Horn. Then she frowned, and said, "I'm sorry for coming off a little hot."

"Skepticism isn't the worst thing we've faced," Beckham said. "You're just trying to look out for your friends and family. Trust me, I can understand that."

Horn just grumbled.

"I don't mean to sound so standoffish, but I know the military brought something here," she said. "It can't be a coincidence that the beasts showed up now."

Sally still didn't look like she was going to back down, and as much as Beckham respected that, he also couldn't spill classified intel just because she was someone willing to fight for it.

"Ma'am, if you were in danger, I would tell you. I believe we're all safe down here," Beckham said. "I wouldn't put my family in harm's way, or yours."

Sally nodded, but didn't seem satisfied.

"Let's leave these men and their families alone now," said Rodman.

Brown nodded and turned his wheelchair, returning to his spot along the wall.

"All right, Dad," Sally said. She turned back to Beckham, but then reached out to help her dad.

Beckham also reached out to assist.

"Sir, if I may," he said.

Frank nodded and his daughter and Beckham helped get him back to his cot.

"Thank you," Sally said.

Beckham nodded and returned to his family where Fischer was talking to Javier.

"Your son was just telling me how he hopes to be a soldier or a scientist someday," Fischer said. "I'm trying to convince him being an engineer—especially a petroleum engineer—isn't such a bad thing."

"Good luck with that," Beckham said.

Fischer smiled and Beckham smiled back.

"Your wife is still in the lab, I take it?" Fischer asked.

"She is," Beckham replied.

"When do we get to see Mom again?" Javier asked.

"Shouldn't be long now," Beckham said.

The dogs wiggled their way through the throng of civilians. Fischer crouched and petted Ginger.

"Good lookin' dogs," he said. "I sure miss having one."

Beckham also bent down, tousling the fur behind Spark's ears. In a quiet voice, he said, "Want to tell me why you came down here?"

"To tell you something I didn't earlier," Fischer said. "This room isn't exactly fit to talk candidly about certain subjects, though."

Beckham checked to make sure the kids weren't listening. Javier had gone back to tapping his foot, bored. The girls were talking to Horn.

"I'll be right back, okay?" Beckham said.

Horn frowned and mumbled something about being a babysitter.

"Kate should be here in about half an hour," Beckham said. "Why don't you guys get out some food?"

Javier went to their bags and started digging in.

"Thanks, buddy," Beckham said. He left with Fischer and his guards before Javier could protest.

The soldiers standing at the shelter door opened it to let them out. They walked up the basement stairs and into the chilly night. Smoke fingered away from chimneys across the outpost skyline.

Beckham pulled his collar up and looked to Fischer.

"All right, so what is it?" he asked.

"There's something I want to tell you that I would regret too much if I didn't, Captain," Fischer replied. "I was told to keep this quiet, but my conscience kicked in and my gut tells me you're someone that I can trust. In a world where even the crack of a branch might mean something's trying to kill you, that means a lot to me."

"And?" Beckham looked at his watch. It was already eight o'clock, and Kate was supposed to be meeting them any minute for her short break.

Fischer looked around like he was making sure no one was listening. Tran and Chase moved outward to give them some space.

"I think this place is compromised," he whispered. "And I think Presley knows it but won't admit it."

"You mean there are collaborators here?"

Fischer nodded. "We believe there are cells at virtually all the outposts."

"I'd be lying if I said I didn't suspect the same thing now," Beckham said. "But I wanted to trust Presley that he had this place locked down."

"He sure thinks he does, but General Cornelius warned me I needed to be cautious. He fears that the collaborators know far more about what we're up to than we could have ever predicted. We need to be vigilant."

Beckham cursed his decision to bring the children here. If there were collaborators here, then Manchester was a ticking time bomb. Especially with the mastermind here.

"Reed!"

The sound of Kate's voice snapped Beckham from his thoughts. He saw his wife jogging down the street with two soldier escorts.

"We'll talk more later," Beckham said to Fischer.

Kate ran to meet Beckham.

"What are you doing outside? Where are the kids?" she asked.

"With Horn. Don't worry, I was just talking to…"

"S.M. Fischer," he said, holding out a hand. "Doctor Lovato, I presume."

"Oh, pleased to meet you," she said, her gaze flitting to Beckham. "I've only got a few minutes. We're making headway, and I need to keep at it."

Beckham nodded and looked to Fischer.

He had an almost wistful look in his eyes as he said, "Go be together with your family, Captain."

"Nice to meet you," Kate said. She gave Beckham a look that told him she knew something was up. He surveyed the quiet outpost one more time, hoping he and Fischer were both wrong about the collaborators.

— 20 —

Dohi stood beneath a line of trees inside the National Accelerator Laboratory campus. A full moon burned away some of the darkness enveloping the scattered buildings and trees.

If he were alone, he would have no issues infiltrating a place like this. There was plenty of cover and shadows to conceal his search for the SDS equipment. But with Mendez and ten Wolfhounds following, sneaking was far more difficult.

He held up a fist to halt the team.

From their vantage in the trees, he surveyed a row of four warehouses lining a road. A large office building loomed on the opposite side of the street. Nearly a dozen SUVs and trucks were parked in a line along the curb.

Mendez paused beside him, and the ten Wolfhounds took shelter between the tree trunks. Using his scope, Dohi glassed the vehicles.

As he suspected, these didn't have rotted tires or rust tracing up the side panels. More telling of recent activity were the pair of Humvees at the end of the line. An M249 was mounted atop each with ammo belts trailing inside.

"People with firepower like that aren't fucking around, amigo," Mendez said.

"Best we don't piss them off then," Dohi said.

"We're already sneaking around their backyard. That would piss *me* off."

Martin moved up next to them, fidgeting with the AK-47 necklace hanging from his neck. He pushed it back behind his armored vest. "Think we should call this in?"

"What don't you understand about radio silence?" Mendez asked.

Martin shrugged.

Dohi remained prone, considering everything he had seen so far. The people who used those vehicles couldn't be far. Normally he could tell if he was being watched. This felt different. It was like these people had disappeared in a hurry.

Maybe the people had seen Ghost and the Wolfhounds, then bailed, he thought.

But why would they leave behind these vehicles?

"Martin, you wait here with the rest of your team," Dohi ordered. "Stay hidden, okay?"

"Yeah, I got it."

"Mendez, you're with me," Dohi whispered.

They peeled away, creeping around the north side of the warehouses through the underbrush. Dohi normally didn't like splitting up, but Martin was clueless. Leaving him behind was better than dragging him along.

Dohi scanned the rooftops for contacts, expecting someone to pop up with an RPG or a machine gun. He used the cover of the vegetation until they made it past the fourth warehouse.

That's when he heard it. Muffled footsteps and the clink of weapons. Someone was headed toward them.

He motioned for Mendez to get down, and they dropped to the grass. Dohi kept his barrel just high enough to fire should they be spotted.

Two men in black fatigues walked through the woods at a hunch. They were no more than a half-dozen yards from Dohi's position. Further north, Dohi spotted another pair. Then beyond them, another.

Mendez tapped Dohi on the shoulder, then pointed toward snipers that had appeared in the windows of the office buildings rising above the trees across the street from the warehouses.

"What are we going to do?" Mendez whispered as they watched the mysterious soldiers continue onward.

Dohi took out his radio. "We should let Fitz know." He opened a private channel. "Ghost 1, this is Ghost 3. Do you read?"

No reply.

"Ghost 1, Ghost 3. Contacts spotted."

Still nothing.

An icy vein of anxiety wormed through Dohi.

"What's the matter?" Mendez asked in a low voice.

"Radio isn't going through."

Dohi tried to open a channel to Martin.

"Wolfhound 2, Ghost 3. Contacts headed your way."

Again, he got no response.

These people had set up an ambush that, thankfully, Dohi had discovered. But they must have a Warlock system operating, which made Team Ghost's comms broke dick.

The implications were nerve wracking. Fitz, Rico, Ace, and all the others were out there, potentially headed straight into another ambush.

"What's our move now, *jefe*?" Mendez asked.

Dohi shook his head, unsure.

"Maybe we should just shoot our way out of this," Mendez suggested. "I can get a drop on those two, you get the other pair. That leaves just two more."

Dohi thought about it but there were too many

contacts to take on without suffering major casualties.

"I say we try making contact," he said. "If nothing else, we'll learn their intentions."

"How about contact with bullets, not words? We got the drop on them. Couple of clean shots, and we got ourselves an escape path."

"And a gunfight. I want to avoid that. Follow me."

They stood quietly and snuck through the trees. Dohi was close enough to the first pair of contacts that he heard them breathing.

With a hand signal, Dohi gestured for Mendez to take the one on the right. He would take the other. The men moved like jaguars through the forest toward their marks.

Mendez slammed the butt of his rifle into the back of his target's head. The man fell unconscious instantly. Dohi took out his buck knife. He locked one hand around his target's mouth and pushed the blade against his throat. The man froze in Dohi's grips.

Pulling him tightly against his body, Dohi took him back into the woods while Mendez dragged his guy. When they were safely out of view and away from the other patrols, Dohi loosened his grip around the man's neck.

"Listen good," Dohi said. "I'm Sergeant Yas Dohi with Delta Force Team Ghost, and I'm not here to harm you. Nod if you understand."

His prisoner hesitated, then nodded.

"We're not here to hurt you. We're here for some old equipment in those warehouses," he said. "That's all we want. Nothing else."

The man didn't reply.

"I'm taking my hand away from your mouth but if you scream, I'll trace this knife across your throat. Got it?"

Another nod.

Dohi turned the guy around enough so he could see the fear in the man's eyes. He trusted that meant the prisoner wouldn't do anything stupid. Then he slowly removed his hand, but kept the blade pressed against his flesh.

"How many of you are there?" Dohi asked.

The man kept his lips tightly closed.

"Seriously, we don't want to hurt you," he repeated. "We want equipment and that's it. If you help us, we're willing to pay."

The man snorted. "Fuck you and whatever you have to offer."

Mendez glanced over, but Dohi kept his gaze on the man.

"You abandoned us out here," he said. "My people have survived on our own, and we aren't giving you shit."

Dohi wanted to curse, but remained calm. "Look, we'll give you whatever you want."

"We want to be left alone," the man snarled. "You're better off leaving and pretending you never set foot here."

Dohi kept the knife at the guy's throat, trying to figure out what to do.

"Who's in charge here?" Dohi asked. "Maybe he'll—"

Muzzle flashes suddenly lit up the night, and bullets plunged into the tree behind him, sending a shower of bark over his back.

Mendez squeezed off a burst of return fire.

The captive held Dohi's gaze, eyes burning with rage. Dohi knew if he took the knife away the man would try to kill him.

But he wasn't about to execute the guy in cold blood

either. Instead, he gripped the man's neck with his free hand, taking him in a sleeper chokehold. The man soon fell unconscious.

Dohi got up and set off with Mendez the way they had come. Rounds chipped at the bark and whistled by their retreat. Keeping low and running fast, they made it back to the Wolfhounds unscathed.

Martin stood suddenly, pointing his barrel at Dohi.

"Friendly!" Dohi hissed.

"What the hell is happening?" Martin said, lowering his rifle.

"Talking with those assholes didn't work," Mendez said.

"We need to fall back to the rally point," Dohi said.

"All the way back to the freeway?" Martin asked.

"Yes," Dohi said. "Now go!"

Mendez still looked like he wanted to stand and fight, but Dohi knew very little about the enemy numbers. They already had entrenched positions in the buildings. The last thing he wanted to do was be flooded by a veritable army with the ground advantage and cut off from the rest of their team without radio contact.

He led his team away from the trees around the warehouses, charging back toward the rally point. They ran through areas that had taken them a couple hours to infiltrate when they'd been sneaking through.

Now Dohi didn't care about stealth. Just about keeping the team alive. The only way to do that was retreat as fast as possible.

A cacophony of curses and hollers rose behind them. Gunfire lanced into trees and lit up the darkness like fireflies.

The group broke from the cover of the trees and

dashed across an open field. Then they passed along a road that took them another half-mile to the parking lots filled with vehicles, apartments, and other buildings they had first seen when approaching the laboratories. They finally made it to a street that would take them another fifty yards to the freeway.

One of the Wolfhounds went down and slid across the asphalt.

Dohi stopped and went back to check the guy, but he was gone, his forehead destroyed by an exit wound. More rounds bit into the ground, and Dohi rolled away, keeping low behind a few cars parked along the street.

On his feet again, he bolted for the highway, hoping Fitz and his team would be ready for them.

Mendez and the others made it to the freeway and started across. They crossed the first few lanes, then dove over the concrete wall of the center median.

"Friendly!" shouted a familiar voice on the other side. *Fitz.*

The crack of gunfire continued.

A second Wolfhound dropped to his knees, clutching his throat.

"Find cover!" Dohi yelled.

Half the team had made it across the center median and into the ditch where Fitz and Singh were waiting. Fitz's team provided covering fire, and Dohi used it to cross the road, keeping low as possible. Martin and the other half of the Wolfhounds were still crossing the freeway.

Muzzle flashes sparked from some of the vehicles in the parking lots and from the windows of the apartments and buildings adjacent to the freeway where a second group of hostiles had set up firing positions.

The Wolfhounds stuck on the road were in the middle of an open killing field. Dohi was right there with them, crouched next to Martin against the center median wall.

"Over here!" Martin yelled.

Another Wolfhound made a run for their position but was cut down. Dohi moved out to help drag him, but rounds peppered the pavement around the man's body.

"Come on!" Dohi said to Martin.

Dohi and Martin climbed over the center median just as a flurry of rounds slammed into the other side. He hit the ground. Ace was standing in a ditch in front of him.

"Run, Dohi!" he shouted.

Martin ran for cover but tripped and went down.

"Shit," Dohi grumbled. He hunched down and went back to help him up.

"Grenade!" someone yelled.

Dohi had just enough time to help Martin to his feet when a fiery blast threw chunks of hot asphalt into them. The concussive force sent him flying forward, and Martin tumbling into a ditch.

Ears ringing, Dohi pushed himself up, engulfed by a cloud of dust. He and Martin scrambled into the ditch. One of the Wolfhounds lay on the slope, chunks of shrapnel jutting from his face.

Ace was sprawled at the bottom of the ditch, coughing. Blood streamed from his nostrils. Rico ran to the older operator, and he threw his arm around her shoulder, limping away.

Martin turned and drained his magazine into the distance.

"Fuck you, assholes!" he shouted.

Dohi grabbed him and yanked him down. The rest of the team was retreating into the woods, helping the injured get away. Fitz remained there, waving.

"Let's move!" he shouted.

Dohi and Martin hurried after. But the Wolfhounds were moving too fast, and he could hardly keep up.

A body suddenly flung into the air up ahead, dangling by a rope. He screamed for help but was silenced by a sniper's round to his chest. He spun, limp, and dead.

"Watch out for the traps!" Dohi yelled.

Having fallen back to help Martin, he couldn't guide the group through the forest. Most of the Wolfhounds started to slow, ducking low as the gunfire blasted into tree trunks, but most kept running.

A scream rang out, fading as a pit swallowed the man.

Dohi barreled ahead, surveying the place for traps as fast as he could, yelling at the Wolfhounds to fall in line. The gunfire soon quieted, and Dohi looked back, expecting to see their ambushers flooding across the freeway.

But instead, only a high-pitched chanting followed them.

Screams, like victorious war cries.

As the team faded back into the forest, terror filled Dohi to his very core. This enemy was more dangerous than the Variants. They were organized, knew the terrain, and were well armed. And they were standing in the way of the SDS equipment that could help prevent the entire Allied States from collapse.

One way or another, Team Ghost would have to make it onto that campus again.

***

Timothy sat on the bench inside his cell, rubbing his neck

where Nick had implanted a chip under his skin. The tracking device, along with the collar around his neck made it pretty much impossible for him to escape.

That meant it would be even more difficult to bring this place down and kill the collaborators. From what he had seen over the past few days, he doubted even the president knew just how well prepared these people and the monsters were for war.

He had to expose this place and these people.

He couldn't do it alone. He needed help.

Not from people like Beckham and Horn though. They had abandoned him and let his dad die.

What Timothy needed were people who were dependable and brave.

"Hey…" mumbled a female voice.

Timothy got off the bench he was sitting on. He went to the bars of his holding cell. The woman who Nick had drugged earlier was standing on shaking legs and looking at him from the opposite cell.

"Hey," Timothy said back. "What's your name?"

"Lilly," she said.

Her sickly pallor was set off by a face that looked like it had once been pretty before the collaborators had gotten here. He feared that was why they'd kept her prisoner.

A frightening thought wormed through his mind. He wondered what the collaborators would do with Tasha if they'd captured her like they had this poor woman.

"Why are you here?" he asked.

She looked down the hall but didn't respond.

"How long have you been in there?" he tried.

She looked at the ground, and then shook her head.

"You don't know?" he asked.

"No, only that it's been a very long time."

Timothy figured that meant at least a few months.

"You have to help me get out of here," she said.

Now he said nothing. This wasn't part of his plan.

Her dark eyes pleaded for help. "I can't live another day like this."

She seemed sincere, but he didn't want to blow his cover. Didn't want to reveal his false allegiance to the collaborators. This could be another test from Pete, Nick, and Alfred.

"I can't," Timothy said. He sat down again and looked away. "I'm sorry."

"Please," she begged, gripping the bars. "They do awful things. They use me like…"

Timothy swallowed hard as he listened.

Everything that he suspected in the back of his mind was true.

But he knew conspiring with her would get them both killed and ruin any chance of carrying out his plan of bringing down the entire organization. That was the only way to truly help her. Until this place was discovered, and shut down, her nightmares wouldn't end.

He focused on coming up with his next steps as the poor woman sobbed.

Pete said Timothy was going to get them into Outpost Portland. Again, he would have to watch, listen, and learn once he was out there. Then maybe he would find an opportunity to fight back or escape.

First, he needed to figure out where this base was located. Then he could tell someone when he was in Portland.

A growling voice snapped him from his thoughts.

"Shut up!" yelled a guard.

The man marched between the cells and hit the bars of Lilly's cell with a baseball bat. She jumped away and then hurried back to her bed, where she squeezed her legs against her chest and hid behind her knees.

"Stupid bitch," growled the man. "You're too damn loud."

Timothy wanted to say something… no, he wanted to take a knife and stick it in the man's neck.

But instead he just sat there, biding his time. Listening to the helpless woman whimper. It was one of the hardest things he'd ever had to do.

The only thing holding him back from yelling at the guard was his thirst for revenge.

Finally, the guard retreated to the other room.

An hour or so later the door to the brig opened and more footsteps echoed. Pete was the first man Timothy saw. Nick and Alfred followed, all three dressed in fatigues, armored vests, and duty belts with holstered pistols, sheathed knives, and extra magazines.

They stopped outside his cell.

"You ready to prove yourself?" Pete asked.

"Yeah, it's about fucking time," Timothy said.

Pete nodded to Alfred, who unlocked the cell.

"Come on," Nick said.

Timothy stepped out and followed the men away from the cells. Lilly gazed up and locked eyes with him, but he didn't give her anything. Not a wink, or a friendly smile, or a nod. Nothing but pity.

Pete took them down a wing of the bunker Timothy hadn't seen before. Most of the paint had flecked away on the walls that were now covered in grime.

Two more men waited at the end of the next corridor armed with M-16 rifles and dressed in fatigues. It took both men to pull open the steel door at the end.

Beyond the door, a mezzanine stretched across a chamber illuminated by lights built into the walls of another silo. Nick went first, his boots clicking on the metal surface. Alfred and Pete escorted Timothy next. He froze in his tracks halfway across, his eyes locked on something below that couldn't possibly be real.

"Move it, fuck head," said one of the guards behind him.

Timothy felt the cold touch of a gun barrel prodding his back, but he didn't move. Even in the dim lighting there was no mistaking the massive missile below the walkway.

Nick twisted back to face him with a wry grin.

"What?" he asked. "Never seen a ballistic missile before?"

"The government lied about a lot of things before the war," Nick said. "The world thought the only nuclear missile silos were in North Dakota and Wyoming."

The butt of a gun slammed Timothy in the back, forcing him forward. He followed Nick to another steel door that the group opened to a narrow metal stairwell.

His mind spun with questions each step up.

Did the missile work?

Were there more?

Was this part of their plan?

The implications nearly took his breath, but he kept his composure. None of that mattered if he screwed up now, and this gave him even more reason to find a way to expose this place.

Alfred opened the door at the top of the stairs, letting in moonlight. This was the first Timothy had seen in days. He waited for his eyes to adjust to the darkness until he could make out a field of knee-high weeds rustling in the cold wind.

The men set off across the clearing toward warehouse-style buildings tucked away in a wooded area.

Timothy covertly studied his surroundings, trying to identify the location. But he didn't recognize this place and had no idea where they might be.

"Eyes ahead," said a guard. He gave Timothy the butt of his rifle again.

Timothy winced.

Heat rose to his face but he couldn't let himself lose control now.

"You don't like that, do you?" the man said. He rammed the rifle butt into Timothy's back again.

This time Timothy couldn't help it. He turned and glared, teeth gritted.

"You better fucking look forward or I'm going to break your face," the man growled.

"Keep walking and don't do anything stupid," Alfred said.

Timothy hesitated just long enough to memorize the man's face. He was going on the list of collaborators he would kill first.

They continued until they got to the warehouses. A tall canopy of trees, some still with their leaves, protected the buildings from a bird's eye view. Camo tarps also helped disguise vehicles and equipment outside.

The double doors to the first warehouse were wide open, revealing another small fleet of vehicles. Pickups, mostly, but a few military-style trucks and a Humvee. There was also a black muscle car.

The collaborators Timothy had seen in the briefing were working inside. Others had joined them. All wore fatigues and body armor with slung rifles and holsters on their hips.

The only man not armed was another guy wearing a collar like Timothy's.

He was on both knees next to a pickup truck, his gaze on the floor. Timothy was brought over to him and instructed to sit.

The collaborators loaded gear and weapons into their vehicles over the next hour. By the time they had finished, ominous storm clouds rolled over the sky, masking the stars and moon. The first clap of thunder sounded, rattling the metal walls of the warehouse.

"All right, listen up," Pete said.

The collaborators clustered around him.

"We're headed back to Outpost Portland to finish the job," Pete said. "We've softened their defenses, and now our job is to blow holes through what they have left so the beasts can get in."

Several hollers broke out.

"Burn it to the fucking ground," one of the men said.

"The heretics deserve to die," said another.

Pete raised a hand, and the space quieted.

"Once Portland is gone, we will all be rewarded with a visit from our master," Pete said. "No more mistakes. Our time is almost here, and once this is complete, we will be headed into the final reckoning."

The men's features transformed from excitement to fear, shadows playing over them with each distant strike of lightning.

"This has been a long time coming," Pete said. "Years of planning have led to this. And we're not the only ones. All across the Land of the New Gods, our brothers and sisters are rising up."

The hollers and hoots came again, their voices rivaling the rolling thunder.

Pete motioned for Nick who walked over to a side door. He opened it and stepped back. Guttural barking sounded outside.

A man wearing what looked like a riot suit entered holding a chain and a club with barbwire wrapped around the shaft. The slack in the chain straightened out, rattling from whatever it was attached to.

The guard yanked on it and in came a muscular beast with a maw covered by a muzzle. It was another freak dog like the one Timothy had seen earlier. Only this one had a collar around its neck.

The creature growled, spine going rigid and hairs spiked like arrow quivers. Saliva dripped out of the muzzle onto the ground.

"It's time to unleash our new weapons," Pete said.

A second guard in riot gear followed the beast into the room. Muffled barks escaped from the muzzle until the man clicked on a remote, zapping the dog into submission. Several more genetically modified canines were brought in and loaded into cages in the backs of pickup trucks.

"Mount up," Nick called out. "We move out soon.'

The men fanned out into vehicles while Nick walked over to Timothy.

"You, my pimple-faced friend, are going to help us get inside the command post," he said.

The man who had hit Timothy with his gun barrel withdrew a black bag and pulled it over Timothy's face. A hand grabbed him and pushed him into a truck. Motors growled to life.

Over the noise came the barking of the dogs in the

back of the pickup trucks.

They sounded nothing like Ginger and Spark, even when the dogs were angry. These canines were starving, anxious to feast on flesh.

Timothy's stomach curdled with the thought of just whose flesh they would be dining on tonight.

— 21 —

Beckham had done exactly what Fischer had expected any hard-headed Delta Force Operator would. He had marched to the forward command point to discuss security again with Colonel Presley. This time Master Sergeant Parker Horn accompanied him, too.

Fischer had joined the meeting, but kept his mouth shut. His men were holding security outside a tent functioning as their command point outside the area where Presley had his desk and war tables.

Beckham was determined to root out the issue immediately as soon as Fischer told him about Cornelius's worries that collaborators had infiltrated Manchester.

"Captain, I understand your concern, but we do not have a collaborator problem," Presley said. "The problem we're facing right now isn't some boogeymen hiding in our base. The problem is finding those packs of juveniles we spotted before. Their trail disappeared an hour ago, and we need to pick it back up. Not waste our time throwing around crazy allegations."

Presley was trying his best to hide his frustration, and Fischer didn't want to add fuel to the fire, but he had no choice.

"Colonel, I regret not bringing this up earlier," Fischer said. "But it seems too much of a coincidence that the juvenile scouts showed up right when work began on the mastermind. Now I'm not a military man, but I've been around long enough to run into my fair share of company spies looking for the next oil or mineral rights to pull a land grab right under my nose."

"This place isn't an oilfield," Presley snapped.

"No, it's not, but I'm telling you that my experience and recent events sure get the gears in my head turning." Fischer gestured toward Beckham. "When I mentioned this to Captain Beckham, he insisted we come back to you, because we both respect what you've done at this outpost."

Presley clenched his jaw. He set the folder he was holding down on a table and motioned for Horn to shut the tent flaps.

"What I'm about to tell you doesn't leave this tent," Presley said.

"Understood," Beckham said.

Fischer and Horn nodded in turn.

"A little over a year ago we discovered a group of terrorists planning to poison our water treatment plant," he said. "They were collaborators, but we never found out much more than that."

"Poison with what?" Beckham asked.

"Poison isn't exactly the accurate word." Presley hesitated, apparently considering his words carefully. "They were planning on infecting the water with VX-99."

"*What?*" Beckham said.

Fischer was equally surprised to hear this. Horn's brow creased, nostrils flaring like a bull ready to charge.

"Why wasn't President Ringgold informed of this?" Beckham asked.

"I informed the proper people," Presley said.

"The president *is* the proper person, *sir*," Horn growled.

Fischer had to admit he agreed. "It seems to me the administration of this country has the right to know about terrorist activity involving VX-99."

"Look, I've taken care of my people here." Presley shook his head. "We don't need any local problems blown out of proportion. If you think back two months ago, even before those attacks, local economies relied on trade between all the outposts. Who wants to trade with an outpost that has a collaborator problem?"

"The president had a right to know," Beckham repeated.

"And I had a right to protect my people. Both from physical and economic harm."

"How can you be sure you've actually protected them?"

"Since those arrests and the following executions, we have not had any problems." Presley shrugged. "Burning people alive in the town square has proved to be a good deterrent. I'm a big believer in making my actions count more than my words… Any potential collaborators knew from then on we meant business, and I made a promise that if we caught more, I would do worse to them than the Variants would."

"You never found out who they were working with?" Horn asked.

"No, none of them would talk," Presley replied. "We used every technique we could and got absolutely nothing from the bastards."

Beckham and Horn exchanged a quick glance.

"If the juveniles know the mastermind is here, it's not because anyone within our walls leaked that intel," Presley said in an argumentative voice. "You might want to take your search for collaborators elsewhere."

"I don't buy it," Beckham said. "I still have more questions."

Presley let out a grunt. "Captain, your concern is noted, but we need to find those juveniles."

"I agree, but they might not be the biggest threat. And I need to ask a few more questions. Sir."

Presley looked exasperated but gave Beckham a nod.

"How many people have gone missing from Outpost Manchester in the past few years?" Beckham asked.

"I… I'm not sure, Captain… We don't exactly keep a running census."

Fischer found himself wondering the same thing Beckham probably was thinking. How could the colonel not know?

"You don't have any idea? Not even a range?" Beckham asked.

"It's a low number, I know that. Less than thirty. I would have to check with my staff for a better total." Presley was agitated.

He walked around the table and called over one of his officers. Then he turned back to Beckham.

"You going to tell me why this information is important?" he asked.

"It's important because collaborators use people by kidnapping their family members and forcing them into serving the Variants," Beckham said. "Or other times, they simply brainwash them. Think Stockholm Syndrome on steroids."

"Happened at our outpost," Horn grumbled.

"I'd recommend putting together a list and checking with the family members of the people still living here,"

Beckham said. "That's one way to see if there's anyone who might be connected."

A female officer opened a tent flap and saluted. Presley spoke to the woman quietly but suddenly went rigid after she said something in response.

"Son of a bitch," he said. He went outside and continued talking with the woman in trenchant voices for minutes.

"That doesn't seem good," Fischer said.

The tent flaps opened again, and Presley walked over to a table with maps draped across the surface. He pulled out a pen and circled a spot.

"We lost a scout a few minutes ago," Presley said. "But we now know where the juveniles are."

Fischer surveyed the location. It was to the east, not even five miles from the outpost perimeter.

Presley looked up from the map. "I recommend getting back to your shelters and hunkering down for the night. Captain, for your benefit, I also charged a team to start looking into what we discussed."

"Thank you, Colonel," Beckham said.

Presley sighed. "I hope you're wrong."

"Me, too," Beckham said.

Fischer followed him and Horn out of the tent. They cradled their rifles as they walked into the street to join Tran and Chase.

"Any update on that monstrosity your wife is working on?" Fischer asked.

"She didn't say much," Beckham said.

"Better get back to the kids," Horn said. "I don't trust that redhead lady we left them with."

"We better try and snag some sleep," Tran said.

"No way I can sleep with everything going on." Chase

spat onto the ground. "I'd go for a beer instead."

"I wouldn't say no to one," Horn said with a chuckle.

"We can drink when we win this war, boys," Fischer said.

"Agreed," Beckham said. "Until then, I'm staying frosty."

The group set off down the empty streets, quiet with the curfew imposed by Presley. When Beckham and Horn got back to their building, they parted ways and headed for the shelter.

Fischer continued down the road with his men, walking for close to an hour. They were almost back when the sound of diesel engines rumbled through the night. A convoy of M-ATVs cruised through the empty streets, stopping at the shelter Fischer had been assigned.

Men in riot gear jumped out of the vehicles and rushed inside. Fischer moved aside with both Tran and Chase getting in front of him when more soldiers hurried over, shouting for their IDs.

"What in the hell are you idiots doing out after curfew?" a guard asked.

"Take it easy," Chase said. "We were just talking to the colonel."

"No need to go Gestapo on us," Tran said.

"Shut the fuck up and show me your ID. *Now*," said one of the guards.

Fischer understood the value of intimidation, but these guys were pissing him off. He and his men hadn't done anything to deserve this kind of treatment.

When he got his ID back, shouting came from the front entrance. The men in riot gear pulled people out, their panicked voices filling the otherwise quiet night.

"Where are you taking me?" one of the men said.

"We didn't do anything!" shouted the woman.

Fischer had expected to hear the shrieks of monsters tonight, but he didn't expect to hear the cries of terrified people at the hands of the base's own guards. He didn't exactly regret going to the colonel about collaborators, but now that he'd seen the results, he worried paranoia and rumors would add a dangerous, unforeseen threat to Outpost Manchester's existence.

"Get inside," said the guard standing by them.

"Calm down, bro," Chase said.

The guard grabbed him and shoved him hard. Tran stepped between the two. "Don't you fucking put another hand on him."

Fischer found his hand inching toward his holstered .357.

Another voice rang out.

"What the fuck is going on here?"

An officer walked over, a vest full of magazines, and a helmet over his black face mask.

"These men were out during curfew," said the soldier who had pushed Chase.

Chase stood next to Tran now, both tense and ready to fight.

"We had a meeting with Colonel Presley, you dumb shit," Fischer said.

The officer motioned for the soldier to return to the truck. After he left, the officer said, "Get back inside the shelter. It's not safe out here."

Fischer glared at the officer but said nothing. Instead, he motioned for his men to move inside. Once they were through the door, the guards locked it, leaving them only a window's view to the street.

The officer got back into an M-ATV and the armored

vehicles pulled away, speeding to the next location.

"I was about to break that dude's face," Chase said.

"Me too," Tran said.

Fischer watched the vehicles round the corner.

"What do we do now?" Tran asked.

"We wait, and we pray I'm wrong about the collaborators," Fischer said. "And if I'm not, we get ready to fight."

***

"Our test today is the most important yet," Kate said. "If we're successful, we can actually figure out what in God's name the Variants are planning."

The mastermind let out a long exhale that rushed over Kate like a storm-born wind, carrying with it the rotten stench of a garbage dump. The two giant, muscular limbs trembled, and its eyelids fluttered.

Nothing Kate had studied during graduate school had prepared her for a test subject like this. In fact, she couldn't imagine anyone in the massive laboratory at Outpost Manchester had ever thought they would be experimenting on a giant monster that wanted nothing more than to have them all killed.

She turned from the half-sleeping beast and joined Sammy, Sean, and Carr at a nearby laboratory workstation. On it lay the bioreactor with a chunk of pulsating red tissue inside of its clear plastic drum-like container. One of the mastermind's tendrils was attached through a port via micro-electric array. On the other end of the tissue, another array connected to Sammy's computer.

Sean looked between the computer and the beast, his

right foot tapping the ground. His fingers traced across the regulator for the monster's sedative IV drip. "Are you sure we have to keep that thing half awake?"

Kate appreciated Sean's caution, but his wariness was holding back their research. It almost seemed like he was purposely trying to slow things down, but they were all tired, and she wasn't working as quickly as normal.

Sammy responded as she typed at her keyboard. "If we put it to sleep, then I'm just talking to a comatose blob. The thing didn't respond last time until we woke it up with enough prodding."

"And we're not going to make any progress if we don't get an actual response from the beast," Kate said.

"We won't be doing ourselves any favors if we're scared to confront the mastermind." Carr leaned over the bioreactor chamber, scrutinizing the tissue within.

Nodding, Kate pointed at Sammy's computer. The technician had done a great job adapting the collaborator's software so they could translate an input signal. That should help them intercept any communications in the Variant network once they hooked up their own computer systems to the webbing.

"We can't just be reactive anymore. We have to be proactive. The way to do that is to send our own signals through the network," Carr said. "Signals that can interfere with Variant-collaborator communications or even lure them into a trap."

"First things first," Sammy cut in. "What kind of messages do we want to send it now?"

"Maybe we should try to trick the monster into thinking it's tapped into the actual Variant network," Kate said. "That might get it to open up more and give us a chance to test how well our messages pass for the real thing."

"Why don't we just tap into the real webbing network?" Sean asked. "We can circumvent the mastermind. Wouldn't that be safer and quicker?"

Sammy laughed, swiveling in her seat. "No way. Not at all. Look, we're trying to play biological hackers here. If we don't know what we're doing and we send a message that makes it obvious it's coming from the outpost, then the Variants will rain hell on us. But if we can fool the mastermind, then maybe we can use what we learn to trick the rest of the Variant network."

"Exactly," Kate said. "So long as we're only connecting the mastermind to this secured bioreactor, it's like we're operating a computer at home with no Internet access. But as soon as we connect to the internet—or in our case, the Variant network—then any beast or collaborator could connect right back to us. Not a good idea."

The mastermind shifted in its restraints. A long growl escaped its bulbous lips. Kate eyed it suspiciously, waiting to see if it would make another move, but it settled back down, its head rolling on its shoulders.

"I really don't like this." Sean tapped on a gauge measuring the sedatives pumping in through one of the massive IV lines into the mastermind. "It's unpredictable. We're playing with fire, just guessing how much we think it needs."

"I trust you'll keep the beast under control, but if all else fails, you have my permission to knock it out," Kate said.

Sean kneaded his fingers together nervously, taking a step back from the lab bench.

"Just focus on taking care of the lab equipment and connections to the mastermind," Kate said.

"Sure," Sean replied.

Truthfully, Kate didn't feel safe either. Not with a monster that could destroy her entire team with a single swipe of its scythe-like claws. Even the dozen soldiers along the walls of the massive lab didn't make her feel much better. She couldn't help but think of Javier and Horn's girls in addition to all the other people sheltering at this outpost.

If the abomination escaped and started attacking from within, she worried how many would fall before they could stop it.

But worries like that wouldn't solve the challenge they faced now.

"Sammy, re-open the connection with the mastermind," Kate ordered.

A few keystrokes and numbers scrolled across the computer monitor. The mastermind's tendrils squirmed like long red snakes slithering from its body.

All around the laboratory, Kate watched technicians and scientists stop what they were doing to watch the giant.

"Connection confirmed," Sammy said. "Ready to proceed on your mark, doctors."

The monster's tendrils undulated as Sammy performed some basic checks.

She input simple commands checking the status of the mastermind.

"Alive?" she typed out.

The response came back, "Yes."

"Where?"

"Location unknown."

"Identify yourself."

"Bio-node Twenty-Two."

From their work with the mastermind, they had determined that the masterminds called themselves Bio-nodes, though they were still unsure who had given them that name.

"Network connection with other Bio-nodes?" Sammy probed.

"Unavailable."

In its half-sedated state, the monster continued to respond robotically. None of the dramatic anger filtered into its responses. For that, Kate was optimistic. It meant Sean had to have dialed down the sedatives at just the right level.

But for the next part, they needed a stronger response from the beast.

"Sean, reduce the sedatives," Kate said. "We need the mastermind in a higher state of consciousness."

Sean's fingers shook as he adjusted the regulators on the IV lines.

The mastermind's eyes blinked, and its arms started to lift, yanking on the thick chains attached to the iron scaffolding.

Simple inquiries like the ones Sammy had tried so far were easy.

But if they were going to disrupt the Variant-collaborator communications, if they were going to send bad intel to compromise the enemy's strategies, then they would need to create significantly more complex messages that would fool even the mastermind.

Now was the moment they had been waiting for. The final test that would determine if they had figured out how to do just that.

To accomplish it, Kate had to rely on Sammy's computer genius to translate regular language through the collaborator's software into signals that the mastermind could understand and react to.

"Let's put your work to the test," Kate said. "Ready, Sammy?"

"Ready," she replied.

"I want to see if the mastermind will listen to our commands. Tell it to stand."

Sammy's fingers worked across the keyboard.

For a second, nothing happened. Then the monster began to push itself up, eyes still roving back and forth like it was drunk. It managed to stand, wavering as it did.

"Damn, I didn't think it would actually listen," Sammy said.

"Tell it to walk forward," Kate said.

Sammy typed in the command, and the monster shivered, huge saucer eyes pulsating, searching around the chamber. Saliva dripped from its toothy maw.

"I think I let the sedatives off too much," Sean said, beginning to twist the regulator.

"Hold on." Kate put up a hand to stay him.

The mastermind took a stumbling step forward. Its eyelids peeled back a little more, and its lips shook into a snarl as it continued to walk forward until the slack in the chains started to disappear, straining against the scaffolds.

With a snarl, the beast reared back one of its claws. Messages scrolled across Sammy's computer screen.

Where am I? What's going on? Enemies everywhere! Where is master? What does he command?

But this time, Kate didn't signal for Sean to knock the creature out.

"Sammy, tell it to stand down. Tell it *we* are the master."

The beast pulled against its restraints. Chains clinked together, and dust fell from the ceiling; iron groaned, echoing around the cavernous room. Sammy's fingers worked across the keyboard.

With a final lurch, the beast stopped and stood, relaxing its limbs.

Master? came the message back on the screen.

"Yes," Sammy typed back. "Sit down."

The beast dropped immediately, a long sigh coming from its flared nostrils. A tremor rocked through the laboratory.

"See?" Sammy asked, looking at Sean. "We got this under control."

Kate nodded. "Good work. What else should we tell it?"

The team began a more complicated conversation with the mastermind, asking about the number of Variants back where they had extracted it in New Orleans and how many other masterminds were out there. It knew pitiful little intel; it was more of a tool than a real 'mind' at all.

Sammy let out an exasperated sigh. "I guess we can think of this Bio-node thing as more of a Wi-Fi router that merely transmits and receives complicated signals. It's not like a hard drive that contains and stores a bunch of data."

While they couldn't drag out more useful intel from the monster, they had at least managed to fool the mastermind into thinking they were on its side. That was good news for weaponizing their technology, Kate thought.

"We should be able to load this software onto other computers," Carr said.

"Then we can install the same language processing applications on other computers. This is our Rosetta Stone," Kate said excitedly. "Wherever Ringgold's armies go, they can hook those computers up to the Variant network to monitor *and* disrupt communications."

The other scientists and engineers around them nodded in agreement, looking pleased with their victory. But Kate noticed one who was not.

"Sammy, what's wrong?" Kate asked. "Is something not working?"

"No, it's all working… Quite well in fact. That's the problem."

"I don't follow," Carr said.

"Think about it." Sammy nodded toward the mastermind.

"Someone or something not only created creatures like this one, but they perfected the webbing network and a neural-biological interface to go along with it," she said. "All in a matter of years. That person, this master that the beast mentioned, must be more intelligent and powerful than these beasts."

"That person is the true mastermind," Kate said. Realization seized all sense of accomplishment.

Sammy nodded. "That's who we have to find and destroy for this nightmare to end."

— 22 —

Daylight glowed over the pine trees casting their shadows across the makeshift camp. Dohi and Mendez were out searching the area, but Fitz, Ace, and Rico were seated around the tree trunks. Dirt covered their fatigues, and deep bruises underscored their eyes, evidence of the lack of sleep they all suffered from.

But exhaustion was the most innocuous thing they had to endure.

Fitz stood, his blades creaking. Rico followed. They walked past a couple of men with bloody bandages. A few Wolfhounds secured the perimeter, their rifles probing the shadows among the woods.

Singh was leaning against a tree with a canteen in his hands, head bowed, either in prayer or asleep.

"Lieutenant," Fitz said.

He looked up and cleared his throat. "Master Sergeant," Singh replied. "Do we have a final head count?"

"Two dead, another six injured. And… three missing." Fitz gritted his teeth together, imagining what had happened to the three who were missing.

Neither of the men needed to think too hard about their fate assuming they'd fallen into those crazy people's hands. These demented, sick people devoured Variants in some ironic twist of fate, and if they did that they would savor the flesh of a normal man.

Singh tugged at his beard, gazing up at the blue sky between the tree branches as if he was looking for an aircraft to come rescue them.

"How long are we going to sit here?" Singh asked. "It can't be safe."

"I've got Dohi off making sure we're not being tracked," Fitz said. "He's also looking for any injured that may have been lost during our retreat."

"We'll know if someone's coming," Rico said, joining them.

"Your man basically walked into a trap before, what makes you think he will…" Singh let his words trail.

But he was right. Dohi had seen this coming too late. If he had failed, that meant these men were damn good.

"We stay here, and stay frosty," Fitz said. "We won't make the same mistake again."

"What about calling in reinforcements?" Singh asked.

Rico let out a wry chuckle. "Reinforcements? What reinforcements? Hate to break it to you, LT, but we're on the other side of the country. We're it. This is on us now."

"Afraid that's true," Fitz said. "When we left for this mission, our defenses around the outposts were already stretched thin. We were the only teams that Cornelius and Ringgold could spare. Even if they changed their mind and granted us reinforcements, it's not going to happen soon enough for Hopkins or the others, especially with all the attacks happening around the outposts."

Rico spat on the ground. "And frankly, I don't want to be responsible for sapping vital defensive forces away from those outposts. They need to be defending the families and strongholds we've got left in the Allied States."

"I agree," Singh said.

Fitz shifted on his blades, happy to hear the Lieutenant was on the same page about that. "We'll get your men back, and in the process, we'll secure the Rolling Stone technology. I'm not leaving California until that happens."

"Future of the Allied States is relying on us," Rico said. Then she leaned forward a bit, a shock of pink hair coming loose. She brushed it back. "You ever seen the tunnels those Variants and Alphas create?"

That caught Singh off-guard. His brow scrunched, and he shook his head.

"You ever see what they do to people in those tunnels? How the beasts string them up to die?" she asked.

Again, Singh shook his head.

"Then count yourself lucky," she continued. "It's a sight that'll haunt my nightmares for the rest of my life. But if we retrieve the SDS equipment, we can make sure those tunnels are a thing of the past."

"Once Dohi returns we'll come up with a game plan to get your men back and get inside this AO," Fitz said.

Singh nodded. If he hadn't been convinced earlier, he was now.

Fitz motioned to Rico, and they joined Ace back under the wide branches of a pine swaying in the wind, isolated from the Wolfhounds.

For a few long moments, the camp was quiet except for the groans of the wounded.

Ace went to get up when Fitz and Rico walked over.

"Sit and rest," Fitz said.

Ace used his finger to comb some of the dirt from his white beard that was also stained from a bloody nose.

"How you doing, brother?" Fitz asked.

"Like I just woke up after drinking the rest of the beer in the Allied States," he grumbled. "And then got hit by a Humvee."

Rico let out a low chuckle, and Fitz grinned.

He sighted movement through the tree line and pointed.

"Dohi's back," Fitz said.

Mendez accompanied the tracker.

"Well?" Fitz asked.

Dohi wiped sweat from his face. "I didn't find any of the missing men, but I did spot some scouts," he said. "They're on the other side of the freeway for now, but come night, I bet they head our way."

"Then we just need to wait and mow those fuckers down," Mendez said. "They caught us with our pants down, and now it's their turn to get ambushed."

Dohi's face appeared mostly expressionless when he replied. "That won't work."

"I agree," Fitz said. "They know we're out here. They'll expect us. We already lost our element of surprise."

"We lost a hell of a lot more than that," Rico said.

"These guys aren't what Cornelius promised," Mendez said. "We need to roll in by ourselves and give these assholes a good taste of their own medicine as mi madre used to say."

"Cool it, bro," Ace said.

Mendez cursed to himself and gestured toward the Wolfhounds.

"Cool it? These guys are like zombies now," he said. "Useless to us."

"They lost some of their brothers today and they trusted us to keep them safe. What do you expect?" Fitz said.

Lincoln, Tanaka, Stevenson, and so many other fallen soldiers flashed through his mind. For a fleeting moment, Fitz felt a white-hot ball of rage.

"So what do you want to do?" Mendez asked. "You trying to say we call this off? That we abandon the mission because they can't handle it?"

Rico kicked at some of the leaves on the ground, shaking her head. "No, that's not what he's saying, Mendez. We're saying to chill out."

"Impossible for me to chill when we're chained to these guys," Mendez replied. "They're a mission hazard. Might as well tie an anchor around our feet and throw us in the damn Pacific."

"What about the men we got back at the plane?" Ace asked. "That might be the next best thing to reinforcements we can get."

"No can do," Rico said, apparently thinking along the same lines. "Imagine that those cannibals find the C-130 without enough of Cornelius' men to defend it."

"They're cannibals?" Dohi asked. "Thought you said they were eating Variants."

"Variants are just very sick, mutated humans," Ace said. "Until ya'll come up with a better word for people that eat Variants, Rico's right on the money. Those people are cannibals with a twisted palate."

"Cannibals or not, we're royally screwed if they take the C-130 or destroy it," Rico added.

"Agreed," Fitz said.

"So what's the plan, boss?" Ace asked.

Fitz looked between the team. "Mendez isn't totally wrong."

"Seriously?" Rico asked.

Mendez patted his rifle. "Hell yes, I'm right."

Fitz looked to Dohi.

"You're going to find us a way into that base and into those warehouses without the cannibals following us," Fitz said. "The Wolfhounds will hold security near the freeway and cover our escape."

"They'll be waiting for us," Dohi said. "It won't be easy."

"No, it won't be easy, but I think we've got a way we can get it done without losing more lives."

Fitz hashed out the details with Team Ghost before he would bring the idea to Singh. As they planned, a piercing cry erupted over the woods.

"What the hell was that?" Ace asked.

"Sounded like a Variant," Mendez said.

Dohi shook his head. "No, that was human."

The voice blasted over the trees once more, a strangulated yell of tortured agony. All around the camp the Wolfhounds got to their feet and readied their weapons.

The screech sounded closer the next time it rang out.

Fitz steeled himself, imagining what terrible things the cannibals were doing to the missing men.

The Wolfhounds all froze in place, as more pained screams traveled through the woods like spirits haunting the forest.

Fitz had promised Singh he would help find his men, but he feared now it was going to be too late. If they were to escape with the SDS equipment from Project Rolling

Stone, they couldn't delay much longer.

He left his team and returned to the lieutenant.

Singh stood stiffly in front of Fitz. The man was different now, his jaw clenched tightly and his face a mask of determination as a result of those screams.

"Those are my men, aren't they?" he asked.

Fitz nodded. "They're trying to frighten us."

"It's working," Singh replied, glancing at his surviving soldiers. "But we didn't come out here to turn tail and run."

The agonized wails echoed once again.

"Good, because tonight my team is going back in, and I need your boys to watch our back," Fitz said.

"Oh, we can do that, brother, and more," Singh said. "I've got an idea on how to keep those cannibals occupied for a while."

***

A cool wind cut through Outpost Manchester's town square. The fiery leaves littering the ground rustled, and the breeze plucked other dead leaves off spindly tree branches.

"Watch this," Horn said to Javier and his daughters. He tossed a stick like a boomerang. It sliced through the air. Ginger and Spark exploded toward it, racing to find it in a pile of leaves.

Beckham and Kate hung out behind a park bench, watching Horn and the kids play with the dogs. Beckham was feeling a bit better after an uneventful night and a quiet morning. A brief phone conversation earlier with President Ringgold had confirmed no other major attacks had occurred elsewhere.

But he wasn't fooled by one peaceful night. He knew the enemy was out there, scheming and waiting to strike like they had for eight years.

The citizens of Outpost Manchester were out this afternoon and didn't seem to be concerned. A glance around the town square and surrounding streets might have looked almost normal to an unwary onlooker.

A long line of people waited patiently for food outside townhall. The sporadic laughter of children and even some adults filled the afternoon with rare sounds of joy.

Kate drank from a mug of steaming coffee, enjoying a brief respite from lab work.

"How's your head feeling?" she asked.

Beckham shrugged. "Just a bump, could have been a lot worse… How are things going in the lab?"

Kate took another sip. "I think we're going to crack the code by tonight."

"That's great. President Ringgold said she'll have a bird ready to evacuate us as soon as you're done."

"And go where?"

Javier tossed a stick, and Ginger leapt into the air, catching it in her teeth.

"Good catch, girl!" Jenny cried out.

Javier smiled proudly and looked to his dad who smiled back.

"I don't know," Beckham said to Kate. "Maybe back to the *Johnson*."

"We have to tell the kids about Timothy, Bo, and Donna soon… But I'd rather wait until we leave this place."

"Agreed." Beckham hated the idea of going back to the warship. And he hated having to tell the kids their friends were dead and their home destroyed.

"Any updates on Fitz and the others?" she asked.

"Nothing new, and the longer we don't…" He let his words trail off. They both knew the more time Ghost spent on the frontier, the less likely they would come home.

Jenny laughed, then threw another stick. "Go get it!"

Both dogs bolted after it, exploding through the piles of leaves while the kids laughed.

"What about the juveniles?" Kate asked quietly, her eyes pinned on the kids.

Beckham kept his voice even lower.

"They took out two Raven scouts. The team that went to locate the Variants didn't find any tracks. It was like they'd vanished into thin air."

Kate kept staring at the kids.

He said what they were both probably thinking.

"This place is a ticking time bomb, Kate. I want to get out of here as soon as you finish your work."

"Me too, and that's a good reminder that break time is over."

"I didn't mean this second…"

"It's okay, Reed." She planted a kiss on his lips and walked over to the kids. "I've got to go, guys, give me a hug."

Javier came running, along with the dogs wagging their tails.

"Good luck," Horn said. He offered a brisk salute.

"Take care of my family," she said to him.

"Always, Kate."

She smiled at Beckham and then returned to the sidewalk where two soldiers were already waiting to escort her. Beckham watched her go before joining the kids.

"Mom sure works a lot now," Javier said.

"I know, buddy, but she's almost done," Beckham replied.

"Awesome. Then do we get to go home?"

"I miss Timothy," Tasha said. "Wish I could at least give him a call."

"And I miss my bed," Jenny said.

Horn raised an eyebrow. "How old are you again?"

Jenny laughed. "Not an old fart like you."

A pair of black Humvees with the Raven logo pulled up outside of the park, a welcome distraction from the questions.

Two men wearing black fatigues got out of the lead Humvee. Several people in the food line watched, others put their heads down, clearly afraid. Not that Beckham blamed them, after last night's raids.

But instead of going toward the line, the soldiers aimed their path at the park.

"Captain Beckham," one called out.

"Yeah…"

"Who's asking?" Horn said.

The men jogged toward him as Horn led the kids over with the dogs.

"Colonel Presley," a soldier said. "He wants to see you."

"About what?" Beckham asked.

"Please, come with us," the other said. "We'll have you back to your family shortly."

"Dad, why do they want you to go again?" Javier asked. He eyed the soldiers suspiciously.

Beckham crouched down on his prosthetic in front of Javier. "I'll be right back."

"I want to come," Javier said.

"Sorry, bud, but this is official business."

Javier frowned and Beckham gave the boy a playful tap on the shoulder. "You stand guard with Big Horn, okay?"

The boy lit up at that. "You got it, Dad."

Beckham nodded at Horn and then went with the Raven soldiers. They drove to a brick complex surrounded by twenty-foot tall metal fences topped with razor wire. Two armored vehicles were parked outside a gate, machine gun turrets occupied by men wearing black face masks.

The gate rolled back, and they drove inside to a parking lot with squad cars sitting in a neat row. Beckham spotted a Raven sign hanging over the main entrance where a police station sign had once been.

"Let's go," said one of the escorts.

Beckham got out of the vehicle.

"Rifle, please," said the other soldier.

Beckham unslung his M4A1 and handed it over. Then he followed them into the building. He was led down a flight of stairs into a basement. From there, they took him to a jail with two dozen cells. Each had only a small window to see through the heavy metal doors. As they walked past, Beckham stole glances into those small windows, surveying the cells' inhabitants.

Realization set in.

Presley wanted to show him the men and women they had taken into custody. People who had probably lost loved ones over the past few months or years that Beckham suggested they investigate.

The two soldiers turned down another wing and stopped to throw up salutes. Colonel Presley stood reading a document with a female staff member in uniform. A second soldier, about a foot taller than Beckham with muscles like Horn's was looking into one of the cells. A black t-shirt clung to his bulging frame and a face mask covered his features. His knuckles were cracked and bloodied, as if he'd just been in a fight.

Presley acknowledged Beckham's escorts with a nod and then handed the document to the woman.

"Captain Beckham, thank you for coming," Presley said. "I need your help. We have someone in custody who we found with this."

Presley held out a small vial.

Beckham leaned closer to look at what appeared to be juvenile acid. The sight of a substance that had all but destroyed his body, leaving him with a prosthetic hand and leg during the great war, made his blood boil.

"I thought you didn't have a collaborator problem," he said, angrily.

"I may have been a little too confident, Captain." He gestured toward a cell door. "We found this on a young man last night."

The guard with the face mask stepped aside so Beckham could look. Inside, a man knelt on the floor, his head hung low. The prisoner must have sensed him and glanced up with a bruised and bloody face.

Beckham turned away from the view. "He's just a kid."

"And he's a stubborn one at that," Presley said. "We can't get him to talk. I thought someone with your experience might have better luck."

"My experience?"

"Before the war, Team Ghost spent time in hot spots around the world. Don't tell me enhanced interrogation techniques were off the table."

"Like I said, that's just a kid," Beckham said. "We

never tortured kids. Even in war."

Presley frowned and handed the vial to a guard. "This isn't the same type of war. Our enemies are monsters."

"You don't fight monsters by becoming one."

"Maybe not. But if we don't try, we might not win this war."

Presley motioned for the man in the t-shirt to open the door. He went inside with the colonel. Beckham followed, instantly smelling urine and body odor.

The kid was maybe twelve. Not that much older than Javier, and much younger than Timothy and Bo. He was kneeling, his hands cuffed behind his back and his feet held to a chain connected to the wall.

"This is Captain Reed Beckham," Presley said. "Sounds like he doesn't want us to hurt you. Unfortunately for you, he's not in charge."

The boy looked up with one eye swollen shut, glaring at Presley.

"Tell us where you got the juvenile acid or things are going to get a lot worse," Presley said.

The boy, quivered, his cracked lips trembling. His brown eyes flitted from Beckham to Presley, and then to the guard with bloody knuckles.

"You know what we did to the last collaborators, right?" Presley asked.

The kid managed a slow nod. "You burned them."

So much for that working, Beckham thought.

"Tell us where you got the acid, or we're going to put you in a barrel of it," Presley said.

The boy glanced down.

Presley sighed, then nodded at the big guy.

"Wait…" Beckham said.

It was too late. The man kicked the kid in the face

with a sickening thud that echoed in the small cell. His head jerked back, nearly snapping his neck.

"Stop!" Beckham shouted as the guard went to throw a punch.

Presley hesitated, then jerked his chin back.

"Tell us where you got the acid," said the colonel.

The kid spat out a tooth onto the concrete floor. Blood drooled from his mouth. He grunted and mumbled something that sounded like a curse.

Presley shrugged. "Okay then."

The soldier walked around the boy and then swung low, hitting him in the ear so hard it split the top.

The boy wailed and then shouted, "You bastard!"

"You *will* talk," Presley said.

Beckham stepped forward and crouched down to meet the kid's gaze.

"Hey," he said. "Look at me."

The boy glanced up.

"Look, whatever the collaborators did to you, whatever they told you they would do, we can help you," Beckham said. "You just have to tell us where they are, and we'll make sure they never hurt you again."

"That's what you don't understand," he grunted. "They didn't hurt me. *He* did."

Beckham glanced back at Presley.

"I *wanted* to help them," the boy said, staring at Presley. "To kill people like this piece of shit."

"See, Captain, he's one of them and there's only one way to deal with the enemy," Presley said.

Beckham stood.

The boy spat more blood. "The brotherhood is right… The Variants are the future. Places like this are meant to burn."

"See what we're up against?" Presley asked.

He nodded at the guard again. This time Beckham closed his eyes as the guard went to work on the kid. Several smacks, wails, and cracks sounded.

Over the noise came a distant wailing sound, but the impact of knuckles on flesh and the kid's yells made it difficult to hear.

"Let me out," Beckham said. He looked at the boy one last time before leaving, his heart breaking at the sight of his bloody features. Collaborator or not, he was just a damn kid.

Beckham walked into the wing to the sound of footsteps. Over the click of boots came the same wail again.

A siren, he realized.

Two guards ran toward the open cell door.

"What the hell is going on?" Beckham demanded.

Neither answered.

"Colonel Presley," said a guard. "You better get to command. We have a problem."

"You want to know where I got the acid?" mumbled the boy.

The guards, colonel, and Beckham all looked in the cell.

The kid glanced up with a twisted, bloody smile.

"You're about to find out…" he said.

— 23 —

The sun had set around six o'clock, forming a golden glow across the horizon. Team Ghost prepared their night vision goggles as they approached their target.

Dohi had spent the better part of the afternoon and early evening leading them into position behind the trees overlooking the easternmost side of the National Accelerator Laboratory Campus. The long circuitous route ensured there were no Variant-eating hostiles lying in wait.

He had already stepped into one ambush. He wasn't about to walk into another.

But what if he was losing his touch?

Back at the freeway the Wolfhounds had been entrenching themselves to the west of the campus, setting up both a covering position and distraction. It was working.

Dohi had spotted dozens of enemy forces moving that way. If all went well, the cannibals would divert most of their forces to defend against the perceived assault.

From what Dohi had seen through, their enemy didn't have near enough to cover the wide swathe of campus, and Team Ghost was using that to their advantage.

Fitz crawled up to Dohi's side to peer over a fallen log.

"Anything?" Fitz whispered.

Dohi shook his head.

Another agonized scream wailed into the night. It

drifted over the buildings like an angered spirit. Dohi tried not to imagine what horrors Hopkins and the other Wolfhounds were enduring at the hands of these cannibals.

The breeze suddenly shifted and cold air swept over Dohi. With it came something else. The distinct smell of a bonfire.

"Anybody else smell that?" he whispered.

"Sure do, bro," Mendez said.

The others nodded.

Strangely, Dohi didn't see the flicker of a fire. The low hanging clouds and dark sky masked most of his ability to see any rising smoke. Maybe these people were using a wood-burning oven or something else to conceal the light of the flames.

But either way, if they had a fire going, then that meant they were cooking. Dohi had no illusions about what was on the menu tonight.

He rose to his feet, keeping low, and signaled for the others to follow. They drew further south, slinking through the trees, closer to the buildings. Dohi halted at a clearing near the parking lot filled with shipping containers.

"This is where my team was before," Fitz whispered to Dohi as he signaled the rest of the team to find cover.

Dohi spotted a flicker of light flaring across his NVGs from the shipping containers. He flipped his goggles and lifted a pair of binoculars to his eyes.

Sure enough, in one container with its doors opened, a fire burned with a spit roast above it. Pipes had been fitted to the top of the container to disperse the smoke, making it less likely to raise in one huge column.

A foot was slowly being rotated above the fire by a

child. Nearby, women and children gnawed on pieces of meat, ripping at the barbecued meal.

Dohi swept the binos over the containers until he saw a man chained against the wall inside one of them. A woman prodded at him with a knife as his face contorted in pain.

A face Dohi recognized.

"Hopkins," Dohi whispered.

Two other Wolfhounds were prisoners in the container. One was either passed out or dead. Probably the latter, Dohi thought when he saw his lower legs were gone. The stumps were blackened and cauterized.

The other prisoner writhed in his chains.

Dohi glassed the rest of the compound until he spotted two men marching between the containers. He used a hand to signal the contacts.

They waited a few more minutes in silence, scoping out the area. Dohi counted another four more men patrolling with rifles. Nothing that Team Ghost couldn't handle, especially if they were the ones doing the ambushing this time.

He continued to survey the cannibals, searching for signs of another trap. But no one appeared in the windows of the adjacent office buildings or in any of the other patches of trees surrounding the complex.

Then something caught Dohi's attention. Two of the patrolling soldiers met each other between the containers. They appeared to be talking in frantic voices, gesturing wildly.

The two men jogged to a squat, square building with antennae protruding out of its roof next to the shipping containers. More guards met them there, opened the door, and were swallowed by white light, leaving the shipping containers patrolled by only a pair of soldiers.

Another scream shot from the shipping container.

"Dohi, I want you and Mendez to take care of the remaining guards, then save Hopkins and the others," Fitz whispered. "The rest of you, follow me. We're going to take that communications post and see if we can destroy their jamming equipment."

Dohi and Mendez split off from the group. They descended from the grass-covered hill maintaining eyes on the two oblivious patrolling guards.

Once they reached the edge of the parking lot, the odor of burning flesh grew sickeningly strong. Dohi could hear laughing in the distance.

Time was running out for Hopkins and the others.

As soon as they were out from cover, Dohi and Mendez rushed toward the shipping containers. The two guards marched their way between the containers, still unaware of Team Ghost.

This time, the cannibal assholes would be the ones walking into an ambush.

Dohi let his rifle fall on its strap and pulled out his knife and hatchet. Mendez unsheathed his knife. They pressed themselves flat against the side of the shipping container.

The two guards passed in front of them. At Dohi's nod, the two operators lunged like wolves, pulling the men into their grasp. Dohi's knife bit into the first man's throat. He felt a bit of resistance as the blade cut through the cartilage and muscle. Then with a swing of his hatchet, he finished the job.

Hot blood poured from the slit in the dying soldier's throat and bubbled between his filed-down teeth. The man crumpled, clutching at his throat.

Mendez dropped his target.

As the two men bled out into growing pools, Dohi and Mendez dragged the bodies into one of the shipping containers that had been turned into a living space. Using a blanket, they covered the two dead soldiers.

Another scream echoed from the container holding the three Wolfhounds.

With the guards dispatched, Dohi hurried to the container with the hostages. The women and children cooking their meals started to stand, a few screeching at the sight of Dohi and Mendez. One dropped a plate of meat, and another backed into the rotating spit, knocking it over into the flames.

"Don't say a word or we'll blow off your fucking heads," Mendez said.

The people grew quiet, shrinking into each other and trembling with fear.

Dohi strode over to the other shipping container and aimed his rifle at a man and woman inside. One held a cleaver and the other a bone saw.

"Drop the tools," he said.

The man hesitated.

Dohi didn't. He dropped him with a suppressed shot to the head. The woman went to her knees, raising her hands, and Dohi knocked her out with a butt to the temple.

He entered the container and held up a hand to signal for Hopkins to be quiet. Tears rolled down his blood-soaked face as he hung suspended by cables. A dirty, blood-soiled cloth covered his ankle stump.

Hopkins groaned in pain.

"Quiet," Dohi said. "We're getting you out of here, brother."

Hopkins grunted something incomprehensible as Dohi undid the restraints.

When Dohi lowered the wounded man gently to the floor, he heard charging footsteps behind him. He swung his rifle up and prepared to fire.

But it was just Fitz.

"We cleared the comms post," he reported. "No luck on the radio jammers, but we did hear they're preparing to attack across the freeway."

"Good, the plan is working," Dohi said. "Now's our chance to find that equipment."

Rico moved in with Ace to help Dohi release the other two Wolfhounds. They had both passed out from the pain. When they were done, Dohi handed the cables that had been restraining the Wolfhounds to Ace.

"Use these to secure the people Mendez is guarding," he said. "Lock 'em in another container but keep the door open. I don't want them to suffocate."

Ace nodded and left with the chains.

Fitz bent down with Dohi to help bandage up the Wolfhounds. The man who had lost his legs was in bad shape, but the bleeding had stopped. Fitz whispered to him and took special care when dressing the cauterized wounds.

Dohi imagined doing so brought back some horrid memories of his own injuries from Iraq.

"No way we can move them," Fitz said. "We'll have to leave them here while we continue the search."

"No, please," Hopkins pleaded, his voice weak. "You can't leave us."

Dohi propped Hopkins into a sitting position against the wall of the shipping container. "Take it easy, man. We're not going to leave you for long."

Ace returned to the front of their shipping container.

"All the women and children are tied up and locked away," he said. "You guys, ready?"

"Don't fucking leave me," Hopkins begged. He grabbed Dohi's sleeve as he went to stand.

"We're not going far," Fitz said. "And your comrades are drawing out the rest of the enemy."

Rico suddenly looked to the sky.

"Do you hear that?" she said.

Dohi strained his ears to what sounded like the thump of helicopter blades in the distance. He pulled free from Hopkins and joined Fitz outside.

Ace stood with his rifle cradled.

"Did someone call in reinforcements?" he asked.

Dohi searched the sky with his binos. Seeing nothing, he pushed his NVGs up to scan the black.

"There," Mendez said. He pointed to the east where helicopters flew low on the skyline.

"They're heading toward the freeway," Dohi said.

"I didn't think reinforcements were coming," Rico said.

"They aren't," Fitz said. "Those aren't ours."

He raised his rifle and took off.

"Where you going?!" Dohi called out.

"To help the Wolfhounds," he said. "They're going to be slaughtered."

Dohi hesitated for a moment as realization sank in. The enemy must have called in reinforcements, and they were headed right for the Wolfhounds.

"Don't leave me," Hopkins whimpered.

Dohi helped him up, and the team followed Fitz away from the containers. They didn't get far before the choppers came in low over the campus, rotor wash blasting the trees as they hovered above the freeway.

Barking machine guns rang out. Gunfire flashed like miniature lightning strikes as tracer rounds lit up the night.

The choppers flew back and forth, pounding the ground with fire, but they weren't just firing at where Dohi judged the Wolfhounds' positions were in the forest. The tracer rounds were cutting into buildings *inside* the campus, presumably where the cannibals were posted.

What the hell… Dohi thought.

One of the Black Hawks launched a blistering volley of rockets into an office building, tossing huge balls of fire into the sky.

For those few seconds, the campus was illuminated like it was the middle of the day. Dohi had never felt so helpless. He crouched with Hopkins, setting him against the side of a container.

If they tried running now and attracted the choppers' attention, they would be shredded. All Team Ghost could do was shelter in the shipping containers and wait for the attack to finish.

The group took cover in the container with Hopkins and the Wolfhounds as the ground thumped from explosions. Dohi remained at the open door, peering out. He raised his rifle at a figure fleeing the battle. The man ran at a tilt, favoring his left leg, long skinny arms pumping.

Dohi moved his finger to the trigger, ready to fire.

But as the man drew closer, he recognized the frightened eyes and lanky body along with the AK-47 necklace dangling from his neck.

"Martin!" Dohi hissed.

The soldier didn't respond and kept running. Dohi let

his rifle drop on his sling and jumped out of the container, tackling Martin. He glanced up to make sure the choppers hadn't seen the man sprinting.

Then he dragged Martin into the shipping container. Writhing, Martin tried to escape, clearly in shock.

"Calm the fuck down," Dohi said.

Martin suddenly froze, staring at Dohi with frightened eyes.

"Where are the rest of the Wolfhounds?" Fitz asked.

Martin's gaze flitted to Fitz.

"Martin," Rico said. "Where's the rest of your team?"

"Where the hell were you?" Martin said, his voice shaking. "You guys left us there. The lieutenant… my brothers… all of them are dead."

***

The convoy had driven for what felt like hours and stopped a few times. Timothy couldn't see what they were doing with the black bag over his head, but he could listen. So far what he had heard allowed him to figure out two things about the collaborators.

The first was they definitely had multiple encampments in Variant territory that they used to refuel and get updates from guards posted there. Timothy had no idea how they still had access to fuel, but he guessed they were stealing it from outposts. It was as if they had developed their own network of resources just like the Allied States.

Another thing he had figured out was that Outpost Portland wasn't very close to the missile silo that the collaborators had turned into a base. Judging by the time that had passed, they were hundreds of miles away.

Rustling sounded in front of him, and his blindfold was suddenly ripped away. Timothy blinked, trying to get his eyes to adjust. Outside, the world was bathed in darkness except for where the moonlight illuminated the convoy.

He sat in the backseat of a dual cab pickup with Alfred on his left, and another prisoner scrunched against the passenger side door.

Timothy looked out the windows, trying to get a sense of where he was, but Nick snapped his fingers from the front seat of the truck to command his attention.

"Here," Nick said. He handed Timothy a water bottle. "Drink."

Holding up his handcuffed hands, Timothy took it and downed a quarter of the bottle.

"Easy," Nick said.

Timothy caught his breath, then drank more before handing the bottle back. Nick fished into a bag and pulled out a couple of sealed energy bars.

"Eat. You'll need your energy," Nick said.

Timothy took a bar, but ate slowly, trying to bide his time to see where they were headed. He couldn't see much in the darkness, especially without the lights on.

The driver wore night vision goggles to see the road.

Smart, he thought.

The convoy turned again, and Timothy got a better view of the truck ahead. Cages were secured to the back of the pickups. Inside each stood the silhouette of a muzzled mutated dog.

He took a bite of the energy bar and chewed for a while, but his appetite was gone. It wasn't hard to figure out what the collaborators had done to these poor beasts. Just like the bats that had been infected with VX-99, these mutant dogs had also been infected with a hybrid variant of the bioweapon.

Timothy forced himself to finish the energy bar, taking the nutrition not because his appetite had returned, but because Nick was right—he needed the energy.

But Nick didn't know what Timothy was going to use it for.

The convoy moved onto a gravel road, and the driver slowed.

Nick turned around with the black bag in hand.

"Bend down," he said.

Alfred took it and just as he was about to slip it over his head, Timothy spotted a sign for Highway 295. The road led directly to Outpost Portland.

Then Alfred secured the bag over Timothy's head and the world went dark again.

Timothy closed his eyes, using the time to think of his dad. He was going to make his old man proud.

The next time the convoy stopped and Timothy's bag was removed, the moon had risen higher into the sky.

It took a few blinks for Timothy's eyes to adjust where he could see enough to know they were in a large park. There was a forest to his left and buildings to the right.

He recognized one with a steeple that stood out under the crescent moon.

They were here.

Outpost Portland.

Armed soldiers popped out of the vehicles and spread out to set up a perimeter while Pete spoke to Alfred. They were on the outskirts of the city.

Nick opened the door and Timothy got out, standing next to the other prisoner, who still hadn't said a single word.

They waited near the truck while the other men unloaded vehicles and prepared their weapons. The growls of the caged dogs filled the night, rising over the low chatter of the soldiers.

Timothy shivered in the cool air. He was freezing even with the sweatshirt they had given him.

There was almost no light pollution over Outpost Portland. Only a few stubborn lights burned away the dark.

By this time tomorrow night, he had a bad feeling there wouldn't be a single light left. If the collaborators were successful, it would be a scrapyard of the dead, torn apart by the mutated dogs.

At least Tasha won't be there, he thought.

Using the weak glow of the moon, he counted thirty-one soldiers and twelve dogs. There were six trucks and the black muscle car with oversized tires.

Nick, Alfred, and Pete walked over to Timothy.

"All right, kid, listen up," Nick said. "We've got a job for you."

"I'm ready," Timothy said confidently.

"Once we attack, you're going in with us," Pete said. "We'll face a lot of resistance from the Army Rangers here. That's where you come in."

Alfred folded his arms over his chest, watching Timothy.

"All you got to do is tell them who you are when you get to the gates," Nick said with a wide grin.

"What do you mean tell them who I am?" Timothy asked.

Nick spat on the dirt. "Don't play me for a fool."

"I'm not," Timothy said. "Why do you think I could get us in?"

Reaching into his pocket, Nick pulled out a wallet.

"We found this on you when the Variants brought you to us," Nick said. He tossed the open wallet at Timothy's feet, exposing his ID that had his full name and address at Peaks Island.

"We know all about you, kid," Nick said. "We know who your dad was and who your friends are."

"Including your little sweetheart Tasha," Pete said, puckering his lips and making a kissing sound.

Timothy boiled with anger, his face warming. The ID, he understood. But Tasha? How in the hell did they know about her?

"You know the soldiers at the command post, too," Pete said. "We heard they even tried looking for you."

Timothy wanted to rip their throats out with his bare hands, but he managed to keep still.

"They're here," someone called.

The welcome distraction got the men to leave Timothy with the other prisoner. As they walked away, the man spoke for the first time.

"Do what they say or they will kill that Tasha girl," he mumbled. "They will kill everyone you love."

They already killed the most important person in the world to me, Timothy thought.

"There is only one way to stop them," the man said. "Destroy Mount Katahdin."

"What?"

Timothy kept his eyes forward, trying to act like he wasn't talking to the other prisoner.

"That's where their base is," he said. "Mount Katahdin. A top-secret nuclear silo that they took over after the war."

Several soldiers walked close by and the man fell silent.

"Get the dogs ready," one yelled.

Timothy tried to process what the prisoner had just told him. If true, he had the location of the collaborators. Something more valuable than their lives.

The dogs growled louder, snapping, saliva spraying from their snarling mouths until they were shocked into submission.

A driver got into the black car, and three men holding rocket launchers piled into the back of a nearby pickup. The two vehicles took off down the street and rounded a corner.

About half of the remaining men marched toward another street and fanned out, jogging toward the city and disappearing into the darkness. The rest of the men waited with the dogs.

"There." A soldier pointed to the tree line.

The other soldiers all watched silently.

Timothy didn't see anything at first. Then he heard the crunching joints, like snapping twigs and popping sucker lips. A pack of Variants bounded through the forest.

Not a pack…

In the moonlight, Timothy saw a small army of the beasts. Cold terror seeped through Timothy's bones, but the beasts ignored the humans. They flowed through the collaborators like a river between stones.

Only one stopped, crouching, and then leaping to the top of a pickup truck. It dented the hood, claws scratching the metal.

Yellow, reptilian eyes darted back and forth in its sunken skull. Bulging lips opened, exposing jagged teeth.

The beast rose, sinewy muscles flexing across its pale, veiny flesh.

A roar sounded from the trees and Timothy saw the

source—an Alpha Variant unlike any he had seen. Matted fur covered the monster, chunks of dirt crumbling off it.

It had huge ears that twitched when it let out a clicking sound. Unmoving, milky white eyes adorned an ugly vaguely ape-like face. Scything black claws curved out over its palms.

The creature on the hood looked over, screeching. Then it jumped to the dirt and bounded away with the other monsters.

"Stupid beast," Alfred muttered.

Pete pointed a remote at Timothy and then pushed the button. A shock brought Timothy to his knees, his body convulsing.

Alfred helped Timothy back up a moment later.

"That's on low," Pete said. "I turn this baby up to high and you'll cook from the inside out."

Timothy shivered, electricity still coursing through his body. He lost control of his muscles, and his bladder voided itself.

Pete put the remote away and then got into the same pickup.

"Let's go," Alfred said.

He grabbed Timothy and the other prisoner, tossing them back in the truck. Nick hopped in the front and looked back.

"Put up his hoodie to surround the collar," he said.

Alfred covered the shock collar while Timothy tried to calm his thumping heart. The rest of the collaborators moved out.

When they were gone, Nick looked at his watch. They waited for a few minutes, then drove onward, winding through abandoned streets. Timothy spotted the old fences that had once been the first layer of defenses protecting the outpost. They had collapsed in the road, and the metal crunched under the truck's tires.

Timothy saw collaborator soldiers marching on the roads and then a pickup and the muscle car hiding out in an open garage. The other teams appeared poised for the attack.

Seconds ticked by, each one getting them closer to their target. Timothy gave up trying to control his rapid breathing and racing heart. Adrenaline and fear had taken control.

Nick turned from the front seat when the pickup stopped outside a warehouse.

"The first standing gate is about a quarter of a mile away," he said. "Go there and get them to open the main gate."

"You try anything, and I'll make sure Tasha dies a very slow and brutal death while her sister watches," Pete said. "Or, you help us, and we'll spare most of the people here. Then you can be with your little girlfriend again."

Timothy nodded. They certainly knew more about him than they had initially let on.

But there were some things these men didn't know.

Tasha wasn't here anymore, he knew where their base was located, and he didn't have a damn thing to lose.

— 24 —

“Go back to your shelter,” Presley had said to Fischer in the command tent. “Let us handle the defenses.”

That had settled it for Fischer. He was sick of doing nothing and waiting for Team Ghost and the Orca soldiers to return with the Project Rolling Stone tech.

For centuries, older men had sent young men off to war. To fight their battles and die on the front lines. He used to be a coward like that, but not anymore. So long as he could wrangle cattle, he could fight for humanity.

So he had marched to the westernmost buildings on the border of Outpost Manchester, and climbed to the top of a twelve-story structure where he stood now with Tran and Chase. They had even managed to get two scoped M4s from the outpost’s armory.

If there was one thing they weren’t short of here, it was weapons.

Two Raven soldiers manned M134 Miniguns on pedestal mounts.

They didn’t seem to mind Fischer’s presence. He figured none of them would turn down an extra set of eyes or rifles tonight, and with Chase and Tran, he’d brought them three extra sets.

Sporadic gunshots echoed into the night, making one of the guards flinch. The bursts were followed by an animalistic scream.

Fischer’s nerves felt like icicles under his flesh as he

searched for the source of the screams beyond the razor wire fence stretching across the streets below.

The noises faded into silence again.

Command had ordered the sirens off after the regular folk were moved to their shelters. The quiet gave the guards a better opportunity to locate and identify the juveniles that had been spotted earlier, but it also made every scream all the more horrifying.

The silence now was eerie. It was the calm before the storm that he had experienced so many times before.

"You boys see anything?" Fischer asked.

One of the Raven soldiers, a bulky middle-aged man named Amir shook his head. "We're still getting mixed reports of juvies. Sometimes I hear two or three packs of no more than five."

"Other times, it's fifty juveniles, all flowing through the trees like ghosts," said Sherman. The blond bearded man grinned. "All I know is I got five thousand rounds a minute to unload on the fuckers."

"They took out two of our scout teams so far, and the rest are pulling back now," Amir said. "Should be heading our way soon."

Fischer glassed the swaying grass and shadows beneath the tree-covered hills again. Occasional spotlights from other rooftops swept over the darkness, dispersing the shadows momentarily.

For several long minutes, they waited in tense silence. Fischer nearly forgot to breathe, trying to remain quiet enough to hear a crunching footstep in the foliage.

"I've got movement," said Amir. He directed the M134 toward the tree line where a shape burst out.

Fischer nearly pulled the trigger, but then recognized the distinct shape of a human.

"That's one of ours!" Sherman said.

Two more people followed after the first. All three limped and stumbled forward. Only the lead soldier seemed to have any weapons. He kept a rifle trained on the woods as he backpedaled to cover the other scouts.

The men stumbled into the street. Spotlights hit their blood-soiled fatigues.

"Open the gate!" one of the men yelled. "They're right behind us!"

Amir grabbed both handholds of the mounted M134 and rotated it into position. "Get ready."

"Contact at three o'clock!" Chase shouted. He fired a burst at something Fischer only glimpsed.

A second later, he too saw movement in the forest. Fischer aimed at a misshapen skull with bulging eyes. Long ropy muscles coursed along the body of the beast stalking the retreating scouts.

Fischer squeezed the trigger as more of the creatures spilled out of the woods, charging after the injured Raven scouts.

Amir and Sherman opened up with the miniguns. The engines whined as the rotating barrels painted the wooded area with rounds. Branches and leaves rained down under the spray.

They eased up and Sherman somewhat calmly spoke into a radio. "Command, Tower 21. We have contacts. Six—no, ten, maybe more."

The two men went back to firing into the forest as the beasts emerged. Gunfire lanced from other rooftops into the incoming monsters. The heavy *whoomph* of a discharging explosive erupted into the night, accompanied by a ball of flames that lit up the landscape.

In that brief second, Fischer caught the explosion

reflecting off the eyes of dozens upon dozens of starving Variants streaming out of the woods. Wrinkled flesh-covered bodies with protruding bones.

Something within his guts sunk at that sight, dropped by the leaden weight of fear. Those were just the beasts he could see, and judging from the sound of gunfire, the monsters were attacking multiple positions.

The M134 rounds chiseled through the juveniles below, sprays of hot red mist exploded from their broken armor. That bought enough time for the three fleeing scouts to finally make it to a nearby gate.

But the soldier that had been manning the gate wasn't there when Fischer looked.

"Son of a bitch, Reynolds must have run! That pussy!" Sherman yelled. He turned to Fischer. "Get down there and open the gate while we cover you."

"You got it," Fischer replied.

The gunfire rattled above them and the sirens blared again as Fischer descended the stairs from the rooftop with Chase and Tran following.

They hit the ground and split up with Tran going to grab their truck while Chase and Fischer ran to the gate.

"Let us the fuck in!" yelled one of the soldiers on the other side. The man with the rifle fired into the distance. The third scout held onto the thick bars of the gate to support his body on his shredded leg.

Fischer unclasped the locks and yanked on a lever that released another locking mechanism. The gate raised up with a clank, pulled by an internal counterweight.

Chase helped the injured man through, blood weeping from long gashes along his right leg that revealed muscle and tendon. It was only sheer adrenaline and fear that had gotten the man this far. The last soldier was still firing, half his face melted away by Variant acid.

Fischer looked away and kept his rifle up to cover them. The growl of the truck engine announced Tran's arrival. As soon as the scouts were through, Fischer slammed the gate down and locked it again.

Tran hopped out from the cab and helped Chase load the men into the bed. Fischer stayed in the pickup bed to help.

"Go, Tran! Now!" Fischer shouted.

The truck peeled away, tires screaming.

Fischer secured a tourniquet on the man with the shredded leg, and Chase cut off parts of his jacket sleeves to use as bandages for the man with the acid-burned face.

Every bump and jostle of the truck made the men groan in pain. The remaining scout sat against the back of the pickup's cab, a thousand-yard stare masking his face.

"They're coming… and we can't stop them," he mumbled.

Fischer saw more clearly the wet sheen soaking through the man's fatigues. The darkness had helped conceal it before, but half the jacket was torn.

Tran called back through the open window of the cab. "We're almost there! Just hang on!"

"I need to look at your side," Fischer said. He slowly pulled the torn jacket back, trying not to gawk at exposed ribs. The man's abdomen had split open, revealing hints of glistening organs.

He tried to look down but Fischer covered the wound.

"You're going to be okay," he said. "We're almost back."

The soldier exhaled, and stared at the sky.

A convoy of armored vehicles screamed past them on their way to the border. Tran took a right, and sped toward the main command building.

"We need medics!" Chase yelled, standing up in the pickup bed. Men and women in scrubs were waiting outside the adjacent hospital with a group of soldiers listening to orders.

Among those people Fischer spotted a familiar face with a lump on his head.

Beckham. The 'retired' Delta Force Operator just couldn't stay out of the center of action, and for that, Fischer was more than grateful.

"Fischer!" Beckham yelled. "What the hell happened?"

"Juveniles." Fischer looked back to the soldier with the torn abdomen. The young man's grip on his hand had loosened, fingers slipping away.

The medics had climbed into the pickup and others waited at the bed to carry off the first two men, but by the time they got to the man with Fischer, he was gone.

Chase reached up and helped Fischer out of the back while they carried the lifeless body away on a stretcher. For a moment, Fischer stood there staring, hands covered in blood.

Distant gunfire filled the night, and the shouts of the medical staff and the cries of wounded joined the din.

He could almost hear his wife's voice in his head again. Just like back in the tunnels under his fields.

Get out! Get out! No one will survive tonight!

Fischer did his best to repress the storm of emotion coursing through him. He had to keep his wits.

"Captain," Fischer said. "What are you doing here?"

"To see what's going on… How bad is it out there?"

Fischer shook his head. "Not good."

They entered the command building together and then went up to the second floor to talk to Colonel Presley.

Inside what had been turned into a CIC, officers relayed reports streaming in from the outpost. Presley stood in front of his war table, eyes darting back and forth. They flitted to Fischer first.

"I told you to get to your damn shelter," Presley said. "And Captain…"

His words trailed off as an officer whispered something to him.

"God dammit," Presley said, upper lip curling. "Deploy all of the strike teams. We have to make sure not a single Variant gets in."

"What about the team guarding the mastermind?" asked an officer.

"*All* the strike teams," Presley repeated.

"No," Beckham said. "You can't do that."

The commander glared at Beckham.

"You aren't in charge here, Captain," Presley said. "I've got the situation under control, and frankly I'm getting sick of you interjecting."

"You also thought you had the collaborator problem under control."

"All due respect, but Captain Beckham's right," Fischer said. "If what I just saw is happening around the outpost, then things aren't even remotely under control. We're straight up shit's creek without a paddle."

Presley stiffened, raising his jaw proudly. He motioned to two guards standing at the doorway.

"Get these men out," Presley said. "They're no longer authorized to be inside any military facility."

Beckham looked at the two guards, then back to Presley.

"You're making a mistake, Colonel. We have to protect the science building at all costs!" he shouted.

Presley nodded at the guards who grabbed Beckham by his upper arms. He shook out of their grip, glaring at Presley.

"Don't make this harder than it has to be," Presley said.

Beckham marched out and Fischer followed him. The door shut behind them, sealing them outside with Tran and Chase.

"What the hell just happened?" Tran asked.

"I reckon the end of Manchester," Fischer said with a sigh.

Beckham was already walking away.

"Captain, where are you going?" Fischer called out.

"To protect my wife and make sure she finishes the job we came here for," he replied. "You're welcome to join me. I might need some help."

After what Fischer had just seen, he had no doubt that the Variants were coming for the mastermind now. He just hoped the scientists had enough time to finish their work before the beasts infiltrated the outpost.

He tapped his holstered .357 revolver.

If it turned out that the scientists didn't have enough time, he would buy some for them. Even if it meant he didn't make it out of here alive.

***

Kate could only hear the chirp and hum of laboratory equipment, but she knew from the reports, there was a battle going on at the border. She had expected as much, but knowing her family was out there put her on edge.

She wasn't the only one.

Guards nervously shuffled around the perimeter of the

massive space. They weren't just concerned about keeping the mastermind in here anymore—they were afraid of what might try to make its way in from the outside.

Several of the soldiers had already left to guard the passages and entrance to the lab. Only four remained in the space. The sergeant in charge assured the science team they were safe.

He stepped over to Kate. "Colonel Presley just told me he's handling the situation, and to keep working."

"What exactly is happening out there?" Carr said. "We deserve to know."

"Just a few isolated attacks," replied the sergeant.

"Get back to work," said another guard.

"Back off with those machine guns, and we will," Carr said firmly.

The sergeant motioned his men back, and Kate huddled with her staff.

"Should I try and get in touch with Reed?" Kate whispered. "He'll know what's really going on."

"They said they have it under control," Sean said.

Kate was surprised by the normally timid lab technician's response.

"We're almost done," Sammy said. "I just need a bit more time to focus."

"We need you here, Doctor Lovato," Carr said. "Trying to track down your husband will take far too long. Besides, he's probably in the shelter with your family, where they're safe."

He was right, and Kate trusted Beckham to show up if there was an issue. He had never let her down in the past.

"Let's finish the job," Kate said.

The other lab techs and engineers scattered

throughout the room back to their assigned stations. Kate went with Sammy, Sean, and Carr back to a computer terminal.

They were so close to finalizing the lexicon they would need to seamlessly communicate between the masterminds.

Kate did her best to concentrate on work and remind herself that Beckham and Horn were looking after the kids, but it was almost impossible.

Sweat dripped down Sammy's forehead behind her plastic mask.

"Okay, my natural language algorithm is in sync with the collaborators' software," she said. "We really just need to run through a few more commands, and then I think we can have the algorithm figured out."

As if in answer, an animalistic howl rumbled from the abomination.

"There isn't a word that this thing has uttered now that I haven't been able to decipher," Sammy said. "I'm operating at one-hundred percent translation success now."

"Good," Kate said. She peered into the bioreactor with the red webbing that was transmitting their signals from Sammy's computer to the tendrils attached to the mastermind.

"What's the current success rate for communicating back?" Carr asked, holding up a tablet to document the data.

"About eighty percent of my commands are being understood successfully," Sammy replied. "The simpler stuff is no problem. More complicated inputs are proving difficult."

"Give me an example."

"Complex information about enemy movements. Sometimes it believes me, sometimes it realizes we're actually the enemy. I'm not quite sure what the difference is between those instances, but with a little more time—"

The mastermind moved again, rattling its chains. The four soldiers paced, watching the beast.

"It's acting like it knows what's happening outside," Kate said.

"How?" Carr asked. "The beast isn't connected to the Variant network, and no way this thing has ESP."

"It can't know," Sean said, nervously eying the IV lines with the sedatives. "It's just agitated."

Kate narrowed her brows at the uncharacteristically overconfident young technician, but then went back to examining the shackled beast. Huge muscled arms dangled slackly against its bulbous sides. The monster's eyes were still half-closed beneath the folds of pink flesh covering its ugly head.

"Just keep the thing under control, okay, Sean?" Kate asked.

Sean glanced between her and the monster.

"We're running out of time," Carr reminded everyone.

Kate checked the attachments on the micro-electronic array attached to the bioreactor. "Re-check everything. Make sure nothing is interfering with Sammy's work."

"And the sedatives?" Sean asked. "Do you think they're holding things back?"

Sammy looked up at him from her computer. "Honestly, maybe. If the thing's brain isn't functioning at full capacity, that might be an issue."

Kate didn't like the idea of pulling back on the sedatives and was surprised Sean suggested it, but they all wanted to finish. Anything to expedite their research now might be worth the risk.

"If you think it can help, then do it," Kate said.

Sean nodded, adjusting the dials on the IV drip.

"What are you doing?" asked a guard.

Kate explained, and the men moved closer, their weapons cradled.

"Please, back up," Sean said as they circled around. "I need some room."

Kate turned her attention back to Sammy's monitor as the computer engineer typed out a few more queries to the mastermind. It took several minutes, but sure enough, the responses started to come back slightly faster, and clearer.

"Ask if it has identified any enemy contacts in its location," Kate said.

Sammy typed in the request.

"I am uncertain of my current whereabouts," said the mastermind's computerized reply that came over the speakers. The monster's eyelids suddenly flipped open and swept the room. "Unfamiliar contacts are holding me prisoner. Hostiles. Ten of them."

Sammy looked up at Kate with a proud grin.

"Now, let's see if this thing really believes we're its master or not," Kate said.

"Those contacts you see are your allies," Sammy typed.

The chains holding the mastermind rustled as it rotated slightly.

"Some are allies, true," came the reply over the computer screen.

"See?" Sammy said, her grin widening.

Kate was too nervous to smile. Her family was out there, in the middle of an attack, and she had no idea what was happening behind the lab walls.

The sound of distant gunfire reverberated, but how was that possible?

The lab was basically soundproof. It had to be her ears playing tricks on her. They would know if there were hostiles in the building.

Kate returned her attention to Sammy. The young technician stared at the computer screen, her smile gone.

"Something isn't right." She tapped at the keyboard. "It just said the connection has been terminated."

The chains rattled again, the clank echoing. The soldiers closed in.

Sean walked over to the sealed door and used his keycard to open it. Before Kate could ask him what he was doing, the door opened, and another soldier walked in.

He handed Sean a rifle. Both men aimed their weapons at the other guards. None of the four soldiers even had a chance to raise their rifles before they crumpled under a spray of automatic bullets.

The gunfire echoed in the space, nearly deafening to Kate. Sammy screamed, and the other techs darted for cover. Carr was the only one that remained standing by Kate.

"What are you doing!" he yelled at Sean.

Sean swung the rifle at Carr. "Shut the fuck up, and don't move."

The soldier that Sean had let in hurried toward the shackles holding the mastermind in place.

"No," Kate said. "You can't do this."

Sean laughed. "You're more naïve than I thought, Kate Lovato."

"Sean, please," Sammy begged. "It's not too late to

stop whatever it is you're doing."

"Shut up, you dumb bitch," Sean said, angling the weapon at her.

The soldier used a key to unlock the first of the shackles on the mastermind.

"Neither of you get it, do you?" Sean said, his voice booming. "You used science to try and save us, but all you did was make them stronger."

He angled his weapon at Kate. "You created the Variants. The new gods."

"That's not true," said Sammy.

"I said shut your mouth!" Sean said.

Kate reached out to the technician just as Sean fired. Sammy slumped to the ground, holding her stomach.

"NO!" Kate shouted. She glared at Sean, nerves firing with anger. "You *monster*."

"Call me what you want, but you created the real monsters." Sean shrugged. Then he backpedaled to the mastermind, holding a gun on them.

Carr and Kate bent down next to Sammy.

"What do we do?" he whispered.

"I don't know," Kate said.

She put pressure on Sammy's wound, the only thing she could do.

The other technicians and engineers hid behind their stations, trembling. They could all storm Sean and the soldier but she wasn't sure they could get there without all being killed.

Kate knew there was no way they could talk Sean and his partner out of what they were doing. The only way to stop them was to fight or hope the rest of the guards got here in time. She thought back to the gunfire she heard earlier.

It must have been real after all.

The man with Sean had killed the other guards. There probably weren't any other men left out there.

"We have to do something," Carr said. He stood and faced Sean again. But before he could even open his mouth Sean shot him through his face.

He hit the ground next to Kate, his eyes still open.

— 25 —

Beckham stopped at Outpost Manchester's civilian shelter on his way to the lab. People clustered around, asking questions about what was happening outside. He waved them off and pushed through the crowd until he found Horn trying to keep the kids calm.

"Dad!" Javier shouted. "Please don't leave again."

"Sorry, buddy," Beckham said. "I promise everything's going to be okay."

"So you'll stay?"

Beckham hesitated, but his son was tough. He would understand. "I've got to go check on your mom. Once she finishes her work, we're all going to leave this place."

"Good," Tasha said.

"Can't wait," Jenny said with a snort.

Once the kids returned to their cots and chairs, Beckham pulled Horn aside. He found a corner they could whisper in without the kids overhearing.

"How bad is it out there?" Horn asked.

"We got hit by a bunch of rogue juveniles. Seems like they're really pressing the defenses now, and Presley kicked me out of the command building."

"That son of a bitch weasel. I had a bad feeling about him."

Beckham thought back to the kid collaborator in the jail. He had a feeling there were more of them out there, waiting to strike.

"I've got good reason to believe this is going to get a lot worse," Beckham said. "We have to get out of here."

"Jesus."

"President Ringgold will send an evac as soon as we call for it," Beckham said. "If things go south, and I can't get back here, you take the kids and the dogs to the tarmac, okay? Leave without me if you have to."

"Screw that," Horn said. "We ain't going anywhere without you."

Horn had a look in his eye that Beckham recognized. Like he wanted to roll outside with the M249 and mow everything down.

"The kids, Big Horn. You've got to stay with them and stay calm."

Horn clenched his jaw, but nodded, finally relenting. "Fine. What are you going to do?"

"I'm going to the lab to make sure Kate's good. She told me they were almost done."

"Okay," Horn said. He put a hand on Beckham's shoulder. "Be careful, boss."

"You, too."

Beckham said goodbye to the kids and dogs before returning to the street where Fischer waited with his men. The sound of distant gunfire rattled in the night, but it was more sporadic now.

"Everyone okay?" Fischer asked.

"For now." Beckham jerked his chin. "Let's go."

They set off with Tran and Chase down the empty road. Even the routine patrols had been called off to other areas.

When Beckham reached the lab building, it wasn't guarded by a single vehicle or soldier. He wanted to march back to the command post and knock Presley out.

Chase halted on the sidewalk. "They didn't even leave a single damn guard outside?"

"That stupid son of a gun," Fischer said. "What in Sam Hill was he thinking?"

"He's lost control, and shits about to hit the fan," Beckham said. "Come on. Let's find a way in."

They tried the front entrance, but it was locked. Knocking didn't help. Beckham cupped his hands over his eyes to peer through the windows in the door. No one stood guard inside either.

He circled around the building and found a side door, but it too was locked and no one answered his knocks.

"I know Presley's acting like a dumbass, but it's still strange *no one* is in there, right?" Chase asked.

"Sure as hell seems strange to me," Tran said.

"Think you can pick it?" Fischer asked him.

"If by pick you mean shoot, sure," Beckham said. He motioned for them to get back. Then he aimed his M4 and fired at the lock. The well-placed round did the trick, and he kicked the door open.

Tran went in first, keeping his rifle angled at the ground, just in case there were friendlies inside. He stopped right in the entrance.

"Why are the lights off?" he asked.

Beckham moved inside. "Something's not right."

Shouldering his rifle, he took the lead. Emergency lights glowed in the nook of the ceilings, providing just enough light to guide him down the hallway.

Every step he took, his pulse raced faster.

God, even Presley wasn't actually bullheaded enough

to leave this place completely unguarded. Something was definitely wrong.

Very wrong.

Please be okay, Kate.

He stopped at an intersection and held up his prosthetic hand. Then he checked the leftward hallway. Seeing it was clear, he looked to the right.

His stomach flipped. Two bodies lay crumpled. Dark blood pooled over the tiled floor, but he didn't see any sign of gashes or torn flesh to indicate Variants were inside.

"Collaborators already got here," he whispered.

Fischer came up next to him to have a look.

"On me," Beckham whispered. "Tran, watch our six. We've got at least one hostile shooter."

Without hesitation, Beckham led the way, his rifle up and finger hovering over the trigger. The lab entrance was at the end of the passage, not far from where the soldiers had fallen.

He kept low, hugging the wall, barrel aimed at the door to the lab. When he reached the bodies, he halted to examine them.

The men had both been shot in the back. They probably never saw the attack coming. One of their weapons was gone, which told Beckham the shooter had probably taken it to give to someone else.

Judging by the looks of things, the shooter had taken the extra weapon straight to the lab.

Beckham swallowed hard and kept walking. A tremor shook the ground as he passed the dead Raven guards. He almost stopped, but pressed on to the windows.

As a defense mechanism against any potential mastermind escapes, the glass to the lab had been made bulletproof. That ruined any plans of shooting the hostiles from behind. They had to get inside if they wanted to take these assholes down.

He crouched under those windows as he made his way to the door.

A roar from the monster confirmed Beckham was going to have more than men with guns to worry about.

He held his breath and got up to scan the room. A cluster of scientists huddled behind lab benches, but he didn't see Kate.

Two men stood near the mastermind, one in a white lab coverall. The man pointed a rifle at another person in the lab. The other gunman was dressed in fatigues and appeared to be unlocking the shackles on the beast.

Shit, shit, shit.

Beckham ducked down before either collaborator could spot him. The creature roared inside the lab again. Fischer crouched next to Beckham.

"What do we do, Captain?" he asked.

"Hold here." Beckham risked another glance to search for Kate. His heart thumped when he saw her. The floor around her was covered in blood from two fallen scientists. She was crouched beside the bodies, crimson staining her white coveralls.

Beckham whispered what he saw to Fischer, Tran, and Chase.

They needed to get in there. Fast. He crawled back to the guards' bodies to search for a lab key card. He found two. He handed one to Fischer.

"There is another entrance on the other side of the lab," Beckham said quietly to Fischer. "You go there with Chase. Tran, you're with me."

Another guttural roar sounded followed by the clanking of chains.

They were running out of time.

Beckham held his position to give Fischer and Chase time to get to the other entrance. The wait was agonizing. Every passing second the beast grew louder and more enraged.

"You take this," Beckham said. He handed the keycard to Tran. "Open the door on my mark. I'll go in first."

A nod from Tran.

"Our targets are at the north side, near the beast. You shoot them, but don't shoot the creature unless I tell you, understood?"

"You got it, Captain."

Beckham waited another beat, then peeked to confirm the gunmen hadn't moved. They were still in the same spot. He glimpsed a blur of motion behind the other door across the lab. Fischer and Chase must have been in place.

"Go time," he said.

Tran moved into position, and with a nod, Beckham gave him the order. He flashed the keycard over the door, and it slid open.

Beckham brought up his rifle, aimed, and fired a shot into the scientist's neck and then two to his chest. Fischer and Chase opened fire across the lab. Their shots lanced into the soldier working on the mastermind's locks. Bullets peppered his body as he tried to rise to his feet with his rifle.

The beast screeched and stomped the floor, a miniature quake vibrating through the floor. Fischer and Chase turned their rifles on the monster, but a scream rang out behind them.

"Don't shoot it!" Kate yelled, streaks of blood over her face. "We haven't finished our work!"

"Get that thing secured!" Beckham shouted.

Tran, Chase, and Fischer approached the loosened shackles cautiously as the monster swiped at them with a free hand.

Fischer fired, painting the clawed hand with bullets. The creature shrieked in pain and lashed out at the final chain holding it in place.

"I said don't shoot!" Kate shouted.

Fischer glanced over with a crazed look. "We have to disable those limbs if you want us to secure the damn thing!"

"Okay, but don't kill it," Kate said.

Beckham hurried over to her, looking between her and the two shot scientists. He recognized the first. It was Carr.

The woman was still alive. She had one hand pressed down over a red spot on her white bunny suit, and her eyes blinked lethargically, her gaze unfocused.

"We need to get her to the hospital," Kate said. "Ron, Leslie, get over here!"

Two technicians bolted over from their hiding position and bent down next to the injured woman while Beckham embraced Kate.

"Are you okay?" Beckham asked.

"The blood's not mine."

He looked her up and down just to be sure. There was no time for hugs or to talk about what happened. "We have to get out of here, Kate. The outpost's under attack. Variants are on their way."

"We're almost done with our work." Kate used the back of her gloved hand to wipe some of the blood from her face. "We're so close. We really can't leave yet. Too many people have already died for this research. It can't be in vain."

Tran, Chase, and Fischer circled the monster, firing at the limbs with short bursts. Blood wept from the dozens of inflicted wounds, its claws starting to twitch uselessly. The enraged creature screeched with each searing round.

Two more shots crippled its knee, and the creature finally collapsed to one leg. That gave the men a chance to yank the chains back in place and secure them to the scaffolds.

Beckham waved Fischer over.

"Have your men hold sentry in the halls," Beckham said. "We have to buy Kate and her team time to finish their work."

"How long is this going to take?" Fischer asked.

"Not long," Kate said. "But I need Sammy."

The other technicians were patching the injured computer scientist up, but Beckham could tell she was in bad shape. She had taken a bullet to the gut. One of the most painful—and potentially deadly—places to be shot. If her guts had been pierced, the resulting bleeding and infection would be devastating.

"I can work," Sammy croaked. "Just help me up."

They got her into a chair after finishing the bandages.

Her face continued to lose color as she tapped at the computer. "We… we about had my algorithm tuned." She looked over at the monster. "Just give me… give me five minutes with this bastard."

"Are you sure you can do this?" Kate asked.

"I *have* to do this." Sammy grimaced. "The thing is agitated which means we're going to get better results… There's no better testing ground for my language processing software."

Beckham kept his rifle up while the injured scientist finetuned her code with repeated queries and answers from the monster. He looked out at the lab's doors with every passing minute, waiting for the eruption of more gunshots.

Fischer joined him there and they spoke quietly while they waited.

Finally, maybe fifteen minutes later, Sammy slowly pushed back from her computer. The bandage around her abdomen had already bled through.

"Done," she said.

"Great work," Kate said. She helped Sammy to her feet.

"We have to call in an evac now, get this data somewhere safe," Beckham said.

She motioned at a phone on the wall. "Ron, see if you can get command on the line."

Kate bent down next to Carr and put a hand on his back.

"We finished the job," she whispered. Then she bowed her head. "I'm sorry you couldn't be here to see it."

"I can't get a signal," Ron said from the phone.

"I've got a better idea," Fischer said, called from the door he was guarding. "I've already got a private plane on the tarmac. We can take it anywhere you want to go."

"Anywhere is better than this place," Beckham said. "Get ready, everyone, we move out in five minutes."

He looked at the beast as he waited for the science team to gather up their gear and move Sammy.

Countless soldiers and multiple scientists had already sacrificed their lives for the intel they had gotten from this abomination, but something told him this was far from over.

***

Timothy hunched behind a shed outside the border of Outpost Portland, trying to find the courage to fight his handlers.

Me or them… he thought.

From his vantage, Timothy saw a blockaded road with a machine gun nest and patrolling guards. Snipers had to be on the adjacent rooftop watching the walled campus.

A second gate blocked off another road with a few guards just beyond it.

The buzz of his collar hit his ears before he felt the pain. The jolt nearly dropped him to his knees. Scorching pain flamed across his neck. When it passed, he took in a deep breath, tears brimming in his eyes.

Time to move.

The collaborators were watching him and if he didn't get going, they would shock him again.

Keeping his hoodie cinched above his neck, he walked out from behind the shed and started off down the road, his hands by his side. He made it three strides before a spotlight hit him.

"Contact!" shouted a soldier.

Timothy raised his hands in the air.

"Get on the ground!" yelled another guard. "And don't fucking move!"

He dropped to his knees. "It's me, Timothy Temper! I live here!"

Footsteps echoed down the street. He blinked to see through the intense light. Two soldiers made their way toward him.

"I live on Peaks Island," Timothy said as calmly as he could.

"All the way on the ground!" shouted one of the soldiers over Timothy's explanation. "Hands behind your head."

Timothy slowly put his hands on his head and went down to his belly.

"Keep your head—" one of them yelled.

Before the soldier could finish, his head flew back from a bullet that blew out the back of his skull. Two rounds hit the other in the chest. He slumped next to Timothy, still alive, gasping for air.

Screeching tires tore down the road. The black muscle car turned a corner. A pickup followed, and a rocket streaked from the bed.

Timothy rolled off the street and into the ditch as the grenade slammed against a mound of sandbags. Another projectile hit two concrete barriers blocking the gate. The explosions shook the ground, and the gate collapsed, clanging against the pavement.

He crawled back up as the muscle car sped toward the flames. It thumped over the fallen gate, and the passenger tossed something out the window. Several soldiers at the secondary checkpoint vanished behind a fiery blast.

The car raced around the wreckage followed by the pickup truck, their tires squealing.

Timothy rose to a kneel. The dual cab pickup that Pete drove pulled up. Alfred jumped out and aimed his rifle down the street. Then he grabbed Timothy.

"Get in," he said, opening the back door.

The other prisoner was gone. Timothy was afraid to ask what had happened to the man who had told him the location of the collaborators' base.

Pete drove toward the sound of gunfire and sparkling muzzle flashes from the rooftops deeper within the outpost.

The high-pitched shriek of a Variant pierced the chaotic noise.

Several of the beasts leapt from the shadows and took to the sides of buildings, scaling them like demonic lizards. Near the monsters, a patch of grass and soil gave way. A hulking monstrosity pushed itself from the crumbling soil, and Timothy nearly gasped at the abomination with wide, bat-like ears and a scrunched face. Fangs hung from its mouth.

It raised its muscled arms, and long tendrils along its back stood straight like the spikes on a porcupine. Red vines clung to parts of the creature's body as it hoisted itself from the earth.

A high-pitched clicking noise sounded and the other Variants burst from the ground where the monster had tunneled, each squirming past the red vines.

Collaborators, Alphas, and all their thralls were descending on Portland.

Timothy couldn't save the outpost, but he could still get the enemy's location to soldiers here.

Nick drove down a side street littered with twisted and torched bodies. The pickup thumped over one with a sickening crunch.

As the truck sped closer to the university campus, an army of Variants bounded along the roads to either side of them. Another Alpha exploded from the ground, rallying the smaller monsters and charging toward the heart of the garrisoned outpost.

"You're going to let the beasts kill them all?" Timothy asked. "You told me if I got you in, you would spare them."

Nick and Pete exchanged a glance, but didn't reply.

"Those that respect the New Gods *will* be spared," Alfred said quietly. "But first the blood of the heretics must be spilled."

Explosions bloomed ahead.

Timothy tried to think of a plan to stop the madness, but the faster they raced into the outpost, the more muddled his mind became. If the attack continued at this rate, Timothy wouldn't have anyone to tell about the base.

"It's almost over," Pete said with a crooked grin. "Soon we'll own this outpost, and our thralls will feast."

The truck stopped at the next intersection with a destroyed checkpoint.

Timothy could see the campus now.

"This is the spot," Pete said. "The others should be here soon."

Fiery blasts and gunfire cut through the night while they waited. It wasn't long until the trucks with the dogs arrived. The guards let the dogs out of their cages, and the abominations took off down the main road into campus.

Alfred opened the truck's door, gesturing for Timothy to get out. Agonized screams wailed between the staccato sound of gunshots and the chorus of mutant hounds.

They set off toward the battle with six other armed collaborators.

Two pickup trucks followed the group as they made their way toward the dormitories.

More shrieks split the air.

As they got closer, Timothy wanted to close his eyes when he saw the scattered bodies. The collaborators were proud of the macabre scene. They watched in silence, their features stoic.

Timothy held back the bile in his throat.

Variants and mutated dogs fed on people who had been caught during their retreat.

An Alpha tore one of the bodies in half and sucked at the corpse's insides. Nearly a dozen people fled in that direction from a side road, oblivious to threats waiting.

He wanted to scream and warn them, but it wouldn't matter.

In the distance, Timothy spotted more people climbing out of windows to escape Variants that had made it into the shelters. A woman jumped from the second floor, only to be torn apart by a pack of prowling beasts outside the building.

A man with a pistol fired at four Variants surrounding him and two women in the parking lot. They backed toward a parked car. A monstrous dog leaped around the bumper and tackled the man. Its teeth tore into his neck, pulling out sinew as the two women screamed in terror.

Pete held a walkie-talkie up to his ear.

Sniper rifles cracked in the distance. The heads of several Variants burst in sprays of bloody mist. One of the Alphas turned in the direction of the gunfire. Bullets plunged through its body, but still it advanced, roaring and gathering a cadre of smaller monsters.

The Rangers were still in this fight.

There might yet be hope to turn the slaughter around.

"They're retreating to the command post." Pete pointed the remote at Timothy. "You're up. The faster you do this, the faster we call off the beasts."

Timothy nodded and set off down the road, doing his best to ignore the mangled and shredded bodies littering his path. He turned into a parking lot. If he remembered correctly, this one led to another where more dormitories were. Command was located between those buildings.

Several Variants and hounds sprinted toward the increasingly sporadic sounds of gunfire. Two diseased dogs ripped apart dead bodies, spilling the organs of carcasses across the asphalt. A few gaunt Variants fought for scraps nearby, shoveling mangled flesh into their mouths.

Why weren't they attacking him?

A bony beast straddling a dead man glanced up at Timothy as he neared the tree line separating the parking lots. Intestines hung from its maw like noodles. But it didn't seem interested in him. Nor did the other creatures.

They simply looked at him and then looked away. He didn't hear the pop of the creature's collar zapping him. No way the beast *knew* that he was one of their allies yet, right?

It struck him then. The chip that Nick had implanted in his neck. That had to be it. These beasts probably had them too, and they were all connected somehow.

Timothy started searching for a weapon as he walked. Several soldiers had fallen in the trees. He spotted a rifle and ran over, fully expecting a zap from his collar.

But none came.

He was out of sight from the collaborators now. They would catch up to him again soon, but for now, he was free.

He picked up the rifle and grabbed another magazine off the vest of a dead soldier. Then he took a knife and slipped it in his waistband. With the blade, he could excise the chip.

That also probably meant the creatures would turn on him if he no longer had it implanted in himself. He stood, armed for the first time since his captivity, conflicted.

Part of him wanted to go back and mow down Nick, Pete, and Alfred. But he also knew there was something more important at stake than revenge. The intel he had about Mount Katahdin, if true, could save other outposts from Portland's fate.

That was his mission now.

He took off for the command post, keeping low until he spotted the building.

Several Army Rangers fired rifles from the rooftop at the monsters surrounding it. He spotted more guns in the windows.

He slunk past the Variants closing in on the building, coming so close to the monsters he could smell their sour flesh and sweat.

They continued to ignore him, and Timothy made his way to a clearing. He thought about calling up to the Rangers, telling them who he was. They probably wouldn't be able to hear him and that might only get him shot in all the chaos.

Two Variants threw themselves at the reinforced door ahead. Another began scaling the wall toward the roof.

Gritting his teeth, Timothy took aim and fired. Bullets stitched up the side of the climbing beast. The other two at the door turned toward Timothy.

They too jerked and collapsed as he unloaded the rest of his first magazine into their bony bodies. Then he rushed between their corpses and started pounding on the door.

"Please, let me in!" he yelled.

He looked over his shoulder for the collaborators. If they were watching now, maybe they would think this was all part of his ploy to get them into the command post.

But even if the collaborators were convinced, six Variants prowling along the edges of the clearing didn't seem to be.

One took a step forward, dropping to all fours.

"Please, help! I'm Timothy Temper! Jake Temper's son!"

He slammed his fist against the door.

The pack of Variants moved in closer. More gunfire rang out from the rooftops. Screams erupted from the parking lot where the monsters feasted.

Timothy levered his hand back, ready to pound again. One Variants twitched its head as it looked between him and the dead monsters at his feet. It looked as if it was figuring out whether he was an ally or traitor.

Then the door flung open.

"Get in, kid!" someone said, grabbing his shoulder.

The door slammed shut behind him, and he was suddenly assaulted with a chaotic din. Down the halls people ran shouting orders. He saw one soldier covered in blood, gashes along both of his cheeks. Somehow the man was standing, but there were many others slumped against the walls. Several looked dead, with bullet wounds or terrible lacerations from Variants covering their bodies.

People in civilian clothes were among the dead and dying. Their wails and pleas for help echoed in the hall.

Timothy staggered forward, trying to look for someone in charge. Lieutenant Niven or Sergeant

Ruckley. Someone who he could tell about Mount Katahdin.

He rounded a corner, the tile slick with blood. The trail led up a stairwell to the higher levels where the boom of gunfire echoed against the walls. A door suddenly opened behind him and screaming echoed deeper in the building.

Turning, he saw two soldiers carrying wounded inside. People pushed and shoved their way into the passage. A female and male soldier came inside last, both carrying children.

He recognized the woman. "Sergeant Ruck—"

A zap from his collar made him drop his rifle.

Another shock burned into his neck. He gritted his teeth, gripping the collar. The new group of Rangers and civilians made their way toward him. He reached up toward them, but they all passed him by.

"Ruckley!" Timothy wailed.

She suddenly stopped, handing the child off to another soldier. Then she made her way over to him. A soiled bandage was wrapped around her right arm and blood streaked down her chest.

"Sergeant," he said. "I have information that…"

A third shock dropped him to the ground.

Timothy's eyes teared up as he battled the pain. The collaborators wanted him to open the door, let them in. This was their reminder.

"Mount… Mount Katahdin," he managed.

"Slow down, kid, where are you hurt?" She reached down and saw his collar, rearing back at the sight.

She screamed for back up while pulling out her pistol and aiming it at his head. Several soldiers ran over, rifles pointed down at him.

Outside, the creatures' howls came in during the respite of gunfire.

Another electric shock coursed through Timothy's body. Ruckley bent over him with her pistol.

"Mount Katahdin," Timothy mumbled. "That's where the collaborators are… that's where their base is."

"Hey, isn't that Jake Temper's son," someone said.

Ruckley looked over her shoulder, then back to Timothy. She moved her gun away from his head.

"Jets are inbound, Sergeant!" shouted a deep voice. "Everyone, find cover!"

"Get him in the shelter," Ruckley said.

Timothy felt people lifting him up. They carried him down the hall, and then down into a basement filled with frightened civilians. He was put up against a wall as another shock coursed through his body.

His vision blurred.

"Timothy, you still with me?" Ruckley asked.

He tried to nod but his muscles were locked rigid, and the pain was too much. Tears streamed over his eyes.

"Incoming!" shouted a voice.

Timothy thought he heard jet engines. He definitely heard the explosions and then felt the floor rumbling from impacts.

Cries. Maybe triumphant. Maybe out of pain.

The electric shocks came again.

Over his own agony, he suddenly focused on one thing—the image of Pete, Nick, Alfred and the other collaborators burning on the ground with their thralls.

Dust rained from the ceiling and the lights winked off, casting darkness over the shelter. The screams that followed were far from triumphant. These were pained wails of agony.

They faded away, but he heard one last thing before he passed out—the shriek of a monster.

— 26 —

Fitz crouched inside the shipping container with Team Ghost and the injured Wolfhounds that had nearly been butchered alive. The gunfire around the National Accelerator Laboratory had grown more sporadic.

But like vultures hovering over carrion, Black Hawks circled the base, their rotors beating the air with a vicious growl. From Fitz's observations, he noticed the birds rotate out, presumably to stay fueled while maintaining eyes in the sky over the base.

It made no sense to Fitz.

Black Hawks were rare for the military, and how the hell did they have fuel?

The collaborators and Variants must have been more organized than command had realized out here.

He shook those concerns aside to focus. Those questions would have to be answered later. For now, he had to keep his team alive.

If he had kept track of the choppers accurately, there were only two now. The third had departed a few minutes earlier. That meant whoever these people were, they had a place to refuel in range.

Fitz risked peering out the cracked-open door. Using his night vision goggles, he spotted a chopper circling nearby, machine guns trained on the ground. He turned back to Rico and Ace who were crouched next to Martin.

The Wolfhound still seethed in anger from the massacre he'd witnessed, his jaw clenched.

Mendez and Dohi were in the back of the container taking care of Hopkins and the other two injured Wolfhounds. The man with the missing legs had woken and groaned in pain. Dohi bent down to keep him quiet.

"We can't stay here forever," Rico said. "What's the plan, Fitz?"

Fitz knew when she used his real name she was worried.

He was too.

The radios were jammed, they didn't have the Rolling Stone tech, and with the Wolfhounds mostly dead and a new enemy out there, he wasn't sure what the right move was.

"Your last plan got all my brothers killed," Martin muttered.

"This ain't our fault, amigo, and you're starting to really piss me off," Mendez said.

"Cool it," Fitz said to Mendez. Then he looked at Martin. "You want to blame us, fine, but if you want to survive, you got to work *with* us."

"So what's your brilliant plan then?" Martin asked.

"Shoot those choppers down," Mendez said. "I could plug 'em with a couple good shots."

"Don't think so," Ace said. "Unless you got something more than that M4."

"Look we still don't even know who they are," Rico said. "We don't know what they've got in store for us."

A chopper boomed overhead, flying in low as its spotlights traced over the ground. The light flashed inside the shipping container door.

"My guess is collaborators," Dohi said. "Someone

compromised our mission."

"I have a bad feeling you're right," Fitz said.

Rico shook her head, like she didn't believe it. "You ever seen collaborators with Black Hawks? Not me… Hell, the Allied States is low on those birds."

Fitz started to reply, but then he heard the crash of metal.

The cannibals they had imprisoned in another shipping container had escaped.

He pushed open the door a little wider and saw the cannibals streaming toward a thicket of trees to the southeast.

The two Black Hawks trained their spotlights on the people and flew over to intercept them.

We might not get a better chance, Fitz thought.

He rose on his blades and looked at Hopkins. The man's eyes were barely staying open.

"Martin, grab Hopkins," Fitz said.

Martin looked ready to protest, but then grabbed his comrade under an arm.

"Mendez and Dohi, you carry those two," Fitz said. "Rico, rearguard. Ace, on me. We're moving. *Now.*"

Mendez hoisted the Wolfhound missing his legs into a fireman's carry, and Dohi gave the other soldier his shoulder, helping the man stand.

Fitz slipped out of the container, hesitating outside. The two Black Hawks soared above the trees where the cannibals had run.

Using the distraction, Fitz led the team away from the containers. Dohi and Mendez managed to keep up, but Martin lagged slightly behind as he helped Hopkins. Rico reached out to assist.

All around the campus, fires raged through the

buildings from the attack. Oily smoke covered the stars and moon.

Fitz signaled to an office building blazing with flames. If his memory served him correctly, going inside and out the back would take them to the warehouses with the Project Rolling Stone tech. With every other route vulnerable to an attack from the choppers, he hoped the structure and the smoke would provide some cover. They would have to cross a wide-open space to get there first.

Dohi jogged next to him, practically carrying the injured Wolfhound. "I saw some Humvees earlier that had M240s behind those warehouses. If I can get to them, I might be able to take out those choppers…"

"Do it," Fitz said. "You too, Mendez. Take those two Wolfhounds with you and get them secured."

Dohi and Mendez took off.

A sudden blast of gunfire made Fitz twist. One of the choppers unleashed a storm of rounds into the trees. Screams sounded, but were quickly silenced.

The other Black Hawk peeled off from the woods and started toward Team Ghost and their injured comrades. Its spotlight raked over the ground, just a few dozen yards from lighting up Martin, Rico, and Hopkins. Those three would be the first to be smeared across the pavement.

The last sputters of the second chopper's machine guns dissipated.

Fire churned through the top of the building ahead. Bricks and chunks of the walls from the crumbling upper floors littered the ground outside the office. Ace was the first there, and crouched with his rifle up. Fitz arrived a moment later and knelt behind a pile of bricks adjacent to Ace.

Dohi and Mendez had already disappeared through the blazing building with the other two Wolfhounds, but Rico, Martin, and Hopkins were still running to catch up.

They weren't going to make it.

Rotor wash blew dust and cinder around the hapless trio.

In mere seconds, they would be dead.

Fitz brought his rifle to his shoulder and fired a burst at the cockpit of the Black Hawk. The bullets sparked off the metal and glass. The 5.56 mm M4 rounds couldn't bring down a chopper. If he was lucky, the best he could do was score a shot that brought down a door gunner.

None of that was the goal, though.

The chopper swerved hard to its right, spotlight sweeping away from Rico and the others. Fitz ran before the light could hit him, using the smoke and scree for cover. Sweat poured down his face as he unleashed another salvo of frantic fire.

Bullets painted the office building in response, trailing after him. He rolled away from the spray, got up, and kept running. Ash and embers lifted into the air above when gunfire raked into the building again.

The second chopper soared far ahead, looking to cut him off. Caught in a pincer movement, he had nowhere else to go but into the building. He lunged sideways, throwing himself through one of the busted windows on the ground floor.

Jagged fragments of glass tore into his flesh like the teeth of hungry Variants. He slammed against a desk, then scrambled over broken glass with his gloved hands and knee pads.

Bullets punched holes into the floor and drywall. Some lanced dangerously past him, close enough he could hear them whooshing past. Dust sprayed from their impact, kicking up a foggy screen.

Fitz scrambled to stand on his blades. Smoke drifted along the ceiling, and he heard the sizzle of burning fire chewing through the building.

Coughing, he stumbled into a hall, ducking under a fallen ceiling beam still smoldering. The choppers were strafing the building, sending in gouts of random gunfire. He might've escaped their sight, but he wasn't safe yet.

Fitz finally made it to the main hallway.

"Fitz!" Rico said.

To his surprise, she now had Hopkins on her back in a fireman's carry. Martin was beside her, chest heaving. Ace had his hands on his knees, trying to catch his breath. Soot covered their fatigues and flesh.

Fitz joined them and took point.

They jogged down the hall, all coughing through the smoke. Behind them, something crashed through the ceiling. Blackened ceiling beams and ash poured through a hole, along with furniture and dry wall still aflame.

"Go, go, go!" Fitz yelled to be heard over the inferno.

They made it to an exit that butted up against a street. Charred cars lined the road. Papers, still burning, fluttered over the asphalt.

Fitz cautiously stepped outside. He spied one Black Hawk patrolling on the southern edge of the building. The other bird sounded like it was on the opposite side of the office building, but he couldn't see with the smoke blocking his view.

The third chopper hadn't yet returned.

He signaled for the others to follow. With Rico now lugging Hopkins on her back, they moved faster, straight toward the building across the street.

The growl of helicopter engines suddenly grew louder. Dark smoke parted with a wave of rotor wash. The first Black Hawk appeared above, spotlights probing the ground.

"Move!" Fitz yelled.

They made it across and into the other building before the helicopter opened fire. Rounds pounded into the doorway, kicking up bits of floor tiles and breaking windows.

Fitz didn't stop until they got to the opposite exit. Through the windows he saw cars parked in front of the warehouses where the SDS equipment should be. The Humvees Dohi had mentioned were farther down the road, but he didn't see Dohi or Mendez.

"Master Sergeant!" a voice shouted.

Fitz turned to his right. Through a doorway leading off the hallway, he saw one of the Wolfhounds.

"In here!" Fitz called to the others as he jogged toward the injured man.

The Wolfhound was propped up behind a desk, his eyes glazed over. Next to him was his comrade, passed out from the agony of his severed legs. The rest of the room was covered in heavy desks and tipped over chairs.

"Dohi… and Mendez ran to the Humvees," the conscious Wolfhound said. "They told me… they told me to tell you they'd be ready when you got here."

Fitz squeezed the Wolfhound's shoulder, kneeling in front of him. "Thanks. You hold tight, and we'll get you guys out of here soon."

Rico lugged Hopkins into the office. She was breathing heavily when she laid him down behind another desk. Martin settled in beside his brothers, and Fitz crouched next to a fallen cabinet.

Ace aimed his rifle out a window.

The helicopters lowered toward the street, spotlights searching the office windows, lighting up the hallways. They were low enough now Fitz could clearly see the forms of the door gunners and the soldiers working the spotlights.

The choppers hovered down the road, passing in front of the warehouses and vehicles, hunting like beasts. But they were hunting in the wrong place.

Down the road, Fitz saw Dohi and Mendez emerge in the turrets of the Humvees. They grabbed the mounted machine guns and fired on the choppers.

Bullets sprayed through the open side doors and into the door gunners. One tumbled out, falling to the street.

The spotlights sparked and burst with incoming gunfire, going dark. Chunks of the glass in the cockpit gave way, fracturing and exploding. The Black Hawk tilted sideways, the pilot dead. The rotor blades broke against the ground, kicking up a wave of sparks as they fractured.

The bird erupted into flames, grinding across asphalt until it slammed against the side of the building. Smoke wafted from inside the other helicopter as it lifted away.

Dohi and Mendez swiveled their M240s and caught it in their stream of tracer rounds. The bird made it out over the trees past the warehouses before it suddenly dropped, disappearing beneath the canopy. An explosion burst from the woods.

Fitz motioned for the team to move out. Rico, Martin, and Ace helped pick up the Wolfhounds. They hurried past the wreckage of the first chopper. Judging by the mangled debris, Fitz doubted anyone had survived, but he kept his rifle up anyway.

Dohi waved from atop his Humvee. Mendez was propped up at the gun of the other. They were about twenty yards from the entrance to the office. Past where those Humvees were parked were the warehouses where Team Ghost would find the SDS equipment. Finally, they could finish their mission and go home.

Then a familiar sound boomed over the horizon.

The sound of another helicopter.

"Oh, shit," Martin said, halting.

Fitz tugged Rico down against the ground. The rest of the team took cover next to them.

"Dohi, Mendez, get the hell out of there!" Fitz yelled.

The third Black Hawk raced over the burning woods, launching a volley of Hydra rockets that streaked through the smoke, and slammed into the warehouses.

Heat crashed into Fitz, and the concussive force from the exploding rockets swept over the group in a scorching wave.

Moments filled with thuds and explosions passed by in what felt like slow motion. Fitz couldn't do anything but crouch down and pray.

Once the bird had expended everything it had, it tore away again.

As the smoke cleared, Fitz got up. It wasn't just the warehouses destroyed. Both the Humvees were nothing but scrap metal.

Fitz's ears rang as he tried to call out to the others. But he saw nothing except rolling smoke.

Their mission had ended, swept away by a deadly inferno. And now, Dohi and Mendez had vanished in the flames. There was nothing left but the smoldering remains of failure.

***

Beckham hated sitting in the comfy leather seat in the private jet while others were dying on the ground.

Fischer had the same guilty look in his eye, and so did Horn. They watched as Kate and a medic tended to Sammy, who had passed out from the pain.

In a separate closed-off section of the plane, Javier, Tasha, Jenny, and the dogs were resting—or were supposed to be. Beckham heard nervous chatter coming from the area.

He peered out of the window as they flew away from Outpost Manchester. The landscape was consumed in darkness except for the orange flashes of gunfire and flames now far in the distance.

After getting the rest of the technicians into another aircraft, Beckham had gladly taken Fischer's offer to take the private plane. But he couldn't help feeling like he was abandoning the people still down there. Just like when he'd been forced to leave Portland.

On another day, he would have considered staying, but Presley didn't want to listen to reason or advice. The colonel wanted to do things his own way, and Beckham could see where that was leading now.

He would be surprised if there was anything left of Outpost Manchester by the time the sun rose again.

Tasha peeked out of the doorway in the back half of the plane. "Are we headed home?"

"Not right now," Horn said. "Can you please go watch Jenny, Javier, and the dogs?"

Tasha looked like she was about to refuse.

"Please, Tasha," Horn said softly. "I need your help."

"Okay." Tasha disappeared into the back of the plane again.

Horn looked at Fischer expectantly. "So, do *you* know where we're going?"

The grizzled older man merely shrugged. "We still haven't received the exact coordinates. Ringgold's security forces won't give them to us until the last minute to be sure no collaborators intercept our comms."

"We have absolutely no idea?" Beckham asked.

"I've got a trajectory," Fischer said. "Headed south toward Long Island until we're told otherwise."

Horn folded his muscular arms over his chest.

"Ringgold's right to be cautious," Beckham said. "We just saw what happens when we underestimate the traitors in our midst."

The pilot's voice broke over the intercom. "Mr. Fischer, we've got an incoming satellite video call."

"Patch it through," Fischer replied.

A screen on the front bulkhead of the passenger cabin sizzled to life. The picture was grainy and the sound filled with the bite of static. To Beckham, that meant the incoming call was being heavily encrypted to prevent prying ears and eyes.

When the image settled, President Ringgold appeared. The wrinkles around her eyes looked especially pronounced, shadowed by dark half-circles.

Beckham had never seen her more exhausted.

"I'm glad to see you…" she started to say. "Where's Dr. Carr and the kids?"

Kate bowed her head. "Carr didn't make it, but the kids are safe."

Ringgold lowered her eyes a moment.

"We completed our work," Kate said. "We now have

everything we need to tap into the collaborator and Variant network."

"I'm happy to hear some good news," Ringgold replied. "I just hope that after the night is over, things aren't worse than we predicted."

Beckham felt dread pooling in his stomach.

Ringgold's voice sounded shaky when she spoke again. "I'm afraid Outpost Manchester wasn't the only place that has been hit hard. Just as we've suspected, our enemy's initial attacks were only testing our defenses. Combined with the collaborator attacks from the inside, we're losing everything."

She used the back of her hand to wipe her eyes. Beckham could see a layer of tears forming.

"I'm so sorry to tell you this, but Outpost Portland is gone. Lieutenant Niven called in an airstrike to take out the collaborators, and a small army of Variants that surrounded the outpost earlier tonight. That was pretty much the end of it, but they had no choice."

"God, no," Horn said, bowing his head.

"Timothy…" came a voice.

Horn looked over his shoulder at Tasha who stood cupping her mouth. He got up and hurried over to her. Beckham felt a tear of his own forming.

"How many outposts are left?" Kate asked.

"General Souza believes we will lose half by morning," Ringgold said.

Beckham wiped at his eye, and kept it together, knowing despair would get him nowhere.

"What about Team Ghost?" he asked. "If they got the SDS technology from Project Rolling Stone, we could hold out, right?"

Ringgold's pause told him all he needed to know.

"What?" he asked "Did something—"

"We lost all radio communications with Team Ghost and the Wolfhounds," Ringgold said.

"How the hell did we lose contact?"

"There seems to be something interfering with radio signals around the lab campus, and we lost contact with the C-130 and the remaining group of the Wolfhounds guarding it about an hour ago."

"They're all dead?" Beckham's insides twisted.

"We're not sure," Ringgold replied.

Beckham slammed his fist against one of the armrests.

Raised voices came from the back of the plane where the kids were with Horn. Beckham should have been back there to console them, but he remained seated to finish the call with Ringgold.

"Without the Rolling Stone technology, the Variants will destroy what's left of civilization wherever they can tunnel," Fischer said.

"There are other threats than tunneling Variants now," she replied. "We're getting reports of animals the collaborators have infected with VX-99. Dogs, the bats… it's a horror show. My advisors are telling me they must have been working on this for years."

"How?" Kate whispered incredulously.

No one had an answer for Kate. It was something Beckham desperately wished he could answer. Trying to figure out how they had missed all this would not help them bring back the outposts or all the thousands that had died.

For now, all they could do was focus on moving forward.

"From what we saw, from everything you're telling us, we need to do something quick, but I'm not sure that tapping into the Variant network will give us the upper hand," Beckham said. "We need something bigger."

"I agree, even if we somehow deployed the SDS equipment soon, there won't be much left for us to defend," Fischer said.

"You're both right," Ringgold said. "That's why we're ordering a mass retreat to concentrate our remaining assets. Air strikes around the country haven't stopped them. Recent intel suggests we may have a better ID on some of their bases, but ultimately, according to our estimates, it won't be enough."

"Won't be enough?" Fischer asked. "Then what in Sam Hill are we going to do?"

"General Souza and I have been in close contact with Cornelius. We've also tried to recruit more foreign aid, but we're not getting much. Even France is calling back the consultants they offered."

"So we're alone," Fischer said.

"It seems that way," Ringgold said. "We've evaluated options, and there is only one that we keep coming back to. One that may be our Hail Mary, and up until now, one that I disagreed with."

Beckham was afraid to ask what the President had in mind, although he sensed where this was going, especially if Cornelius was involved.

His gut was right.

"I agree with Cornelius now," Ringgold said, lacing her fingers together. "As hard as this is for me to say, we need to deploy what's left of our active nuclear arsenal to hammer the Variants where they are the strongest. Targets will include all major cities where hives are suspected and collaborator locations have been identified."

Fischer tugged on his mustache, but didn't say a word.

"I don't harbor any illusions about what this great country of ours will look like if we survive," Ringgold said. "We'll be turning our cities into radioactive festering ruins, but there's no taking them back from what's there now."

"All due respect, but we're not just talking about radioactive craters," Beckham said. "Don't forget what happened in Europe when the Variants were exposed to radiation."

"That was mostly due to fallout from nuclear power plants," Kate said. "Nuking the bastards will kill them before they can mutate further."

Initially Beckham was surprised at his wife's tone. But after all they'd been through, he realized he shouldn't have been.

"There are communities of people out there, living on their own," Beckham said. "Not to mention refugees. The collaborators have taken our people captive, too. All of them will be condemned to die."

Ringgold's face fizzled in and out of existence. "Yes, I'm all too aware of the sacrifices that will be made if we choose this course of action, but we have given the stranded outside of our outposts every opportunity to join us in this fight."

"You said this is the best option, but what are the others?" Beckham asked.

"One is to stay the course."

"We already know where that one leads," Beckham said, picturing the beasts swarming Outpost Portland and Manchester. "What else?"

"We try to evacuate whoever we can. Escape across the ocean."

"Maybe," Kate said. "But then we're giving North America to these monsters. They'll continue to propagate and grow in strength. Eventually they'll make the journey, too."

"It doesn't sound like our so-called allies are willing to help us now, either," Fischer said. "So why would they take us in, especially if there's a risk we're bringing along collaborators?"

"There is no guarantee," Ringgold said. "That's why I'm leaning toward the nuclear option."

Beckham hated the idea of launching nukes on their soil and cities. The home he had fought for, that he had sacrificed so much for. The place where he had raised a family, where he had done everything in his power to protect his friends and rebuild a better and free civilization.

For eight years they had accomplished that. Creating outposts where citizens could live in peace after a lifetime of violence.

But as soon as they launched those nukes, the country as he knew it would permanently be gone. The United States and now the Allied States would be just a memory.

"If we do this," Beckham said finally. "Everything we know will be left in ashes."

There had to be a better way.

He took a moment to think.

"What if we attack the major hubs, but hold back most of our nukes?" Beckham asked. "Maybe we give Team Ghost a chance to complete the mission, pull everyone back to the safest and most defendable outposts. Then, if Ghost fails, we launch everything we've got at those animals?"

"What do you think, Kate?" Ringgold asked.

She managed a nod and then reached out for Beckham's hand.

"Okay," Ringgold said. "By the time you reach our secured location, the nuclear weapons will be deployed on select targets."

"And then we're back to where we started nearly a decade ago," Fischer said. "Back underground, hiding from the monsters."

Ringgold grimaced as she turned her eyes downward. When she raised them, Beckham saw a new wave of confidence.

"No," Ringgold said. "We're not launching these weapons just to hide."

She unfolded her fingers and sat up straighter, staring at the camera with raw determination.

"We're launching them to fight back. Once the smoke clears, and the ashes settle, we return to the battlefield and throw every last man, woman, and bullet at the beasts to save what's left of our country."

End of Book 2

Extinction Cycle Dark Age Book 3:
Extinction Ashes, coming very soon!

About the Authors

Nicholas Sansbury Smith is the New York Times and USA Today bestselling author of the Hell Divers series. His other work includes the Extinction Cycle series, the Trackers series, and the Orbs series. He worked for Iowa Homeland Security and Emergency Management in disaster planning and mitigation before switching careers to focus on his one true passion—writing. When he isn't writing or daydreaming about the apocalypse, he enjoys running, biking, spending time with his family, and traveling the world. He is an Ironman triathlete and lives in Iowa with his wife, their dogs, and a house full of books.

Anthony J Melchiorri is a scientist with a PhD in bioengineering. Originally from the Midwest, he now lives in Texas. By day, he develops cellular therapies and 3D-printable artificial organs. By night, he writes apocalyptic, medical, and science-fiction thrillers that blend real-world research with other-worldly possibility, including works like *The Tide* and *Eternal Frontier.* When he isn't in the lab or at the keyboard, he spends his time running, reading, hiking, and traveling in search of new story ideas.

Join Nicholas on social media:

Facebook Fan Club:
facebook.com/groups/NSSFanclub

Facebook Author Page:
facebook.com/pages/Nicholas-Sansbury-Smith/124009881117534

Twitter: @greatwaveink

Website: NicholasSansburySmith.com

Instagram: instagram.com/author_sansbury

Email: Greatwaveink@gmail.com

Sign up for Nicholas's spam-free newsletter and receive special offers and info on his latest new releases.

Join Anthony on social media:

Facebook: facebook.com/anthonyjmelchiorri

Email: ajm@anthonyjmelchiorri.com

Website: anthonyjmelchiorri.com

Did we mention Anthony also has a newsletter?
http://bit.ly/ajmlist

Made in the USA
Coppell, TX
11 August 2020

33107976R00232